MW00526662

WHOLE FAMILY

A Novel by Twelve Authors

WILLIAM DEAN HOWELLS
MARY E. WILKINS FREEMAN
MARY HEATON VORSE
MARY STEWART CUTTING
ELIZABETH JORDAN
JOHN KENDRICK BANGS
HENRY JAMES
ELIZABETH STUART PHELPS
EDITH WYATT
MARY RAYMOND SHIPMAN ANDREWS
ALICE BROWN
HENRY VAN DYKE

Foreword by June Howard

Introduction by Alfred Bendixen

Duke University Press   *Durham and London 2001*

Foreword, introduction, and appendix
©2001 Duke University Press
All rights reserved
Printed in the United States of America
on acid-free paper
Library of Congress Cataloging-in-Publication Data
appear on the last printed page of this book.

CONTENTS

ILLUSTRATIONS

Illustrations follow page numbers given

FOREWORD

BY JUNE HOWARD

In a sense, all writing is collaboration. We do not invent our own words but learn them from others, and when we make sentences we talk back to other people. All human language is full of history—shaped by the past, it carries both that past and our present inventions into the future.

The composite novel *The Whole Family* remains interesting nearly one hundred years after it was written, partly because it is a remarkable document of collaboration. Twelve creative individuals, shaped by different backgrounds and holding different opinions, worked together to tell a story. Each chapter incorporates the vital issues of the day. For example, William Dean Howells, the eminent author and critic who started the project in 1906, suggested the theme of coeducation, a well-established practice that was being debated again at that moment. He also described one of the members of this fictional family as an "old maid." Mary Wilkins Freeman, herself a famous author, was to write from that character's point of view; she thought the image ridiculously old-fashioned and turned the unmarried Aunt

Elizabeth into an up-to-date independent woman, with "men at [her] feet"—including the man her coeducated niece is engaged to marry. Alfred Bendixen's introduction describes the uproar among the authors that followed, reminding us that collaboration is not necessarily harmonious. In fact, Elizabeth Jordan, the editor of *Harper's Bazar* (as the magazine's name was then spelled), in which the chapters of the novel appeared month by month, wrote later: "This wholly unexpected twist of the tale proved to be the explosion of a bombshell on our literary hearthstone."[1]

The Whole Family dramatizes, almost literalizes, cultural critics' notion of the "social text": narrative as a site on which struggles between historical positions are played out. The early twentieth century was a period of profound change and perceived crisis in the family. Professionals in the emerging fields of the social sciences went to work on the problem. In December 1908, just as the serial was published in book form, the American Sociological Society organized its third annual meeting around the topic of the family.[2] The *Bazar's* book review of *The Whole Family* perhaps exaggerated in claiming that "never before has the American family, as an institution, been so subtly discussed,"[3] yet the collaborators engage the topic in richly varied ways. They implicitly debate models of the family—what some consider domestic bliss, others see as claustrophobic misery. The themes of coeducation and spinsterhood confront them with the controversial figure of the "new woman," and pose the question of what happens if not only men but women embrace the modern notion of individual freedom. Will women voluntarily—can they legitimately—choose lives outside the marriage relationship? Does that mean rejecting the family or redefining it? Readers of *The Whole Family* may find the novel surprisingly contemporary, both in its suggestion that the family is endangered, and in its strenuous defense of that vexed, complex institution.

Each author wrote from the viewpoint of one member of the novel's fictional family. As the project unfolded, the contributors began to call themselves a family as well. Allusions to the troubles on their "literary hearthstone" even crept into the text itself. That hearthstone was located in what its inhabitants and publishing historians alike refer to as "the House of Harper": the family business Harper & Brothers, located at Franklin Square in New York City. The rhetoric of family pervaded the ways that the owners and staff at Harper's wrote about their corporate solidarity, as well as the collaboration and the novel. Publishing what they constantly called a "family of magazines" addressed to different audiences, and an immense number of books, Harper's was one of the most important American literary institutions of the nineteenth century; its subsequent story has embodied the multiple transformations of the culture industry in the twentieth century. *The Whole Family* originated in the clearinghouse at Franklin Square. Only the firm's far-reaching connections and prestige, accumulated over decades of solid respectability, made the project possible. Yet it was also a circulation-building novelty for the *Bazar*, a modern marketing strategy. In all these ways, the publishing house is virtually one of the authors of *The Whole Family*.

To understand this novel, then, we must give up any notion that the business of publishing is separate from the art of writing. Several contributors take on the relations of commerce and culture as a theme, notably Henry James. He writes from the perspective of the eldest son, making him an artist unhappily employed in the family business, unable (his character claims) to design an ice pitcher ugly enough to sell to his father's "unspeakable market" (p. 149) but without enough money to get away to Paris to paint. One of the many surprising things about *The Whole Family* is finding Henry James contributing to a women's fashion magazine. Even Alice Brown, whose impressively crafted next-to-last chapter finds a path to the happy ending, thought so when she looked back years later, writing in a letter to Jordan: "I think he's the funniest figure possible among us amount-to-nothings, like Dr. Johnson at a village sewing circle. . . . O Henry James! why *did* he go picknicking with us!"[4] The installments were published anonymously, with a list of the participating authors and an invitation to the reader to guess who was responsible for the current contribution—so James, the serious, self-conscious artist and idiosyncratic stylist, gave up being "the Master" long enough to allow his signature to float over other people's chapters, and theirs over his. Here and elsewhere James's late work consistently elaborates the impossibility of insulating any zone of human activity—whether the family or aesthetics—from exchange and publicity. Both the story and the text of *The Whole Family* suggest that literature and the marketplace can never be disentangled. Similarly, they remind us that men's and women's literary histories cannot be separated. The conversation of *The Whole Family* is specifically heterosocial, including both men and women and consistently inflected by gender.

The reasons to read *The Whole Family* are many. It is, as I have begun to show, a revealing document of the American middle class at the beginning of the twentieth century, from its representations of gender relations and taste to its glaringly casual racism, its contribution to the image of the American boy, and other topics I have not addressed here.[5] It is a fascinating case study in the social relations of literary production. It is a chance to glimpse the work of forgotten authors who deserve to be revived, and unexpected efforts by famous ones. And the novel is not only thought-provoking but entertaining. As the advertisements in Harper publications proclaimed when the book was first published, it is a "strangely exciting story."

Notes

1. Freeman's letter is in the Jordan collection at the New York Public Library; Jordan quotes it in her autobiography, *Three Rousing Cheers* (New York: D. Appleton-Century, 1938), on p. 266. The quotation from Jordan is from p. 264 of that book.
2. See volume three of the *Papers and Proceedings of the American Sociological Society* (third annual meeting, general topic: The Family; At-

lantic City, N.J., 28–30 December 1908; published for the Society by the University of Chicago Press, 1909). On the history of the family, see Stephanie Coontz's *The Way We Never Were: American Families and the Nostalgia Trap* (New York: Basic Books/HarperCollins, 1992).

3. The notice appeared in the December 1908 issue (vol. 42, no. 12).

4. Brown's letter is in the Jordan collection at the New York Public Library. Though undated, its contents and handwriting indicate that it was written late in her life.

5. For more on the heterosociality of the novel, see Karen L. Kilcup, "The Conversation of 'The Whole Family': Gender, Politics, and Aesthetics in Literary Tradition," in *Soft Canons: American Women Writers and Masculine Tradition,* ed. Karen L. Kilcup (Iowa City: University of Iowa Press, 1999), 1–24. I have written at greater length about the topics discussed or mentioned in this foreword in *Publishing the Family* (Durham, N.C.: Duke University Press, 2001).

INTRODUCTION:
The Whole Story Behind
The Whole Family

The Whole Family is the result of one of the most fascinating literary experiments in the history of American writing.[1] It was William Dean Howells who first thought of bringing together a dozen of the leading American writers to collaborate on a novel. As the leading critical voice for American realism and the unofficial Dean of American Literature, Howells had served as editor, adviser, and friend to most of the important writers in America. He felt sure that he could persuade eleven distinguished authors to join him in writing a book. In the spring of 1906, he suggested the project to Elizabeth Jordan, the energetic editor of *Harper's Bazar*. She responded with enthusiasm and eagerly agreed to undertake the editorial work. The chapters would appear serially in *Harper's Bazar* and then be collected into a book. It seemed like an editor's dream. It turned out to be an editor's nightmare.

The story of *The Whole Family* is one of great expectations and great frustrations. Jordan acted as the editor, but Howells served as an adviser and developed the initial plans—plans which were to undergo a series of dramatic changes. Howells originally conceived of the novel as a realistic portrait of a typical American family "in middling circumstances, of average culture and experiences." Each author would write one chapter focusing on one member of the family, except for the final chapter, which would be a summation by a female "Friend of the Family." Initially, Howells seems to have placed more emphasis on characters than plot. He, however, suggested: "The family might be in some such moment of vital agitation as that attending the Young Girl's engagement, or pending engagement, and each witness could treat of it in character. There could be fun enough, but each should try seriously to put himself or herself really into the personage's place. I think the more seriously the business was treated, the better."[2]

Howells thought that the book should open with an account of The Grandmother and then proceed through the other members of the family in a logical order. In a letter to Jordan, he suggested the book might consist of:

The Grandmother

The Father

The Mother

The Son

The Daughter-in-law

The Daughter

The Son-in-law

THE WHOLE FAMILY

The Little Girl

The Small Boy

The Maiden Aunt (on the Father's side or the Mother's)

The Young Girl

The Friend (female) of the Family.

The novel would thus be framed by the accounts of the grandmother and the female friend, and the intervening chapters would be grouped in pairs encouraging comparison and contrast: the father and mother, the son and his wife, the daughter and her husband, the little girl and the small boy, and the maiden aunt and the engaged young girl.[3]

Once the characters were chosen, the next step was to select the right authors and persuade them to contribute. In her autobiography, *Three Rousing Cheers* (1938), Jordan explains that she hoped "to bring together what P. T. Barnum would have called the greatest, grandest, most gorgeous group of authors ever collaborating on a literary production."[4] Although she made most of the final decisions, Jordan relied heavily on Howells's advice and consulted other members of the staff at Harper's. It seems clear that Jordan and Howells focused on writers who published with Harper's or at least contributed regularly to *Harper's Magazine* and *Harper's Bazar*. *The Whole Family* was designed to be a showplace for Harper's family of authors.

Howells volunteered to do the father, suggested that Mark Twain would enjoy doing the small boy, and in-

vited Jordan to write one of the chapters. He also suggested that Jordan complete the group with Margaret
Deland, Mary E. Wilkins Freeman, May Isabel Fisk,
John Kendrick Bangs, Thomas Allibone Janvier, and
"four other women writers."[5] The emphasis on women
writers presumably reflects Howells's awareness of the
Bazar's audience. Not all of the facts behind the selec-
tion process are known, but it is clear that it was Jordan, not Howells, who thought of inviting Henry James
to participate.[6] Jordan also decided to assign specific
chapters to the authors instead of following Howells's
suggestion that the authors be allowed to choose the
characters they wrote about.[7]

Jordan found that gathering her family of authors together proved more difficult than she had expected.
Almost every writer had other commitments and con-
tracts to fulfill. Some could not undertake a chapter for
two years. Others pleaded for the chance to write a
chapter that had already been assigned to someone
else.[8] Furthermore, several of the writers wanted to be
paid much more than Jordan anticipated. Some simply
declined to take part in the project. Margaret Deland
flatly refused to write the mother's chapter, stating that:
"I am dazzled at the distinguished names that have entered your domestic circle; but it doesn't seem to me
that you are, any of you, taking the rank that belongs
to you in literature when you make yourselves into this
pleasant sandwich."[9] Deland was even a bit offended
by Jordan's suggestion that a contribution would entail
no more work than the writing of a short story. She
told Jordan: "I am no smart New York author, that can
reel off stories and papers every few minutes; I am

nothing but a Bostonian, who plods, and plods, and plods; and it would certainly take me a summer and probably a winter, to write a short story for any magazine."[10]

Mark Twain did not respond with the enthusiasm that Jordan and Howells had expected. Twain later confided to Jordan that he had foreseen the ultimate outcome of *The Whole Family*. But his reservations about the project were based primarily on his belief that writing must be a completely natural process. He was both unwilling and unable to turn out a work of fiction designed to fit an abstract and artificial scheme. Nevertheless, Twain agreed to read the early chapters of *The Whole Family* and promised to contribute if he found himself inspired by them. Unfortunately, his examination of the chapters prepared by Howells and Freeman did not motivate him to take part. In a letter dated August 4, 1906, Mark Twain explained to Jordan that even if the schoolboy "has a story to tell he is not moved to tell it through me. I could compel him, but the children of the fancy are sensitive, and I do not offend them with compulsion. So I have given him up, and dismissed the thought of him from my mind—permanently."[11] The loss of Mark Twain was a serious blow to the project. Jordan pleaded with Howells to use his influence on Twain, but Howells politely refused, explaining that "a friend of his youth ought not to afflict his age."[12]

In spite of the disappointing responses of Margaret Deland and Mark Twain, Jordan managed to bring together a respectable group of authors in a remarkably short time. She began inviting contributers in late May

1906 and received commitments from most of the authors by the middle of June.[13] Although she did not have a complete family of authors, Jordan had enough commitments to move ahead. It is not precisely clear when Henry James agreed to join Jordan's family, but Mary E. Wilkins Freeman was among the first to agree to participate. Freeman was probably picked to write the old-maid aunt's chapter because of her memorable portraits of New England spinsters in stories like "A New England Nun" and "A Village Singer." Jordan also heard promptly and favorably from Alice Brown, who had established her reputation with some distinguished local color tales of New England, and from her choice for the Friend of the Family, Dr. Henry van Dyke, whose moralistic essays and romantic tales were then extremely popular. Jordan had discarded Howells's suggestion that the family friend be female. John Kendrick Bangs, a prolific and popular humorist who could always be counted on for an amusing piece, agreed to take on the role of the son-in-law.

Some of the authors chosen have been virtually forgotten today, but Jordan had a good reason for each of her selections. For instance, Mary Stewart Cutting had established a popular following by specializing in short stories about married life. It was logical for Jordan to ask her to write the daughter-in-law's chapter. When she was invited to write the grandmother's chapter, Mary Heaton Vorse had not yet published a book, but she had written some impressive short stories and had shown an interest in the elderly which eventually resulted in her novel, *The Autobiography of an Elderly Woman* (1911). Jordan chose Edith Wyatt to do the mother's chapter on the advice of Howells, who greatly admired Wyatt's stories of Chicago.

Howells suggested some other authors for Jordan's consideration, including Brander Matthews, William Allen White, Henry B. Fuller, Robert Grant, Brand Whitlock, Hamlin Garland, Francis Hopkinson Smith, Elia Wilkinson Peattie, and Thomas Bailey Aldrich.[14] Jordan attempted to persuade at least some of these writers to take part in *The Whole Family*, but without success. Frances Hodgson Burnett also declined to contribute, praising the project but explaining that she could not write about characters and situations created by others.[15] Finding someone to take Mark Twain's place proved especially difficult. It was apparently not until the end of April 1907 that Mary Raymond Shipman Andrews agreed to write the schoolboy's chapter. Andrews had gained national attention with her short story about Abraham Lincoln, "The Perfect Tribute," but she was probably chosen because of her skillful depiction of young boys and the outdoor life in *Bob and the Guides* (1906).

Unfortunately for Jordan, some writers initially agreed to provide a chapter but then bowed out. For example, Kate Douglas Wiggin, the author of *Rebecca of Sunnybrook Farm* (1903), originally promised to write the married daughter's chapter, proclaiming *The Whole Family* "the only interesting scheme ever propounded me by an editor!"[16] Wiggin, however, later dropped out, pleading other commitments including the editorship of a series of children's classics. Her letters also indicate that she was not really satisfied with the amount of money Jordan offered for her contribution. Wiggin may have also been intimidated by the prospect of rapidly producing a work which would appear in the company of more distinguished authors, and she felt that Howells's account of the married daughter in the first chapter had given her little to work with. She urged Jordan to find someone "who would know *just* how to do it, for whom it has no terrors, and to whom it would be merely a pleasant fortnight's work."[17] Jordan eventually persuaded Elizabeth Stuart Phelps to write the married daughter's chapter. Phelps is remembered today mostly for her sentimentalization of the heavenly afterlife in *The Gates Ajar* (1868), but she was an ardent feminist and social reformer who produced some powerful work.

The most distinguished writers on the final list of contributors were, of course, Howells and James. Of the other writers, only Mary E. Wilkins Freeman produced work that is still widely read and anthologized. Although the literary reputations of the others have not fared well, they were all capable and successful writers. In fact, some of them may be unjustly neglected. Incidentally, there is absolutely no relationship between the current reputation of these authors and the amount of money they received for their contributions to *The Whole Family*. Howells was not really paid anything, because his Harper's contract included a salary which covered his contributions to their periodicals. Henry James expressed "perfect satisfaction" with his fee of $400.[18] Freeman asked for $250, her usual sum for a short story. Some of the other writers were more demanding. Henry van Dyke complained when Jordan sent him a check for only $350 instead of the $600 he expected and eventually received. Jordan was clearly surprised when Mary Stewart Cutting insisted on $350, Alice Brown asked for $500, and Elizabeth Stuart Phelps demanded no less than $750.

The editing of *The Whole Family* proved much more complex and difficult than Jordan expected. While assembling her literary family, Jordan found that the order of chapters would have to be based on the schedules of her writers. The logical arrangement that Howells originally contemplated had to be abandoned. While Jordan was seeking commitments from the writers, Howells set to work on his chapter. He found himself producing an introductory piece which clearly had to be the first chapter. Howells thus discarded his own plan to open *The Whole Family* with the grandmother. Howells apparently hoped that the mother's chapter would follow his, but unfortunately for his plans for the novel, Mary E. Wilkins Freeman was the only author able to go to work immediately. Freeman had consented to take on the maiden aunt of the family, a relatively minor character in Howells's original scheme. Little did Howells or anyone else suspect what Freeman would do to *The Whole Family* when she wrote the second chapter.

Howells almost certainly expected *The Whole Family* to be an illustration of his views of literary realism. The focus would be on the ordinary, commonplace, everyday life of a more-or-less average American family, and the book's strength would depend on the careful and realistic portrayal of character. There would be, as he told Jordan, "full space for the light and humorous play of anybody's preference in the treatment of characters."[19] Howells repeatedly insisted on his willingness to go along with the wishes of the other writers, stating that: "They must be left in entire freedom."[20] He even offered to revise his chapter to meet the demands of the other authors. Nevertheless, by the time he wrote the first chapter, Howells had developed a clear picture of what *The Whole Family* would be.

Howells envisioned a serious treatment of the effect of marriage on a family:

> What I wish to imply is that an engagement or a marriage is much more a family affair, and much less a personal affair than Americans usually suppose. As we live on, we find that family ties, which held us very loosely in youth, or after we ceased to be children, are really almost the strongest things in life. A marriage cannot possibly concern the married pair alone; but it is in the notion that it can that most of our marriages are made. It is also in this notion that most of them are unmade.

Howells's chapter also introduced at least one other serious theme. He explained: "I wish to indicate in my advocacy of coeducation that young people ought to know at least the workings of the male and female mind as fully as they can. Their natures are diverse enough, though not so diverse as we like to pretend, and the difference is exaggerated by the separate training."[21]

Howells had accepted the difficult task of preparing the way for eleven other writers. He carefully provided a setting, the rough outlines of a dramatic situation, and an introduction to the main characters. His affectionate and homely portrait of the family opened a number of possibilities for the writers who would follow him, but it did not provide them with a real plot. The closest thing to an issue of conflict in the opening chapter concerned the propriety of publishing a wedding announcement in the local newspaper. Furthermore, Howells had sketched in a few details about the various members of the family, but he had not breathed life into them. He had not even provided most of the family members with names. The conversation between the father and his new neighbor, the town's newspaper editor, served as a frame for a less than memorable catalog of characters. The opening chapter illustrated Howells's belief in a literature focused on the quiet and commonplace details of everyday life, but it was, at best, unexciting.

Howells himself had reservations about the chapter. He recognized that it was hardly a masterpiece and would need some revision to suit the aims of the other authors, but he thought that the chapter would serve to get the project started. He warned Jordan that putting too much emphasis on the engagement could easily trivialize the novel. Howells suggested that the other authors should be concerned primarily with portraying their individual characters, mentioning the engagement only when necessary and appropriate. Howells had other worries, too. He told Jordan that he did not want "to appear in co-operation with young or unimportant writers."[22] He also clearly felt that the whole project would either be a brilliant success or a dismal failure, and he hoped that Jordan would quickly drop the project if it did not prove promising.

THE WHOLE FAMILY

And then along came Mary E. Wilkins Freeman. She clearly felt the need to start the plot moving, to give the story some momentum. She had a great deal of respect and admiration for Howells, but apparently his remarks on women in the first chapter, particularly his treatment of the old-maid aunt, irritated her. Freeman felt that Howells's conception of the aunt was based on outdated values that condemned a single woman in her thirties to an eternal and dowdy spinsterhood. In her letters to Jordan, Freeman explained that the unmarried woman, who once "put on caps, and renounced the world" when she turned thirty, now lived a full life and "men are at their feet." Freeman went on to declare that: "Single women have caught up with, and passed, old bachelors in the last half of the century."[23] She even asserted that a young man would find a modern, intelligent, mature woman more attractive than a young girl. It must be noted that in 1902, at the age of forty nine, Freeman had married a man who was seven years younger than herself.

Freeman gave most of the characters names and took possession of the novel. She made the old-maid aunt into a thoroughly modern and bold woman who relished the attention of men and refused to be confined by the family's old-fashioned notions. Instead of the relatively minor figure she was in Howells's original plan, the aunt became the moving force behind the novel. The quiet world Howells had created in the first chapter was shattered by Freeman's revelations that the young man who had just become engaged to the daughter, Peggy, was really hopelessly in love with the aunt. Freeman could not resist taking a few other shots at

THE WHOLE FAMILY

Howells's first chapter: she even suggested that Ned Temple, the newspaper editor and narrator of chapter 1, had once been infatuated with the aunt. Suddenly, *The Whole Family* had become an entirely different book.

Jordan greeted Freeman's chapter with enthusiasm and soon rushed off proofs of it to the other authors— a mistake she regretted almost immediately. When she had sent out Howells's chapter to the authors, they had responded respectfully. Freeman's chapter proved, however, to be what Jordan called "the explosion of a bomb-shell on our literary hearthstone."[24] Jordan claimed that every one of the authors immediately wrote to her, some to praise Freeman's daring chapter, others to condemn. Henry van Dyke wrote: "Heavens! what a catastrophe! Who would have thought that the maiden aunt would go mad in the second chapter? Poor lady. Red hair and a pink hat and boys in beau-knots all over the costume. What *will* Mr. Howells say?"[25] What Mr. Howells said in his letter to Jordan was so severe that Jordan asserted it "almost scorched the paper it was written on."[26] Howells hated Freeman's chapter and urged Jordan not to publish it. He pleaded with her: "Don't, *don't* let her ruin our beautiful story!"[27]

Jordan now faced a real dilemma. Any decision she made would upset either Freeman or Howells, both of whom were important authors to Harper's. She consulted others at Harper's, including Henry Mills Alden, the editor of *Harper's Magazine;* Colonel George Harvey, the president of the publishing firm; and Frederick A. Duneka, the general manager. They shared her admiration of Freeman's story and agreed that it gave *The Whole Family* "the push it needed for cumulative interest."[28] Jordan, a single woman in her early forties, also accepted Freeman's argument about the vitality of contemporary single women. Jordan wrote to Howells, explaining as tactfully as she could that Freeman's story would be published. She noted: "He took the decision like the scholar and gentleman he was; but he let me see that he thought the novel was wrecked and that he himself lay buried among the ruins."[29]

Howells's disappointment is understandable. After all, his entire conception of the novel had been demolished. Moreover, there was the clear danger that *The Whole Family* would turn into an absurd farce. Mark Twain, who had been sent the first two chapters in the hopes they would inspire him to collaborate, greatly preferred Howells's chapter to Freeman's. He found Howells's contribution to be natural and "well-done," but complained that Freeman's failed because it was "a piece of pure literary manufacture and has the shop-marks all over it."[30] Some of the contributors were quite dismayed by the complications Freeman had introduced. Alice Brown wrote to Jordan: "Again I thought we were to take Mr. Howells's key, being good. He struck it clearly. We had one of his dear entirely natural families of 'folks' we should all delight in living with. I understood them at once. I wanted to make them a visit. But in Mrs. Freeman's chapter I had a facer." Brown even declared that: "When I met Aunt Elizabeth, powder-puff to powder-puff, face to face, I was on the point of writing you that I should have to give up the job. I frankly didn't see any un-farcical way out."[31]

On the other hand, some of the contributors to *The*

Whole Family realized that Freeman had provided the book with vitality and movement. Indeed, there is much to be said for Freeman's lively chapter. It found the comic potential in what threatened to become a dull story. It gave the plot a strong sense of direction without overly confining the future contributors. In fact, "The Old-Maid Aunt" will come as a delightful surprise to those readers who know Freeman only as the author of grim stories of New England life. Her chapter is filled with wit, insight, and irony. Although she may have been annoyed by Howells's comments on old maids, Freeman did not allow her feelings to mar her art. In Freeman's hands, the old-maid aunt became a remarkably complex figure who is capable of seeing all the absurdities in the world except her own. In fact, Alice Brown was first horrified by Freeman's chapter, but later came to believe that it was really "a delicate and too-convincing satire on the present woman who 'getting on in years,' continues to play not only as hard but according to the rules of twenty. . . ."[32]

The controversy generated by Freeman's chapter proved to be only the beginning. Jordan quickly discovered that twelve individual literary talents do not readily form a common vision. She soon regretted that she had established a policy of sending the authors copies of the proofs for each chapter. She welcomed the advice of Howells and was pleased when he continued to provide comments even after his pleas to stop Freeman's chapter were rejected.[33] But she was distressed to find that the other authors often interpreted the proofs she sent as invitations to offer their own views, comments, and criticisms. Jordan was almost overwhelmed by her need to respond tactfully to a wide range of strongly held opinions.

In her autobiography, Jordan described her problems vividly:

> The mail was as active as our family setter, Freckles, bringing in bones—the bones of authors, dug up, as it were, by other authors. Almost every author seemed to consider the chapters before his merely as material leading up to his own work, and to judge it solely in its relation to his individual plans. Also, any later departures from the values or leads in his chapter grieved him sorely. . . . When it came to the point of considering the book as a whole, the authors were very much like members of a theatrical cast listening to the reading of a new play. Each judged it from the viewpoint of his own part and each had grave doubts about the abilities of his associates.[34]

Moreover, some of the authors shared their strong opinions with others. The turmoil surrounding the creation of *The Whole Family* became a major subject of literary gossip in New York.

As *The Whole Family* developed, the plot increasingly focused on family misunderstandings and family rivalries, which were mirrored by the artistic rivalries of the authors. The writing of the novel became as much a contest as it was a collaboration, with each author trying hard to impose his vision on the entire work. The authors often revealed a deep sympathy for their assigned characters, and they often tried to manipulate the plot to turn their characters into central figures. Of course, the writing of the novel allowed for a certain amount of good-natured fun. In assuming the role of a character, an author could easily use the persona to make remarks directed at least partly at the other writers. For example, the opening of John Kendrick Bangs's chapter clearly refers to both the fictional family of the novel and the literary family that was writing the novel:

> On the whole I am glad our family is no larger than it is. It is a very excellent family as families go, but the infinite capacity of each individual in it for making trouble, and adding to complications already sufficiently complex, surpasses anything that has ever come before into my personal or professional experience.

To a certain extent, the twelve authors were playing a game, but it was a game for professionals and it was played, for the most part, with utmost seriousness.

Jordan's work had a few rewarding moments. She was pleased that the chapter she contributed to *The Whole Family* won the approval of all the other authors. In particular, she relished the praise of Henry James, who said of her treatment of the schoolgirl: "Allow me to congratulate you on your big little Girl: full of nature and truth!"[35] Often, however, Jordan found herself the frustrated head of a literary family which showed more inclination toward conflict than cooperation. The stature of these writers made it difficult for her to offer criticism. As she explained in her autobiography,

> The appalling candor with which editors of to-day discuss the work of their authors was then undreamed of.

Occasionally I passed on hints, always tentatively and
with many preliminary tributes and apologies.

"It has been suggested that. . . ." "What would you
think of. . . ." "Does it strike you—perhaps. . . ."

It rarely struck them. It was really not expected that
it would.[36]

There were times, however, when Jordan had to do a
good deal more than merely pass on hints.

The most troublesome member of the family was
Edith Wyatt, whose original chapter was deemed so
awful that it had to be completely rewritten. "The
Mother" was originally scheduled to appear as the sev-
enth chapter. Jordan seems to have rushed the proofs
of Wyatt's chapter to the other authors before she had
a chance to read it.[37] It was a mistake she soon regretted. Wyatt's original chapter apparently contradicted the
entire development of *The Whole Family*. Instead of a
first-person narrative, Wyatt relied on a series of letters
by various characters in the novel. She defended this
decision to Jordan by arguing that monologue would be
an inappropriate form for Mrs. Talbert, the mother of
the family. The mother, Wyatt suggested, would not
be likely to talk about herself at length and even her
thoughts would be focused on others. Wyatt also tried
to justify her introduction of a new character, Mrs.
Evarts, the family's great aunt.[38] Wyatt's changes were
not well received. In fact, Jordan notes that "the mother's chapter caused as great a convulsion among the
authors as the old maid's did."[39] The harshest criticism
of the chapter probably came from Frederick A. Duneka, the general manager of Harper's, who wrote: "This

chapter of *The Whole Family* is simply awful—confused, dull, stupid, vapid, meaningless, halting, lame, holding up the action and movement of the story which has run along so splendidly thus far."[39] He warned Jordan that "this cruelly incompetent drivel" could ruin her potentially great book, suggested that the chapter was so hopelessly bad that revision was not even possible, and advised her to pay the author, if necessary, but not to publish the work.[40]

Jordan had a great deal of difficulty in persuading Wyatt to undertake the thorough rewriting that she deemed necessary. Finally, a brief message was sent to Wyatt, bluntly telling her that her chapter could not be used, that she had been paid, and that she would not be troubled further. Jordan even lined up Alice French to take Wyatt's place. Wyatt, however, did not accept her dismissal from the family. She wrote a long, carefully written letter, protesting the way she had been treated and noting her willingness to make reasonable changes.[41] Jordan relented and Wyatt finally produced a chapter which could be used. Howells thought the revised chapter was "charming—delicately true to nature and abounding in fine bits of observation."[42] James, however, despised the chapter, lamenting that Wyatt had reduced a potentially interesting character to "a positive small convulsion of debility!—without irony, without fancy, without anything!"[43]

Henry James clearly valued his own contribution to *The Whole Family*. His chapter, "The Married Son," has been ignored by most of his critics, but it deserves attention from anyone interested in James's view of the artistic spirit and American society. It is a delightfully comic and thoroughly Jamesean confrontation with the agonies of an aesthetic nature trapped in a materialistic environment. Howells justly praised the "phosphorescent play of James's humor" and applauded "his delicate treatment of it, his perfect intelligence, and ironical ease."[44] James himself believed for a while that he had saved the novel by giving the story a more meaningful direction, and he was deeply troubled when the authors who followed him failed to appreciate it. Jordan asserts that James even seriously suggested that he write all the final chapters himself.[45] He explained to Jordan:

> I can't help saying now that I wish I might have been suffered to take upon myself to *save* the stuff—which would have interested & amused me, & which I would have done ingeniously &—well, *cheap!* I saw a way, & this even though I hadn't ever thought the hare originally started (the Aunt's flirtation, or whatever, with the niece's *fiance*—no gleam of light, shed by any pen, has ever shone on *what* it was!) would at the best run very far, or was indeed anything *of* a hare. Still, I had engaged to play the game & take over the elements as they were & hated to see them so helplessly muddled away when, oh, one could one's self (according to one's fatuous thought!) have made them *mean* something, given them sense, direction, and form. It was, & still is, I confess, for me, the feeling of a competent cook who sees good vittles messed—& all the more that he has been named as having had a hand in the dinner. I wince at the vision of the dinner being served—& this particular cook will at any rate, thereunder, stick very

tight in the kitchen. Don't think, however, I mean too
tactlessly to discompose you as the hostess.[46]

"The Married Son" was about twice as long as most
of the other chapters. Jordan and James discussed the
possibility of making cuts in it, but James was clearly
delighted at Jordan's final decision not to cut his chapter.[47] In spite of the length of his contribution, James
regretted that he was unable to do more. When he sent
Jordan his chapter dealing with the married son, Charles
Edward, James emphasized his disappointment at being
unable to work in a direct treatment of the old-maid
aunt. He explained: "She is the person, in the whole
thing, to have been, *objectively,* done; Miss Wilkins
making her, to my sense, too subjectively sentimental.
My own restricted effort, with C.E., was, frankly, to
objectify them all as much as possible."[48]

James had plenty of advice for his successors, but
he, unfortunately, had no control over them. In fact,
he did not even know who they would be. Part of the
problem was that James had lost his list of contributors.
He wrongly believed that there would be only two or
three chapters after his, including one written by Mark
Twain. Incidentally, James was not thrilled at the idea
of preparing the way for Twain's chapter, noting that
"that will be sure to be a clarionet *[sic]* solo only, and
won't naturally do much to crown my edifice."[49] He
also hoped that someone "more potent than" Wyatt
would write the chapter following his.[50] At one point,
James suggested that that chapter should focus on the
fiancé, Harry Goward, "reporting on C.E., from his
view, on all the rest of it, and above all on the frolic

Aunt."[51] Nevertheless, in a later letter, James explained: "The person whom I have imagined presenting in *her* recital what C.E. did in N.Y.—did with Eliza & H.G.—is the Mother herself (his whole reference to his mother *prepares* for that;) & ah me how I sh[ou]ld like to 'do' the Mother—verily!—(under a false, an extemporized name!!)"[52]

Unfortunately for James, the next chapter was "The Married Daughter," by Elizabeth Stuart Phelps, who found James's chapter "long and heavy" and promptly discarded almost everything James had developed.[53] James felt frustrated by the way the final contributors ignored his work. He explained to Jordan that he had attempted to offer them much to build on, including:

> the picture of Charles Edward's action & passion (so to speak) there, his dealings with Eliza & the young man, his "line taken" on behalf of & in the interest of his Mother &c—with more other things &c than I can say. I tried to suggest some *values* for this & to *leave* them suggested: his confrontation with the kidnapped & "compromised" youth in the Park as a Value, his then meeting, his "having it out," with Eliza &, as it were, *disposal* of her, as a Value; & I left them these Values, fairly dangling there, to my best ability, as it were, for my successors to catch at. But alas they haven't, by my vision, caught much—& my vision, such as it was, of the elements, such as *they* were, has fallen to the ground.[54]

James was particularly upset by Wyatt's treatment of "The Mother." His own chapter had emphasized the relationship between Charles Edward and his mother and suggested that the mother possessed extraordinary qualities. James complained to Jordan that the chapter, "The Mother," should have been "a thing of the highest value," and wondered: "Does your public *want* that so completely lack-lustre domestic sentimentality?"[55]

The early months of 1907 must have been dreadful for Jordan. Wyatt had submitted a manuscript that could not be used and was reluctant to make changes. James had written a chapter that was much longer than Jordan wanted and that provided a direction that some of the other authors neither understood nor particularly liked. Furthermore, Jordan still needed to find someone to take Mark Twain's place and write "The Schoolboy." To make matters worse, Elizabeth Stuart Phelps began to create a whole new set of complications. Phelps complained that she did not know what to do with her assigned character, Maria, the married daughter, and even threatened to quit the family. She did not know where James's chapter could lead, and she objected to James's suggestion that the old-maid aunt "posed as moving in better society than she did." Phelps also tried to persuade Jordan to invite her husband, Herbert Ward, a younger writer without a substantial literary reputation, to write the chapter—either on his own or in collaboration with Phelps. After Jordan rejected that proposal, Phelps ultimately found a way of handling her character. She decided to "defend Maria from the aspersions of being 'a manager,' " noting that: "Such people are often the very back-bone of family life."[56] What Phelps did was to replace James's vision of the novel with her own.

THE WHOLE FAMILY

In spite of all the disagreements, *The Whole Family* was finally completed. Unraveling the plot, however, proved to be a tricky issue for the final contributors, largely because the authors had never reached any real agreement about the characters. Several of the contributers felt that Harry Goward, the young man engaged to the daughter, was clearly an unworthy match for the heroine. In her remarkable chapter, "The School-boy," Mary Raymond Shipman Andrews attempted to address that problem by finding a new lover for Peggy. Andrews's solution moved the novel into a surprisingly new direction, but Alice Brown quickly moved the book out of it in the penultimate chapter.

It is Alice Brown who deserves most of the credit for finally resolving the plot complications. She recognized that the story was still working out the complexities introduced by Freeman and that the main problem was the old-maid aunt. Brown shared her thoughts with Jordan:

> Now, gradually, it seems to me, we have been working out from the impressionist purple shadow of Aunt Elizabeth though we have not yet escaped. One after another has thrown an illuminating ray upon her, and, seen in the light, she is not so formidable. But she is still the knot in the puzzle. If she is mad she can be grappled with. We can pack her off to a symbolic asylum and let the erotic fervor which follows her tracks die with the fancy that created it. Or is she sane? And has she lied about her age or has she not? Is she still "eligible"?[57]

THE WHOLE FAMILY

Brown finally decided that Freeman's portrait was really a brilliant satire and disposed of the aunt accordingly. She was also able to tie up most of the other loose ends, leaving van Dyke little to do in the last chapter except provide a happy ending. Brown's achievement is best expressed in Jordan's statement that every one of the other authors liked her chapter.[58]

The Whole Family appeared in *Harper's Bazar* in twelve installments from December 1907 to November 1908. Instead of identifying the authors of individual chapters, each issue simply listed the names of all twelve authors and provided the following note:

> Each chapter of this novel was written by one of the twelve authors whose names appear above. The intelligent reader will experience no difficulty in determining which author wrote each chapter—perhaps.

The guessing game kept the readers of *Harper's Bazar* intrigued for a whole year. Then, towards the end of 1908, *The Whole Family* was published in book form, where it met with good sales and polite reviews.

Almost all the reviewers compared the book to some kind of game, most said they found it amusing, and many wondered who was responsible for persuading so many distinguished writers to take part. *The Bookman* called *The Whole Family* a "monument to its anonymous projector and editor," but felt that the authors had not all played the game fairly. The reviewer argued that there ought to be clear rules forbidding each author of a chapter from taking a "sly fling" at one of his predecessors or laying a trap for one of his successors. The reviewer for *The Nation* remarked: "One fancies Mr. James hypnotically persuaded to take his place in the circle between facetious Mr. Bangs and soulful Elizabeth Stuart Phelps, and caused to produce an excellent parody of himself, as if in spite of himself." *The North American Review* was more reverent; it found the book "faithful to certain homely yet spiritual ideals that lie at the base of American life." It also predicted that the book would be "keenly enjoyed by all readers of today, and the future critic who writes the literary history of this period will not be likely to pass over it in silence."[59]

In her autobiography, Elizabeth Jordan summed up her feelings with a brief but eloquent statement. She said: *"The Whole Family* was a mess!"[60] Her statement reflects the frustration that built up while she was trying to serve as editor, adviser, mediator, critic, and friend to twelve very different literary talents. The project had aroused the energy of a dozen successful writers and left most of them, including Howells and James, feeling helplessly frustrated. *The Whole Family* was a fascinating experiment, but its ultimate lesson was that twelve literary visions were more likely to clash than harmonize.

Nevertheless, *The Whole Family* remains an intriguing book. It has to be regarded as one of the most interesting experiments with multiple points of view and the novel form in early twentieth-century literature.[61] Although *The Whole Family* has been largely ignored by critics of American literature, it deserves attention from anyone interested in Howells, James, or Freeman. Furthermore, modern readers may be pleasantly surprised by the chapters of some of the now neglected writers.

THE WHOLE FAMILY

The Whole Family has been almost completely forgotten, but the book offers both an entertaining story about family rivalries and an important record of artistic rivalries.

NOTES

1. The letters in the Elizabeth Jordan Papers in the Rare Books and Manuscripts Division of the New York Public Library are the principal sources for information on *The Whole Family*. I want to thank the New York Public Library for providing me with access to this material and for allowing me to use it in preparing this introduction.

There is surprisingly little published information on *The Whole Family*. Elizabeth Jordan offered a lively, but not completely accurate, account of the creation of *The Whole Family* in chapter 16 of her autobiography, *Three Rousing Cheers* (New York: D. Appleton-Century Co., 1938), pp. 258–280. Jordan repressed certain facts, such as the details behind her difficulties with Edith Wyatt and the demands of many of the writers for more money than Jordan offered. She also took editorial liberties with the letters she quoted, omitting phrases and occasionally quoting lines out of context. Typographical errors also mar the text of some of the letters she cites, particularly those of Henry James. The letters in the New York Public Library suggest that, in preparing her autobiography, Jordan was often willing to sacrifice accuracy of detail to the creation of an entertaining story.

THE WHOLE FAMILY

Jordan's account of Henry James's role in the production of the novel is particularly misleading. Leon Edel and Lyall H. Powers pointed out some of the problems with Jordan's account and provided an accurate text of James's letters in "Henry James and the *Bazar* Letters," originally printed in the February 1958 *Bulletin* of the New York Public Library and reprinted in the pamphlet, *Howells and James: A Double Billing* (New York: New York Public Library, 1958), pp. 27–55. The pamphlet is cited hereafter as *Bazar Letters*.

Established as a weekly in 1867, *Harper's Bazar* was originally intended to be an American version of the German magazine, *Der Bazar*, which provided women with cultural resources as well as fashion plates. Elizabeth Jordan became editor in 1900, transformed the *Bazar* into a monthly in 1901, and guided the development of the magazine until 1913 when it was sold to Hearst. The spelling of *Bazar* was changed to *Bazaar* in 1929. The original spelling of *Bazar* apparently caused some confusion. For instance, Henry James's letters to Jordan invariably misspelled the title as *Bazaar*.

2. Howells, letter to Jordan, 21 May 1906; published in *Selected Letters of W. D. Howells*, ed. William C. Fischer (Boston: Twayne Publishers, 1983), Vol. V, pp. 179–180. This volume is cited hereafter as *Selected Letters*.

3. Ibid.

4. Jordan, p. 258.

5. Howells, letter to Jordan, 21 May 1906; published in *Selected Letters*, p. 179. The version of the letter published in *Selected Letters* incorrectly prints "Mrs. Donnell" instead of

THE WHOLE FAMILY

"Mrs. Deland." Howells misspelled Fisk's last name as "Fiske."

Freeman and Bangs agreed to take part in the project, while Deland refused. It is not clear whether Jordan invited Fisk and Janvier to contribute. Deland (1857–1945) was highly regarded for her realistic tales of life in a Pennsylvania town, such as those collected in *Old Chester Tales* (1898) and *Dr. Lavendar's People* (1903), and for her novel, *The Awakening of Helena Ritchie* (1906), the rights to which Jordan had acquired for Harper's. Janvier (1849–1913) was the author of satiric stories about Philadelphia, *The Uncle of an Angel* (1891) and *The Passing of Thomas* (1901), but he also produced fiction set in Mexico, France, and New York City. Fisk (1885–19 ?) specialized in monologues, many of which focused on women; her collections include *Monologues* (1903) and *The Talking Woman* (1907).

6. In an unpublished letter to Jordan, dated 6 June 1906, Howells says that he does not think that either Henry James or Edith Wharton would be interested in participating.

7. Howells had made that suggestion in a letter to Jordan, 21 May 1906; see *Selected Letters*, p. 179.

8. On p. 261 of her autobiography, Jordan writes: "The mother selected yearned to contribute the chapter of the married daughter; the selected son-in-law passionately preferred to be the friend of the family. Every author except Mr. Howells desired to write a final chapter, and have the benefit of the literary spading done by his predecessors." It must be noted that the letters in the Jordan Papers do not provide evidence supporting these statements. In fact, none of the letters indicate that any of the contributors preferred to undertake a different chapter, and only James expressed a desire to write a final chapter. It is, of course, possible that the letters supporting Jordan's claims have simply not survived.

9. Deland, letter to Jordan, 5 June 1906; published in Jordan, pp. 261–262. This letter is not in the Elizabeth Jordan Papers, but it was clearly Deland's second letter of refusal. The Jordan Papers contain an earlier letter, dated 1 June 1906, in which Deland politely declines to participate and a much later letter, dated 15 March 1938, in which she praises Jordan's autobiography and notes the wisdom of her decision not to take part.

10. Ibid.

11. Quoted in Jordan, p. 259. The letter is not in the Jordan Papers, but two unpublished letters from Twain, dated 6 July 1906 and 30 July 1906, express an eagerness to see the early chapters. Mark Twain's response to Howells's and Freeman's contributions may be found in Alan Gribben's invaluable book, *Mark Twain's Library: A Reconstruction* (Boston: G. K. Hall, 1980), Vol. I, pp. 245–246 and 328. See also Earl F. Briden, "Samuel L. Clemens and Elizabeth Jordan: An Unpublished Letter," *Mark Twain Journal*, 17 (Summer 1974), 11–13.

12. Howells, letter to Jordan, 8 August 1906; quoted in *Selected Letters*, p. 180 fn. Jordan's account on p. 259 of her autobiography implies a slightly different picture. She writes that she and Howells "used on him all our powers of persuasion, and then drew on reservoirs we had not suspected lay within us." In her autobiography, Jordan also took a remark Henry James later made about Mark Twain, changed some words and distorted the context, making it seem as if James had responded to Twain's refusal by writing "soothingly" to Jordan: "His chapter would be a clarionet solo only, and wouldn't do much to crown *my* edifice!" (p. 260). (For the accurate text and context of James's remark about Mark Twain, see *Bazar Letters*, p. 45.)

13. Jordan's autobiography implies that James and van Dyke immediately agreed to participate and that it took her much longer to assemble the other writers. The dates of the letters of acceptance in the Jordan Papers provide a more complete and accurate account: Freeman, 31 May 1906; Brown, 1 June 1906; van Dyke, 2 June 1906; Bangs, 8 June 1906; Cutting, 9 June 1906; Wyatt, 12 June 1906. There are no letters from Vorse in the Jordan Papers, but Vorse apparently accepted the assignment by the middle of June 1906. The first letter from Andrews in the Jordan Papers is dated 26 April 1907; it could be the letter of acceptance, but there may have been an earlier acceptance letter which has not survived. It is also difficult to tell exactly when Phelps agreed to join the family. The first letter from her in the Jordan Papers which refers to *The Whole Family* is obviously incorrectly dated 28 January 1906, and should probably read 1907. Phelps's letters to Jordan did not offer a clear commitment to the project; in fact, they often express serious reservations about the project and about her willingness and ability to take part in it.

Dating James's entry into the family proves difficult. In her autobiography, Jordan writes: "Henry James at once consented to write the married son's chapter, as I had counted on him to do" (p. 259). Nevertheless, the first mention of *The Whole Family* in James's letters in the Jordan Papers does not occur until a letter dated 16 October 1906, in which James acknowledges the arrival of "your interesting letter on the subject of 'The Whole Family,' " and the first three chapters and writes: "I *incline* meanwhile, I may also say, to 'close' with you on the question of the Married Son; but can't be sure I see my way until I have read *all* of what leads up to him" (quoted in *Bazar Letters*, p. 41). In his letters (dated 27 June, 17 July, 20 July, and 27 July 1906) James refers to articles he was writing for the *Bazar*, but makes no mention of the composite novel. Moreover, the Jordan Papers includes an early list of contributors, in which James's name does not appear and Henry B. Fuller is listed as writing the married son's chapter. The list, which appears to have been prepared in June 1906, also suggests that Fuller was scheduled to hand in his chapter sometime between July 15 and September 1, and that his chapter probably would have been the fourth in the book. In short, the list implies that James was one of the last authors to join *The Whole Family* and that he was actually a replacement for Fuller who apparently dropped out.

14. These names appear in unpublished letters from Howells in the Jordan Papers. In a letter dated 6 June 1906, Howells mentions Matthews, White, Fuller, and Edith Wyatt, who eventually wrote the mother's chapter. His interest in the last three names can be partly explained by his desire to include some midwesterners. White (1868–1944) was a famous newspaper editor in Kansas; Howells admired his portrait of small town life, *In Our Town* (1906). A remark in Howells's letter of 8 August 1906 implies that Jordan approached White, but found he wanted much more money than she was willing to spend. Fuller (1857–1929) is best

known for his realistic stories about Chicago, including *Under the Skylights* (1901) which focuses on Chicago artists. Fuller may have actually agreed to write the married son's chapter; see note 13. Matthews (1852–1929) taught literature and drama at Columbia University and wrote plays, criticism, and fiction about New York City. In a letter, dated 12 June 1906, Matthews told Jordan he was too busy to participate.

Howells mentioned most of the other names in his letter of 4 July 1906. Grant (1852–1940) was a Boston judge who also wrote fiction focusing on moral and legal issues; *The Undercurrent* (1904) and *The Orchid* (1905) deal with divorce. Whitlock (1869–1934) was a lawyer, journalist, and the reform mayor of Toledo as well as the author of novels devoted to political reform. Garland (1860–1940) achieved fame with his stories about the hardships of life among midwestern farmers, most notably *Main-Travelled Roads* (1891). Smith (1838–1915) relied on a wide range of settings for his fiction, some of which focuses on artists. An undated letter in the Jordan papers suggests that he was asked to participate, but declined. Peattie (1862–1935) was a Chicago journalist, literary critic, and author, whose fiction ranged from historical romances to realistic portrayals of small town life.

In his letter of 9 August 1906, Howells praised Aldrich's *The Story of a Bad Boy* (1870) and suggested that Jordan consider him as a replacement for Mark Twain, who had just given his final refusal. Aldrich (1836–1907) was also a famous editor, poet, and short-story writer.

15. In an unpublished letter, dated 20 August 1906, Burnett praises the project but refuses politely to do the daughter-in-law. Since that chapter had been assigned to Cutting in June, the letter is somewhat puzzling. It may mean that

THE WHOLE FAMILY

Jordan was considering making some changes in the assignments. Burnett (1849–1924) is now remembered mostly for her books for children, such as *Little Lord Fauntleroy* (1886), but her novels for adults once sold well and some were highly regarded.

16. Wiggin, letter to Jordan, 13 June 1906; published in Jordan, p. 260. The version in the autobiography omits a passage in which Wiggin expresses concern with the financial arrangements.

17. Wiggin, letter to Jordan, 21 June 1906; published in Jordan, p. 278. Jordan omits Wiggin's complaints about the fee offered her. Wiggin's brief comments on Howells's chapter appear in the letter, dated 22 June 1906, in which she finally resigned from the family. Jordan does not mention them and implies that Wiggin's departure from the family did not occur until much later. Incidentally, Wiggin had collaborated with three friends on a composite novel, *The Affair at the Inn* (1904); the four later produced another novel together, *Robinetta* (1911).

18. James, letter to Jordan, 18 February 1907; published in *Bazar Letters*, p. 47. All information on the fees requested by the other writers comes from unpublished letters in the Jordan Papers.

19. Howells, letter to Jordan, 4 June 1906; quoted in *Life in Letters of William Dean Howells*, ed. Mildred Howells (Garden City: Doubleday, Doran, 1928), Vol. II, p. 223. *Selected Letters* includes much of this letter in footnotes on pp. 280–281, including some parts of a postscript omitted in Mildred Howells's edition. The full text of the letter has not been published.

20. Ibid.

21. Ibid. The editor of *Selected Letters* notes that Howells's interest in the marriage theme may have stemmed from the pain his family suffered from the broken engagement of his daughter, Mildred.

22. Howells, postscript to letter, dated 4 June 1906; quoted in *Selected Letters*, p. 281. Some information in this paragraph is drawn from Howells's unpublished letters in the Jordan Papers, dated 23 May, 4 June, 6 June, and 13 June 1906.

23. Freeman, letter to Jordan, 1 August 1906; quoted in Jordan, p. 266. Freeman's unpublished letters in the Jordan Papers are informative. When she agreed to take part, she thought that the assignment would be relatively easy, because she found the monologue a congenial form (16 June 1906). Her next letter, however, expresses her uneasiness at following a writer as distinguished as Howells. She also expresses her admiration for the chapter, but notes the need to do something drastic to create a sense of action (16 June 1906). The note accompanying her chapter explains that "such an innovation in the shape of a maiden aunt rather frightened me" (26 July 1906; quoted in Jordan, p. 265 with letter incorrectly dated as 24 July). Then Freeman writes a long, almost passionately defensive letter justifying her act (1 August 1906; Jordan made some editorial changes in the version she published, pp. 265–266).

24. Jordan, p. 264.

25. Van Dyke, undated letter to Jordan; published in Jordan, pp. 266–267. I have restored the original hyphen in "beau-knots." If, as Jordan claims, every author wrote to her about Freeman's chapter, then most of those letters have not survived or did not find their way into the Jordan Papers. Jordan states that Andrews, Vorse, and, "to a degree," Henry James admired Freeman's chapter (p. 264).

26. Jordan, p. 264. Howells's letter is not in the Jordan Papers and presumably has not survived.

27. Ibid.

28. Ibid., p. 267

29. Ibid.

30. Quoted in Gribben, Vol. I, p. 245.

31. Brown, letter to Jordan, 10 February 1907; published in Jordan, p. 275.

32. Ibid. Freeman's letters to Jordan clearly deny any intention of producing that kind of a satire. In an undated letter, apparently written in 1938 after Brown read Jordan's autobiography, Brown again noted the impact of Freeman's old-maid aunt on the family and wondered if the aunt was Freeman's subconscious response to growing old.

33. In his letters, Howells praised the chapters by Vorse, James, and Wyatt. He objected to Andrews's treatment of the small boy, noting that: "He seems to me not so much like a boy as like what a girl would be if she were a boy" (Letter to Jordan, 23 June 1907; published in Jordan, p. 269).

34. Jordan, pp. 279–280.

35. James, letter to Jordan, 27 November 1906; published in *Bazar Letters*, p. 42.

36. Jordan, p. 280.

37. James, letter to Jordan, 2 January 1907; see *Bazar Letters*, pp. 43–44.

38. Wyatt, unpublished letter to Jordan, dated 21 December 1906.

39. Jordan, p. 273.

40. Duneka, letter to Jordan, 19 December 1906; quoted in Jordan, p. 273. The edited version Jordan cites omits Duneka's comment that revision would be impossible and his suggestion that Jordan pay the author, if necessary. Duneka obviously did not know who had written the chapter, because he also wonders in the letter if Bangs wrote it.

41. Wyatt had submitted her original chapter in mid-December 1906. She and Jordan apparently exchanged some letters before the message dismissing her from the family was sent on 8 March 1907. Wyatt's protest to this action is dated 13 March 1907. Wyatt finally sent her new chapter to Jordan on 18 April 1907.

An unpublished letter, dated 14 March 1907, from Alice French accepts Jordan's invitation to join the family. French (1850–1934) was known for her local color stories about the midwest, some of which focus on labor problems.

42. Howells, letter to Jordan, 23 June 1907; published in Jordan, p. 269.

43. James, letter to Jordan, 13 August 1907; published in *Bazar Letters*, p. 52.

44. Howells, letter to Jordan, 21 February 1907; published in *Selected Letters*.

45. Jordan, p. 279.

46. James, letter to Jordan, 2 October 1907; published in *Bazar Letters*, pp. 52–53.

47. James's view of the possible cuts appears in his letters dated 25 January, 18 February, 5 March, and 14 March 1907; see *Bazar Letters*, pp. 45–49.

48. James, letter to Jordan, 25 January 1907; published in *Bazar Letters*, p. 46.

49. James, letter to Jordan, 22 January 1907; published in *Bazar Letters*, p. 45.

50. James, letter to Jordan, 25 January 1907; published in *Bazar Letters*, p. 46.

51. Ibid.

52. James, letter to Jordan, 5 March 1907; published in *Bazar Letters*, p. 48.

53. Phelps, letter to Jordan, 18 February 1907; quoted in Jordan, p. 277.

54. James, letter to Jordan, 13 August 1907; published in *Bazar Letters*, p. 51.
Sergio Perosa offers an accurate assessment of the problems James's chapter caused for his successors in *Henry James and the Experimental Novel* (Charlottesville: University Press of Virginia, 1978), pp. 107–130, noting that: "No one but him could have carried the story forward once he had put his skillful hand to it. If James's chapter in *The Whole Family*

is a perfect example of his latter style and technique, seen from another angle it did prove a stumbling block for anyone else having to start from there. James's contribution froze the action, stopped all movement, and brought the novel to a standstill" (p. 117).

55. *Bazar Letters,* pp. 51–52.

56. This paragraph is based largely on unpublished letters to Jordan from Phelps, dated 1 February, 18 February, and 23 February 1907; quotations are from Jordan, p. 277. I have restored Phelps's original phrase "very back-bone" instead of using Jordan's "backbone."

57. Brown, letter to Jordan, 10 February 1907; published in Jordan, p. 275. I have restored Brown's original: Jordan's version incorrectly says "fever" instead of fervor and adds an "ic" to "impressionist."

58. Jordan, p. 277.

59. *Bookman,* Vol. 28, January 1909, 422–424. *Nation,* Vol. 87, 3 December 1908, 552–553. *North American Review,* Vol. 188, December 1908, 928–930.

60. Jordan, p. 280. In spite of these feelings, Jordan later went on to edit another composite novel, *The Sturdy Oak* (1917), which was written by fourteen American authors who donated their talents and all the royalty fees to the suffrage cause. Vorce was the only writer to contribute chapters to both composite novels.

61. *The Whole Family* is the most interesting composite novel in American literature, but it is not the only one. Six authors, including Harriet Beecher Stowe and Edward Ev-

erett Hale, collaborated on *Six of One by Half a Dozen of the Other* (1872). Fourteen authors collaborated on *The Sturdy Oak* (1917), which Jordan also edited. The detective novel, *Bobbed Hair* (1925), was the work of "twenty famous authors" including Dorothy Parker, Alexander Woollcott, Louis Bromfield, Rube Goldberg, and George Palmer Putnam. *The Whole Family* is the most uneven, the most surprising, and the most intriguing of these novels.

Among the other literary stunts which have attracted talented American writers is *A House Party* (1901) a volume of short stories held together by a frame narrative. The book was edited by Paul Leicester Paul, with contributions by John Kendrick Bangs, Frank R. Stockton, Alice French, Sarah Orne Jewett, Owen Wister, George Washington Cable and others. The authors of each story were not identified and readers were invited to try to win a thousand dollars by guessing the correct authors.

THE WHOLE FAMILY

THE WHOLE FAMILY

I

THE FATHER

By William Dean Howells

As soon as we heard the pleasant news—I suppose the news of an engagement ought always to be called pleasant—it was decided that I ought to speak first about it, and speak to the father. We had not been a great while in the neighborhood, and it would look less like a bid for the familiar acquaintance of people living on a larger scale than ourselves, and less of an opening for our own intimacy if they turned out to be not quite so desirable in other ways as they were in the worldly way. For the ladies of the respective families first to offer and receive congratulations would be very much more committing on both sides; at the same time, to avoid the appearance of stiffness, some one ought to speak, and speak promptly. The news had not come to us directly from our neighbors, but au-

3

thoritatively from a friend of theirs, who was also a friend of ours, and we could not very well hold back. So, in the cool of the early evening, when I had quite finished rasping my lawn with the new mower, I left it at the end of the swath, which had brought me near the fence, and said across it, "Good-evening!"

My neighbor turned from making his man pour a pail of water on the earth round a freshly planted tree, and said, "Oh, good-evening! How d'ye do? Glad to see you!" and offered his hand over the low coping so cordially that I felt warranted in holding it a moment.

"I hope it's in order for me to say how very much my wife and I are interested in the news we've heard about one of your daughters? May I offer our best wishes for her happiness?"

"Oh, thank you," my neighbor said. "You're very good indeed. Yes, it's rather exciting—for us. I guess that's all for to-night, Al," he said, in dismissal of his man, before turning to lay his arms comfortably on the fence top. Then he laughed, before he added, to me, "And rather surprising, too."

"Those things are always rather surprising, aren't they?" I suggested.

"Well, yes, I suppose they are. It oughtn't be so in our case, though, as we've been through it twice before: once with my son—he oughtn't to have counted, but he did—and once with my eldest

4

daughter. Yes, you might say you never do quite expect it, though everybody else does. Then, in this case, she was the baby so long, that we always thought of her as a little girl. Yes, she's kept on being the pet, I guess, and we couldn't realize what was in the air."

I had thought, from the first sight of him, that there was something very charming in my neighbor's looks. He had a large, round head, which had once been red, but was now a russet silvered, and was not too large for his manly frame, swaying amply outward, but not too amply, at the girth. He had blue, kind eyes, and a face fully freckled, and the girl he was speaking of with a tenderness in his tones rather than his words, was a young feminine copy of him; only, her head was little, under its load of red hair, and her figure, which we had lately noticed flitting in and out, as with a shy consciousness of being stared at on account of her engagement, was as light as his was heavy on its feet.

I said, "Naturally," and he seemed glad of the chance to laugh again.

"Well, of course! And her being away at school made it all the more so. If we'd had her under our eye, here— Well, we shouldn't have had her under our eye if she had *been* here; or if we had, we shouldn't have seen what was going on; at least *I* shouldn't; maybe her mother would. So it's just as well it happened as it did happen, I guess.

5

We shouldn't have been any the wiser if we'd known all about it." I joined him in his laugh at his paradox, and he began again. "What's that about being the unexpected that happens? I guess what happens is what ought to have been expected. We might have known when we let her go to a co-educational college that we were taking a risk of losing her; but we lost our other daughter that way, and *she* never went to *any* kind of college. I guess we counted the chances before we let her go. What's the use? Of course we did, and I remember saying to my wife, who's more anxious than I am about most things—women are, I guess—that if the worst came to the worst, it might not be such a bad thing. I always thought it wasn't such an objectionable feature, in the coeducational system, if the young people did get acquainted under it, and maybe so well acquainted that they didn't want to part enemies in the end. I said to my wife that I didn't see how, if a girl was going to get married, she could have a better basis than knowing the fellow through three or four years' hard work together. When you think of the sort of hit-or-miss affairs most marriages are that young people make after a few parties and picnics, coeducation as a preliminary to domestic happiness doesn't seem a bad notion."

"There's something in what you say," I assented.

"Of course there is," my neighbor insisted. "I

couldn't help laughing, though," and he laughed, as if to show how helpless he had been, "at what my wife said. She said she guessed if it came to that they would get to know more of each other's looks than they did of their minds. She had me there, but I don't think my girl has made out so very poorly even as far as books are concerned."

Upon this invitation to praise her, I ventured to say, "A young lady of Miss Talbert's looks doesn't need much help from books."

I could see that what I had said pleased him to the core, though he put on a frown of disclaimer in replying, "I don't know about her looks. She's a *good* girl, though, and that's the main thing, I guess."

"For her father, yes, but other people don't mind her being pretty," I persisted. "My wife says when Miss Talbert comes out into the garden, the other flowers have no chance."

"Good for Mrs. Temple!" my neighbor shouted, joyously giving himself away.

I have always noticed that when you praise a girl's beauty to her father, though he makes a point of turning it off in the direction of her goodness, he likes so well to believe she is pretty that he cannot hold out against any persistence in the admirer of her beauty. My neighbor now said with the effect of tasting a peculiar sweetness in my words, "I guess I shall have to tell my wife, that."

Then he added, with a rush of hospitality, "Won't you come in and tell her yourself?"

"Not now, thank you. It's about our tea-time."

"Glad it isn't your *dinner*-time!" he said, heartily.

"Well, yes. We don't see the sense of dining late in a place like this. The fact is, we're both village-bred, and we like the mid-day dinner. We make rather a high tea, though."

"So do we. I always want a dish of something hot. My wife thinks cake is light, but I think meat is."

"Well, cake is the New England superstition," I observed. "And I suppose York State, too."

"Yes, more than pie is," he agreed. "For supper, anyway. You may have pie at any or all of the three meals, but you have *got* to have cake at tea, if you are anybody at all. In the place where my wife lived, a woman's social standing was measured by the number of kinds of cake she had."

We laughed at that, too, and then there came a little interval and I said, "Your place is looking fine."

He turned his head and gave it a comprehensive stare. "Yes, it is," he admitted. "They tell me it's an ugly old house, and I guess if my girls, counting my daughter-in-law, had their way, they would have that French roof off, and something Georgian—that's what they call it—on, about as quick as the carpenter could do it. They want a

8

kind of classic front, with pillars and a pediment; or more the Mount Vernon style, body yellow, with white trim. They call it Georgian after Washington?" This was obviously a joke.

"No, I believe it was another George, or four others. But I don't wonder you want to keep your house as it is. It expresses something characteristic." I saved myself by forbearing to say it was handsome. It was, in fact, a vast, gray-green wooden edifice, with a mansard-roof cut up into many angles, tipped at the gables with rockets and finials, and with a square tower in front, ending in a sort of lookout at the top, with a fence of iron filigree round it. The taste of 1875 could not go further; it must have cost a heap of money in the depreciated paper of the day.

I suggested something of the kind to my neighbor, and he laughed. "I guess it cost all we had at the time. We had been saving along up, and in those days it used to be thought that the best investment you could make was to put your money in a house of your own. That's what we did, anyway. I had just got to be superintendent of the Works, and I don't say but what we felt my position a little. Well, we felt it more than we did when I got to be owner." He laughed in good-humored self-satire. "My wife used to say we wanted a large house so as to have it big enough to hold *me*, when I was feeling my best, and we built the largest we could for all the money we had. She had a plan of her own, which she took partly from the house of a girl friend of hers where she had been visiting, and we got a builder to carry out her idea. We did have some talk about an architect, but the builder said he didn't want any architect bothering around *him*, and I don't know as *she* did, either. Her idea was plenty of chambers and plenty of room in them, and two big parlors one side of the front door, and a library and dining-room on the other; kitchen in the L part, and girl's room over that; wide front hall, and black-walnut finish all through the first floor. It was considered the best house at the time in Eastridge, and I guess it was. But now, I don't say but what it's old-fashioned. I have to own up to that with the girls, but I tell them so are we, and that seems to make it all right for a while. I guess we sha'n't change."

He continued to stare at the simple-hearted edifice, so simple-hearted in its out-dated pretentiousness, and then he turned and leaned over the top of the fence where he had left his arms lying, while contemplating the early monument of his success. In making my journalistic study, more or less involuntary, of Eastridge, I had put him down as materially the first man of the place; I might have gone farther and put him down as the first man intellectually. We folk who have to do more constantly with reading and writing are apt to think that the other folk who have more to do with making and marketing have not so much mind, but I fancy we make a mistake in that now and then. It is only another kind of mind which they have quite as much of as we have of ours. It was intellectual force that built up the Plated-Ware Works of Eastridge, where there was no other reason for their being, and it was mental grip that held constantly to the management, and finally grasped the ownership. Nobody ever said that Talbert had come unfairly into that, or that he had misused his money in buying men after he began to come into it in quantity. He was felt in a great many ways, though he made something of a point of not being prominent in politics, after being president of the village two terms. The minister of his church was certainly such a preacher as he liked; and nothing was done in the church society without him; he gave the town a library building, and a soldier's monument; he was foremost in getting the water brought in, which was natural enough since he needed it the most; he took a great interest in school matters, and had a fight to keep himself off the board of education; he went into his pocket for village improvements whenever he was asked, and he was the chief contributor to the public fountain under the big elm. If he carefully, or even jealously guarded his own interests, and held the leading law firm in the hollow of his hand, he was not oppressive, to the general knowledge. He was a despot, perhaps, but he was Blackstone's ideal of the head of a state, a good despot. In all his family relations he was of the exemplary perfection which most other men attain only on their tombstones, and I had found him the best of neighbors. There were some shadows of diffidence between the ladies of our families, mainly on the part of my wife, but none between Talbert and me. He showed me, as a newspaper man with ideals if not abilities rather above the average, a deference which pleased my wife, even more than me.

It was the married daughter whom she most feared might, if occasion offered, give herself more consequence than her due. She had tried to rule her own family while in her father's house, and now though she had a house of her own, my wife believed that she had not wholly relinquished her dominion there. Her husband was the junior member of the law firm which Talbert kept in his pay, to the exclusion of most other clients, and he was a very good fellow, so far as I knew, with the modern conception of his profession which, in our smaller towns and cities, has resulted in corporation lawyers and criminal lawyers, and has left to a few aging attorneys the faded traditions and the scanty affairs of the profession. My wife does not mind his standing somewhat in awe of his father-in-law, but she thinks poorly of his spirit in relation to that managing girl he has married. Talbert's son is in the business with him, and will probably succeed him in it; but it is well known in the place that he will never be the man his father is, not merely on account of his college education, but also on account of the easy temperament, which if he had indulged it to the full would have left him no better than some kind of artist. As it is, he seems to leave all the push to his father; he still does some sketching outside, and putters over the æsthetic details in the business, the new designs for the plated ware, and the illustrated catalogues which the house publishes every year; I am in hopes that we shall get the printing, after we have got the facilities. It would be all right with the young man in the opinion of his censors if he had married a different kind of woman, but young Mrs. Talbert is popularly held just such another as her husband, and easy-going to the last degree. She was two or three years at the Art Students' League, and it was there that her husband met her before they both decided to give up painting and get married.

The two youngest children, or the fall chickens as they are called in recognition of the wide interval between their ages and those of the other children, are probably of the indeterminate character proper to their years. We think the girl rather inclines to a hauteur based upon the general neglect of that quality in the family, where even the eldest sister is too much engaged in ruling to have much force left for snubbing. The child carries herself with a vague loftiness, which has apparently not awaited the moment of long skirts for keeping pretenders to her favor at a distance. In the default of other impertinents to keep in abeyance we fancy that she exercises her gift upon her younger brother, who, so far as we have been able to note, is of a disposition which would be entirely sweet if it were not for the exasperations he suffers from her. I like to put myself in his place, and to hold that he believes himself a better judge than she of the sort of companions he chooses, she being disabled by the mental constitution of her sex, and the defects of a girl's training, from knowing the rare quality of boys who present themselves even to my friendly eyes as dirty, and, when not patched, ragged. I please myself in my guesses at her character with the conjecture that she is not satisfied with her sister's engagement to a fellow-student in a co-educational college, who is looking forward to a professorship.

In spite of her injustice in regard to his own companions, this imaginable attitude of hers impresses the boy, if I understand boys. I have no doubt he reasons that she must be right about something, and as she is never right about boys, she must be right about brothers-in-law, potential if not actual. This one may be, for all the boy knows, a sissy; he inclines to believe, from what he understands of the matter, that he is indeed a sissy, or he would never have gone to a college where half the students are girls. He himself, as I have heard, intends to go to a college, but whether Harvard, or Bryant's Business College, he has not yet decided. One thing he does know, though, and that is there are not going to be any girls in it.

We have not allowed our invention so great play in regard to the elder members of our neighbor's family perhaps because we really know something more about them. Mrs. Talbert duly called after we came to Eastridge, and when my wife had self-respectfully waited a proper time, which she made a little more than a week lest she should feel that she had been too eager for the acquaintance, she returned the call. Then she met not only Mrs. Talbert, but Mrs. Talbert's mother, who lives with them, in an anxiety for their health which would impair her own if she were not of a constitution such as you do not find in these days of unladylike athletics. She was inclined to be rather strict with my wife about her own health, and mine too, and told her she must be careful not to let me work too hard, or overeat, or leave off my flannels before the weather was settled in the spring. She said she had heard that I had left a very good position on a

Buffalo paper when I bought the Eastridge *Banner*, and that the town ought to feel very much honored. My wife suppressed her conviction that this was the correct view of the case, in a deprecatory expression of our happiness in finding ourselves in Eastridge, and our entire satisfaction with our prospects and surroundings. Then Mrs. Talbert's mother inquired, as delicately as possible, what denominations, religious and medical, we were of, how many children we had, and whether mostly boys or girls, and where and how long we had been married. She was glad, she said, that we had taken the place next them, after our brief sojourn in the furnished house where we had first lived, and said that there was only one objection to the locality, which was the prevalence of moths; they obliged you to put away your things in naphtha-balls almost the moment the spring opened. She wished to know what books my wife was presently reading, and whether she approved of women's clubs to the extent that they were carried to in some places. She believed in book clubs, but to her mind it was very questionable whether the time that ladies gave to writing papers on so many different subjects was well spent. She thought it a pity that so many things were canned, nowadays, and so well canned that the old arts of pickling and preserving were almost entirely lost. In the conversation, where she bore a leading part as long as she remained in the room, her mind took a wide range, and visited more human interests than my wife was at first able to mention, though afterward she remembered so many that I formed the notion of something encyclopedic in its compass. When she reached the letter Z, she rose and took leave of my wife, saying that now she must go and lie down, as it appeared to be her invariable custom to do (in behalf of the robust health which she had inherited unimpaired from a New England ancestry), at exactly half-past four every afternoon. It was this, she said, more than any one thing that enabled her to go through so much as she did; but through the door which she left open behind her my wife heard Talbert's voice saying, in mixed mockery and tenderness, "Don't forget your tonic, mother," and hers saying, "No, I won't, Cyrus. I never forget it, and it's a great pity you don't take it, too."

It was our conclusion from all the facts of this call, when we came to discuss them in the light of some friendly gossip which we had previously heard, that the eldest daughter of the Talberts came honestly by her love of ruling if she got it from her grandmother, but that she was able to indulge it oftener, and yet not so often as might have been supposed from the mild reticence of her mother. Older if not shrewder observers than ourselves declared that what went in that house was what Mrs. Talbert said, and that it went all the more effectively because what she said Talbert said too. That might have been because she said so little. When her mother left the room she let a silence follow in which she seemed too embarrassed to speak for a while on finding herself alone with my wife, and my wife decided that the shyness of the girl whose engagement was soon afterward reported, as well as the easy-goingness of the eldest son, had come from their mother.   As soon as Mrs. Talbert could command herself, she began to talk, and every word she said was full of sense, with a little gust of humor in the sense which was perfectly charming.   Absolutely unworldly as she was, she had very good manners; in her evasive way she was certainly qualified to be the leader of society in Eastridge, ard socially Eastridge thought fairly well of itself.   She did not obviously pretend to so much literature as her mother, but she showed an even nicer intelligence of our own situation in Eastridge.   She spoke with a quiet appreciation of the improvement in the *Banner*, which, although she quoted Mr. Talbert, seemed to be the result of her personal acquaintance with the paper in the past as well as the present.   My wife pronounced her the ideal mother of a family, and just what the wife of such a man as Cyrus Talbert ought to be, but no doubt because Mrs. Talbert's characteristics were not so salient as her mother's, my wife was less definitely descriptive of her.

18

From time to time, it seemed that there was a sister of Mr. Talbert's who visited in the family, but was now away on one of the many other visits in which she passed her life. She was always going or coming somewhere, but at the moment she was gone. My wife inferred from the generation to which her brother belonged that she had long been a lady of that age when ladies begin to be spoken of as maiden. Mrs. Talbert spoke of her as if they were better friends than sisters-in-law are apt to be, and said that she was to be with them soon, and she would bring her with her when she returned my wife's call. From the general impression in Eastridge we gathered that Miss Talbert was not without the disappointment which endears maiden ladies to the imagination, but the disappointment was of a date so remote that it was only matter of pathetic hearsay, now. Miss Talbert, in her much going and coming, had not failed of being several times in Europe. She especially affected Florence, where she was believed to have studied the Tuscan school to unusual purpose, though this was not apparent in any work of her own. We formed the notion that she might be uncomfortably cultured, but when she came to call with Mrs. Talbert afterward, my wife reported that you would not have thought, except for a remark she dropped now and then, that she had ever been out of her central New York village, and so far from putting on airs of art, she did not speak of any gallery abroad, or of the pensions in which she stayed in Florence, or the hotels in other cities of Italy where she had stopped to visit the local schools of painting.

In this somewhat protracted excursion I have not forgotten that I left Mr. Talbert leaning against our party fence, with his arms resting on the top, after a keen if not critical survey of his dwelling. He did not take up our talk at just the point where we had been in it, but after a reflective moment, he said, "I don't remember just whether Mrs. Temple told my mother-in-law you were homœopaths or allopaths."

"Well," I said, "that depends. I rather think we are homœopaths of a low-potency type." My neighbor's face confessed a certain disappointment. "But we are not bigoted, even in the article of appreciable doses. Our own family doctor in our old place always advised us, in stress of absence from him, to get the best doctor wherever we happened to be, so far as we could make him out, and not mind what school he was of. I suppose we have been treated by as many allopaths as homœopaths, but we're rather a healthy family, and put it all together we have not been treated a great deal by either."

Mr. Talbert looked relieved. "Oh, then you will have Dr. Denbigh. He puts your rule the other way, and gets the best patient he can, no matter whether he is a homœopath or an allopath. We have him, in all our branches; he is the best doctor in Eastridge, and he is the best man. I want you to know him, and you can't know a doctor the way you ought to, unless he's your family physician."

"You're quite right, I think, but that's a matter I should have to leave two-thirds of to my wife: women are two-thirds of the patients in every healthy family, and they ought to have the ruling voice about the doctor." We had formed the habit already of laughing at any appearance of joke in each other, and my neighbor now rolled his large head in mirth, and said:

"That's so, I guess. But I guess there won't be any trouble about Mrs. Temple's vote when she sees Denbigh. His specialty is the capture of sensible women. They all swear by him. You met him, didn't you, at my office, the other day?"

"Oh yes, and I liked him so much that I wished I was sick on the spot!"

"That's good!" my neighbor said, joyfully. "Well, you could meet the doctor there almost any afternoon of the week, toward closing-up hours, and almost any evening at our house here, when he isn't off on duty. It's a generally understood thing that if he isn't at home, or making a professional visit, he's at one place or the other. The farmers round stop for him with their buggies, when they're in a hurry, and half our calls over the 'phone are for Dr. Denbigh. The fact is he likes to talk, and if there's any sort of man that *I* like to talk with better than another, it's a doctor. I never knew one yet that didn't say something worth while within five minutes' time. Then, you know that you can be free with them, be yourself, and that's always worth while, whether you're worth while yourself or not. You can say just what you think about anybody or anything, and you know it won't go farther. You may not be a patient, but they've always got their Hippocratic oath with them, and they're safe. That so?"

My neighbor wished the pleasure of my explicit assent; my tacit assent he must have read in my smile. "Yes," I said, "and they're always so tolerant and compassionate. I don't want to say anything against the reverend clergy; they're oftener saints upon earth than we allow; but a doctor is more solid comfort; he seems to understand you experientially."

"That's it! You've hit it! He's seen lots of other cases like yours, and next to a man's feeling that he's a peculiar sufferer, he likes to know that there are other fellows in the same box."

We both laughed at this; it was, in fact, a joke we were the joint authors of.

"Well, we don't often talk about my ailments; I haven't got a great many; and generally we get on some abstract topic. Just now we're running the question of female education, perhaps because it's impersonal, and we can both treat of it without prejudice."

"The doctor isn't married, I believe?"

"He's a widower of long standing, and that's the best kind of doctor to have: then he's a kind of a bachelor with practical wisdom added. You see, I've always had the idea that women, beginning with little girls and ending with grandmothers, ought to be brought up as nearly like their brothers as can be—that is, if they are to be the wives of other women's brothers. It don't so much matter how an old maid is brought up, but you can't have her destiny in view, though I believe if an old maid could be brought up more like an old bachelor she would be more comfortable to herself, anyway."

"And what does Dr. Denbigh say?"

"Well, you must hear him talk. I guess he rather wants to draw me out, for the most part."

"I don't wonder at that. I wish you'd draw yourself out. I've thought something in the direction of your opinion myself."

"Have you? That's good! We'll tackle the doctor together sometime. The difficulty about putting a thing like that in practice is that you have to co-operate in it with women who have been brought up in the old way. A man's wife is a woman—"

"Generally," I assented, as if for argument's sake.

He gave himself time to laugh. "And she has the charge of the children as long as they're young, and she's a good deal more likely to bring up the boys like girls than the girls like boys. But the boys take themselves out of her hands pretty soon, while the girls have to stay under her thumb till they come out just the kind of women we've always had."

"We've managed to worry along with them."

"Yes, we have. And I don't say but what we fancy them as they are when we first begin to 'take notice.' One trouble is that children are sick so much, and their mothers scare you with that, and you haven't the courage to put your theories into practice. I can't say that any of my girls have inherited my constitution but this one." I knew he meant the one whose engagement was the origin of our conversation. "If you've heard my mother-in-law talk about her constitution you would think she belonged to the healthiest family that ever got out of New England alive, but the fact is there's always something the matter with her, or she thinks there is, and she's taking medicine for it, anyway. I can't say but what my wife has always been strong enough, and I've been satisfied to have the children take after her; but when I saw this one's sorrel-top, as we used to call it before we admired red hair, I knew she was a Talbert, and I made up my mind to begin my system with her." He laughed as with a sense of agreeable discomfiture. "I can't say it worked very well, or rather that it had a chance. You see, her mother had to apply it; I was always too busy. And a curious thing was that though the girl looked like me, she was a good deal more like her mother in temperament and character."

"Perhaps," I ventured, "that's the reason why she was your favorite."

He dropped his head in rather a shamefaced way, but lifted it with another laugh. "Well, there may be something in that. Not," he gravely retrieved himself, "that we have ever distinguished between our children."

"No, neither have we. But one can't help liking the ways of one child better than another; one will rather take the fancy more than the rest."

"Well," my neighbor owned, "I don't know but it's that kind of shyness in them both. I suppose one likes to think his girl looks like him, but doesn't mind her being like her mother. I'm glad she's got my constitution, though. My eldest daughter is more like her grandmother in looks, and I guess she's got her disposition too, more. I don't know," he said, vaguely, "what the last one is going to be like. She seems to be more worldly. But," he resumed, strenuously, as if the remembrance of old opposition remained in his nerves, "when it came to this going off to school, or college, or whatever, I put my foot down, and kept it down. I guess her mother was willing enough to do my way, but her sister was all for some of those colleges where girls are educated with other girls and not with young men. She said they were more ladylike, and a lot more stuff and nonsense, and were more likely to be fit for society. She said this one would meet a lot of jays, and very likely fall in love with one; and when we first heard of this affair of Peggy's I don't believe but what her sister got more satisfaction out of it than I did. She's quick enough! And a woman likes to feel that she's a prophetess at any time of her life. That's about all that seems to keep some of them going when they get old." I knew that here he had his mother-in-law rather than his daughter in mind, and I didn't interrupt the sarcastic silence into which he fell. "You've never met the young man, I believe?" he asked, at quite another point, and to the negation of my look he added, "To be sure! We've hardly met him ourselves; he's only been here once; but you'll see him —you and Mrs. Temple. Well!" He lifted his head, as if he were going away, but he did not lift his arms from the fence, and so I knew that he had not emptied the bag of his unexpected confidences; I did not know why he was making them to me, but I liked him the better for them, and tried to feel that I was worthy of them. He began with a laugh, "They both paid it into me so," and now I knew that he meant his eldest daughter as well as her grandmother, "that my wife turned round and took my part, and said it was the very best thing that could happen; and she used all the arguments that I had used with her, when she had her misgivings about it, and she didn't leave them a word to say. A curious thing about it was, that though my arguments seemed to convince them, they didn't convince me. Ever notice, how when another person repeats what you've said, it sounds kind of weak and foolish?" I owned that my reasons had at times some such way of turning against me from the mouths of others, and he went on: "But they seemed to silence her own misgivings, and she's been enthusiastic for the engagement ever since. What's the reason," he asked, "why a man, if he's any way impetuous, wants to back out of a situation just about the time a woman has got set in it like the everlasting hills? Is it because she feels the need of holding fast for both, or is it because she knows she hasn't the strength to keep to her conclusion, if she wavers at all, while a man can let himself play back and forth, and still stay put."

"Well, in a question like that," I said, and I won my neighbor's easy laugh, "I always like to give my own sex the benefit of the doubt, and I haven't any question but man's inconsistency is always attributable to his magnanimity."

"I guess I shall have to put that up on the doctor,"

my neighbor said, as he lifted his arms from the fence at last, and backed away from it.

I knew that he was really going in-doors now, and that I must come out with what was in my mind, if I meant to say it at all, and so I said, "By-the-way, there's something. You know I don't go in much for what's called society journalism, especially in the country press, where it mostly takes the form of 'Miss Sadie Myers is visiting with Miss Mamie Peters,' but I realize that a country paper nowa-days must be a kind of open letter to the neighbor-hood, and I suppose you have no objection to my mentioning the engagement?"

This made Mr. Talbert look serious; and I fancy my proposition made him realize the affair as he had not before, perhaps. After a moment's pause, he said, "Well! That's something I should like to talk with my wife about."

"Do so!" I applauded. "I only suggest it—or chiefly, or partly—because you can have it reach our public in just the form you want, and the Rochester and Syracuse papers will copy my paragraph; but if you leave it to their Eastridge correspondents—"

"That's true," he assented. "I'll speak to Mrs. Talbert—" He walked so inconclusively away that I was not surprised to have him turn and come back before I left my place. "Why, certainly! Make the announcement! It's got to come out. It's a kind of a wrench, thinking of it as a public affair; because a man's daughter is always a little girl to him, and he can't realize— And this one— But of course!"

"Would you like to suggest any particular form of words?" I hesitated.

"Oh no! Leave that to you entirely. I know we can trust you not to make any blare about it. Just say that they were fellow-students—I should like that to be known, so that people sha'n't think I don't like to have it known—and that he's looking forward to a professorship in the same college— How queer it all seems!"

"Very well, then, I'll announce it in our next. There's time to send me word if Mrs. Talbert has any suggestions."

"All right. But she won't have any. Well, good-evening."

"Good-evening," I said from my side of the fence; and when I had watched him definitively in-doors, I turned and walked into my own house.

The first thing my wife said was, "You haven't asked him to let you announce it in the *Banner?*"

"But I have, though!"

"Well!" she gasped.

"What is the matter?" I demanded. "It's a public affair, isn't it?"

"It's a family affair—"

"Well, I consider the readers of the *Banner* a part of the family."

29

II

THE OLD-MAID AUNT

By Mary E. Wilkins Freeman

I AM relegated here in Eastridge to the position
in which I suppose I properly belong, and I dare
say it is for my best spiritual and temporal good.
Here I am the old-maid aunt. Not a day, not an
hour, not a minute, when I am with other people,
passes that I do not see myself in their estimation
playing that rôle as plainly as if I saw myself in a
looking-glass. It is a moral lesson which I presume
I need. I have just returned from my visit at the
Pollards' country-house in Lancaster, where I most
assuredly did not have it. I do not think I deceive
myself. I know it is the popular opinion that old
maids are exceedingly prone to deceive themselves
concerning the endurance of their youth and charms,
and the views of other people with regard to them.
But I am willing, even anxious, to be quite frank
with myself. Since—well, never mind since what
time—I have not cared an iota whether I was considered an old maid or not. The situation has
seemed to me rather amusing, inasmuch as it has
involved a secret willingness to be what everybody

has considered me as very unwilling to be. I have regarded it as a sort of joke upon other people.

But I think I am honest—I really mean to be, and I think I am—when I say that outside East-ridge the rôle of an old-maid aunt is the very last one which I can take to any advantage. Here I am estimated according to what people think I am, rather than what I actually am. In the first place, I am only fifteen years older than Peggy, who has just become engaged, but those fifteen years seem countless æons to the child herself and the other members of the family. I am ten years younger than my brother's wife, but she and my brother regard me as old enough to be her mother. As for Grandmother Evarts, she fairly looks up to me as her superior in age, although she *does* patronize me. She would patronize the prophets of old. I don't believe she ever says her prayers without infusing a little patronage into her petitions. The other day Grandmother Evarts actually inquired of me, of *me!* concerning a knitting-stitch. I had half a mind to retort, "Would you like a lesson in bridge, dear old soul?" She never heard of bridge, and I suppose she would have thought I meant bridge-building. I sometimes wonder why it is that all my brother's family are so singularly unsophisticated, even Cyrus himself, able as he is and dear as he is.

Sometimes I speculate as to whether it can be due to the mansard-roof of their house. I have always had a theory that inanimate things exerted more of an influence over people than they dreamed, and a mansard-roof, to my mind, belongs to a period which was most unsophisticated and fatuous, not merely concerning æsthetics, but simple comfort. Those bedrooms under the mansard-roof are miracles not only of ugliness, but discomfort, and there is no attic. I think that a house without a good roomy attic is like a man without brains. Possibly living in a brainless house has affected the mental outlook of my relatives, although their brains are well enough. Peggy is not exactly remarkable for hers, but she is charmingly pretty, and has a wonderful knack at putting on her clothes, which might be esteemed a purely feminine brain, in her fingers. Charles Edward really has brains, although he is a round peg in a square hole, and as for Alice, her brains are above the normal, although she unfortunately knows it, and Billy, if he ever gets away from Alice, will show what he is made of. Maria's intellect is all right, although cast in a petty mould. She repeats Grandmother Evarts, which is a pity, because there are types not worth repeating. Maria if she had not her husband Tom to manage, would simply fall on her face. It goes hard with a purely patronizing soul when there is nobody to manage; there is apt to be an explosion. However, Maria *has* Tom. But none of my brother's family, not even my dear sister-in-law, Cyrus's wife, have the right point of view with regard to the present, possibly on account of the mansard-roof which has overshadowed them. They do not know that to-day an old-maid aunt is as much of an anomaly as a spinning-wheel, that she has ceased to exist, that she is prehistoric, that even grandmothers have almost disappeared from off the face of the earth. In short, they do not know that I am not an old-maid aunt except under this blessed mansard-roof, and some other roofs of Eastridge, many of which are also mansard, where the influence of their fixed belief prevails. For instance, they told the people next door, who have moved here recently, that the old-maid aunt was coming, and so, when I went to call with my sister-in-law, Mrs. Temple saw her quite distinctly. To think of Ned Temple being married to a woman like that, who takes things on trust and does not use her own eyes! Her two little girls are exactly like her. I wonder what Ned himself will think. I wonder if he will see that my hair is as red-gold as Peggy's, that I am quite as slim, that there is not a line on my face, that I still keep my girl color with no aid, that I wear frills of the latest fashion, and look no older than when he first saw me. I really do not know myself how I have managed to remain so intact; possibly because I have always grasped all the minor sweets of life, even if I could not have the really big worth-while ones. I honestly do not think that I have had the latter. But I have not taken the position of some people, that if I cannot have what I want most I will have nothing. I have taken whatever Providence chose to give me in the way of small sweets, and made the most of them. Then I have had much womanly pride, and that is a powerful tonic.

For instance, years ago, when my best lamp of life went out, so to speak, I lit all my candles and kept my path. I took just as much pains with my hair and my dress, and if I was unhappy I kept it out of evidence on my face. I let my heart ache and bleed, but I would have died before I wrinkled my forehead and dimmed my eyes with tears and let everybody else know. That was about the time when I met Ned Temple, and he fell so madly in love with me, and threatened to shoot himself if I would not marry him. He did not. Most men do not. I wonder if he placed me when he heard of my anticipated coming. Probably he did not. They have probably alluded to me as dear old Aunt Elizabeth, and when he met me (I was staying at Harriet Munroe's before she was married) nobody called me Elizabeth, but Lily. Miss Elizabeth Talbert, instead of Lily Talbert, might naturally set him wrong. Everybody here calls me Elizabeth. Outside Eastridge I am Lily. I dare say Ned Temple has not dreamed who I am. I hear that he is quite brilliant, although the poor fellow must be limited as to his income. However, in some respects it must be just as well. It would be a great trial to a man with a large income to have a wife like Mrs. Temple, who could make no good use of it. You might load that poor soul with crown jewels and she would make them look as if she had bought them at a department store for ninety-eight cents. And the way she keeps her house must be maddening, I should think, to a brilliant man. Fancy the books on the table being all arranged with the large ones under the small ones in perfectly even piles! I am sure that he has his meals on time, and I am equally sure that the principal dishes are preserves and hot biscuits and cake. That sort of diet simply shows forth in Mrs. Temple and her children. I am sure that his socks are always mended, but I know that he always wipes his feet before he enters the house, that it has become a matter of conscience with him; and those exactions are to me pathetic. These reflections are uncommonly like the popular conception as to how an old-maid aunt should reflect, had she not ceased to exist. Sometimes I wish she were still existing and that I carried out her character to the full. I am not at all sure but she, as she once was, coming here, would not have brought more happiness than I have. I must say I thought so when I saw poor Harry Goward turn so pale when he first saw me after my arrival. Why, in the name of commonsense, Ada, my sister-in-law, when she wrote to me at the Pollards', announcing Peggy's engagement, could not have mentioned who the man was, I cannot see.

Sometimes it seems to me that only the girl and the engagement figure at all in such matters. I suppose Peggy always alluded to me as "dear Aunt Elizabeth," when that poor young fellow knew me at the Abercrombies', where we were staying a year ago, as Miss Lily Talbert. The situation with regard to him and Peggy fairly puzzles me. I simply do not know what to do. Goodness knows I never lifted my finger to attract him. Flirtations between older women and boys always have seemed to me contemptible. I never particularly noticed him, although he is a charming young fellow, and there is not as much difference in our ages as in those of Harriet Munroe and her husband, and if I am not mistaken there is more difference between the ages of Ned Temple and his wife. Poor soul! she looks old enough to be his mother, as I remember him, but that may be partly due to the way she arranges her hair. However, Ned himself may have changed; there must be considerable wear and tear about matrimony, taken in connection with editing a country newspaper. If I had married Ned I might have looked as old as Mrs. Temple does. I wonder what Ned will do when he sees me. I know he will not turn white, as poor Harry Goward did. That really worries me. I am fond of little Peggy, and the situation is really rather awful. She is engaged to a man who is fond of her aunt and cannot conceal it. Still, the affection of most male things is curable. If Peggy has sense enough to retain her love for frills and bows, and puts on her clothes as well, and arranges her hair as prettily, after she has been married a year—no, ten years (it will take at least ten years to make a proper old-maid aunt of me)—she may have the innings. But Peggy has no brains, and it really takes a woman with brains to keep her looks after matrimony.

Of course, the poor little soul has no danger to fear from me; it is lucky for her that her *fiancé* fell in love with me; but it is the principle of the thing which worries me. Harry Goward must be as fickle as a honey-bee. There is no assurance whatever for Peggy that he will not fall headlong in love —and headlong is just the word for it—with any other woman after he has married her. I did not want the poor fellow to stick to me, but when I come to think of it that is the trouble. How short-sighted I am! It is his perverted fickleness rather than his actual fickleness which worries me. He has proposed to Peggy when he was in love with another woman, probably because he was in love with another woman. Now Peggy, although she is not brilliant, in spite of her co-education (perhaps because of it), is a darling, and she deserves a good

37

husband. She loves this man with her whole heart, poor little thing! that is easy enough to be seen, and he does not care for her, at least not when I am around or when I am in his mind. The question is, is this marriage going to make the child happy? My first impulse, when I saw Harry Goward and knew that he was poor Peggy's lover, was immediately to pack up and leave. Then I really wondered if that was the wisest thing to do. I wanted to see for myself if Harry Goward were really in earnest about poor little Peggy and had gotten over his mad infatuation for her aunt and would make her a good husband. Perhaps I ought to leave, and yet I wonder if I ought. Harry Goward may have turned pale simply from his memory of what an uncommon fool he had been, and the consideration of the embarrassing position in which his past folly has placed him, if I chose to make revelations. He might have known that I would not; still, men know so little of women. I think that possibly I am worrying myself needlessly, and that he is really in love with Peggy. She is quite a little beauty, and she does know how to put her clothes on so charmingly. The adjustments of her shirt-waists are simply perfection. I may be very foolish to go away; I may be even insufferably conceited in assuming that Harry's change of color signified anything which could make it necessary. But, after all, he must be fickle and ready to turn from one to

another, or deceitful, and I must admit that if
Peggy were my daughter, and Harry had never
been mad about me six weeks ago, but about some
other woman, I should still feel the same way.

Sometimes I wonder if I ought to tell Ada. She
is the girl's mother. I might shift the responsibility
on to her. I almost think I will. She is alone in
her room now, I know. Peggy and Harry have
gone for a drive, and the rest have scattered. It is
a good chance. I really don't feel as if I ought to
bear the whole responsibility alone. I will go this
minute and tell Ada.

Well, I have told Ada, and here I am back in my
room, laughing over the result. I might as well
have told the flour-barrel. Anything like Ada's
ease of character and inability to worry or even
face a disturbing situation I have never seen. I
laugh, although her method of receiving my tale
was not, so to speak, flattering to me. Ada was in
her loose white kimono, and she was sitting at her
shady window darning stockings in very much the
same way that a cow chews her cud; and when I
told her, under promise of the strictest secrecy, she
just laughed that placid little laugh of hers and
said, taking another stitch, "Oh, well, boys are
always falling in love with older women." And
when I asked if she thought seriously that Peggy
might not be running a risk, she said: "Oh dear, no;

Harry is devoted to the child. You can't be foolish enough, Aunt Elizabeth, to think that he is in love with you *now?*"

I said, "Certainly not." It was only the principle involved; that the young man must be very changeable, and that Peggy might run a risk in the future if Harry were thrown in much with other women.

Ada only laughed again, and kept on with her darning, and said she guessed there was no need to worry. Harry seemed to her very much like Cyrus, and she was sure that Cyrus had never thought of another woman besides herself (Ada).

I wonder if another woman would have said what I might have said, especially after that imputation of the idiocy of my thinking that a young man could possibly fancy *me*. I said nothing, but I wondered what Ada would say if she knew what I knew, if she would continue to chew her cud, that Cyrus had been simply mad over another girl, and only married her because he could not get the other one, and when the other died, five years after he was married to Ada, he sent flowers, and I should not to this day venture to speak that girl's name to the man. She was a great beauty, and she had a wonderful witchery about her. I was only a child, but I remember how she looked. Why, I fell in love with her myself! Cyrus can never forget a woman like that for a cud-chewing creature like Ada, even if she does keep his house in order and make a good mother to his children. The other would not have kept the house in order at all, but it would have been a shrine. Cyrus worshipped that girl, and love may supplant love, but not worship. Ada does not know, and she never will through me, but I declare I was almost wicked enough to tell her when I saw her placidly darning away, without the slightest conception, any more than a feather pillow would have, of what this ridiculous affair with me might mean in future consequences to poor, innocent little Peggy. But I can only hope the boy has gotten over his feeling for me, that he has been really changeable, for that would be infinitely better than the other thing.

Well, I shall not need to go away. Harry Goward has himself solved that problem. He goes himself to-morrow. He has invented a telegram about a sick uncle, all according to the very best melodrama. But what I feared is true—he is still as mad as ever about me. I went down to the post-office for the evening mail, and was coming home by moonlight, unattended, as any undesirable maiden aunt may safely do, when the boy overtook me. I had heard his hurried steps behind me for some time. Up he rushed just as we reached the vacant lot before the Temple house, and caught my arm and poured forth a volume of confessions and avowals, and, in short, told me he did not love

Peggy, but me, and he never would love anybody but me. I actually felt faint for a second. Then I talked. I told him what a dishonorable wretch he was, and said he might as well have plunged a knife into an innocent, confiding girl at once as to have treated Peggy so. I told him to go away and let me alone and write friendly letters to Peggy, and see if he would not recover his senses, if he had any to recover, which I thought doubtful; and then when he said he would not budge a step, that he would remain in Eastridge, if only for the sake of breathing the same air I did, that he would tell Peggy the whole truth at once, and bear all the blame which he deserved for being so dishonorable, I arose to the occasion. I said, "Very well, remain, but you may have to breathe not only the same air that I do, but also the same air that the man whom I am to marry does." I declare that I had no man whatever in mind. I said it in sheer desperation. Then the boy burst forth with another torrent, and the secret was out.

My brother and my sister-in-law and Grandmother Evarts and the children, for all I know, have all been match-making for me. I did not suspect it of them. I supposed they esteemed my case as utterly hopeless, and then I knew that Cyrus knew about—well, never mind; I don't often mention him to myself. I certainly thought that they all would have as soon endeavored to raise the dead as to marry me, but it seems that they have been thinking that while there is life there is hope, or rather, while there are widowers there is hope. And there is a widower in Eastridge—Dr. Denbigh. He is the candle about which the mothlike dreams of ancient maidens and widows have fluttered, to their futile singeing, for the last twenty years. I really did not dream that they would think I would flutter, even if I was an old-maid aunt. But Harry cried out that if I were going to marry Dr. Denbigh he would go away. He never would stay and be a witness to such sacrilege. "That *old* man!" he raved. And when I said I was not a young girl myself he got all the madder. Well, I allowed him to think I was going to marry Dr. Denbigh (I wonder what the doctor would say), and as a consequence Harry will flit to-morrow, and he is with poor little Peggy out in the grape-arbor, and she is crying her eyes out. If he dares tell her what a fool he is I could kill him. I am horribly afraid that he will let it out, for I never saw such an alarmingly impetuous youth. Young Lochinvar out of the west was mere cambric tea to him. I am really thankful that he has not a gallant steed, nor even an automobile, for the old-maid aunt might yet be captured as the Sabine women were.

Well, thank fortune, Harry has left, and he cannot have told, for poor little Peggy has been sitting with me for a solid hour, sniffing, and sounding his praises. Somehow the child made me think of myself at her age. I was about a year older when my tragedy came and was never righted. Hers, I think, will be, since Harry was not such an ass as to confess before he went away. But all the same, I am concerned for her happiness, for Harry is either fickle or deceitful. Sometimes I wonder what my duty is, but I can't tell the child. It would do no more good for me to consult my brother Cyrus than it did to consult Ada. I know of no one whom I can consult. Charles Edward and his wife, who is just like Ada, pretty, but always with her shirt-waist hunching in the back, sitting wrong, and standing lopsided, and not worrying enough to give her character salt and pepper, are there. (I should think she would drive Charles Edward, who is really an artist, only out of his proper sphere, mad.) Tom and Maria are down there, too, on the piazza, and Ada at her everlasting darning, and Alice bossing Billy as usual. I can hear her voice. I think I will put on another gown and go for a walk.

I think I will put on my pink linen, and my hat lined with pink chiffon and trimmed with shaded roses. That particular shade of pink is just right for my hair. I know quite well how I look in that gown and hat, and I know, also, quite well how I shall look to the members of my family assembled below. They all unanimously consider that I should dress always in black silk, and a bonnet with a neat little tuft of middle-aged violets, and black ribbons tied under my chin. I know I am wicked to put on that pink gown and hat, but I shall do it. I wonder why it amuses me to be made fun of. Thank fortune, I have a sense of humor. If I did not have that it might have come to the black silk and the bonnet with the tuft of violets, for the Lord knows I have not, after all, so very much compared with what some women have. It troubles me to think of that young fool rushing away and poor, dear little Peggy; but what can I do? This pink gown is fetching, and how they will stare when I go down!

Well, they did stare. How pretty this street is, with the elms arching over it. I made quite a commotion, and they all saw me through their eye-glasses of prejudice, except, possibly, Tom Price, Maria's husband. I am certain I heard him say, as I marched away, "Well, I don't care; she does look stunning, anyhow," but Maria hushed him up. I heard her say, "Pink at her age, and a pink hat, and a parasol lined with pink!" Ada really looked more disturbed than I have ever seen her. If I had been Godiva, going for my sacrificial ride through the town, it could not have been much worse. She made her eyes round and big, and asked, in a voice which was really agitated, "Are you going out in that dress, Aunt Elizabeth?" And Aunt Elizabeth replied that she certainly was, and she went after she had exchanged greetings with the family and kissed Peggy's tear-stained little face. Charles Edward's wife actually straightened her spinal column, she was so amazed at the sight of me in my rose-colored array. Charles Edward, to do him justice, stared at me with a bewildered air, as if he were trying to reconcile his senses with his traditions. He is an artist, but he will always be hampered by thinking he sees what he has been brought up to think he sees. That is the reason why he has settled down uncomplainingly in Cyrus's "Works," as he calls them, doing the very slight æsthetics possible in such a connection. Now Charles Edward would think that sunburned grass over in that field is green, when it is pink, because he has been taught that grass is green. If poor Charles Edward only knew that grass was green not of itself, but because of occasional conditions, and knew that his aunt looked—well, as she does look—he would flee for his life, and that which is better than his life, from the "Works," and be an artist, but he never will know or know that he knows, which comes to the same thing.

Well, what does it matter to me? I have just met a woman who stared at me, and spoke as if she thought I were a lunatic to be afield in this array. What does anything matter? Sometimes, when I am with people who see straight, I do take a certain pleasure in looking well, because I am a woman, and nothing can quite take away that pleasure from me; but all the time I know it does not matter, that nothing has really mattered since I was about Peggy's age and Lyman Wilde quarrelled with me over nothing and vanished into thin air, so far as I was concerned. I suppose he is comfortably settled with a wife and family somewhere. It is rather odd, though, that with all my wandering on this side of the water and the other I have never once crossed his tracks. He may be in the Far East, with a harem. I never have been in the Far East. Well, it does not matter to me where he is. That is ancient history. On the whole, though, I like the harem idea better than the single wife. I have what is left to me—the little things of life, the pretty effects which go to make me pretty (outside Eastridge); the comforts of civilization, travelling and seeing beautiful things, also seeing ugly things to enhance the beautiful. I have pleasant days in beautiful Florence. I have friends. I have everything except—well, except everything. That I must do without. But I will do without it gracefully, with never a whimper, or I don't know myself. But now I *am* worried over Peggy. I wish I could consult with somebody with sense. What a woman I am! I mean, how feminine I am! I wish I could cure myself of the habit of being feminine. It is a horrible nuisance; this wishing to consult with somebody when I am worried is so disgustingly feminine.

Well, I have consulted. I am back in my own room. It is after supper. We had three kinds of cake, hot biscuits, and raspberries, and—a concession to Cyrus—a platter of cold ham and an egg salad. He will have something hearty, as he calls it (bless him! he is a good-fellow), for supper. I am glad, for I should starve on Ada's New England menus. I feel better, now that I have consulted, although, when I really consider the matter, I can't see that I have arrived at any very definite issue. But I have consulted, and, above all things, with Ned Temple! I was walking down the street, and I reached his newspaper building. It is a funny little affair; looks like a toy house. It is all given up to the mighty affairs of the Eastridge *Banner*. In front there is a piazza, and on this piazza sat Ned Temple. Changed? Well, yes, poor fellow! He is thin. I am so glad he is thin instead of fat; thinness is not nearly so disillusioning. His hair is iron-gray, but he is, after all, distinguished-looking, and his manners are entirely sophisticated. He shows at a glance, at a word, that he is a brilliant man, although he is stranded upon such a petty little editorial island. And—

and he saw *me* as I am. He did not change color. He is too self-poised; besides, he is too honorable. But he saw *me*. He rose immediately and came to speak to me. He shook hands. He looked at my face under my pink-lined hat. He saw it as it was; but bless him! that stupid wife of his holds him fast with his own honor. Ned Temple is a good man. Sometimes I wonder if it would not have been better if he, instead of Lyman— Well, that is idiotic.

He said he had to go to the post-office, and then it was time for him to go home to supper (to the cake and sauce, I suppose), and with my permission he would walk with me. So he did. I don't know how it happened that I consulted with him. I think he spoke of Peggy's engagement, and that led up to it. But I could speak to him, because I knew that he, seeing me as I really am, would view the matter seriously. I told him about the miserable affair, and he said that I had done exactly right. I can't remember that he offered any actual solution, but it was something to be told that I had done exactly right. And then he spoke of his wife, and in such a faithful fashion, and so lovingly of his two commonplace little girls. Ned Temple is as good as he is brilliant. It is really rather astonishing that such a brilliant man can be so good. He told me that I had not changed at all, but all the time that look of faithfulness for his wife never left his handsome face, bless him! I believe I am nearer loving him for his love for another woman than I ever was to loving him for himself.

And then the inconceivable happened. I did what I never thought I should be capable of doing, and did it easily, too, without, I am sure, a change of color or any perturbation. I think I could do it, because faithfulness had become so a matter of course with the man that I was not ashamed should he have any suspicion of me also. He and Lyman used to be warm friends. I asked if he knew anything about him. He met my question as if I had asked what o'clock it was, just the way I knew he would meet it. He knows no more than I do. But he said something which has comforted me, although comfort at this stage of affairs is a dangerous indulgence. He said, very much as if he had been speaking of the weather, "He worshipped you, Lily, and wherever he is, in this world or the next, he worships you now." Then he added: "You know how I felt about you, Lily. If I had not found out about him, that he had come first, I know how it would have been with me, so I know how it is with him. We had the same views about matters of that kind. After I did find out, why, of course, I felt different—although always, as long as I live, I shall be a dear friend to you, Lily. But a man is unfaithful to himself who is faithful to a woman whom another man loves and whom she loves."

"Yes, that is true," I agreed, and said something about the hours for the mails in Eastridge. Lyman Wilde dropped out of Ned's life as he dropped out of mine, it seems. I shall simply have to lean back upon the minor joys of life for mental and physical support, as I did before. Nothing is different, but I am glad that I have seen Ned Temple again, and realize what a good man he is.

Well, it seems that even minor pleasures have dangers, and that I do not always read characters rightly. The very evening after my little stroll and renewal of friendship with Ned Temple I was sitting in my room, reading a new book for which the author should have capital punishment, when I heard excited voices, or rather an excited voice, below. I did not pay much attention at first. I supposed the excited voice must belong to either Maria or Alice, for no others of my brother's family ever seem in the least excited, not to the extent of raising their voices to a hysterical pitch. But after a few minutes Cyrus came to the foot of the stairs and called. He called Aunt Elizabeth, and Aunt Elizabeth, in her same pink frock, went down. Cyrus met me at the foot of the stairs, and he looked fairly wild. "What on earth, Aunt Elizabeth!" said he, and I stared at him in a daze.

"The deuce is to pay," said he. "Aunt Elizabeth, did you ever know our next-door neighbor
before his marriage?"

"Certainly," said I; "when we were both infants.
I believe they had gotten him out of petticoats and
into trousers, but much as ever, and my skirts were
still abbreviated. It was at Harriet Munroe's before she was married."

"Have you been to walk with him?" gasped poor
Cyrus.

"I met him on my way to the post-office last
night, and he walked along with me, and then as far
as his house on the way home, if you call that walking out," said I. "You sound like the paragraphs
in a daily paper. Now, what on earth do you mean,
if I may ask, Cyrus?"

"Nothing, except Mrs. Temple is in there raising
a devil of a row," said Cyrus. He gazed at me in a
bewildered fashion. "If it were Peggy I could
understand it," he said, helplessly, and I knew how
distinctly he saw the old-maid aunt as he gazed at
me. "She's jealous of you, Elizabeth," he went
on in the same dazed fashion. "She's jealous of
you because her husband walked home with you.
She's a dreadfully nervous woman, and, I guess,
none too well. She's fairly wild. It seems Temple
let on how he used to know you before he was
married, and said something in praise of your looks,
and she made a regular header into conclusions.

You have held your own remarkably well, Elizabeth, but I declare—" And again poor Cyrus gazed at me.

"Well, for goodness' sake, let me go in and see what I can do," said I, and with that I went into the parlor.

I was taken aback. Nobody, not even another woman, can tell what a woman really is. I thought I had estimated Ned Temple's wife correctly. I had taken her for a monotonous, orderly, dull sort of creature, quite incapable of extremes; but in reality she has in her rather large, flabby body the characteristics of a kitten, with the possibilities of a tigress. The tigress was uppermost when I entered the room. The woman was as irresponsible as a savage. I was disgusted and sorry and furious at the same time. I cannot imagine myself making such a spectacle over any mortal man. She was weeping frantically into a mussy little ball of handkerchief, and when she saw me she rushed at me and gripped me by the arm like a mad thing.

"If you can't get a husband for yourself," said she, "you might at least let other women's husbands alone!"

She was vulgar, but she was so wild with jealousy that I suppose vulgarity ought to be forgiven her.

I hardly know myself how I managed it, but, somehow, I got the poor thing out of the room and the house and into the cool night air, and then I talked to her, and fairly made her be quiet and listen. I told her that Ned Temple had made love to me when he was just out of petticoats and I was in short dresses. I stretched or shortened the truth a little, but it was a case of necessity. Then I intimated that I never would have married Ned Temple, anyway, and *that* worked beautifully. She turned upon me in such a delightfully inconsequent fashion and demanded to know what I expected, and declared her husband was good enough for any woman. Then I said I did not doubt that, and hinted that other women might have had their romances, even if they did not marry. That immediately interested her. She stared at me, and said, with the most innocent impertinence, that my brother's wife had intimated that I had had an unhappy love-affair when I was a girl. I did not think that Cyrus had told Ada, but I suppose a man *has* to tell his wife everything.

I hedged about the unhappy love-affair, but the first thing I knew the poor, distracted woman was sobbing on my shoulder as we stood in front of her gate, and saying that she was so sorry, but her whole life was bound up in her husband, and I was so beautiful and had so much style, and she knew what a dowdy she was, and she could not blame poor Ned if— But I hushed her.

"Your husband has no more idea of caring for

IT ACTUALLY ENDED IN MY SHOWING NED'S WIFE **HOW**
TO DO UP HER HAIR LIKE MINE

another woman besides you than that moon has
of travelling around another world," said I; "and
you are a fool if you think so; and if you are dowdy
it is your own fault. If you have such a good
husband you owe it to him not to be dowdy. I know
you keep his house beautifully, but any man would
rather have his wife look well than his house, if he
is worth anything at all."

Then she gasped out that she wished she knew
how to do up her hair like mine. It was all highly
ridiculous, but it actually ended in my going into
the Temple house and showing Ned's wife how to
do up her hair like mine. She looked like another
woman when it was puffed softly over her forehead
—she has quite pretty brown hair. Then I taught
her how to put on her corset and pin her shirt-waist
taut in front and her skirt behind. Ned was not
to be home until late, and there was plenty of time.
It ended in her fairly purring around me, and
saying how sorry she was, and ashamed, that she
had been so foolish, and all the time casting little
covert, conceited glances at herself in the looking-
glass. Finally I kissed her and she kissed me, and
I went home. I don't really see what more a
woman could have done for a rival who had sup-
planted her. But this revelation makes me more
sorry than ever for poor Ned. I don't know,
though; she may be more interesting than I thought.
Anything is better than the dead level of small books

on large ones, and meals on time. It cannot be exactly monotonous never to know whether you will find a sleek, purry cat, or an absurd kitten, or a tigress, when you come home. Luckily, she did not tell Ned of her jealousy, and I have cautioned all in my family to hold their tongues, and I think they will. I infer that they suspect that I must have been guilty of some unbecoming elderly prank to bring about such a state of affairs, unless, possibly, Maria's husband and Billy are exceptions. I find that Billy, when Alice lets him alone, is a boy who sees with his own eyes. He told me yesterday that I was handsomer in my pink dress than any girl in his school.

"Why, Billy Talbert!" I said, "talking that way to your old aunt!"

"I suppose you *are* awful old," said Billy, bless him! "but you are enough-sight prettier than a girl. I hate girls. I hope I can get away from girls when I am a man."

I wanted to tell the dear boy that was exactly the time when he would not get away from girls, but I thought I would not frighten him, but let him find it out for himself.

Well, now the deluge! It is a week since Harry Goward went away, and Peggy has not had a letter, although she has haunted the post-office, poor child! and this morning she brought home a letter for *me* from that crazy boy. She was white as chalk when she handed it to me.

"It's Harry's writing," said she, and she could barely whisper. "I have not had a word from him since he went away, and now he has written to you instead of me. What has he written to you for, Aunt Elizabeth?"

She looked at me so piteously, poor, dear little girl! that if I could have gotten hold of Harry Goward that moment I would have shaken him. I tried to speak, soothingly. I said:

"My dear Peggy, I know no more than you do why he has written to me. Perhaps his uncle is dead and he thought I would break it to you."

That was rank idiocy. Generally I can rise to the occasion with more success.

"What do I care about his old uncle?" cried poor Peggy. "I never even saw his uncle. I don't care if he is dead. Something has happened to Harry. Oh, Aunt Elizabeth, what is it?"

I was never in such a strait in my life. There was that poor child staring at the letter as if she could eat it, and then at me. I dared not open the letter before her. We were out on the porch. I said:

"Now, Peggy Talbert, you keep quiet, and don't make a little fool of yourself until you know you have some reason for it. I am going up to my own room, and you sit in that chair, and when I have

read this letter I will come down and tell you about
it."

"I know he is dead!" gasped Peggy, but she sat
down.

"Dead!" said I. "You just said yourself it was
his handwriting. Do have a little sense, Peggy."
With that I was off with my letter, and I locked my
door before I read it.

Of all the insane ravings! I put it on my hearth
and struck a match, and the thing went up in flame
and smoke. Then I went down to poor little Peggy
and patched up a story. I have always been averse
to lying, and I did not lie then, although I must
admit that what I said was open to criticism when
it comes to exact verity. I told Peggy that Harry
thought that he had done something to make her
angry (that was undeniably true) and did not dare
write her. I refused utterly to tell her just what
was in the letter, but I did succeed in quieting her
and making her think that Harry had not broken
faith with her, but was blaming himself for some
unknown and imaginary wrong he had done her.
Peggy rushed immediately up to her room to write
reassuring pages to Harry, and her old-maid aunt
had the horse put in the runabout and was driven
over to Whitman, where nobody knows her—at
least the telegraph operator does not. Then I sent
a telegram to Mr. Harry Goward to the effect that
if he did not keep his promise with regard to writing

F. L. to P. her A. would never speak to him again; that A. was about to send L., but he must keep his promise with regard to P. by next M.

It looked like the most melodramatic Sunday personal ever invented. It might have meant burglary or murder or a snare for innocence, but I sent it. Now I have written. My letter went in the same mail as poor Peggy's, but what will be the outcome of it all I cannot say. Sometimes I catch Peggy looking at me with a curious awakened expression, and then I wonder if she has begun to suspect. I cannot tell how it will end.

III

THE GRANDMOTHER

By Mary Heaton Vorse

THE position of an older woman in her daughter's house is often difficult. It makes no difference to me that Ada is a mother herself; she might be even a great-grandmother, and yet in my eyes she would still be Ada, my little girl. I feel the need of guiding her and protecting her just as much this minute as when she was a baby in the nursery; only now the task is much more difficult. That is why I say that the position of women placed as I am is often hard, harder than if I lived somewhere else, because although I am with Ada I can no longer protect her from anything—not even from myself, my illnesses and weaknesses. It sometimes seems to me, so eagerly do I follow the lights and shadows of my daughter's life, as if I were living a second existence together with my own. Only as I grow older I am less fitted physically to bear things, even though I take them philosophically.

When Ada and the rest of my children were little, I could guard against the menaces to their happiness; I could keep them out of danger; if their little friends didn't behave, I sent them home. When it was needed, I didn't hesitate to administer a good wholesome spanking to my children. There isn't one of these various things but needs doing now in Ada's house. I can't, however, very well spank Cyrus, nor can I send Elizabeth home. All I *can* do is to sit still and hold my tongue, though I don't know, I'm sure, what the end of it all is to be.

Life brings new lessons at every turn in the road, and one of the hardest of all is the one we older people have to learn—to sit still while our children hurt themselves, or, what is worse, to sit still while other people hurt our children. It is especially hard for me to bear, when life is made difficult for my Ada, for if ever any one deserved happiness my daughter does. I try to do justice to every one, and I hope I am not unfair when I say that the best of men, and Cyrus is one of them, are sometimes blind and obstinate. Of all my children, Ada gave me the least trouble, and was always the most loving and tender and considerate. Indeed, if Ada has a fault, it is being too considerate. I could, if she only would let me, help her a great deal more around the house; although Ada is a very good housekeeper, I am constantly seeing little things that need doing. I do my best to prevent the awful waste of soap that goes on, and there are a

great many little ways Ada could let me save for
her if she would. When I suggest this to her she
laughs and says, "Wait till we need to save as badly
as that, mother," which doesn't seem to me good
reasoning at all. "Waste not, want not," say I,
and when it comes to throwing out perfectly good
glass jars, as the girls would do if I didn't see to it
they saved them, why, I put my foot down. If
Ada doesn't want them herself to put things up in,
why, some poor woman will. I don't believe in
throwing things away that may come in handy
sometime. When I kept house nobody ever went
lacking strings or a box of whatever size, to send
things away in, or paper in which to do it up, and
I can remember in mother's day there was never
a time she hadn't pieces put by for a handsome
quilt. Machinery has put a stop to many of our
old occupations, and the result is a generation of
nervous women who haven't a single thing in life
to occupy themselves with but their own feelings,
while girls like Peggy, who are active and useful,
have nothing to do but to go to school and keep
on going to school. If one wanted to dig into the
remote cause of things, one might find the root of
our present trouble in these changed conditions,
for Cyrus's sister, Elizabeth, is one of these unoccupied women. Formerly in a family like ours
there would have been so much to do that, whether
she liked it or not, and whether she had married

or not, Elizabeth would have had to be a useful woman—and now the less said the better.

It is hard, I say, to see the causes for unhappiness set in action and yet do nothing, or, if one speaks, to speak to deaf ears. Oh, it is very hard to do this, and this has been the portion of older women always. Our children sometimes won't even let us dry their tears for them, but cry by themselves, as I know Ada has been doing lately—though in the end she came to me, or rather I went to her, for, after all, I am living in the same world with the rest of them. I have not passed over to the other side *yet*, and while I stay I am not going to be treated as if I were a disembodied spirit. I have eyes of my own, and ears too, and I can see as well as the next man when things go wrong.

I have always known that no good would come of sending Peggy to a coeducational college. I urged Ada to set her foot down, for Ada didn't wish to send Peggy there, naturally enough, but she wouldn't.

"Well," said I, "*I'm* not afraid to speak my mind to your husband." Now I very seldom open my mouth to Cyrus, or to any one else in this house, for it is more than ever the fashion for people to disregard the advice of others, and the older I get the more I find it wise to save my breath to cool my porridge—there come times, however, when I feel it my duty to speak.

"Mark my words, Cyrus," I said. "You'll be sorry you sent Peggy off to a boys' school. Girls at her age are impressionable, and if they aren't under their mothers' roofs, where they can be protected and sheltered, why, then send them to a seminary where they will see as few young men as possible."

Cyrus only laughed and said:

"Well, mother, you can say 'I told you so' if anything bad comes of it."

"It's all very well to laugh, Cyrus," I answered, "but *I* don't believe in putting difficulties into life that aren't there already, and that's what sending young men and young women off to the same college seems to *me!*"

When Peggy came home engaged, after her last year, everybody was surprised.

"I'm sure I don't know what Cyrus expected," I said to Ada. "You can't go out in the rain without getting wet. Let us pray that this young man will turn out to be all right, though we know so little about him." For all we knew was what Peggy told us, and you know the kind of things young girls have to tell one about their sweethearts. Peggy didn't even know what church his people went to! I couldn't bear the thought of that dear child setting out on the long journey of marriage in such a fashion. I looked forward with fear to what Ada might have to go through if it didn't turn out all right.

For one's daughter's sorrows are one's own; what she suffers one must suffer, too. It is hard for a mother to see a care-free, happy young girl turn into a woman before her eyes. Even if a woman is very happy, marriage brings many responsibilities, and a woman who has known the terror of watching beside a sick child can never be quite the same, I think. We ourselves grew and deepened under such trials, and we wouldn't wish our daughters to be less than ourselves; but, oh, how glad I should be to have Peggy spared some things! How happy I should be to know that she was to have for her lot only the trials we all must have! I do not want to see my Ada having to bear the unhappiness of seeing Peggy unhappy. Even if Peggy puts up a brave face, Ada will know—she will know just as I have known things in my own children's lives; and I shall know, too. This young man has it in his hands to trouble my old age.

No mother and daughter can live together as Ada and I have without what affects one of us affecting the other. When her babies were born I was with her; I helped her bring them up; as I have grown older, though she comes to me less and less, wishing to spare me, I seem to need less telling; for I know myself when anything ails her.

It amazed me to see how Ada took Peggy's engagement, and when young Henry Goward came to visit, I made up my mind that he should not go away again without our finding out a little, at any rate, of what his surroundings had been, and what his own principles were. As we grow older we see more and more that character is the main thing in life, and I would rather have a child of mine marry a young man of sound principles whom she respected than one of undisciplined character and lax ideas whom she loved. When I said things like this to Ada, she replied:

"I'm afraid you're prejudiced against that poor boy because he and Peggy happened to meet at college."

I answered: "I am not prejudiced at all, Ada, but I feel that all of us, you especially, should keep our eyes and ears open. Wait! is all I say."

I know my own faults, for I have always believed that one is never too old for character-building, and I know that being prejudiced is not one of them. I realize too keenly that as women advance in years they are very apt to get set in their ways unless they take care, and I am naturally too fair-minded to judge a man before I have seen him. Maria and Alice *were* prejudiced, if you like. Maria, indeed, had so much to say to Ada that I interfered, though it is contrary to my custom.

"I should think, Maria," I said, "that however old you are, you would realize that your father and mother are *even* better able to judge than you as to their children's affairs." I cannot imagine where

Maria gets her dominant disposition. It is very unlike the women of our family.

When he came, however, Mr. Goward's manners and appearance impressed me favorably. Neither Ada nor Cyrus, as far as I could see, tried in the least to draw him out. I sat quiet for a while, but at last for Peggy's sake I felt I would do what I could to find out his views on important things. I was considerably relieved to hear that his mother was a Van Horn, a very good Troy family and distant connection of mother's.

When I asked him what he was, "My *people* are Episcopalians," he replied.

"I suppose that means *you* are something else?" I asked him.

"I'm afraid it means I'm nothing else," he answered; and while I was glad he was so honest, I couldn't help feeling anxious at having Peggy engaged to a man so unformed in his beliefs. I do not care so much *what* people believe, for I am not bigoted, as that they should believe *something*, and that with their whole hearts. There are a great many young men like Henry Goward, to-day, who have no fixed beliefs and no established principles beyond a vague desire to be what they call "decent fellows." One needs more than that in this world.

However, I found the boy likable, and everything went smoothly for a time, when all at once I felt something had gone wrong—what, I didn't know.

Mr. Goward received a telegram and left suddenly. Ada, I could see, was anxious; Peggy, tearful; and, as if this wasn't enough, Mrs. Temple, our new neighbor, who had seemed a sensible body to me, had some sort of a falling-out with Aunt Elizabeth, who pretended that Mrs. Temple was jealous of her! After Mrs. Temple had gone home, Elizabeth Talbert went around pleased as Punch and swore us all to solemn secrecy never to tell any one about "Mrs. Temple's absurd jealousy."

"You needn't worry about me, Aunt Elizabeth," I said. "I'm not likely to go around proclaiming that *another* woman has made a fool of herself."

Elizabeth Talbert is one of those women who live on a false basis. She is a case of arrested development. She enjoys the same amusements that she did fifteen years ago. She is like a young fruit that has been put up in a preserving fluid and gives the illusion of youth; the preserving fluid in her case is the disappointment she suffered as a girl. I like useful women—women who, whether married or unmarried, bring things to pass in this world, and Elizabeth does not. Still, I can't help feeling sorry for her, poor thing; in the end our own shortcomings and vanities hurt us more than they hurt any one else. I heartily wish she would get married —I have known women older than Elizabeth, and worse-looking, to find husbands—both for her own sake and for Ada's, for her comings and goings complicate life for my daughter.   She diffuses around her an atmosphere of criticism—I do not think she ever returns from a visit to the city without wishing that we should have dinner at night, and Alice is beginning to prick up her ears and listen to her. She spends a great deal of time over her dress, and, if she has grown no older, neither have her clothes —not a particle.   She dresses in gowns suitable for Peggy, but which Maria, who is years younger than her aunt, would not think of wearing.   Elizabeth is the kind of woman who is a changed being at the approach of a man; she is even different when Cyrus or Billy is around; she brightens up and exerts herself to please them; but when she is alone with Ada and me she is frankly bored and looks out of the window in a sad, far-away manner.   The presence of men has a most rejuvenating effect on Aunt Elizabeth, although she pretends she has never been interested in any man since her disappointment years ago.   When she got back and found Harry Goward here, instead of relapsing into her lack-lustre ways, as she generally does, she kept on her interested air.

I have always thought that houses have their atmosphere, like people, and this house lately has seemed bewitched.   After Mr. Goward left, although every one tried to pretend things were as they should be, the situation grew more and more uncomfortable.   I felt it, though no one told me a thing.   I fancy that most older people have the same experience often that I have had lately. All at once you are aware something is wrong. You can't tell why you feel this; you only know that you are living in the cold shadow of some invisible unhappiness. You see no tears in the eyes of the people you love, but tears have been shed just the same. Why? You don't know, and no one thinks of telling you. It is like seeing life from so far off that you cannot make out what has happened. I have sometimes leaned out of a window and have seen down the street a crowd of gesticulating people, but I was too far off to know whether some one was hurt or whether it was only people gathered around a man selling something. When I see such things my heart beats, for I am always afraid it is an accident, and so with the things I don't know in my own household. I always fancy them worse than they are. There are so many things one can imagine when one doesn't *know*, and now I fancied everything. Such things, I think, tell on older people more than on younger ones, and at last I went to my room and kept there most of the time, reading William James's *Varieties of Religious Experience*. It is an excellent work in many ways. I am told it is given in sanitariums for nervous people to read, for the purpose of getting their minds off themselves. I found it useful to get my mind off others, for of late I have gotten to an almost morbid alertness, and I know by the very way Peggy ran up the stairs

"TELL MOTHER WHAT'S WORRYING YOU, DEAR"

that something ailed her even before I caught a glimpse of her face, which showed me that she was going straight to her room to cry.

This sort of thing had happened too often, and I made up my mind I would not live in this moral fog another moment. So I went to Ada.

"Ada," I said, "I am your mother, and I think I have a right to ask you a question. I want to know this: what has that young man been doing?"

"I suppose you mean Harry," Ada answered. "He hasn't been doing anything. Peggy's a little upset because he isn't a good correspondent. You know how girls feel—"

"Don't tell *me*, Ada," said I. "I know better. There's more in it than that. Peggy's a sensible girl. There's something wrong, and I want you to tell me what it is." Younger people don't realize how bad it can be to be left to worry alone in the dark.

Ada sat down with a discouraged air such as I have seldom seen her with. I went over to her and took her hand in mine.

"Tell mother what's worrying you, dear," I said, gently.

"Why, it's all so absurd," Ada answered. "I can't make head or tail of it. Aunt Elizabeth came to me full of mystery soon after she came back, and told me that Harry Goward had become infatuated with her when she was off on one of her visits—"

I couldn't help exclaiming, "Well, of all things!"

"That's not the queerest part," Ada went on. "She told me as confidently as could be that he is still in love with her."

"Ada," said I, "Elizabeth Talbert must be daft! Does she think that all the men in the world are in love with her—at her age? First Mrs. Temple making such a rumpus, and now this—"

"At first I thought just as you do," Ada said, helplessly. "Of course there can't be anything in it—and yet—I'm sure I don't understand the situation at all. You know Harry left quite unexpectedly—soon after Elizabeth came; he didn't write for a week—and then to her, and Peggy's only had one short note from him—"

I can see through a hole in a millstone as well as any one, and a light dawned on me.

"You can depend upon it, Ada," I said, "Aunt Elizabeth has been making trouble! I don't know what she's been up to, but she's been up to something! I wondered why she had been having such a contented look lately — and now I know."

"Oh, mother, I can't believe that!" Ada protested. "I thought Elizabeth was a little vain and silly, and, though everything is so incomprehensible, I don't believe for a moment that Aunt Elizabeth would do anything to hurt Peggy."

My Ada is a truly good woman—so good that it

is almost impossible for her to believe ill of any one, and she was profoundly shocked at what I suggested.

"I don't think in the beginning Elizabeth intended to hurt Peggy," I answered her, gently, "but when you've lived as long in the world as I have you'll realize to what lengths a woman will go to show the world she's still young. Just look at it for yourself. Everything was going smoothly until Elizabeth came. Now it's not. Elizabeth has told you she's had goings-on with Harry Goward. I don't see, Ada, how you can be so blind as not to be willing to look the truth in the face. If it's not Elizabeth's fault, whose is it? I don't suppose you believe Henry Goward's dying for love of Aunt Elizabeth when he can look at Peggy! Oh, I'd like to hear his side of the story! For you may be sure that there is one!"

"Mother," said Ada, "if I believed Elizabeth had done anything to mar that child's happiness—" She stopped for fear, I suppose, of what she might be led to say. "We mustn't judge before we know," she finished. But I knew by the look on her face that, if Aunt Elizabeth has made trouble, Ada will never forgive her.

"What does Cyrus say to all this?" I asked, by way of diversion.

"Oh, I haven't told Cyrus anything about it. I didn't intend to tell any one—about Aunt Elizabeth's part in it. I think Cyrus is a little uneasy himself, but he's been so busy lately—"

"Well," I said, "*I* think Cyrus ought to be told! And you're the one to do it. Don't let's judge, to be sure, before we know everything, but I think Cyrus ought to know the mischief his sister is making! Elizabeth simply makes a convenience of this house. It's her basis of departure to pack her trunk from, that's all your home means to her. She's never lifted a finger to be useful beyond re-arranging the furniture in a different way from what you'd arranged it. She acts exactly as if she were a young lady boarder. She's nothing what-ever to do in this world except make trouble for others. I think Cyrus should know, and then if he prefers his sister's convenience to his wife's happi-ness, well and good!" It's not often I speak out, but now and then things happen which I can't very well keep silent about. It did me good to ease my mind about Elizabeth Talbert for once.

Ada only said, "Elizabeth and I have always been such good friends, and she's so fond of Peggy."

Ada doesn't realize that with some women vanity is stronger than loyalty. She kissed me. "It's done me good to talk to you, mother," she said, "because now it doesn't seem, when I put it outside myself, that there's very much of anything to worry about."

Ada has always been like that—she seems to get

rid of her troubles just by telling them. Now she had passed her riddle on to me, and I could not keep Peggy and her affairs from my mind. I tried to tell myself that it would be better for every one to find out now than later if Henry Goward was not worthy to be Peggy's husband. But, oh, for all their sakes, how I hoped this cloud, whatever it was, would blow over! I have a very good constitution and I know how to take care of it, but when several more days passed without Peggy's hearing from Henry again I gave way, but I tried to keep up on Ada's account. I began to see how much this young man's honor and faithfulness meant to Peggy, and I took long excursions back into the past to remember how I felt at her age. Mail-time was the difficult time for all three of us. Before the postman came Peggy would brighten up; not that she was drooping at any time, only I knew how tensely she waited, because Ada and I waited with her. When the man came, and again no letters, Peggy held up her head bravely as could be, but I could see, all the same, how the light had gone out. The worst of it was, everybody knew about it. It would have been twice as easy for the child if she could have borne it alone, but Elizabeth Talbert watched the mail like a cat, and even manœuvred to try and get the letters before Peggy, while Alice went around with her nose in the air, and I heard Maria saying to Ada:

"What's all this about Harry Goward's not writing?"

To escape it all I took to my room, coming down only for meals. I couldn't eat a thing, and Cyrus noticed it—it is queer how observant men are about some things and how unobservant about others He didn't tell me what he was going to do, but in the afternoon Dr. Denbigh came to see me. That's the way they do—I'm liable to have the doctor sent in to look me over any time, whether I want him or not. Dr. Denbigh is an excellent friend and a good doctor, but at my time of life I should be lacking in intelligence if I didn't understand my constitution better than any doctor can. They seem to think that there's more virtue in a pill or a powder because a doctor gives it to one than because one's common-sense tells one to take it. That afternoon I didn't need him any more than a squirrel needs a pocket, and I told him so. He laughed, and then grew serious.

"You're not looking as well as you did, Mrs. Evarts," he said, "and Talbert told me that you had all the preliminary symptoms of one of your attacks and wanted me to 'nip it in the bud,' he said."

"Dr. Denbigh," said I, "if the matter with me could be cured by the things you know, there are other people in this house who need your attention more than I." I wanted to add that if Cyrus

76

would always be as far-sighted as he has been about me there wouldn't be anything the matter to-day, but I held my tongue.

"I see you're worried about something," the doctor said, very kindly. "Mental anxiety pulls you down quicker than anything."

Then as he sat chatting with me so kind and good—there's something about Dr. Denbigh that makes me think of my own father, although he is young enough to be my son—I told him the whole thing, all except Aunt Elizabeth's share in it. I merely told him that Henry Goward had written to her and not to Peggy.

I felt very much better. He took what I told him seriously, and yet not in the tragic way we did. He has a way of listening that is very comforting.

"It seems absurd, I know, for an old woman like me to get upset just because her grandchild does not get letters from her sweetheart," I told him. "But you see, doctor, no one suffers alone in a family like ours. An event like this is like a wave that disturbs the whole surface of the water. Every one of us feels anything that happens, each in his separate way. Why, I can't be sick without its causing inconvenience to Billy." And it is true; people in this world are bound up together in an extraordinary fashion; and I wondered if Henry Goward's mother was unhappy too, and was wondering what it was Peggy had done to her boy, for she, of course, will think whatever happens is Peggy's fault. The engagement of these two young people has been like a stone thrown into a pond, and it takes only a very little pebble to ruffle the water farther than one would believe it possible.

After the doctor left, Ada came to sit with me. We were sewing quietly when I heard voices in the hall. I heard Peggy say, "I want you to tell mother." Then Billy growled:

"I don't see what you're making such a kick for. I wouldn't have told you if I'd known you'd be so silly."

And I heard Peggy say again:

"I want you to tell mother." Her tone was perfectly even, but it sounded like Cyrus when he is angry. They both came in. Peggy was flushed, and her lips were pressed firmly together. She looked older than I have ever seen her.

"What's the matter?" Ada asked them.

"Tell her," Peggy commanded. Billy didn't know what it all was about.

"Why, I just said I wondered what Aunt Elizabeth was telegraphing Harry Goward about, and now she drags me in here and makes a fuss," he said, in an aggrieved tone.

"He was over at Whitman playing around the telegraph-office—he had driven over on the express-wagon—and when Aunt Elizabeth drove up he hid because he didn't want her to see him. Then

78

he heard the operator read the address aloud," Peggy explained, evenly.

"Is this so ?" Ada asked.

"Sure," Billy answered, disgustedly, and made off as fast as he could.

"Now," said Peggy, "I want to know why Harry wrote to Aunt Elizabeth, and why she telegraphed him—over there where no one could see her!" She stood up very straight. "I think I ought to know," she said, gently.

"Yes, dear," Ada answered, "I think you ought."

I shall be sorry for Elizabeth Talbert if she has been making mischief.

IV

THE DAUGHTER-IN-LAW

By Mary Stewart Cutting

I HAVE never identified myself with my husband's family, and Charles Edward, who is the best sort ever, doesn't expect me to. Of course, I want to be decent to them, though I know they talk about *me*, but you can't make oil and water mix, and I don't see the use of pretending that you can. I know they never can understand how Charles Edward married me, and they never can get used to my being such a different type from theirs. The Talberts are all blue-eyed, fair-haired, and rosy, and I'm dark, thin, and pale, and Grandmother Evarts always thinks I can't be well, and wants me to take the medicine she takes.

But, really, I see very little of the family, except Alice and Billy, who don't count. Billy comes in at any time he feels like it to get a book and something to eat, though the others don't know it, and Alice has fits of stopping in every afternoon on her way from school, and then perhaps doesn't come near me for weeks. Alice is terribly discontented at home, and I think it's a very good thing that she is; anything is better than sinking to that dreadful dead level. She doesn't quite know whether to take up the artistic life or be a society queen, and she feels that nobody understands her at home. It makes her nearly wild when Aunt Elizabeth comes back from one of her grand visits and acts as if *she* wasn't anything. She came over right after the row, of course, and told me all about it—she had on her new white China silk and her hat with the feathers. She said she was so excited about everything that she couldn't stop to think about what she put on; she looked terribly dressed up, but she had come all through the village with her waist unfastened in the middle of the back— she said she couldn't reach the hooks. Aunt Elizabeth had gone away that morning for over- night, so nobody could get at her to find out about her actions with Mr. Goward, and the telegram she had sent to him, until the next day, and every one was nearly crazy. They talked about it for two hours before Maria went home. Then Peggy had locked herself in her room, and her mother had gone out, and her grandmother was sitting now on the piazza, rocking and sighing, with her eyes shut. Alice said each person had got dreadfully worked up, not only about Aunt Elizabeth, but about all the ways every other member of the family had hurt that person at some time. Maria said that

Peggy never would take *her* advice, and Peggy returned that Maria had hurt her more than any one by her attitude toward Harry Goward, that she was so suspicious of him that it had made him act unnaturally from the first—that nothing had hurt her so much since the time Maria took away Peggy's doll on purpose when she was a little girl—the doll she used to sleep with—and burned it; it was something she had *never* got over.

Then her mother, who hadn't been talking very much, said that Peggy didn't realize the depth of Maria's affection for her, and what a good sister she had been, and how she had taken care of Peggy the winter that Peggy was ill—and then she couldn't help saying that, bad as was this affair about Harry Goward, it wasn't like the anxiety one felt about a sick child; there were times when she felt that she could bear anything if Charles Edward's health were only properly looked after. Of course Lorraine was young and inexperienced, but if she would only use her influence with him—

Alice broke off suddenly, and said she had to go— it was just as Dr. Denbigh's little auto was coming down the street. She dashed out of the door and bowed to him from the crossing, quite like a young lady, for all her short skirts—she really did look fetching! Dr. Denbigh smiled at her, but not the way he used to smile at Peggy. I really thought he cared for Peggy once, though he's so much older that nobody else seemed to dream of such a thing.

Of course, after Alice went, I just sat there in the chair all humped up, thinking of her last words.

The family are always harping on "Lorraine's influence." If they wanted their dear Charles Edward made different from the way he is, why on earth didn't they do it themselves, when they had the chance? That's what I want to know! I know they mean to be nice to me, but they take it for granted that every habit Charles Edward has or hasn't, and everything he does or doesn't, is because I didn't do something that I ought to have done, or condoned something that I ought not. They seem to think that a man is made of soft, kindergarten clay, and all a wife has to do is to sit down and mould him as she pleases. Well, some men may be like that, but Peter isn't. The family never really have forgiven me for calling their darling "Charles Edward" Peter. I perfectly loathe that long-winded Walter-Scotty name, and I don't care how many grandfathers it's descended from. I'm sorry, of course, if it hurts their feelings, but as long as *I* don't object to their calling him what *they* like, I don't see why they mind. And as for my managing Peter, they know perfectly well that, though he's a darling, he's just mulishly obstinate. He's had his own way ever since he was born; the whole family simply adore him. His mother has always waited on him hand and foot, though she's sensible enough with the other children. If he looks sulky she is perfectly miserable. I am really very fond of my mother-in-law—that is, I am fond of her *in spots*. There are times when she understands how I feel about Peter better than any one else—like that dreadful spring when he had pneumonia and I was nearly wild. I know she is dreadfully unselfish and kind, but she *will* think—they all do—that they know what Peter needs better than I do, and whenever they see me alone it's to hint that I ought to keep him from smoking too much and being extravagant, and that I should make him wear his overcoat and go to bed early and take medicine when he has a cold. And through everything else they hark back to that everlasting, "If you'd only exert your influence, Lorraine dear, to make Charles Edward take more interest in the business—his father thinks so much of that."

If I were to tell them that Charles Edward perfectly detests the business, and will *never* be interested in it and never make anything out of it, they'd all go straight off the handle; yet they all know it just as well as I do. That's the trouble—you simply can't tell them the truth about anything; they don't want to hear it. I never talk at all any more when I go over to the big house, for I can't seem to without horrifying somebody.

I thought I should die when I first came here;

it was so different from the way it is at home, where you can say or do anything you please without caring what anybody thinks. Dad has always believed in not restricting individuality, and that girls have just as much right to live their own lives as boys — which is a fortunate thing, for, counting Momsey, there are four of us.

We never had any system about anything at home, thank goodness! We just had atmosphere. Dad was an artist, you know, and he does paint such lovely pictures; but he gave it up as a profession when we were little, and went into business, because, he said, he couldn't let his family starve— and we all think it was so perfectly noble of him! *I* couldn't give up being an artist for anybody, no matter *who* starved, and Peter feels that way, too. Of course we both realize that we're not *living* here in this hole, we're simply existing, and nothing matters very much until we get out of it. In six months, when Charles Edward is twenty-five, there's a little money coming to him—three thousand dollars—and then we're going to Paris to live our own lives; but nobody knows anything about that. One day I said something, without thinking, to my mother-in-law about that money; I've forgotten what it was, but she looked so horrified and actually gasped:

"You wouldn't think of Charles Edward's using his *principal*, Lorraine?"

And I said: "Why not? It's his own principal."

Well, I just made up my mind afterward that I'd never open my mouth again, while I live here, about *anything* I was interested in, even about Peter!

His father might have let him go to Paris that year before we met, when he was in New York at the Art League, just as well as not, but the family all consulted about it, Peter says, and concluded it wasn't "necessary." That is the blight that is always put on everything we want to do—it isn't necessary. Oh, how Alice hates that word! She says she supposes it's never "necessary" to be happy.

Well, Peter heard that when the Paris scheme came up—he'd written home that he couldn't work without the art atmosphere—Grandmother Evarts said:

"Why, I'm sure he has the Metropolitan Museum to go to; and there's Wanamaker's picture-gallery, too. Has he been to Wanamaker's?"

I thought I should throw a fit when Peter told me that!

I know, of course, that the family pity Peter for living in a house that's all at sixes and sevens, and for not having everything the way he has been used to having it; and I know they think I keep him from going to see them all at home, when the truth is—although, as usual, I can't say it—sometimes

86

I absolutely have to *hound* him to go there; though, of course, he's awfully fond of them all, and his mother especially; but he gets dreadfully lazy, and says they're his own people, anyway, and he can do as he pleases about it. It's their own fault, because they've always spoiled him. And if they only knew how he hates just that way of living he's been always used to, with its little, petty cast-iron rules and regulations, and the stupid family meals, where everybody is expected to be on time to the minute! My father-in-law pulls out his chair at the dinner-table exactly as the clock is striking one, and if any member of the family is a fraction late all the rest are solemn and strained and nervous until the culprit appears. Peter says the way he used to suffer—he was *never* on time.

The menu for each day of the week is as fixed as fate, no matter what the season of the year: hot roast beef, Sunday; cold roast beef, Monday; beefsteak, Tuesday; roast mutton, Wednesday; mutton pot-pie, Thursday; corned beef, Friday; and beefsteak again on Saturday. My father-in-law never eats fish or poultry, so they only have either if there is state company. There's one sacred apple pudding that's been made every Wednesday for nineteen years, and if you can imagine anything more positively dreadful than that, *I* can't.

Every time, as soon as we sit down to the table, Grandmother Evarts always begins, officially:

"Well, Charles Edward, my dear boy, we don't have you here very often nowadays. I said to your mother yesterday that it was two whole weeks since you had been to see her. What have you been doing with yourself lately?"

And when he says, as he always does, "Nothing, grandmother," I know she's disappointed, and then she starts in and tells what she has been doing, and Maria — Maria always manages to be there when we are—Maria tells what *she* has been doing, with little side digs at me because I haven't been pickling or preserving or cleaning. Once, when I first went there, Maria asked me at dinner what days I had for cleaning. And I said, as innocently as possible, that I hadn't any; that I perfectly loathed cleaning, and that we never cleaned at home! Of course it wasn't true, but we never talk about it, anyway. Peter said he nearly shrieked with joy to hear me come out like that.

It was almost as bad as the time I wore that sweet little yellow Empire gown. It's a dear, and Lyman Wilde simply raved over it when he painted me in it (not that he can really paint, but he has a *touch* with everything he does). I noticed that everybody seemed solemn and queer, but I never dreamed that I was the cause until my mother-in-law came to me afterward, blushing, and told me that Mr. Talbert never allowed any of the family to wear Mother Hubbards around the house.

88

Mother Hubbards! I could have moaned. Well, when I go around there now I never care what I have on, and I never pretend to talk at meals; I just sit and try and make my mind a blank until it's over. You *have* to make your mind a blank if you don't want to be driven raving crazy by that dining-room. It has a hideous black-walnut sideboard, an "oil-painting" of pale, bloated fruit on one side, and pale, bloated fish on the other, and a strip of black-and-white marbled oil-cloth below.

I feel sometimes as if I could hardly live until my father-in-law rises from his chair and kisses his wife good-bye before going off to the factory. She always blushes so prettily when he kisses her—as if it were for the first time. Then everybody looks pained when Peter and I just nod at each other as he goes out—I cannot be affectionate to him before them—and then, thank Heaven! the rest of us escape from the dining-room.

How Peggy, who has been away from home and seen and done things, can stand it there now as it is, is a continual wonder to me.

Peggy is a dear little thing. Peter has always been awfully fond of her, but she doesn't seem to have an idea in her head beyond her clothes and Harry Goward, though she'll *have* to have something more to her if she's going to keep *him*. The moment I saw that boy, of course I knew that he had the artistic temperament; I've seen so much

89

of it. He's the kind that's always awfully gloomy until eleven o'clock in the morning, and has to make love intensely to somebody every evening. What it must have been to that boy, after indulging in a romantic dream with poor little earnest, downright Peggy, to wake up and find the engagement taken seriously not only by her, but by all her relatives—find himself being welcomed into the family, introduced to them all as a future member— what it must have been to him I can't imagine! Peggy has no more temperament than a cow—the combination of Maria and Tom, and Grandmother Evarts, and Billy with his face washed clean, and Alice with three enormous bows on her hair, all waiting to welcome him, standing by the pictorial lamp on the brown worsted mat on the centre-table, made me fairly howl when I sat at home and thought of it—and that was before I'd *seen* Harry.

The family were, of course, quite "hurt" that Peter and I wouldn't assist at the celebration. I cannot see why people *will* want you to do things when they *know* you don't care to!

The next evening, however, we had to go, when Peggy herself came around and asked us. Of course Mr. Goward was with Peggy most of the time. They certainly looked charming together, but rather conscious and stiff. Every member of the family was watching his every motion. Oh, I've been there! I know what it is!

Some of the neighbors were there, too. Peter hardly ever plays on the big, old-fashioned grand-piano, but that night he was so bored he had to. The family always *think* they're very musical—you can know the style when I tell you that after Peter has been rambling through bits from Schumann and Richard Strauss they always ask him if he won't "play something." Well, after Peggy had gone into the other room with her mother to do the polite to Mrs. Temple, Mr. Goward gravitated over to where I sat in the big bay-window behind the piano; he had that "be-good-to-me,-won't-you?" air that I know so well! Then we got to talking and listening in between whiles—he knows lots of girls in the Art League—till Peter began playing that heart-breaking "Im Herbst" from the Franz Songs, and then he said:

"You're going to be my sister, aren't you? Won't you let me hold your hand while your husband's playing that? It makes me feel so lonely!"

I answered, promptly, "Certainly; hold both hands if you like!"

And we laughed, and Peter turned around for a moment and smiled, too. Oh, it *was* nice to meet somebody of one's own kind! You get so sick of having everything taken seriously.

That night, after we'd left the house, Harry caught up with us at the corner on his way to the hotel, and went home with us, and we all talked until three o'clock in the morning. We simply ate all over the house—goodness! how hungry we were! At Peter's home it's an unheard-of thing to eat anything after half-past six—almost a crime, unless it's a wedding or state reception. We began now with coffee in the dining-room, and jam and cheese, and ended by gradual stages at hot lobster in the chafing-dish in the studio—the darky was out all night, as usual.

Then Harry and Peter concluded that it was too late to go to bed at all—it was really daylight—so they took bath-towels and went down to the river and had a swim, and Harry slipped back to the house at six o'clock. He said we'd repeat it all the next night, but of course we didn't. He's the kind that, as soon as he's promised to do a thing, feels at once that he doesn't really want to do it.

The next day Peter's Aunt Elizabeth came on the scene, and of course we stayed away as much as we could. She loves Peter—they all do—but she hasn't any use for me, and shows it. She thinks I'm perfectly dumb and stupid. I simply don't exist, and I've never tried to undeceive her—it's too much trouble. She always wants to tell people how to do their hair and put on their clothes.

Miss Elizabeth Talbert is a howling swell; she only just endures it here. I've heard lots of things about her from Bell Pickering, who knows the Munroes—Lily Talbert, they call her there. She thinks she's fond of Art, but she really doesn't know the first thing about it—she doesn't like anything that isn't expensive and elegant and *à la mode*.

The only time she ever came to see me she actually *picked* her way around the house when I was showing it to her—there's no other word to use—just because there was a glass of jelly on the sofa, and the painting things were all over the studio with Peter's clothes. I perfectly hated her that day, yet I do love to look at her, and I can see how she might be terribly nice if you were any one she thought worth caring for. There have been times when I've seen a look on her face, like the clear ethereal light beyond the sunset, that just *pulled* at me. She is very fond of Peggy; I know she would never do anything to injure Peggy.

Poor little Peggy! When I think of this affair about Harry Goward I don't believe she ever felt sure of him; that is why she is so worked up over this matter now. I know there was something that I felt from the first through all her excitement, something that wasn't quite happy in her happiness. I feel atmospheres at once; I just can't help it. And when I get feeling other people's atmospheres too much I lose my own, and then I can't paint. I began so well the other day with the picture of that Armenian peddler, and now since Alice left I can't do a thing with it; his bare yellow knees look just like ugly grape-fruit. I wish Sally was in. She

93

can't cook, but she can do a song-and-dance that's
worth its weight in gold when you're down in the
mouth.

—Just then I looked out of the window and saw
my mother-in-law coming in. For a minute I was
frightened. I'd never seen her look like that before
—so white and almost *old;* she seemed hardly able
to walk, and I ran to the door and helped her in,
and put her in a chair and her feet on a footstool,
and got her my dear little Venetian bottle of smell-
ing-salts with the long silver chain; it's so beautiful
it makes you feel better just to look at it. I whisked
Peter's shoes out into the hall, and when I sat down
by her she put her hand out to me and said, "Dear
child," and I got all throaty, the way I do when any
one speaks like that to me, for, oh, I *have* been lonesome for Dad and Momsey and my own dear home!
though no one ever seems to imagine it, and I said:

"Oh, can't I do something for you, Madonna?"
I usually just call her "you," but once in a great
while, when there's nobody else around, I call her
Madonna, and I know she likes it, even if she does
think it a little Romish or sacrilegious or something
queer.

But she said she didn't want anything, only to rest
a few minutes, and that there was something she
wanted me to tell Peter. She couldn't come in the
evening to see him without every one wanting to
know why she came. There was some terrible

"OH, CAN'T I DO SOMETHING FOR YOU, MADONNA?"

trouble about Peggy's engagement. She flushed up and hesitated, and when I broke in to say, "You needn't bother to explain, I know all about the whole thing," she didn't seem at all surprised or ask how I knew—she only seemed relieved to find that she could go right on. I never can be demonstrative to her before people, but I just put my arms around her now when she said:

"It's a great comfort to be able to come to you, Lorraine, and speak out. At home your dear grandmother considers me so much — she only thinks of everything as it affects me, but it makes it so that I can't always show what I feel, for if I do she gets ill. All *I* can think of is Peggy. If you knew what it was to me just now when my little Peggy went away from me and locked herself in her room—Peggy, who all her life has always come to me for comfort—"

She stopped for a minute, and I patted her. It was so unlike my mother-in-law to speak in this way; she's uually so self-contained that it made me sort of awestruck. After a moment she went on in a different voice:

"They all want me to tell Cyrus—your father—that Aunt Elizabeth has been trying to take Mr. Goward's affections away from Peggy. I'm afraid it's just what she has been doing, though it seems incredible that she should have any attraction for a young man. I was glad Elizabeth had gone away overnight, for Maria is in such a state I don't know what might have happened."

"And don't you want to tell—father?" I gulped, but I knew I must say it. "Why not, Madonna?"

She shook her head, with that look that makes you feel sometimes that she isn't just the gentle and placid person that she appears to be. I seemed to catch a glimpse of something very clear and strong. If I could paint her with an expression like that I'd make my fortune.

"No, Lorraine. If it was about anybody but your aunt Elizabeth I would, but I can't speak against her. It's her home as well as mine; I've always realized that. I made up my mind, when I married, that I never would come between brother and sister, and I never have. Aunt Elizabeth doesn't know how many times I have smoothed matters over for her, how many times Cyrus has been provoked because he thought she didn't show enough consideration for me. I have always loved Aunt Elizabeth, and I believed she loved us—but when I saw my Peggy to-day, Lorraine, I couldn't go and tell your father about Aunt Elizabeth while I feel as I do now! I couldn't be just. If I made him angry with her—"

She stopped, and I didn't need to have her go on. My father-in-law is one of those big, kind, sensible, good-natured men who, when they do get angry, go clear off the handle, and are so absolutely furious and unreasonable you can't do anything with them. He got that way at Peter once—but it makes me so furious myself when I think of it that I never do.

"And, Lorraine," Madonna went on, quite simply, "bringing all this home to Aunt Elizabeth and making her pay up for it really has nothing to do with Peggy's happiness. It is my child's happiness that I want, Lorraine. There may be a misunderstanding of some kind — misunderstandings are very cruel things sometimes, Lorraine. I cannot believe that boy doesn't care for her—why, he loved her dearly! It seems to me far the best and most dignified thing to just write to Mr. Goward himself and find out the truth."

"I think so, too!" said I. "Oh, Madonna, you're a Jim Dandy!"

"And so," she went on, "I want you to ask Charles Edward to write to-night. I'll leave the address with you. As Peggy's brother, it will be more suitable for him to attend to the matter."

Charles Edward! I simply gasped. The idea of Peter's writing to Harry Goward to ask him the state of his affections! If Peter's mother couldn't realize how perfectly impossible it was for even *me* to make Peter do a thing that— Well—I was knocked silly.

Dear Madonna is the survival of a period when a woman always expected some man to face any crisis for her. All I could do was to say, resignedly:

"I'll give him the address." And when she got up I went to the gate with her. She was as dear as she could be; I just loved her until she happened to say:

"When I came in I thought you might be lying down, for I looked up and saw the shades were pulled down in your room, as they are now."

"Oh," I said, "I don't suppose anybody has been back in the room since we got up." And I was downright scared, she looked at me so strangely and began to tremble all over. "What *is* the matter?" I cried. "Do come into the house again!" But she only grasped my arm and said, tragically:

"Lorraine, it isn't *possible* that you haven't made your bed at four o'clock in the afternoon!" And I answered:

"Oh, I always make it up before I sleep in it." And then I knew that I'd said just the wrong thing. What difference it can make to *anybody* what time you make your *own* bed I can't see! She tried to make me promise I'd always make it up before ten o'clock in the morning. Why, I wouldn't even promise to always feel fond of Peter at ten o'clock in the morning! I *never* have anything to do with the family without always feeling on edge afterward. Why, when she was so sweet and strong about Peggy and Aunt Elizabeth and all the rest of it, *why* should she get upset about such a trifle?

I stood there by the gate just glowering as she

went off. I knew she thought I was going to perdition. I was sick of "the engagement." What business was it of Peter's and mine, anyhow? It had nothing to do with us, really. Then I thought of the time Peter and I quarrelled, and how *dear* Lyman Wilde was about it, and how he brought Peter back to me—just to say the name of Lyman Wilde always makes me feel better. I adore him, and always shall, and Peter knows it. If I could only go back to the Settlement and hear him say, "Little girl," in that coaxing voice of his! He is one of those men who are always working so hard for other people that you forget he hasn't anything for himself.

Thinking of him made me quite chipper again, and I went in and got his picture and stuck it up in the mantel-piece and put flowers in front of it. When Peter came in I told him about everything, and of course he refused to write to Harry Goward, as I knew he would. He said it was all rot, anyway, and that Harry was a nice boy, but not worth making such a fuss over. He didn't know that he was particularly stuck on Peggy's marrying Harry Goward, anyway—but there was no use in any one's interfering. Peggy was the person to write. Finally he said he'd telephone to Harry the next day to come out and stay at our house over Sunday, and then he and Peggy could have a chance to settle it. But Peter didn't telephone. He was late at the

Works the next day—though not nearly so late as he often is; but Mr. Talbert has a perfect fad about every one's getting there on time; it's one of the things there's always been a tug about between him and Peter. I should think he'd have realized long ago that Peter *never* will be on time, and just make up his mind to it, but he won't. Well, Peter came back again to the house a little after nine, perfectly white; he said he'd never enter the factory again. . . .

His father was in a towering rage when Peter went in; he spoke to Peter so that every one could hear him, and then— Oh, it was a dreadful time! . . .

Alice told me afterward that Maria had found her father in the garden before breakfast. She insinuated, in *her* way, all kinds of dreadful things about Harry Goward and Aunt Elizabeth, and there was a scene at the breakfast-table—and Peggy was taken so ill that they had to send for Dr. Denbigh. I don't know what will happen when Aunt Elizabeth comes home.

V

THE SCHOOL-GIRL

By Elizabeth Jordan

EXCEPT for Billy, who is a boy and does not count, I am the youngest person in our family; and when I tell you that there are eleven of us— well, you can dimly imagine the kind of a time *I* have. Two or three days ago I heard Grandma Evarts say something to the minister about "the down-trodden and oppressed of foreign lands," and after he had gone I asked her what they were. For a wonder, she told me; usually when Billy and I ask questions you would think the whole family had been struck dumb. But this time she an- swered and I remember every word—for if ever anything sounded like a description of Billy and me it was what Grandma Evarts said that day. I told her so, too; but, of course, she only looked at me over her spectacles and didn't understand what I meant. Nobody ever does except Billy and Aunt Elizabeth, and they're not much comfort. Billy is always so busy getting into trouble and having me get him out of it, and feeling sorry for himself, that he hasn't time to sympathize with me. Besides, as I've said before, he's only a boy, and you know what boys are and how they lack the delicate feelings girls have, and how their minds never work when you want them to. As for Aunt Elizabeth, she is lovely sometimes, and the way she remembers things that happened when she was young is simply wonderful. She knows how girls feel, too, and how they suffer when they are like Dr. Denbigh says I am—very nervous and sensitive and high-strung. But she admitted to me to-day that she had never before really made up her mind whether I am the "sweet, unsophisticated child" she calls me, or what Tom Price says I am, *The Eastridge Animated and Undaunted Daily Bugle and Clarion Call*. He calls me that because I know so much about what is going on; and he says if Mr. Temple could get me on his paper as a regular contributor there wouldn't be a domestic hearth-stone left in Eastridge. He says the things I drop will break every last one of them, anyhow, beginning with the one at home. That's the way he talks, and though I don't always know exactly what he means I can tell by his expression that it is not very complimentary.

Aunt Elizabeth is different from the others, and she and I have inspiring conversations sometimes—serious ones, you know, about life and responsibility and careers; and then, at other times, just when I'm revealing my young heart to her the way girls do in books, she gets absent-minded or laughs at me, or stares and says, "You extraordinary infant," and changes the subject. At first it used to hurt me dreadfully, but now I'm beginning to think she does it when she can't answer my questions. I've asked her lots and lots of things that have made her sit up and gasp, I can tell you, and I have more all ready as soon as I get the chance.

There is another thing I will mention while I think of it. Grandma Evarts is always talking about "rules of life," but the only rule of life I'm perfectly sure I have is to always mention things when I think of them. Even that doesn't please the family, though, because sometimes I mention things they thought I didn't know, and then they are annoyed and cross instead of learning a lesson by it and realizing how silly it is to try to keep secrets from me. If they'd *tell* me, and put me on my honor, I could keep their old secrets as well as anybody. I've kept Billy's for years and years. But when they all stop talking the minute I come into a room, and when mamma and Peggy go around with red eyes and won't say why, you'd better believe I don't like it. It fills me with the "intelligent discontent" Tom is always talking about. Then I don't rest until I know what there is to know, and usually when I get through I know more than anybody else does, because I've got all the different sides—Maria's and Tom's and Lorraine's and

Charles Edward's and mamma's and papa's and grandma's and Peggy's and Aunt Elizabeth's. It isn't that they intend to tell me things, either; they all try not to. Every one of them keeps her own secrets beautifully, but she drops things about the others. Then all I have to do is to put them together like a patch-work quilt.

You needn't think it's easy, though, for the very minute I get near any of the family they waste most of the time we're together by trying to improve me. You see, they are all so dreadfully old that they have had time to find out their faults and youthful errors, and every single one of them thinks she sees *all* her faults in me, and that she must help me to conquer them ere it is too late. Aunt Elizabeth says they mean it kindly, and perhaps they do. But if you have ever had ten men and women trying to improve you, you will know what my life is. Tom Price, who married my sister Maria, told Dr. Denbigh once that "every time a Talbert is unoccupied he or she puts Alice or Billy, or both, on the family moulding-board and kneads awhile." I heard him say it and it's true. All *I* can say is that if they keep on kneading and moulding me much longer there won't be anything left but a kind of a pulpy mass. I can see what they have done to Billy already; he's getting pulpier every day, and I don't believe his brain would ever work if I didn't keep stirring it up.

However, the thing I want to say while I think of it is this. It is a question, and I will ask it here because there is no use of asking it at home: Why is it that grown-up men and women never have anything really interesting to say to a girl fifteen years old? Then, if you can answer that, I wish you would answer another: Why don't they ever listen or understand what a girl means when she talks to them? Billy and I have one rule now when we want to say something serious. We get right in front of them and fix them with a glittering eye, the way the Ancient Mariner did, you know, and speak as slowly as we can, in little bits of words, to show them it's very important. Then, sometimes, they pay attention and answer us, but usually they act as if we were babies gurgling in cunning little cribs. And the rude way they interrupt us often and go on talking about their own affairs—well, I will not say more, for dear mamma has taught me not to criticise my elders, and I never do. But I watch them pretty closely, just the same, and when I see them doing something that is not right my brain works so hard it keeps me awake nights. If it's anything very dreadful, like Peggy's going and getting engaged, I point out the error, the way they're always pointing errors out to me. Of course it doesn't do any good, but that isn't my fault. It's because they haven't got what my teacher calls "receptive minds."

I'm telling you all this before I tell you what has happened, so you will be sorry for Billy and me. If you are sorry already, as well indeed you may be, you will be a great deal more sorry before I get through. For if ever any two persons were "down-trodden and oppressed" and "struggling in dark-ness" and "feeling the chill waters of affliction," it's Billy and me to-night—all because we tried to help Peggy and Lorraine and Aunt Elizabeth after they had got everything mixed up! I told them I was just trying to help, and Tom Price said right off that there was only one thing for Billy and me to do in future whenever the "philanthropic spirit began to stir" in us, and that was to get on board the suburban trolley-car and go as far away from home as our nickels would take us, and not hurry back. So you see he is not a bit grateful for the interesting things I told Maria.

I will now tell what happened. It began the day Billy heard the station agent at Whitman read Aunt Elizabeth's telegram to Harry Goward. The telegram had a lot of silly letters and words in it, so Billy didn't know what it meant, and, of course, he didn't care. The careless child would have forgotten all about it if I hadn't happened to meet him at Lorraine's after he got back from Whitman. He is always going to Lorraine's for some of Sallie's cookies—she makes perfectly delicious ones, round and fat and crumbly, with currants on the top.

Billy had taken so many that his pockets bulged out on the sides, and his mouth was so full he only nodded when he saw me. So, of course, I stopped to tell him how vulgar that was, and piggish, and to see if he had left any for me, and he was so anxious to divert my mind that as soon as he could speak he began to talk about seeing Aunt Elizabeth over in Whitman. That interested me, so I got the whole thing out of him, and the very minute he had finished telling it I made him go straight and tell Peggy. I told him to do it delicately, and not yell it out. I thought it would cheer and comfort Peggy to know that some one was doing something, instead of standing around and looking solemn, but, alas! it did not, and Billy told me with his own lips that it was simply awful to see Peggy's face. Even he noticed it, so it must have been pretty bad. He said her eyes got so big it made him think of the times she used to imitate the wolf in Red Riding-Hood and scare us 'most to death when we were young.

When Billy told me that, I saw that perhaps we shouldn't have told Peggy, so the next day I went over to Lorraine's again to ask her what she thought about it. I stopped at noon on my way home from school, and I didn't ring the bell, because I never do. I walked right in as usual, falling over the books and teacups and magazines on the floor, and I found Lorraine sitting at the tea-table with her head down among the little cakes and bits of toast left over from the afternoon before. She didn't look up, so I knew she hadn't heard me, and I saw her shoulders shake, and then I knew that she was crying. I had never seen Lorraine cry before, and I felt dreadfully, but I didn't know just what to do or what to say, and while I stood staring at her I noticed that there was a photograph on the table with a lot of faded flowers. The face of the photograph was up and I saw that it was a picture of Mr. Wilde—the one that usually stands on the mantel - piece. Lorraine is always talking about him, and she has told me ever and ever so much about how nice and kind he was to her when she was studying art in New York. But, of course, I didn't know she cared enough for him to cry over his picture, and it gave me the queerest feelings to see her do it—kind of wabbly ones in my legs, and strange, sinking ones in my stomach. You see, I had just finished reading *Lady Hermione's Terrible Secret*. A girl at school lent it to me. So when I saw Lorraine crying over a photograph and faded flowers I knew it must mean that she had learned to love Mr. Wilde with a love that was her doom, or would be if she didn't hurry and get over it. Finally I crept out of the house without saying a word to her or letting her know I was there, and I leaned on the gate to think it over and try to imagine what a girl in a book would do. In *Lady*

I FOUND LORRAINE WITH HER HEAD DOWN AMONG THE
LITTLE CAKES

Hermione her sister discovered the truth and tried to save the rash woman from the sad consequences of her love, so I knew that was what I must do, but I didn't know how to begin. While I was standing there with my brain going round like one of Billy's paper pinwheels some one stopped in front of me and said, "Hello, Alice," in a sick kind of a way, like a boy beginning to recite a piece at school. I looked up. It was Harry Goward!

You'd better believe I was surprised, for, of course, when he went away nobody expected he would come back so soon; and after all the fuss and the red eyes and the mystery *I* hoped he wouldn't come back at all. But here he was in three days, so I said, very coldly, "How do you do, Mr. Goward," and bowed in a distant way; and he took his hat off quickly and held it in his hand, and I waited for him to say something else. All he did for a minute was to look over my head. Then he said, in the same queer voice: "Is Mrs. Peter in? I wanted to have a little talk with her," and he put his hand on the gate to open it. I suppose it was dreadfully rude, but I stayed just where I was and said, very slowly, in icy tones, that he must kindly excuse my sister-in-law, as I was sure she wouldn't be able to receive him. Of course I knew she wouldn't want him or any one else to come in and see her cry, and besides I never liked Harry Goward and I never expect to. He looked very much surprised at first, and then his face got as red as a baby's does when there's a pin in it somewhere, and he asked if she was ill. I said, "No, she is not ill," and then I sighed and looked off down the street as if I would I were alone. He began to speak very quickly, but stopped and bit his lip. Then he turned away and hesitated, and finally he came back and took a thick letter from his pocket and held it out to me. He was smiling now, and for a minute he really looked nice and sweet and friendly.

"Say, Alice," he said, in the most coaxing way, "don't *you* get down on me, too. Do me a good turn—that's a dear. Take this letter home and deliver it. Will you? And say I'm at the hotel waiting for an answer."

Now, you can see yourself that this was thrilling. The whole family was watching every mail for a letter from Harry Goward and here he was offering me one! I didn't show how excited I was; I just took the letter and turned it over so I couldn't see the address and slipped it into my pocket, and said, coldly, that I would deliver it with pleasure. Harry Goward was looking quite cheerful again, but he said, in a worried tone, that he hoped I wouldn't forget, because it was very, very important. Then I dismissed him with a haughty bow, the way they do on the stage, and this time he put his hat on and really went.

Of course after that I wanted to go straight home with the letter, but I knew it wouldn't do to leave Lorraine bearing her terrible burden without some one to comfort her. While I was trying to decide what to do I saw Billy a block away with Sidney Tracy, and I whistled to him to come, and beckoned with both hands at the same time to show it was important. I had a beautiful idea. In that very instant I "planned my course of action," as they say in books. I made up my mind that I would send the letter home by Billy, and that would give me time to run over to Maria's and get something to eat and ask Maria to go and comfort Lorraine. Maria and Lorraine don't like each other very much, but I knew trouble might bring them closer, for Grandma Evarts says it always does. Besides, Maria is dreadfully old and knows everything and is the one the family always sends for when things happen. If they don't send she comes anyhow and tells everybody what to do. So I pinned the letter in Billy's pocket, so he couldn't lose it, and I ordered him to go straight home with it. He said he would. He looked queer and I thought I saw him drop something near a fence before he came to me, but I was so excited I didn't pay close attention. As soon as Billy started off I went to Maria's.

She was all alone, for Tom was lunching with some one at the hotel. When we were at the table I told her about Lorraine, and if ever any one was excited and really listened this time it was sister Maria. She pushed back her chair, and spoke right out before she thought, I guess.

"Charles Edward's wife crying over another man's picture!" she said. "Well, I like that! But I'm not surprised. I always said no good would come of *that* match!"

Then she stopped and made herself quiet down, but I could see how hard it was, and she added: "So *that* was the matter with Charles Edward when I met him this morning rushing along the street like a cyclone."

I got dreadfully worried then and begged her to go to Lorraine at once, for I saw things were even more terrible than I had thought. But Maria said: "Certainly not! I must consult with father and mother first. This is something that affects us all. After I have seen them I will go to Lorraine's." Then she told me not to worry about it, and not to speak of it to any one else. I didn't, either, except to Billy and Aunt Elizabeth; and when I told Aunt Elizabeth the man's name I thought she would go up into the air like one of Billy's skyrockets. But that part does not belong here, and I'm afraid if I stop to talk about it I'll forget about Billy and the letter.

After luncheon Maria put her hat on and went straight to our house to see mother, and I went back to school. When I got home I asked, the first thing, if Billy had delivered the letter from Harry Goward, and for the next fifteen minutes you would have thought every one in our house had gone crazy. That wretched boy had not delivered it at all! They had not even seen him, and they didn't know anything about the letter. After they had let me get enough breath to tell just how I had met Harry and exactly what he had said and done, mother rushed off to telephone to father, and Aunt Elizabeth came down-stairs with a wild, eager face, and Grandma Evarts actually shook me when she found I didn't even know whom the letter was for. I hadn't looked, because I had been so excited. Finally, after everybody had talked at once for a while, Grandma Evarts told me mamma had said Billy could go fishing that afternoon, because the weather was so hot and she thought he looked pale and overworked. The idea of Billy Talbert being overworked! I could have told mamma something about *that*.

Well, I saw through the whole thing then. Billy hadn't told me, for fear I would want to go along; so he had sneaked off with Sidney Tracy, and if he hadn't forgotten all about the letter he had made up his mind it would do as well to deliver it when he came home. That's the way Billy's mind works— like Tom Price's stop-watch. It goes up to a certain instant and then it stops short. You'd better believe I was angry. And it didn't make it any easier for me to remember that while I was having this dreadful time at home, and being reproached by everybody, Billy and Sidney Tracy were sitting comfortably under the willows on the edge of the river pulling little minnows out of the water. I knew exactly where they would be—I'd been there with Billy often enough. Just as I thought of that I looked at poor Peggy, sitting in her wrapper in papa's big easy-chair, leaning against a pillow Grandma Evarts had put behind her back, and trying to be calm. She looked so pale and worn and worried and sick that I made up my mind I'd follow those boys to the river and get that letter and bring it home to Peggy—for, of course, I was sure it was for her. I wish you could have seen her face when I said I'd do it, and the way she jumped up from the chair and then blushed and sank back and tried to look as if it didn't matter—with her eyes shining all the time with excitement and hope.

I got on my bicycle and rode off, and I made good time until I crossed the bridge. Then I had to walk along the river, pushing the bicycle, and I came to those two boys so quietly that they never saw me until I was right behind them. They were fishing still, but they had both been swimming—I could tell that by their wet hair and by the damp, mussy look of their clothes. When Billy saw me he turned red and began to make a great fuss over his line. He didn't say a word; he never does when he's surprised or ashamed, so he doesn't speak very often, anyhow; but I broke the painful silence by saying a few words myself. I told Billy how dreadful he had made everybody feel and how they were all blaming me, and I said I'd thank him for that letter to take home to his poor suffering sister. Billy put down his rod, and all the time I talked he was going through his pockets one after the other and getting redder and redder. I was so busy talking that I didn't understand at first just what this meant, but when I stopped and held out my hand and looked at him hard I saw in his guilty face the terrible, terrible fear that he had lost that letter; and I was so frightened that my legs gave way under me, and I sat down on the grass in my fresh blue linen dress, just where they had dripped and made it wet.

All this time Sidney Tracy was going through *his* pockets, too, and just as I was getting up again in a hurry he took off his cap and emptied his pockets into it. I wish you could have seen what that cap held then—worms, and sticky chewing-gum, and tops, and strings, and hooks, and marbles, and two pieces of molasses candy all soft and messy, and a little bit of a turtle, and a green toad, and a slice of bread-and-butter, and a dirty, soaking, hand-kerchief that he and Billy had used for a towel. There was something else there, too—a dark, wet, pulpy, soggy-looking thing with pieces of gum and molasses candy and other things sticking to it.

Sidney took it out and held it toward me in a proud, light-hearted way:

"There's your letter, all right," he said, and Billy gave a whoop of joy and called out, "Good-bye, Alice," as a hint for me to hurry home. I was so anxious to get the letter that I almost took it, but I stopped in time. I hadn't any gloves on, and it was just too dreadful. If you could have seen it you would never have touched it in the world. I got near enough to look at it, though, and then I saw that the address was so dirty and so covered with gum and bait and candy that all I could read was a capital "M" and a small "s" at the beginning and an "ert" at the end; the name between was hidden. I covered my eyes with my hand and gasped out to the boys that I wanted the things taken off it that didn't belong there, and when I looked again Sidney had scraped off the worst of it and was scrubbing the envelope with his wet handkerchief to make it look cleaner. After that you couldn't tell what *any* letter was, so I just groaned and snatched it from his hands and left those two boys in their disgusting dirt and degradation and went home.

When I got back mamma and Grandma Evarts and Tom Price and Peggy and Aunt Elizabeth were in the parlor, looking more excited than ever, because Maria had been there telling the family about Lorraine. Then she had gone on to Lorraine's and Tom had dropped in to call for her and was waiting to hear about the letter. They were all watching the door when I came in, and Peggy and Aunt Elizabeth started to get up, but sat down again. I stood there hesitating because, of course, I didn't know who to give it to, and Grandma Evarts shot out, "Well, Alice! Well, Well!" as if she was blowing the words at me from a little pea-shooter. Then I began to explain about the address, but before I could say more than two or three words mamma motioned to me and I gave the letter to her.

You could have heard an autumn leaf fall in that room. Mamma put on her glasses and puzzled over the smear on the envelope, and Peggy drew a long breath and jumped up and walked over to mamma and held out her hand. Mamma didn't hesitate a minute.

"Certainly it must be for you, my dear," she said, and then she added, in a very cold, positive way, "For whom else could it possibly be intended?" No one spoke; but just as Peggy had put her finger under the flap to tear it open, Aunt Elizabeth got up and crossed the room to where mamma and Peggy stood. She spoke very softly and quietly, but she looked queer and excited.

"Wait one moment, my dear," she said to Peggy. "Very probably the letter *is* for you, but it is just possible that it may be for some one else. Wouldn't it be safer—wiser—for *me* to open it?"

Then Peggy cried out, "Oh, Aunt Elizabeth, how dreadful! How can you say such a thing!" Mother had hesitated an instant when Aunt Elizabeth spoke, but now she drew Peggy's head down to her dear, comfy shoulder, and Peggy stayed right there and cried as hard as she could—with little gasps and moans as if she felt dreadfully nervous. Then, for once in my life, I saw my mother angry. She looked over Peggy's head at Aunt Elizabeth, and her face was so dreadful it made me shiver.

"Elizabeth," she said, and she brought her teeth right down hard on the word, "this is the climax of your idiocy. Have you the audacity to claim here, before me, that this letter from my child's affianced husband is addressed to you?"

Aunt Elizabeth looked very pale now, but when she answered she spoke as quietly as before.

"If it is, Ada," she said, "it is against my wish and my command. But—it may be." Then her voice changed as if she were really begging for something.

"Let me open it," she said. "If it is for Peggy I can tell by the first line or two, even if he does not use the name. Surely it will do no harm if I glance at it."

Mother looked even angrier than before.

"Well," she said, "it could do no harm, you think, if you read a letter intended for Peggy, but you don't dare to risk letting Peggy read a letter addressed by Harry Goward to you. This is intolerable, Elizabeth Talbert. You have passed the limit of my endurance—and of my husband's."

She brought out the last words very slowly, looking Aunt Elizabeth straight in the eyes, and Aunt Elizabeth looked back with her head very high. She has a lovely way of using such expressions as "For the rest" and "As to that," and she did it now.

"As to that," she said, "my brother must speak for himself. No one regrets more bitterly than I do this whole most unpleasant affair. I can only say that with all my heart I am trying to straighten it out."

Grandma Evarts sniffed just then so loudly that we all looked at her, and then, of course, mamma suddenly remembered that I was still there, regarding the scene with wide, intelligent young eyes, and she nodded toward the door, meaning for me to go out. My, but I hated to! I picked up grandma's ball of wool and drew the footstool close to her feet, and looked around to see if I couldn't show her some other delicate girlish attention such as old ladies love, but there wasn't anything, especially as grandma kept motioning for me to leave. So I walked toward the door very slowly, and before I got there I heard Tom Price say:

"Oh, come now; we're making a lot of fuss about nothing. There's a very simple way out of all this.

Alice says Goward's still at the hotel. I'll just run down there and explain, and ask him to whom that letter belongs."

Then I was at the door, and I *had* to open it and go out. The voices went on inside for a few minutes, but soon I saw Tom come out and I went to him and slipped my arm inside of his and walked with him across the lawn and out to the sidewalk. I don't very often like the things Tom says, but I thought it was clever of him to think of going to ask Harry Goward about the letter, and I told him so to encourage him. He thanked me very politely, and then he stopped and braced his back against the lamp-post on the corner and "fixed me with a stern gaze," as writers say.

"Look here, Clarry," he said ("Clarry" is short, he says, for *Daily Bugle and Clarion Call*, which is "too lengthy for frequent use"), "you're doing a lot of mischief to-day with your rural delivery system for Goward and your news extras about Lorraine. What's this cock-and-bull story you've got up about her, anyway?"

I told him just what I had seen. When I got through he said there was "nothing in it."

"That bit about her head being among the toast and cake," he went on, "would be convincing circumstantial evidence of a tragedy if it had been any other woman's head, but it doesn't count with Lorraine—I mean it doesn't represent the complete abandonment to grief which would be implied if it happened in the case of any one else. You must remember that when Lorraine wants to have a comfortable cry she's got to choose between putting her head in the jam on the sofa, or among the wet paint and brushes in the easy-chair, or among the crumbs on the tea-table. As for that photograph, it probably fell off the mantel-piece to the tea-table, instead of falling, as usual, into the coal-hod. To sum up, my dear Clarry, if you had remembered the extreme emotionalism of your sister Lorraine's temperament and the—er—eccentricity of her house-keeping, you would not have permitted yourself to be so sadly misled. Not remembering it, you've done a lot of mischief. All these things being so, no one will believe them. And to-night, when you are safely tucked into your little bed, if you hear the tramping of many feet on the asphalt walks you may know what it will mean. It will mean that your mother and father, and Elizabeth, and Grandma Evarts and Maria and Peggy will be dropping in on Lorraine, each alone and quite casually, of course, to find out what there really is in this terrible rumor. And some of them will believe to their dying day that there was something in it."

Well, that made me feel very unhappy. For I could see that under Tom's gay exterior and funny way of saying things he really meant every word. Of course I told him that I had wanted to help

Lorraine and Peggy because they were so wretched, and he made me promise on the spot that if ever I wanted to help him I'd tell him about it first. Then he went off to the hotel looking more cheerful, and I was left alone with my sad thoughts.

When I got into the house the first thing I saw was Billy sneaking out of the back door. I had meant to have a long and earnest talk with Billy the minute he got home, and point out some of his serious faults, but when I looked at him I saw that mamma or grandma had just done it. He looked red eyed and miserable, and the minute he saw me he began to whistle. Billy never whistles except just before or just after a whipping, so my heart sank, and I was dreadfully sorry for him. I started after him to tell him so, but he made a face at me and ran; and just then Aunt Elizabeth came along the hall and dragged me up to her room and began to ask me all over again about Mr. Goward and all that he said—whether I was perfectly *sure* he didn't mention any name. She looked worried and unhappy. Then she asked about Lorraine, but in an indifferent voice, as if she was really thinking about something else. I told her all I knew, but she didn't say a word or pay much attention until I mentioned that the man in the photograph was Mr. Lyman Wilde. Then—well, I wish you had seen Aunt Elizabeth! She made me promise afterwards that I'd never tell a single soul what happened, and I won't. But I do wish sometimes that Billy and I lived on a desert island, where there wasn't anybody else. I just can't bear being home when everybody is *so* unhappy, and when not a single thing I do helps the least little bit!

VI

THE SON-IN-LAW

By John Kendrick Bangs

ON the whole I am glad our family is no larger
than it is. It is a very excellent family as
families go, but the infinite capacity of each individual in it for making trouble, and adding to
complications already sufficiently complex, surpasses
anything that has ever before come into my personal
or professional experience. If I handle my end of
this miserable affair without making a break of
some kind or other, I shall apply to the Secretary
of State for a high place in the diplomatic service,
for mere international complications are child's-
play compared to this embroglio in which Goward
and Aunt Elizabeth have landed us all. I think
I shall take up politics and try to get myself elected
to the legislature, anyhow, and see if I can't get a
bill through providing that when a man marries
it is distinctly understood that he marries his wife
and not the whole of his wife's family, from her
grandmother down through her maiden aunts,
sisters, cousins, little brothers, *et al.*, including the

latest arrivals in kittens. In my judgment it ought to be made a penal offence for any member of a man's wife's family to live on the same continent with him, and if I had to get married all over again to Maria—and I'd do it with as much delighted happiness as ever—I should insist upon the interpolation of a line in the marriage ceremony, "Do you promise to love, honor, and obey your wife's relatives," and when I came to it I'd turn and face the congregation and answer "No," through a megaphone, so loud that there could be no possibility of a misunderstanding as to precisely where I stood.

If anybody thinks I speak with an unusual degree of feeling, I beg to inform him or her, as the case may be, that in the matter of wife's relations I have an unusually full set, and, as my small brother-in-law says when he orates about his postage-stamp collection, they're all uncancelled. Into all lives a certain amount of mother-in-law must fall, but I not only have that, but a grandmother-in-law as well, and maiden-aunt-in-law, and the Lord knows what else-in-law besides. I must say that as far as my mother-in-law is concerned I've had more luck than most men, because Mrs. Talbert comes pretty close to the ideal in mother-in-legal matters. She is gentle and unoffending. She prefers minding her own business to assuming a trust control of other people's affairs, but *her* mother—well, I don't wish any ill to Mrs. Evarts, but if anybody is ambitious to adopt an orphan lady, with advice on tap at all hours in all matters from winter flannels to the conversion of the Hottentots, I will cheerfully lead him to the goal of his desires, and with alacrity surrender to him all my right, title, and interest in her. At the same time I will give him a quit-claim deed to my maiden-aunt-in-law—not that Aunt Elizabeth isn't good fun, for she is, and I enjoy talking to her, and wondering what she will do next fills my days with a living interest, but I'd like her better if she belonged in some other fellow's family.

I don't suppose I can blame Maria under all the circumstances for standing up for the various members of her family when they are attacked, which she does with much vigorous and at times aggressive loyalty. We cannot always help ourselves in the matter of our relations. Some are born relatives, some achieve relatives, and others have relatives thrust upon them. Maria was born to hers, and according to all the rules of the game she's got to like them, nay, even cherish and protect them against the slings and arrows of outrageous criticism. But, on the other hand, I think she ought to remember that while I achieved some of them with my eyes open, the rest were thrust upon me when I was defenceless, and when I find some difficulty in adapting myself to circumstances, as is frequently the case, she should be more lenient to my incapacity. The fact that I am a lawyer makes it necessary for me to toe the mark of respect for the authority of the courts all day, whether I am filled with contempt for the court or not, and it is pretty hard to find, when I return home at night, that another set of the judiciary in the form of Maria's family, a sort of domestic supreme court, controls all my private life, so that except when I am rambling through the fields alone, or am taking my bath in the morning, I cannot give my feelings full and free expression without disturbing the family *entente;* and there isn't much satisfaction in skinning people to a lonesome cow, or whispering your indignant sentiments into the ear of a sponge already soaked to the full with cold water. I have tried all my married life to agree with every member of the family in everything he, she, or it has said, but, now that this Goward business has come up, I can't do that, because every time anybody says "Booh" to anybody else in the family circle, regarding this duplex love-affair, a family council is immediately called and "Booh" is discussed, not only from every possible stand-point, but from several impossible ones as well.

When that letter of Goward's was rescued from the chewing-gum contingent, with its address left behind upon the pulpy surface of Sidney Tracy's daily portion of peptonized-paste, it was thought best that I should call upon the writer at his hotel and find out to whom the letter was really written. My own first thought was to seek out Sidney Tracy and see if the superscription still remained on the chewing-gum, and I had the good-fortune to meet the boy on my way to the hotel, but on questioning him I learned that in the excitement of catching a cat-fish, shortly after Alice had left the lads, Sidney had incontinently swallowed the rubber-like substance, and nothing short of an operation for appendicitis was likely to put me in possession of the missing exhibit. So I went on to the hotel, and ten minutes later found myself in the presence of an interesting case of nervous prostration. Poor Goward! When I observed the wrought-up condition of his nerves, I was immediately so filled with pity for him that if it hadn't been for Maria I think I should at once have assumed charge of his case, and, as his personal counsel, sued the family for damages on his behalf. He did not strike me as being either old enough, or sufficiently gifted in the arts of philandery, to be taken seriously as a professional heart-breaker, and to tell the truth I had to restrain myself several times from telling him that I thought the whole affair a tempest in a teapot, because, in wanting consciously to marry two members of the family, he had only attempted to do what I had done un-consciously when I and the whole tribe of Talberts, remotely and immediately connected, became one. Nevertheless, I addressed him coldly.

"Mr. Goward," I said, when the first greetings were over, "this is a most unfortunate affair."

"It is terrible," he groaned, pacing the thin-carpeted floor like a poor caged beast in the narrow confines of the Zoo. "You don't need to tell me how unfortunate it all is."

"As a matter of fact," I went on, "I don't exactly recall a similar case in my experience. You will doubtless admit yourself that it is a bit unusual for a man even of your age to flirt with the maiden aunt of his *fiancée,* and possibly you realize that we would all be very much relieved if you could give us some reasonable explanation of your conduct."

"I'll be only too glad to explain," said Goward, "if you will only listen."

"In my own judgment the best solution of the tangle would be for you to elope with a third party at your earliest convenience," I continued, "but inasmuch as you have come here it is evident that you mean to pursue some course of action in respect to one of the two ladies—my sister or my aunt. Now what *is* that course? and which of the two ladies may we regard as the real object of your vagrom affections? I tell you frankly, before you begin, that I shall permit no trifling with Peggy. As to Aunt Elizabeth, she is quite able to take care of herself."

"It's—it's Peggy, of course," said Goward. "I admire Miss Elizabeth Talbert very much indeed, but I never really thought of—being seriously engaged to her."

"Ah!" said I, icily. "And did you think of being frivolously engaged to her?"

"I not only thought of it," said Goward, "but I was. It was at the Abercrombies', Mr. Price. Lily—that is to say, Aunt Elizabeth—"

"Excuse me, Mr. Goward," I interrupted. "As yet the lady is *not* your Aunt Elizabeth, and the way things look now I have my doubts if she ever is your Aunt Elizabeth."

"Miss Talbert, then," said Goward, with a heart-rending sigh. "Miss Talbert and I were guests at the Abercrombies' last October—maybe she's told you—and on Hallowe'en we had a party —apple-bobbing and the mirror trick and all that, and somehow or other Miss Talbert and I were thrown together a great deal, and before I really knew how, or why, we—well, we became engaged for—for the week, anyhow."

"I see," said I, dryly. "You played the farce for a limited engagement."

"We joked about it a great deal, and I—well, I got into the spirit of it—one must at house-parties, you know," said Goward, deprecatingly.

"I suppose so," said I.

"I got into the spirit of it, and Miss Talbert christened me Young Lochinvar, Junior," Goward went on, "and I did my best to live up to the title.

IT IS A BIT UNUSUAL FOR A MAN TO FLIRT WITH THE MAIDEN
AUNT OF HIS FIANCÉE

Then at the end of the week I was suddenly called home, and I didn't have any chance to see Miss Talbert alone before leaving, and—well, the engagement wasn't broken off. That's all. I never saw her again until I came here to meet the family. I didn't know she was Peggy's aunt."

"So that in reality you *were* engaged to both Peggy and Miss Talbert at the same time," I suggested. "That much seems to be admitted."

"I suppose so," groaned Goward. "But not seriously engaged, Mr. Price. I didn't suppose she would think it was serious—just a lark—but when she appeared that night and fixed me with her eye I suddenly realized what had happened."

"It was another case of 'the woman tempted me and I did eat,' was it, Goward?" I asked.

Goward's pale face flushed, and he turned angrily.

"I haven't said anything of the sort," he retorted. "Of all the unmanly, sneaking excuses that ever were offered for wrong-doing, that first of Adam's has never been beaten."

"You evidently don't think that Adam was a gentleman," I put in, with a feeling of relief at the boy's attitude toward my suggestion.

"Not according to my standards," he said, with warmth.

"Well," I ventured, "he hadn't had many opportunities, Adam hadn't. His outlook was rather provincial, and his associations not broadening. You wouldn't have been much better yourself brought up in a zoo. Nevertheless, I don't think myself that he toed the mark as straight as he might have."

"He was a coward," said Goward, with a positiveness born of conviction. And with that remark Goward took his place in my affections. Whatever the degree of his seeming offence, he was at least a gentleman himself, and his unwillingness to place any part of the blame for his conduct upon Aunt Elizabeth showed me that he was not a cad, and I began to feel pretty confident that some reasonable way out of our troubles was looming into sight.

"How old are you, Goward?" I asked.

"Twenty-one," he answered, "counting the years. If you count the last week by the awful hours it has contained I am older than Methuselah."

At last I thought I had it, and a feeling of wrath against Aunt Elizabeth began to surge up within me. It was another case of that intolerable "only a boy" habit that so many women of uncertain age and character, married and single, seem nowadays to find so much pleasure in. We find it too often in our complex modern society, and I am not sure that it is not responsible for more deviations from the path of rectitude than even the offenders themselves imagine. Callow youth just from college is susceptible to many kinds of flattery, and at the age of adolescence the appeal which lovely woman makes to inexperience is irresistible.

I know whereof I speak, for I have been there myself. I always tell Maria everything that I conveniently can—it is not well for a man to have secrets from his wife—and when I occasionally refer to my past flames I find myself often growing more than pridefully loquacious over my early affairs of the heart, but when I thought of the serious study that I once made in my twentieth year of the dozen easiest, most painless methods of committing suicide because Miss Mehitabel Flanders, *ætat* thirty-eight, whom I had chosen for my life's companion, had announced her intention of marrying old Colonel Barrington—one of the wisest matches ever as I see it now—I drew the line at letting Maria into that particular secret of my career. Miss Mehitabel was indeed a beautiful woman, and she took a very deep and possibly maternal interest in callow youth. She invited confidence and managed in many ways to make a strong appeal to youthful affections, but I don't think she was always careful to draw the line nicely between maternal love and that other which is neither maternal, fraternal, paternal, nor even filial. To my eye she was no older than I, and to my way of thinking nothing could have been more eminently fitting than that we should walk the Primrose Way hand in hand forever.

While I will not say that the fair Mehitabel trifled with my young affections, I will say that she let me believe—nay, induced me to believe by her manner—that even as I regarded her she regarded me, and when at the end she disclaimed any intention to smash my heart into the myriad atoms into which it flew—which have since most happily reunited upon Maria—and asserted that she had let me play in the rose-garden of my exuberant fancy because I was "only a boy," my bump upon the hard world of fact was an atrociously hard one. Some women *pour passer le temps* find pleasure in playing thus with young hopes and hearts as carelessly as though they were mere tennis-balls, to be whacked about and rallied, and volleyed hither and yon, without regard to their constituent ingredients, and then when trouble comes, and a catastrophe is imminent, the refuge of "only a boy" is sought as though it really afforded a sufficient protection against "responsibility." The most of us would regard the hopeless infatuation of a young girl committed to our care, either as parents or as guardians, for a middle-aged man of the world with such horror that drastic steps would be taken to stop it, but we are not so careful of the love-affairs of our sons, and view with complaisance their devotion to some blessed damozel of uncertain age, comforting ourselves with the reflection that he is "only a boy" and will outgrow it all in good time. (There's another mem. for my legislative career—a Bill for the Protection of Boys, and the Suppression of Old Maids Who Don't Mean Anything By It.)

I don't mean, in saying all this, to reflect in any way upon the many helpful friendships that exist between youngsters developing into manhood and their elders among women who are not related to them. There have been thousands of such friendships, no doubt, that have worked for the upbuilding of character; for the inspiring in the unfolding consciousness of what life means in the young boy's being of a deeper, more lasting, respect for womanhood than would have been attained to under any other circumstances, but that has been the result only when the woman has taken care to maintain her own dignity always, and to regard her course as one wherein she has accepted a degree of responsibility second only to a mother's, and not a by-path leading merely to pleasure and for the idling away of an unoccupied hour. Potential manhood is a difficult force to handle, and none should embark upon the parlous enterprise of arousing it without due regard for the consequences. We may not let loose a young lion from its leash, and, when dire consequences follow, excuse ourselves on the score that we thought the devastating creature was "only a cub."

These things flashed across my mind as I sat in

Goward's room watching the poor youth in his nerve-distracting struggles, and, when I thought of the tangible evidence in hand against Aunt Elizabeth, I must confess if I had been juryman sitting in judgment of the case I should have convicted her of kidnapping without leaving the box. To begin with, there was the case of Ned Temple. I haven't quite been able to get away from the notion that however short-sighted and *gauche* poor Mrs. Temple's performance was in going over to the Talberts' to make a scene because of Aunt Elizabeth's attentions to Temple, she thought she was justified in doing so, and Elizabeth's entire innocence in the premises, in view of her record as a man-snatcher, has not been proven to my satisfaction. Then there was that Lyman Wilde business, which I never understood and haven't wanted to until they tried to mix poor Lorraine up in it. Certain it is that Elizabeth and Wilde were victims of an affair of the heart, but what Lorraine has had to do with it I don't know, and I hope the whole matter will be dropped at least until we have settled poor Peggy's affair. Then came Goward and this complication, and through it all Elizabeth has had a weather-eye open for Dr. Denbigh. A rather suggestive chain of evidence that, proving that Elizabeth seems to regard all men as her own individual property. As Mrs. Evarts says, she perks up even when Billie comes into the room—or Mr.

Talbert, either; and as for me—well, in the strictest
confidence, if Aunt Elizabeth hasn't tried to flirt
even with me, then I don't know what flirtation is,
and there was a time—long before I was married,
of course—when I possessed certain well-developed
gifts in that line.   I know this, that when I was
first paying my addresses to Maria, Aunt Elizabeth
was staying at the Talberts' as usual, and Maria
and I had all we could do to get rid of her.   She
seemed to be possessed with the idea that I came
there every night to see her, and not a hint in the
whole category of polite intimations seemed capable
of conveying any other idea to her mind, although
she showed at times that even a chance remark
fell upon heeding ears, for once when I observed
that pink was my favorite color, she blossomed out
in it the next day and met me looking like a peach-
tree in full bloom, on Main Street as I walked from
my office up home.   And while we are discussing
other people's weaknesses I may as well confess my
own, and say that I was so pleased at this unexpected revelation of interest in my tastes that when
I called that evening I felt vaguely disappointed to
learn that Aunt Elizabeth was dining out—and I
was twenty-seven at the time, too, and loved Maria
into the bargain!   And after the wedding, when we
came to say good-bye, and I kissed Aunt Elizabeth
—I kissed everybody that day in the hurry to get
away, even the hired man at the door—and said,

"Good-bye, Aunty," she pouted and said she didn't like the title " a little bit."

Now, of course, I wouldn't have anybody think that I think Aunt Elizabeth was ever in love with me, but I mention these things to show her general attitude toward members of the so-called stronger sex. The chances are that she does not realize what she is doing, and assumes this coy method with the whole masculine contingent as a matter of thoughtless habit. What she wants to be to man I couldn't for the life of me even guess—mother, sister, daughter, or general manager. But that she does wish to grab every male being in sight, and attach them to her train, is pretty evident to me, and I have no doubt that this is what happened in poor Harry Goward's case. She has a bright way of saying things, is unmistakably pretty, and has an unhappy knack of making herself appear ten or fifteen years younger than she is if she needs to. She is chameleonic as to age, and takes on always something of the years of the particular man she is talking to. I saw her talking to the dominie the other night, and a more spiritual-looking bit of demure middle-aged piety you never saw in a nunnery, and the very next day when she was conversing with young George Harris, a Freshman at Yale, at the Barbers' reception, you'd have thought she was herself a Vassar undergraduate. So there you are. With Goward she had assumed that same youthful manner, and backed by all the power of her thirty-seven years of experience he was mere putty in her hands, and she played with him and he lost, just as any other man, from St. Anthony down to the boniest ossified man of to-day would have lost, and it wasn't until he saw Peggy again and realized the difference between the real thing and the spurious that he waked up.

With all these facts marshalled and flashing through my brain much more rapidly than I can tell them, like the quick succession of pictures in the cinematograph, I made up my mind to become Goward's friend in so far as circumstances would permit. With Aunt Elizabeth out of the way it seemed to me that we would find all plain sailing again, but how to get rid of her was the awful question. Poor Peggy could hardly be happy with such a Richmond in the field, and nothing short of Elizabeth's engagement to some other man would help matters any. She had been too long unmarried, anyhow. Maiden aunthood is an unhappy estate, and grows worse with habit. If I could only find Lyman Wilde and bring him back to her, or, perhaps, Dr. Denbigh—that was the more immediate resource, and surely no sacrifice should be too great for a family physician to make for the welfare of his patients. Maria and I would invite Dr. Denbigh to dinner and have Aunt Elizabeth as the only other guest. We could leave them alone on some pretext

or other after dinner, and leave the rest to fate—
aided and abetted by Elizabeth herself.

Meanwhile there was Goward still on my hands.

"Well, my boy," I said, patting him kindly on
the shoulder, "I hardly know what to say to *you*
about this thing. You've got yourself in the
dickens of a box, but I don't mind telling you I
think your heart is in the right place, and, whatever
has happened, I don't believe you have intention-
ally done wrong. Maybe at your age you do not
realize that it is not safe to be engaged to two people
at the same time, especially when they belong to the
same family. Scientific heart-breakers, as a rule,
take care that their *fiancées* are not only not related,
but live in different sections of the country, and as
I have no liking for preaching I shall not dwell further upon the subject."

"I think I realize my position keenly enough
without putting you to the trouble," said Goward,
gazing gloomily out of the window.

"What I will say, however," said I, "is that I'll
do all I can to help you out of your trouble. As one
son-in-law to another, eh?"

"You are very kind," said he, gripping me by the
hand.

"I will go to Mrs. Talbert—she is the best one
to talk to—first, and tell her just what you have
told me, and it is just possible that she can explain
it to Peggy," I went on.

"I—I think I could do that myself if I only had the chance," he said, ruefully.

"Well, then—I'll try to make the chance. I won't promise that I will make it, because I can't answer for anybody but myself. Some day you will find out that women are peculiar. But what I can do I will," said I. "And, furthermore, as the general attorney for the family I will cross-examine Aunt Elizabeth—put her through the third degree, as it were, and try to show her how foolish it is for her to make so serious a matter of a trifling flirtation."

"I wouldn't, if I were you," said Goward, with a frown. "She needn't be involved in the affair any more than she already is. She is not in the least to blame."

"Nevertheless," said I, "she may be able to help us to an easy way out—"

"She can't," said Goward, positively.

"Excuse me, Mr. Goward," said I, chilling a trifle in my newly acquired friendliness, "but is there any real reason why I should not question Miss Talbert—"

"Oh no, none at all," he hastened to reply. "Only I—I see no particular object in vexing her further in a matter that must have already annoyed her sufficiently. It is very good of you to take all this trouble on my account, and I don't wish you to add further to your difficulties, either," he added.

I appreciated his consideration, with certain reservations. However, the latter were not of such character as to make me doubt the advisability of standing his friend, and when we parted a few minutes later I left him with the intention of becoming his advocate with Peggy and her mother, and at the same time of having it out with Aunt Elizabeth.

I was detained at my office by other matters, which our family troubles had caused me to neglect, until supper-time, and then I returned to my own home, expecting to have a little chat over the affair with Maria before acquainting the rest of the family with my impressions of Goward and his responsibility for our woe. Maria is always so full of good ideas, but at half-past six she had not come in, and at six-forty-five she 'phoned me that she was at her father's and would I not better go there for tea. In the Talbert family a suggestion of that sort is the equivalent of a royal command in Great Britain, and I at once proceeded to accept it. As I was leaving the house, however, the thought flashed across my mind that in my sympathy for Harry Goward I had neglected to ask him the question I had sought him out to ask, "To whom was the letter addressed?" So I returned to the 'phone, and ringing up the Eagle Hotel, inquired for Mr. Goward.

"Mr. Goward!" came the answer.

"Yes," said I. "Mr. Henry Goward."

"Mr. Goward left for New York on the 5.40 train this afternoon," was the reply.

The answer, so unexpected and unsettling to all my plans, stunned me first and then angered me.

"Bah!" I cried, impatiently. "The little fool! An attack of cold feet, I guess—he ought to spell his name with a C."

I hung up the receiver with a cold chill, for frankly I hated to go to the Talberts' with the news. Moreover, it would be a humiliating confession to make that I had forgotten to ask Goward about the letter, when everybody knew that that was what I had called upon him for, and when I thought of all the various expressions in the very expressive Talbert eyes that would fix themselves upon me as I mumbled out my confession, I would have given much to be well out of it. Nevertheless, since there was no avoiding the ordeal, I resolved to face the music, and five minutes later entered the dining-room at my father-in-law's house with as stiff an upper lip as I could summon to my aid in the brief time at my disposal. They were all seated at the table already—supper is not a movable feast in that well-regulated establishment—save Aunt Elizabeth. Her place was vacant.

"Sorry to be late," said I, after respectfully saluting my mother-in-law, "but I couldn't help it. Things turned up at the last minute and they had to be attended to. Where's Aunt Elizabeth?"

"She went to New York," said my mother-in-law, "on the 5.40 train."

VII

THE MARRIED SON

By Henry James

IT'S evidently a great thing in life to have got hold of a convenient expression, and a sign of our inordinate habit of living by words. I have sometimes flattered myself that I live less exclusively by them than the people about me; paying with them, paying with them only, as the phrase is (there I am at it, exactly, again!) rather less than my companions, who, with the exception, perhaps, a little —sometimes!—of poor Mother, succeed by their aid in keeping away from every truth, in ignoring every reality, as comfortably as possible. Poor Mother, who is worth all the rest of us put together, and is really worth two or three of poor Father, deadly decent as I admit poor Father mainly to be, sometimes meets me with a look, in some connection, suggesting that, deep within, she dimly understands, and would really understand a little better if she weren't afraid to: for, like all of us, she lives surrounded by the black forest of the "facts of life" very much as the people in the heart of Africa live in their dense wilderness of nocturnal terrors, the mysteries and monstrosities that make them seal themselves up in the huts as soon as it gets dark. She, quite exquisite little Mother, would often understand, I believe, if she dared, if she knew *how* to dare; and the vague, dumb interchange then taking place between us, and from the silence of which we have never for an instant deviated, represents perhaps her wonder as to whether I mayn't on some great occasion show her how.

The difficulty is that, alas, mere intelligent useless wretch as I am, I've never hitherto been sure of knowing how myself; for am I too not as steeped in fears as any of them? My fears, mostly, are different, and of different dangers—also I hate having them, whereas they love them and hug them to their hearts; but the fact remains that, save in this private precinct of my overflow, which contains, under a strong little brass lock, several bad words and many good resolutions, I have never either said or done a bold thing in my life. What I seem always to feel, doubtless cravenly enough, under her almost pathetic appeal, has been that it isn't yet the occasion, the really good and right one, for breaking out; than which nothing could more resemble of course the inveterate argument of the helpless. *Any* occasion is good enough for the helpful; since there's never any that hasn't weak sides for their own strength to make up. However, if there *could* be conceivably a good one, I'll be hanged if I don't seem to see it gather now, and if I sha'n't write myself here "poor" Charles Edward in all truth by failing to take advantage of it. (They have in fact, I should note, one superiority of courage to my own: this habit of their so constantly casting up my poverty at me—poverty of character, of course I mean, for they don't, to do them justice, taunt me with having "made" so little. They don't, I admit, take their lives in their hands when they perform that act; the proposition itself being that I haven't the spirit of a fished-out fly.)

My point is, at any rate, that I designate *them* as Poor only in the abysmal confidence of these occult pages: into which I really believe even my poor wife—for it's universal!—has never succeeded in peeping. It will be a shock to me if I some day find she has so far adventured—and this not on account of the curiosity felt or the liberty taken, but on account of her having successfully disguised it. She knows I keep an intermittent diary—I've confessed to her it's the way in which I work things in general, my feelings and impatiences and difficulties, off. It's the way I work off my nerves— that luxury in which poor Charles Edward's natural narrow means—narrow so far as ever acknowledged —don't permit him to indulge. No one for a moment suspects I have any nerves, and least of all what they themselves do to them; no one, that is, but poor little Mother again—who, however, again, in her way, all timorously and tenderly, has never mentioned it: any more than she has ever mentioned her own, which she would think quite indecent. This is precisely one of the things that, while it passes between us as a mute assurance, makes me feel myself more than the others verily *her* child: more even than poor little Peg at the present strained juncture.

But what I was going to say above all is that I don't care that poor Lorraine—since that's my wife's inimitable name, which I feel every time I write it I must apologize even to myself for!—should quite discover the moments at which, first and last, I've worked *her* off. Yet I've made no secret of my cultivating it as a resource that helps me to hold out; this idea of our "holding out," separately and together, having become for us—and quite comically, as I see—the very basis of life. What does it mean, and how and why and to what end are we holding? I ask myself that even while I feel how much we achieve even by just hugging each other over the general intensity of it. This is what I have in mind as to our living to that extent by the vain phrase; as to our really from time to time winding ourselves up by the use of it, and winding each other. What should we do if we didn't hold out, and of what romantic, dramatic, or simply perhaps quite prosaic, collapse would giving in, in contradistinction, consist for us? We haven't in the least formulated that—though it perhaps may but be one of the thousand things we are afraid of.

At any rate we don't, I think, ever so much as ask ourselves, and much less each other: we're so quite sufficiently sustained and inflamed by the sense that we're just doing it, and that in the sublime effort our union is our strength. There must be something in it, for the more intense we make the consciousness—and haven't we brought it to as fine a point as our frequently triumphant partnership at bridge?—the more it positively does support us. Poor Lorraine doesn't really at all need to understand in order to believe; she believes that, failing our exquisite and intimate combined effort of resistance, we should be capable together of something—well, "desperate." It's in fact in this beautiful desperation that we spend our days, that we face the pretty grim prospect of new ones, that we go and come and talk and pretend, that we consort, so far as in our deep-dyed hypocrisy we do consort, with the rest of the Family, that we have Sunday supper with the Parents and emerge, modestly yet virtuously shining, from the ordeal; that we put in our daily appearance at the Works—for a utility nowadays so vague that I'm fully aware (Lorraine isn't so much) of the deep amusement I excite there, though I also recognize how wonderfully, how quite charitably, they manage not to break out with it: bless, for the most part, their dear simple hearts!

It is in this privately exalted way that we bear in short the burden of our obloquy, our failure, our resignation, our sacrifice of what we should have liked, even if it be a matter we scarce dare to so much as name to each other; and above all of our insufferable reputation for an abject meekness. We're really not meek a bit—we're secretly quite ferocious; but we're held to be ashamed of ourselves not only for our proved business incompetence, but for our lack of first-rate artistic power as well: it being now definitely on record that we've never yet designed a single type of ice-pitcher—since that's the damnable form Father's production more and more runs to; his uncanny ideal is to turn out more ice-pitchers than any firm in the world—that has "taken" with their awful public. We've tried again and again to strike off something hideous enough, but it has always in these cases appeared to us quite beautiful compared to the object finally turned out, on their improved lines, for the unspeakable market; so that we've only been able to be publicly rueful and depressed about it, and to plead practically, in extenuation of all the extra trouble we saddle them with, that such things are, alas, the worst we can do.

We so far succeed in our plea that we're held at least to sit, as I say, in contrition, and to understand how little, when it comes to a reckoning, we really pay our way. This actually passes, I think for the main basis of our humility, as it's certainly the basis of what I feel to be poor Mother's unuttered yearning. It almost broke her heart that we *should* have to live in such shame—she has only got so far as that yet. But it's a beginning; and I seem to make out that if I don't spoil it by any wrong word, if I don't in fact break the spell by any wrong breath, she'll probably come on further. It will glimmer upon her—some day when she looks at me in her uncomfortable bewildered tenderness, and I almost hypnotize her by just smiling inscrutably back—that she isn't getting all the moral benefit she somehow ought out of my being so pathetically wrong; and then she'll begin to wonder and wonder, all to herself, if there mayn't be something to be said for me. She has limped along, in her more or less dissimulated pain, on this apparently firm ground that I'm so wrong that nothing will do for either of us but a sweet, solemn, tactful agreement between us never to mention it. It falls in so richly with all the other things, all the "real" things, we never mention.

Well, it's doubtless an odd fact to be setting down even here; but I *shall* be sorry for her on the day when her glimmer, as I have called it, broadens— when it breaks on her that if I'm as wrong as this comes to, why the others must be actively and ab-

solutely right. She has never had to take it quite
that way—so women, even mothers, wondrously get
on; and heaven help her, as I say, when she shall.
She'll be immense—"tactfully" immense, with
Father about it—she'll manage that, for herself
and for him, all right; but where the iron will enter
into her will be at the thought of her having for
so long given *raison*, as they say in Paris—or as
poor Lorraine at least says they say—to a couple like
Maria and Tom Price. It comes over her that she
has taken it largely from *them* (and she *has*) that
we're living in immorality, Lorraine and I: ah *then*,
poor dear little Mother—! Upon my word I believe I'd go on lying low to this positive pitch of
grovelling—and Lorraine, charming, absurd creature, would back me up in it too—in order precisely
to save Mother such a revulsion. It will be really
more trouble than it will be worth to her; since it
isn't as if our relation weren't, of its kind, just as we
are, about as "dear" as it can be.

I'd literally much rather help her not to see than
to see; I'd much rather help her to get on with the
others (yes, even including poor Father, the fine
damp plaster of whose composition, renewed from
week to week, can't be touched anywhere without
letting your finger in, without peril of its coming to
pieces) in the way easiest for her—if not easiest *to*
her. She couldn't live with the others an hour—
no, not with one of them, unless with poor little

Peg—save by accepting all their premises, save by making in other words all the concessions and having all the imagination. I ask from her nothing of this—I do the whole thing with her, as she has to do it with them; and of this, *au fond*, as Lorraine again says, she is ever so subtly aware—just as, *for* it, she's ever so dumbly grateful. Let these notes stand at any rate for my fond fancy of that, and write it here to my credit in letters as big and black as the tearful alphabet of my childhood; let them do this even if everything else registers meaner things. I'm perfectly willing to recognize, as grovellingly as any one likes, that, as grown-up and as married and as preoccupied and as disillusioned, or at least as battered and seasoned (by adversity) as possible, I'm in respect to *her* as achingly filial and as feelingly dependent, all the time, as when I used, in the far-off years, to wake up, a small blubbering idiot, from frightening dreams, and refuse to go to sleep again, in the dark, till I clutched her hands or her dress and felt her bend over me.

She used to protect me then from domestic derision—for she somehow kept such passages quiet; but she can't (it's where *her* ache comes in!) protect me now from a more insidious kind. Well, now I don't care! I feel it in Maria and Tom, constantly, who offer themselves as the pattern of success in comparison with which poor Lorraine and I are nowhere. I don't say they do it with malice prepense, or that they plot against us to our ruin; the thing operates rather as an extraordinary effect of their mere successful blatancy. They're blatant, truly, in the superlative degree, and I call them successfully so for just this reason, that poor Mother is to all appearance perfectly unaware of it. Maria is the one member of all her circle that has got her really, not only just ostensibly, into training; and it's a part of the general irony of fate that neither she nor my terrible sister herself recognizes the truth of this. The others, even to poor Father, think they manage and manipulate her, and she can afford to let them think it, ridiculously, since they don't come anywhere near it. She knows they don't and is easy with them; playing over Father in especial with finger-tips so lightly resting and yet so effectively tickling, that he has never known at a given moment either where they were or, in the least, what they were doing to him. That's enough for Mother, who keeps by it the freedom of her soul; yet whose fundamental humility comes out in its being so hidden from her that her eldest daughter, to whom she allows the benefit of every doubt, does damnably boss her.

This is the one case in which she's not lucid; and, to make it perfect, Maria, whose humility is neither fundamental nor superficial, but whose avidity is both, comfortably cherishes, as a ground of complaint—nurses in fact, beatifically, as a wrong—

the belief that she's the one person without influence. Influence?—why she has so much on *me* that she absolutely coerces me into making here these dark and dreadful remarks about her! Let my record establish, in this fashion, that if I'm a clinging son I'm, in that quarter, to make up for it, a detached brother. Deadly virtuous and deadly hard and deadly charmless—also, more than anything, deadly *sure!*—how does Maria fit on, by consanguinity, to such amiable characters, such *real* social values, as Mother and me at all? If that question ceases to matter, sometimes, during the week, it flares up, on the other hand, at Sunday supper, down the street, where Tom and his wife, overwhelmingly cheerful and facetious, contrast so favorably with poor gentle sickly (as we doubtless appear) Lorraine and me. We can't meet them—that is I can't meet Tom— on that ground, the furious football-field to which he reduces conversation, making it echo as with the roar of the arena—one little bit.

Of course, with such deep diversity of feeling, we simply loathe each other, he and I; but the sad thing is that we get no good of it, none of the *true* joy of life, the joy of our passions and perceptions and desires, by reason of our awful predetermined geniality and the strange abysmal necessity of our having so eternally to put up with each other. If we could intermit that vain superstition somehow, for about three minutes, I often think the air might clear (as by the scramble of the game of General Post, or whatever they call it) and we should all get out of our wrong corners and find ourselves in our right, glaring from these positions a happy and natural defiance. Then I shouldn't be thus nominally and pretendedly (it's too ignoble!) on the same side or in the same air as my brother-in-law; whose value is that he has thirty "business ideas" a day, while I shall never have had the thirtieth fraction of one in my whole life. He just hums, Tom Price, with business ideas, whereas I just gape with the impossibility of them; he moves in the densest buzzing cloud of them—after the fashion in which we carry our heads here on August evenings, each with its own thick nimbus of mosquitoes. I'm but too conscious of how, on the other hand, I'm desolately outlined to all eyes, in an air as pure and empty as that of a fine Polar sunset.

It was Lorraine, dear quaint thing, who some time ago made the remark (on our leaving one of those weekly banquets at which we figure positively as a pair of social skeletons) that Tom's *facetiæ* multiply, evidently, in direct proportion to his wealth of business ideas; so that whenever he's enormously funny we may take it that he's "on" something tremendous. He's sprightly in proportion as he's in earnest, and innocent in proportion as he's going to be dangerous; dangerous, I mean, to the competitor and the victim. Indeed when I reflect that his jokes are probably each going to cost certain people, wretched helpless people like myself, hundreds and thousands of dollars, their abundant flow affects me as one of the most lurid of exhibitions. I've sometimes rather wondered that Father can stand so much of him, Father who has after all a sharp nerve or two in him, like a razor gone astray in a valise of thick Jäger underclothing; though of course Maria, pulling with Tom shoulder to shoulder, would like to see any one *not* stand her husband.

The explanation has struck me as, mostly, that business genial and cheerful and even obstreperous, without detriment to its *being* business, has been poor Father's ideal for his own terrible kind. This ideal is, further, that his home-life shall attest that prosperity. I think it has even been his conception that our family tone shall by its sweet innocence fairly register the pace at which the Works keep ahead: so that he has the pleasure of feeling us as funny and slangy here as people can only be who have had the best of the bargains other people are having occasion to rue. We of course don't know —that is Mother and Grandmamma don't, in any definite way (any more than I do, thanks to my careful stupidity) how exceeding small some of the material is consciously ground in the great grim, thrifty mill of industrial success; and indeed we grow about as many cheap illusions and easy comforts in the faintly fenced garden of our little life as could very well be crammed into the space.

Poor Grandmamma—since I've mentioned her—appears to me always the aged wan Flora of our paradise; the presiding divinity, seated in the centre, under whose pious traditions, *really* quite dim and outlived, our fond sacrifices are offered. Queer enough the superstition that Granny is a very solid and strenuous and rather grim person, with a capacity for facing the world, that we, a relaxed generation, have weakly lost. She knows as much about the world as a tin jelly-mould knows about the dinner, and is the oddest mixture of brooding anxieties over things that don't in the least matter and of bland failure to suspect things that intensely do. She lives in short in a weird little waste of words—over the moral earnestness we none of us cultivate; yet hasn't a notion of any effective earnestness herself except on the subject of empty bottles, which have, it would appear, noble neglected uses. At this time of day it doesn't matter, but if there could have been dropped into her empty bottles, at an earlier stage, something to strengthen a little any wine of life they were likely to contain, she wouldn't have figured so as the head and front of all our sentimentality.

I judge it, for that matter, a proof of our flat "modernity" in this order that the scant starch holding her together is felt to give her among us

this antique and austere consistency. I don't talk
things over with Lorraine for nothing, and she does
keep for me the flashes of perception we neither of us
waste on the others. It's the "antiquity of the age
of crinoline," she said the other day à propos of a
little carte-de-visite photograph of my ancestress as
a young woman of the time of the War; looking as
if she had been violently inflated from below, but
had succeeded in resisting at any cost, and with a
strange intensity of expression, from her waist up.
Mother, however, I must say, is as wonderful about
her as about everything else, and arranges herself,
exactly, to appear a mere contemporary illustration
(being all the while three times the true picture) in
order that her parent shall have the importance of
the Family Portrait. I don't mean of course that
she has told me so; but she cannot see that if she
hasn't that importance Granny has none other; and
it's therefore as if she pretended she had a ruff, a
stomacher, a farthingale and all the rest—grand old
angles and eccentricities and fine absurdities: the
hard white face, if necessary, of one who has seen
witches burned.

She hasn't any more than any one else among
us a gleam of fine absurdity: that's a product that
seems unable, for the life of it, and though so indispensable (say) for literary material, to grow here;
but, exquisitely determined she shall have Character lest she perish—while it's assumed we still need

her—Mother makes it up for her, with a turn of the hand, out of bits left over from her own, far from economically as her own was originally planned; scraps of spiritual silk and velvet that no one takes notice of missing. And Granny, as in the dignity of her legend, imposes, ridiculous old woman, on every one—Granny passes for one of the finest old figures in the place, while Mother is never discovered. So is history always written, and so is truth mostly worshipped. There's indeed one thing, I'll do her the justice to say, as to which she has a glimmer of vision—as to which she had it a couple of years ago; I was thoroughly with her in her deprecation of the idea that Peggy should be sent, to crown her culture, to that horrid co-educative college from which the poor child returned the other day so preposterously engaged to be married; and, if she had only been a little more actively with *me* we might perhaps between us have done something about it. But she has a way of deprecating with her long, knobby, mittened hand over her mouth, and of looking at the same time, in a mysterious manner, down into one of the angles of the room— it reduces her protest to a feebleness: she's incapable of seeing in it herself more than a fraction of what it has for her, and really thinks it would be wicked and abandoned, would savor of Criticism, which is the cardinal sin with her, to see all, or to follow any premise to it in the right direction.

Still, there was the happy chance, at the time
the question came up, that she had retained, on the
subject of promiscuous colleges, the mistrust of
the age of crinoline: as to which in fact that little
old photograph, with its balloon petticoat and its
astonishingly flat, stiff "torso," might have imaged
some failure of the attempt to blow the heresy into
her. The true inwardness of the history, at the
crisis, was that our fell Maria had made up her mind
that Peg should go—and that, as I have noted, the
thing our fell Maria makes up her mind to among
us is in nine cases out of ten the thing that is done.
Maria still takes, in spite of her partial removal to a
wider sphere, the most insidious interest in us, and
the beauty of her affectionate concern for the welfare of her younger sisters is the theme of every
tongue. She observed to Lorraine, in a moment of
rare expansion, more than a year ago, that she had
got their two futures perfectly fixed, and that as
Peggy appeared to have "some mind," though how
much she wasn't yet sure, it should be developed,
what there was of it, on the highest modern lines:
Peggy would never be thought generally, that is
physically, attractive anyway. She would see about
Alice, the brat, later on, though meantime she had
her idea—the idea that Alice was really going to
have the looks and would at a given moment break
out into beauty: in which event she should be
run for that, and for all it might be worth,

and she, Maria, would be ready to take the contract.

This is the kind of patronage of us that passes, I believe, among her more particular intimates, for "so sweet" of her; it being of course Maria all over to think herself subtle for just reversing, with a "There—see how original I am?" any benighted conviction usually entertained. I don't know that any one has ever thought Alice, the brat, intellectual; but certainly no one has ever judged her even potentially handsome, in the light of no matter which of those staggering girl-processes that suddenly produce features, in flat faces, and "figure," in the void of space, as a conjurer pulls rabbits out of a sheet of paper and yards of ribbon out of nothing. Moreover, if any one *should* know, Lorraine and I, with our trained sense for form and for "values," certainly would. However, it doesn't matter; the whole thing being but a bit of Maria's system of bluffing in order to boss. Peggy hasn't more than the brain, in proportion to the rest of her, of a small swelling dove on a window-sill; but she's extremely pretty and absolutely nice, a little rounded pink-billed presence that pecks up gratefully any grain of appreciation.

I said to Mother, I remember, at the time—I took that plunge: "I hope to goodness you're not going to pitch that defenceless child into any such bear garden!" and she replied that to make a bear-garden you first had to have bears, and she didn't suppose the co-educative young men could be so described. "Well then," said I, "would you rather I should call them donkeys, or even monkeys? What I mean is that the poor girl—a perfect little *decorative* person, who ought to have iridescent-gray plumage and pink-shod feet to match the rest of her —shouldn't be thrust into any general menagerie-cage, but be kept for the dovecote and the garden, kept where we may still hear her coo. That's what, at college, they'll make her unlearn; she'll learn to roar and snarl with the other animals. Think of the vocal sounds with which she may come back to us!" Mother appeared to think, but asked me, after a moment, as a result of it, in which of the cages of the New York Art League menagerie, and among what sort of sounds, I had found Lorraine— who was a product of co-education if there ever had been one, just as our marriage itself had been such a product.

I replied to this—well, what I could easily reply; but I asked, I recollect, in the very forefront, if she were sending Peg to college to get married. She declared it was the last thing she was in a hurry about, and that she believed there was no danger, but her great argument let the cat out of the bag. "Maria feels the want of it—of a college education; she feels it would have given her more confidence"; and I shall in fact never forget the little look of strange supplication that she gave me with these words. What it meant was: "Now don't ask me to go into the question, for the moment, any further: it's in the acute stage—and you know how soon Maria can *bring* a question to a head. She has settled it with your Father—in other words has settled it *for* him: settled it in the sense that we didn't give *her*, at the right time, the advantage she ought to have had. It would have given her confidence—from the want of which, acquired at that age, she feels she so suffers; and your Father thinks it fine of her to urge that her little sister shall profit by her warning. Nothing works on him, you know, so much as to hear it hinted that we've failed of our duty to any of you; and you can see how it must work when he can be persuaded that Maria—!"

"Hasn't colossal cheek?"—I took the words out of her mouth. "With such colossal cheek what *need* have you of confidence, which is such an inferior form—?"

The long and short was of course that Peggy went; believing on her side, poor dear, that it might for future relations give her the pull of Maria. This represents, really, I think, the one spark of guile in Peggy's breast: the smart of a small grievance suffered at her sister's hands in the dim long-ago. Maria slapped her face, or ate up her chocolates, or smeared her copy-book, or something of that sort; and the sound of the slap still reverberates in

Peg's consciousness, the missed sweetness still haunts her palate, the smutch of the fair page (Peg writes an immaculate little hand and Maria a wretched one—the only thing she can't swagger about) still affronts her sight. Maria also, to do her justice, has a vague hankering, under which she has always been restive, to make up for the outrage; and the form the compunction now takes is to get her away. It's one of the facts of our situation all round, I may thus add, that every one wants to get some one else away, and that there are indeed one or two of us upon whom, to that end, could the conspiracy only be occult enough—which it can never!—all the rest would effectively concentrate.

Father would like to shunt Granny—it *is* monstrous his having his mother-in-law a fixture under his roof; though, after all, I'm not sure this patience doesn't rank for him as one of those domestic genialities that allow his conscience a bolder and tighter business hand; a curious service, this sort of thing, I note, rendered to the business conscience throughout our community. Mother, at any rate, and small blame to her, would like to "shoo" off Eliza, as Lorraine and I, in our deepest privacy, call Aunt Elizabeth; the Tom Prices would like to extirpate *us*, of course; we would give our most immediate jewel to clear the sky of the Tom Prices; *und so weiter*. And I think we should really all band together, for once in our lives, in an unnatural alliance to get rid of Eliza. The beauty as to *this* is, moreover, that I make out the rich if dim, dawn of that last-named possibility (which I've been secretly invoking, all this year, for poor Mother's sake); and as the act of mine own right hand, moreover, without other human help. But of that anon; the *immediately* striking thing being meanwhile again the strange stultification of the passions in us, which prevents anything ever from coming to an admitted and avowed head.

Maria can be trusted, as I have said, to bring on the small crisis, every time; but she's as afraid as any one else of the great one, and she's moreover, I write it with rapture, afraid of Eliza. Eliza is the one person in our whole community she does fear —and for reasons I perfectly grasp; to which moreover, this extraordinary oddity attaches, that I positively feel I don't fear Eliza in the least (and in fact promise myself before long to show it) and yet don't at all avail by that show of my indifference to danger to inspire my sister with the least terror in respect to myself. It's very funny, the *degree* of her dread of Eliza, who affects her, evidently, as a person of lurid "worldly" possibilities—the one innocent light in which poor Maria wears for me what Lorraine calls a weird pathos; and perhaps, after all, on the day I shall have justified my futile passage across this agitated scene, and my questionable utility here below every way, by converting our aunt's lively presence into a lively absence, it may come over her that I *am* to be recognized. I in fact dream at times, with high intensity, that I see the Prices some day quite turn pale as they look at each other and find themselves taking me in.

I've made up my mind at any rate that poor Mother shall within the year be relieved in one way or another of her constant liability to her sister-in-law's visitations. It isn't to be endured that her house should be so little her own house as I've known Granny and Eliza, between them, though after a different fashion, succeed in making it appear; and yet the action to take will, I perfectly see, never by any possibility come from poor Father. He accepts his sister's perpetual re-arrivals, under the law of her own convenience, with a broad-backed serenity which I find distinctly irritating (if I may use the impious expression) and which makes me ask myself how he sees poor Mother's "position" at all. The truth is poor Father never does "see" anything of that sort, in the sense of conceiving it in its relations; he doesn't know, I guess, but what the prowling Eliza *has* a position (since this is a superstition that I observe even my acute little Lorraine can't quite shake off). He takes refuge about it, as about everything, truly, in the cheerful vagueness of that general consciousness on which I have already touched: he likes to come home from the Works every day to see how good he really is, after all—and it's what poor Mother thus has to demonstrate for him by translating his benevolence, translating it to himself and to others, into "housekeeping." If he were only good to *her* he mightn't be good enough; but the more we pig together round about him the more blandly patriarchal we make him feel.

Eliza meanwhile, at any rate, is spoiling for a dose—if ever a woman required one; and I seem already to feel in the air the gathering elements of the occasion that awaits me for administering it. All of which it is a comfort somehow to maunder away on here. As I read over what I have written the aspects of our situation multiply so in fact that I note again how one has only to look at any human thing very straight (that is with the minimum of intelligence) to see it shine out in as many aspects as the hues of the prism; or place itself, in other words, in relations that positively stop nowhere. I've often thought I should like some day to write a novel; but what would become of me in that case— delivered over, I mean, before my subject, to my extravagant sense that everything is a part of something else? When you paint a picture with a brush and pigments, that is on a single plane, it can stop at your gilt frame; but when you paint one with a pen and words, that is in *all* the dimensions, how are you to stop? Of course, as Lorraine says, "Stopping, that's art; and what are we artists like, my dear, but those drivers of trolley-cars, in New York, who, by some divine instinct, recognize in the forest of pillars and posts the white-striped columns at which they may pull up? Yes, we're drivers of trolley-cars charged with electric force and prepared to go any distance from which the consideration of a probable smash ahead doesn't deter us."

That consideration deters me doubtless even a little here—in spite of my seeing the track, to the next bend, so temptingly clear. I should like to note for instance, for my own satisfaction (though no fellow, thank God, was ever less a prey to the ignoble fear of inconsistency) that poor Mother's impugnment of my acquisition of Lorraine didn't in the least disconcert me. I did pick Lorraine—then a little bleating stray lamb collared with a blue ribbon and a tinkling silver bell—out of our New York bear-garden; but it interests me awfully to recognize that, whereas the kind of association is one I hate for my small Philistine sister, who probably has the makings of a nice, dull, dressed, amiable, insignificant woman, I recognize it perfectly as Lorraine's native element and my own; or at least don't at all mind her having been dipped in it. It has tempered and plated us for the rest of life, and to an effect different enough from the awful metallic wash of our Company's admired ice-pitchers. We artists are at the best children of despair—a certain divine despair, as Lorraine nat-

LORRAINE'S NATIVE ELEMENT AND MY OWN

ura^{ll}y says; and what jollier place for laying it in abundantly than the Art League? As for Peg, however, I won't hear of her having anything to do with this; she shall despair of nothing worse than the "hang" of her skirt or the moderation of her hat— and not often, if I can help her, even of those.

That small vow I'm glad to register here: it helps somehow, at the juncture I seem to feel rapidly approaching, to do the indispensable thing Lorraine is always talking about—to define my position. She's always insisting that we've never sufficiently defined it—as if I've ever for a moment pretended we have! We've *re*fined it, to the last intensity— and of course, now, shall have to do so still more; which will leave them all even more bewildered than the boldest definition would have done. But that's quite a different thing. The furthest we have gone in the way of definition—unless indeed this too belongs but to our invincible tendency to refine—is by the happy rule we've made that Lorraine shall walk with me every morning to the Works, and I shall find her there when I come out to walk home with me. I see, on reading over, that this is what I meant by "our" in speaking above of our little daily heroism in that direction. The heroism is easier, and becomes quite sweet, I find, when she comes so far on the way with me and when we linger outside for a little more last talk before I go in.

It's the drollest thing in the world, and really the most precious note of the mystic influence known in the place as "the force of public opinion"—which is in other words but the incubus of small domestic conformity; I really believe there's nothing we do, or don't do, that excites in the bosom of our circle a subtler sense that we're "au fond" uncanny. And it's amusing to think that this is our sole tiny touch of independence! That she should come forth with me at those hours, that she should hang about with me, and that we should have last (and, when she meets me again, first) small sweet things to say to each other, as if we were figures in a chromo or a *tableau vivant* keeping our tryst at a stile—no, this, quite inexplicably, transcends their scheme and baffles their imagination. They can't conceive how or why Lorraine gets out, or should wish to, at such hours; there's a feeling that she must violate every domestic duty to do it; yes, at bottom, really, the act wears for them, I discern, an insidious immorality, and it wouldn't take much to bring "public opinion" down on us in some scandalized way.

The funniest thing of all, moreover, is that that effect resides largely in our being husband and wife —it would be absent, wholly, if we were engaged or lovers; a publicly parading gentleman friend and lady friend. What is it we *can* have to say to each other, in that exclusive manner, so particularly, so frequently, so flagrantly, and as if we hadn't chances enough at home? I see it's a thing Mother might accidentally do with Father, or Maria with Tom Price; but I can imagine the shouts of hilarity, the resounding public comedy, with which Tom and Maria would separate; and also how scantly poor little Mother would permit herself with poor big Father any appearance of a grave leave-taking. I've quite expected her—yes, literally poor little Mother herself—to ask me, a bit anxiously, any time these six months, what it is that at such extraordinary moments passes between us. So much, at any rate, for the truth of this cluster of documentary impressions, to which there may some day attach the value as of a direct contemporary record of strange and remote things, so much I here superadd; and verily with regret, as well, on behalf of my picture, for two or three other touches from which I must forbear.

There has lately turned up, on our scene, one person with whom, doors and windows closed, curtains drawn, secrecy sworn, the whole town asleep and something amber-colored a-brewing—there has recently joined us one person, I say, with whom we might really pass the time of day, to whom we might, after due deliberation, tip the wink. I allude to the Parents' new neighbor, the odd fellow Temple, who, for reasons mysterious and which his ostensible undertaking of the native newspaper don't at all make plausible, has elected, as they say, fondly to sojourn among us. A journalist, a rolling stone, a man who has seen other life, how can one not suspect him of some deeper game than he avows —some such studious, surreptitious, "sociological" intent as alone, it would seem, could sustain him through the practice of leaning on his fence at even-tide to converse for long periods with poor Father? Poor Father indeed, if a real remorseless sociologist were once to get well hold of him! Lorraine freely maintains that there's more in the Temples than meets the eye; that they're up to something, at least that *he* is, that he kind of feels us in the air, just as we feel him, and that he would sort of reach out to us, by the same token, if we would in any way give the first sign. This, however, Lorraine contends, his wife won't let him do; his wife, according to mine, is quite a different proposition (much more *really* hatted and gloved, she notes, than any one here, even than the belted and trinketed Eliza) and with a conviction of her own as to what their stay is going to amount to. On the basis of Lorraine's similar conviction about ours it would seem then that we ought to meet for an esoteric revel; yet some-how it doesn't come off. Sometimes I think I'm quite wrong and that he can't really be a child of light: we should in this case either have seen him collapse or have discovered what inwardly sustains him. We *are* ourselves inwardly collapsing— there's no doubt of that: in spite of the central fires, as Lorraine says somebody in Boston used to say somebody said, from which we're fed. From what central fires is Temple nourished? I give it up; for, on the point, again and again, of desperately stopping him in the street to ask him, I recoil as often in terror. He may be only plotting to *make* me do it—so that he may give me away in his paper!

"Remember, he's a mere little frisking prize ass; stick to that, cling to it, make it your answer to everything: it's all you now know and all you need to know, and you'll be as firm on it as on a rock!" This is what I said to poor Peg, on the subject of Harry Goward, before I started, on the glorious impulse of the moment, five nights ago, for New York; and, with no moment now to spare, yet wishing not to lose my small silver clue, I just put it here for one of the white pebbles, or whatever they were, that Hop o' my Thumb, carried off to the forest, dropped, as he went, to know his way back. I was carried off the other evening in a whirlwind, which has not even yet quite gone down, though I am now at home and recovering my breath; and it will interest me vividly, when I have more freedom of mind, to live over again these strange, these wild successions. But a few rude notes, and only of the first few hours of my adventure, must for the present suffice. The *mot*, of the whole thing, as Lorraine calls it, was that at last, in a flash, we recognized what we had so long been wondering about—what supreme advantage we've been, all this latter time in particular, "holding out" for.

Lorraine had put it once again in her happy way only a few weeks previous; we were "saving up," she said—and not meaning at all our poor scant dollars and cents, though we've also kept hold of some of *them*—for an exercise of strength and a show of character that would make us of a sudden some unmistakable sign. We should just meet it rounding a corner as with the rush of an automobile —a chariot of fire that would stop but long enough to take us in, when we should know it immediately for the vehicle of our fate. That conviction had somehow been with us, and I had really heard our hour begin to strike on Peg's coming back to us from her co-educative adventure so preposterously "engaged." I didn't believe in it, in such a manner of becoming so, one little bit, and I took on myself to hate the same; though that indeed seemed the last thing to trouble any one else. Her turning up in such a fashion with the whole thing settled before Father or Mother or Maria or any of us had so much as heard of the young man, much less seen the tip of his nose, had too much in common, for my taste, with the rude betrothals of the people, with some maid-servant's announcement to her employer that she has exchanged vows with the butcher-boy.

I was indignant, quite artlessly indignant I fear, with the college authorities, barbarously irresponsible, as it struck me; for when I broke out about them to poor Mother she surprised me (though I confess she had sometimes surprised me before), by her deep fatalism. "Oh, I suppose they don't pretend not to take their students at the young people's own risk: they can scarcely pretend to control their affections!" she wonderfully said; she seemed almost shocked, moreover, that I could impute either to Father or to herself any disposition to control Peggy's. It was one of the few occasions of my life on which I've suffered irritation from poor Mother; and yet I'm now not sure, after all, that she wasn't again but at her old game (even then, for she has certainly been so since) of protecting poor Father, by feigning a like flaccidity, from the full appearance, not to say the full dishonor, of his failure *ever* to meet a domestic responsibility. It came over me that there would be absolutely nobody to meet this one, and my own peculiar chance glimmered upon me therefore on the spot. I can't retrace steps and stages; suffice it that my opportunity developed and broadened, to my watching eyes, with each precipitated consequence of the wretched youth's arrival.

He proved, without delay, an infant in arms; an infant, either, according to circumstances, crowing and kicking and clamoring for sustenance, or wailing and choking and refusing even the bottle, to the point even, as I've just seen in New York, of immi-

nent convulsions. The "arms" most appropriate
to his case suddenly announced themselves, in fine,
to our general consternation, as Eliza's: but it was
at this unnatural vision that my heart indeed leaped
up. I was beforehand even with Lorraine; she was
still gaping while, in three bold strokes, I sketched
to her our campaign. "I take command—the
others are flat on their backs. I save little pathetic
Peg, even in spite of herself; though her just re-
sentment is really much greater than she dares,
poor mite, recognize (amazing scruple!). By which
I mean I guard her against a possible relapse. I
save poor Mother—that is I rid her of the deadly
Eliza—forever and a day! Despised, rejected, misunderstood, I nevertheless intervene, in its hour of
dire need, as the good genius of the family; and you,
dear little quaint thing, I take advantage of the
precious psychological moment to whisk *you* off to
Europe. We'll take Peg with us for a year's true
culture; she wants a year's true culture pretty
badly, but she doesn't, as it turns out, want Mr.
Goward a 'speck.' And I'll do it all in my own
way, before they can recover breath; they'll recover
it—if we but give them time—to bless our name;
but by that moment we shall have struck for freedom!"

Well, then, my own way—it was "given me," as
Lorraine says—was, taking the night express, without a word to any one but Peg, whom it was charming, at the supreme hour, to feel glimmeringly, all-

wonderingly, with us: my own way, I say, was to go, the next morning, as soon as I had breakfasted, to the address Lorraine had been able, by an immense piece of luck, to suggest to me as a possible clue to Eliza's whereabouts. "She'll either be with her friends the Chataways, in East Seventy-third Street —she's always swaggering about the Chataways, who by her account are tremendous 'smarts,' as she has told Lorraine the right term is in London, leading a life that is a burden to them without her; or else they'll know where she is. That's at least what I *hope!*" said my wife with infinite feminine subtlety. The Chataways as a subject of swagger presented themselves, even to my rustic vision, oddly; I may be mistaken about New York "values," but the grandeur of this connection was brought home to me neither by the high lopsided stoop of its very, very East Side setting, nor by the appearance of a terrible massive lady who came to the door while I was in quite unproductive parley with an unmistakably, a hopelessly mystified menial, an outlandish young woman with a face of dark despair and an intelligence closed to any mere indigenous appeal. I was to learn later in the day that she's a Macedonian Christian whom the Chataways harbor against the cruel Turk in return for domestic service; a romantic item that Eliza named to me in rueful correction of the absence of several indeed that are apparently prosaic enough.

The powder on the massive lady's face indeed
transcended, I rather thought, the bounds of prose,
did much to refer her to the realm of fantasy, some
fairy-land forlorn; an effect the more marked as the
wrapper she appeared hastily to have caught up,
and which was somehow both voluminous and tense
(flowing like a cataract in some places, yet in others
exposing, or at least defining, the ample bed of the
stream) reminded me of the big cloth spread in a
room when any mess is to be made.   She apologized
when I said I had come to inquire for Miss Talbert
—mentioned (with play of a wonderfully fine fat
hand) that she herself was "just being manicured in
the parlor"; but was evidently surprised at my
asking about Eliza, which plunged her into the
question—it suffused her extravagant blondness
with a troubled light, struggling there like a sunrise
over snow—of whether she had better, confessing to
ignorance, relieve her curiosity or, pretending to
knowledge, baffle mine.   But mine of course carried
the day, for mine showed it could wait, while hers
couldn't; the final superiority of women to men
being in fact, I think, that we are more *patiently*
curious.

"Why, is she in the city ?"

"If she isn't, dear madam," I replied, "she ought
to be.   She left Eastridge last evening for parts unknown, and should have got here by midnight."   Oh,
how glad I was to let them both in as far as I possibly

178

could! And clearly now I had let Mrs. Chataway, if such she was, in very far indeed.

She stared, but then airily considered. "Oh, well—I guess she's somewheres."

"I guess she is!" I replied.

"She hasn't got here yet—she has so many friends in the city. But she always wants *us*, and when she does come—!" With which my friend, now so far relieved and agreeably smiling, rubbed together conspicuously the pair of plump subjects of her "cure."

"You feel then," I inquired, "that she *will* come?"

"Oh, I guess she'll be round this afternoon. We wouldn't forgive her—!"

"Ah, I'm afraid we *must* forgive her!" I was careful to declare. "But I'll come back on the chance."

"Any message then?"

"Yes, please say her nephew from Eastridge—!"

"Oh, her nephew—!"

"Her nephew. She'll understand. I'll come back," I repeated. "But I've got to find her!" And, as in the fever of my need, I turned and sped away.

I roamed, I quite careered about, in those up-town streets, but instinctively and confidently west-ward. I felt, I don't know why, miraculously sure of some favoring chance and as if I were floating in the current of success. I was on the way to our reward, I was positively on the way to Paris, and New York itself, vast and glittering and roaring, much noisier even than the Works at their noisiest, but with its old rich thrill of the Art League days again in the air, was already almost Paris for me— so that when I at last fidgeted into the Park, where you get so beautifully away from the town, it was surely the next thing to Europe, and in fact *had* to be, since it's the very antithesis of Eastridge. I regularly revelled in that sense that Eliza couldn't have done a better thing for us than just not be, that morning, where it was supremely advisable she should have been. If she had had two grains of sense she would have put in an appearance at the Chataways' with the lark, or at least with the mani-cure, who seems there almost as early stirring. Or rather, really, she would have reported herself as soon as their train, that of the "guilty couple," got in; no matter how late in the evening. It was at any rate actually uplifting to realize that I had got thus, in three minutes, the pull of her in regard to her great New York friends. My eye, as Lorraine says, how she *has*, on all this ground of those people, been piling it on! If Maria, who has so bowed her head, gets any such glimpse of what her aunt has been making her bow it *to*—well, I think I shall then entertain something of the human pity for Eliza, that I found myself, while I walked about, fairly en-tertaining for my sister.

What were they, what *are* they, the Chataways, anyhow? I don't even yet know, I confess; but now I don't want to—I don't care a hang, having no further use for them whatever. But on one of the Park benches, in the golden morning, the wonderment added, I remember, to my joy, for we hadn't, Lorraine and I, been the least bit over- whelmed about them: Lorraine only pretending a little, with her charming elfish art, that she oc- casionally was, in order to see how far Eliza would go. Well, that brilliant woman *had* gone pretty far for us, truly, if, after all, they were only in the manicure line. She was a-doing of it, as Lorraine says, my massive lady was, in the "parlor" where I don't suppose it's usually done; and aren't there such places, precisely, *as* Manicure Parlors, where they do nothing else, or at least are supposed to? Oh, I do hope, for the perfection of it, that this may be what Eliza has kept from us! Otherwise, by all the gods, it's just a boarding-house: there was exactly the smell in the hall, *the* boarding-house smell, that pervaded my old greasy haunt of the League days: that boiled atmosphere that seems to belong at once, confusedly, to a domestic "wash" and to inferior food—as if the former were perhaps being prepared in the saucepan and the latter in the tubs.

There also came back to me, I recollect, that note of Mrs. Chataway's queer look at me on my saying

I was Eliza's nephew—the droll effect of her making on her side a discovery about *me*. Yes, she made it, and as against me, of course, against all of us, at sight of me; so that if Eliza has bragged at Eastridge about New York, she has at least bragged in New York about Eastridge. I didn't clearly, for Mrs. Chataway, come up to the brag—or perhaps rather didn't come down to it: since I dare say the poor lady's consternation meant simply that my aunt has confessed to me but as an unconsidered trifle, a gifted child at the most; or as young and handsome and dashing at the most, and not as—well, as what I *am*. Whatever I am, in any case, and however awkward a document as nephew to a girlish aunt, I believe I really tasted of the joy of life in its highest intensity when, at the end of twenty minutes of the Park, I suddenly saw my absurd presentiment of a miracle justified.

I could of course scarce believe my eyes when, at the turn of a quiet alley, pulling up to gape, I recognized in a young man brooding on a bench ten yards off the precious personality of Harry Goward! There he languished alone, our feebler fugitive, handed over to me by a mysterious fate and a well-nigh incredible hazard. There is certainly but one place in all New York where the stricken deer may weep—or even, for that matter, the hart ungalled play; the wonder of my coincidence shrank a little, that is, before the fact that

when young ardor or young despair wishes to com-
mune with immensity it can *only* do so either in a
hall bedroom or in just this corner, practically,
where I pounced on my prey. To sit down, in short,
you've *got* to sit there; there isn't another square
inch of the whole place over which you haven't got,
as everything shrieks at you, to step lively. Poor
Goward, I could see at a glance, wanted very much
to sit down—looked indeed very much as if he
wanted never, *never* again to get up.

I hovered there—I couldn't help it, a bit gloat-
ingly—before I pounced; and yet even when he
became aware of me, as he did in a minute, he
didn't shift his position by an inch, but only took
me and my dreadful meaning, with his wan stare,
as a part of the strange burden of his fate. He
didn't seem even surprised to speak of; he had
waked up—premising his brief, bewildered de-
lirium—to the sense that something *natural* must
happen, and even to the fond hope that something
natural *would ;* and I was simply the form in which
it was happening. I came nearer, I stood before
him; and he kept up at me the oddest stare—which
was plainly but the dumb yearning that I would
explain, explain! He wanted everything told him—
but every single thing; as if, after a tremendous fall,
or some wild parabola through the air, the effect of
a violent explosion under his feet, he had landed at
a vast distance from his starting-point and required

to know where he was. Well, the charming thing was that this affected me as giving the very sharpest point to the idea that, in asking myself how I should deal with him, I had already so vividly entertained.

VIII

THE MARRIED DAUGHTER

By Elizabeth Stuart Phelps

WE start in life with the most preposterous of all human claims—that one should be understood. We get bravely over that after awhile; but not until the idea has been knocked out of us by the hardest. I used to worry a good deal, myself, because nobody—distinctly not one person—in our family understood me; that is, me in my relation to themselves; nothing else, of course, mattered so much. But that was before I was married. I think it was because Tom understood me from the very first eye-beam, that I loved him enough to marry him and learn to understand *him*. I always knew in my heart that he had the advantage of me in that beautiful art: I suppose one might call it the soul-art. At all events, it has been of the least possible consequence to me since I had Tom, whether any one else in the world understood me or not.

I suppose—in fact, I know—that it is this unfortunate affair of Peggy's which has brought up all that old soreness to the surface of me.

185

Nobody knows better than I that I have not been a popular member of this family. But nobody knows as well as I how hard I have tried to do my conscientious best by the whole of them, collectively and individually considered. An older sister, if she have any consciousness of responsibility at all, is, to my mind, not in an easy position. Her extra years give her an extra sense. One might call it a sixth sense of family anxiety which the younger children cannot share. She has, in a way, the intelligence and forethought of a mother without a mother's authority or privilege.

When father had that typhoid and could not sleep — dear father! in his normal condition he sleeps like a bag of corn-meal—who was there in all the house to keep those boys quiet? Nobody but me. When they organized a military company in our back yard directly under father's windows —two drums, a fish-horn, a jews-harp, a fife, and three tin pans—was there anybody but me to put a stop to it? It was on this occasion that the pet name Moolymaria, afterward corrupted into Messymaria, and finally evolved into Meddlymaria, became attached to me. To this day I do not like to think how many cries I had over it. Then when Charles Edward got into debt and nobody dared to tell father; and when Billy had the measles and there wasn't a throat in the house to read to him four hours a day except my unpopular throat; and when Charles Edward had that quarrel over a girl with a squash-colored dress and cerise hair-ribbons; or when Alice fell in love with an automobile, the chauffeur being incidentally thrown in, and took to riding around the country with him—who put a stop to it ? Who was the only person in the family that *could* put a stop to it ?

Then again—but what's the use ? My very temperament I can see now (I didn't see it when I lived at home) is in itself an unpopular one in a family like ours. I forecast, I foresee, I provide, I plan—it is my "natur' to." I can't go sprawling through life. I must know where I am to set my foot. Dear mother has no more sense of anxiety than a rice pudding, and father is as cool as one of his own ice-pitchers. We all know what Charles Edward is, and I didn't count grandmother and Aunt Elizabeth.

There has been my blunder. I ought to have counted Aunt Elizabeth. I ought to have fathomed her. It never occurred to me that she was deep enough to drop a plummet in. I, the burden-bearer, the caretaker, the worrier; I, who am opprobriously called "the manager" in this family—I have failed them at this critical point in their household history. I did not foresee, I did not forecast, I did not worry, I did not manage. It did not occur to me to manage after we had got Peggy safely graduated and engaged, and now this dreadful thing has gaped beneath us like the fissures at San Francisco or Kingston, and poor little Peggy has tumbled into it. A teacupful of "management" might have prevented it; an ounce of worry would have saved it all. I lacked that teacupful; I missed that ounce. The veriest popular optimist could have done no worse. I am smothered with my own stupidity. I have borne this humiliating condition of things as long as I can. I propose to go over to that house and take the helm in this emergency. I don't care whether I am popular or unpopular for it. But something has got to be done for Peggy, and I am going to do it.

I have been over and I have done it. I have taken the "management" of the whole thing—not even discouraged by this unfortunate word. I own I am rather raw to it. But the time has come when, though I bled beneath it, I must act as if I didn't. At all events I must *act.* . . . I have acted. I am going to New York by the early morning express— the 7.20. I would go to-night—in fact, I really ought to go to-night. But Tom has a supper "on" with some visitors to the Works. He won't be home till late, and I can't go without seeing Tom. It would hurt his feelings, and that is a thing no wife ought to do, and my kind of wife can't do.

I found the house in its usual gelatinous condition. There wasn't a back-bone in it, scarcely an ankle-joint to stand upon: plenty of crying, but no thinking; a mush of talk, but no decision. To cap the situation, Charles Edward has gone on to New York with a preposterous conviction that *he* can clear it up. . . . *Charles Edward!* If there is a living member of the household— But never mind that. This circumstance was enough for me, that's all. It brought out all the determination in me, all the manager, if you choose to put it so.

I shall go to New York myself and take the whole thing in hand. If I needed anything to padlock my purpose those dozen words with Peggy would have turned the key upon it. When I found that she wasn't crying; when I got face to face with that soft, fine excitement in the eyes which a girl wears when she has a love-affair, not stagnant, but in action—I concluded at once that Peggy had her reservations and was keeping something from me. On pretence of wanting a doughnut I got her into the pantry and shut both doors.

"Peggy," I said, "what has Charles Edward gone to New York for? Do you know?"

Peggy wound a big doughnut spinning around her engagement finger and made no reply.

"If it has anything to do with you and Harry Goward, you must tell me, Peggy. You must tell me instantly."

Peggy put a doughnut on her wedding finger and observed, with pained perplexity, that it would not spin, but stuck.

189

"What is Charles Edward up to?" I persisted.

The opening rose-bud of Peggy's face took on a furtive expression, like that of certain pansies, or some orchids I have seen. "He is going to take me to Europe," she admitted, removing both her doughnut rings.

"*You!* To *Europe!*"

"He and Lorraine. When this is blown by. They want to get me away."

"Away from what? Away from Harry Goward?"

"Oh, I suppose so," blubbered Peggy.

She now began, in a perfectly normal manner, to mop her eyes with her handkerchief.

"Do you want to be got away from Harry Goward?" I demanded.

"I never said I did," sobbed Peggy. "I never said so, not one little bit. But oh, Maria! Moolymaria! You can't think how dreadful it is to be a girl, an engaged girl, and not know what to do!"

Then and there an active idea—one with bones in it—raced and overtook me, and I shot out: "Where is that letter?"

"Mother has it," replied Peggy.

"Have you opened it?"

"No."

"Has Aunt Elizabeth opened it?"

"Oh no!"

"Did Charles Edward take it with him?"

"PEGGY," I SAID, "WHAT HAS CHARLES EDWARD GONE TO
NEW YORK FOR?"

"I don't think he did. I will go ask mother."

"Go ask mother for that letter," I commanded, "and bring it to me."

Peggy gave me one mutinous look, but the instinct of a younger sister was in her and she obeyed me. She brought the letter. I have this precious document in my pocket. I asked her if she would trust me to find out to whom that letter was addressed. After some hesitation she replied that she would. I reminded her that she was the only person in the world who could give me this authority —which pleased her. I told her that I should accept it as a solemn trust, and do my highest and best with it for her sake.

"Peggy," I said, "this is not altogether a pleasant job for me, but you are my little sister and I will take care of you. Kiss your old Meddlymaria, Peggy."

She took down her sopping handkerchief and lifted her warm, wet face. So I kissed Peggy. And I am going on the 7.20 morning train.

It is now ten o'clock. My suit-case is packed, my ticket is bought, but Tom has not come back, and the worst of it is he can't get back to-night. He telephoned between courses at his dinner that he had accepted an invitation to go home for the night with one of the men they are dining. It seems he is a "person of importance"—there is a big order behind the junket, and Tom has gone home with him to talk it over. The ridiculous thing about it is that I forget where he was going. Of course I could telephone to the hotel and find out, but men don't like telephoning wives—at least, my man doesn't. It makes it rather hard, going on this trip without kissing Tom good-bye. I had half made up my mind to throw the whole thing over, but Peggy is pretty young; she has a long life before her; there is a good deal at stake. So Tom and I kissed by electricity, and he said that it was all right, and to go ahead, and the other absurd thing about that is that Tom didn't ask me for my New York address, and I forgot to tell him. We are like two asteroids spinning through space, neither knowing the other's route or destination. In point of fact, I shall register at "The Sphinx," that nice ladies' hotel where mere man is never admitted.

I have always supposed that the Mrs. Chataway Aunt Elizabeth talks about kept a boarding-house. I think Aunt Elizabeth rolls in upon her like a spent wave between visits. I have no doubt that I shall be able to trace Aunt Elizabeth by her weeds upon this beach. After that the rest is easy. I must leave my address for Tom pinned up somewhere. Matilda's mind wouldn't hold it if I stuck it through her brain with a hat-pin. I think I will glue it to his library table, and I'll do it this minute to make sure. . . . I have directed Matilda to give him chicken croquettes for his luncheon, and I have written out the menu for every meal till I get home. Poor Tom! He isn't used to eating alone. I wish I thought he would mind it as much as I do.

Eleven o'clock.—I am obsessed with an idea, and I have yielded to it; whether for good or ill, for wisdom or folly, remains to be proved. I have telephoned Dr. Denbigh and suggested to him that he should go to New York, too. Considered in any light but that of Peggy's welfare— But I am not considering anything in any light but that of Peggy's welfare. Dr. Denbigh used to have a little *tendresse* for Peggy—it was never anything more, I am convinced. She is too young for him. A doctor sees so many women; he grows critical, if not captious. Character goes for more with him than with most men; looks go for less; and poor little Peggy—who can deny?—up to this point in her development is chiefly looks.

I intimated to the doctor that my errand to New York was of an important nature: that it concerned my younger sister; that my husband was, unfortunately, out of town, and that I needed masculine advice. I am not in the habit of flattering the doctor, and he swallowed this delicate bait, as I thought he would. When I asked him if he didn't think he needed a little vacation, if he didn't think he could get the old doctor from Southwest Eastridge to take his practice for two days, he said he didn't know but he could.   The grippe epidemic had gone down, nothing more strenuous than a few cases of measles stood in the way; in fact, Eastridge at the present time, he averred, was lamentably healthy. When he had committed himself so far as this, he hesitated, and very seriously said:

"Mrs. Price, you have never asked me to do a foolish thing, and I have known you for a good many years.   It is too late to come over and talk it out with you.   If you assure me that you consider your object in making this request important I will go.   We won't waste words about it.   What train do you take?"

I am not a person of divination or intuition.   I think I have rather a commonplace, careful, pains-taking mind.   But if ever I had an inspiration in my life I think I have one now.   Perhaps it is the novelty of it that makes me confide in it with so little reflection.   My inspiration, in a word, is this:

Aunt Elizabeth has reached the point where she is ready for a new man.   I know I don't understand her kind of woman by experience.   I don't suppose I do by sympathy.   I have to reason her out.

I have reasoned Aunt Elizabeth out to this con-clusion: She always has had, she always must have, she always will have, the admiration of some man or men to engross her attention.   She is an attractive woman; she knows it; women admit it; and men feel it. I don't think Aunt Elizabeth is a heartless person; not an irresponsible one, only an idle and unhappy one. She lives on this intoxicant as other women might live on tea or gossip, as a man would take his dram or his tobacco. She drinks this wine because she is thirsty, and the plain, cool, spring-water of life has grown stale to her. It is corked up in bottles like the water sold in towns where the drinking-supply is low. It has ceased to be palatable to her.

My interpretation is, that there is no man on her horizon just now except Harry Goward, and I won't do her the injustice to believe that she wouldn't be thankful to be rid of him just for her own sake; to say nothing of Peggy's.

Aunt Elizabeth, I repeat, needs a new man. If Dr. Denbigh is willing to fill this rôle for a few days (of course I must be perfectly frank with him about it) the effect upon Harry Goward will be instantaneous. His disillusion will be complete; his return to Peggy in a state of abject humiliation will be assured. I mean, assuming that the fellow is capable of manly feeling, and that Peggy has aroused it. That, of course, remains for me to find out.

How I am to fish Harry Goward out of the ocean of New York city doesn't trouble me in the least. Given Aunt Elizabeth, he will complete the equation. If Mrs. Chataway should fail me— But I won't suppose that Mrs. Chataway will fail. I must be sure and explain to Tom about Dr. Denbigh.

"*The Sphinx,*" *New York*, 10 *P.M.*—I arrived—that is to say, we arrived in this town at ten minutes past one o'clock, almost ten hours ago. Dr. Denbigh has gone somewhere—and that reminds me that I forgot to ask him where. I never thought of it until this minute, but it has just occurred to me that it may be quite as well from an ignorant point of view that "The Sphinx" excludes mere man from its portals.

He was good to me on the train, very good indeed. I can't deny that he flushed a little when I told him frankly what I wanted of him. At first I thought that he was going to be angry. Then I saw the corners of his mustache twitch. Then our sense of humor got the better of us, and then I laughed, and then he laughed, and I felt that the crisis was passed. I explained to him while we were in the Pullman car, as well as I could without being overheard by a fat lady with three chins, and a girl with a permit for a pet poodle, what it was that I wanted of him. I related the story of Peggy's misfortune—in confidence, of course; and explained the part he was expected to play—confidentially, of course; in fact, I laid my plot before him from beginning to end.

"If the boy doesn't love her, you see," I suggested, "the sooner we know it the better. She must break it off, if her heart is broken in the process. If he does love her—my private opinion is he thinks he does—I won't have Peggy's whole future wrecked by one of Aunt Elizabeth's flirtations. The reef is too small for the catastrophe. I shall find Aunt Elizabeth. Oh yes, I shall find Aunt Elizabeth! I have no more doubt of that than I have that Matilda is putting too much onion in the croquettes for Tom this blessed minute. If I find her I shall find the boy; but what good is that going to do me, if I find either of them or both of them, if we can't disillusionize the boy ?"

"In a word," interrupted the doctor, rather tartly, "all you want of me is to walk across the troubled stage—"

"For Peggy's sake," I observed.

"Of course, yes, for Peggy's sake. I am to walk across this fantastic stage in the inglorious capacity of a philanderer."

"That is precisely it," I admitted. "I want you to philander with Aunt Elizabeth for two days, one day; two hours, one hour; just long enough, only long enough to bring that fool boy to his senses."

"If I had suspected the nature of the purpose I am to serve in this complication"—began the doctor, without a smile. "I trusted your judgment, Mrs. Price, and good sense—I have never known either to fail before. However," he added, manfully, "I am in for it now, and I would do more disagreeable things than this for Peggy's sake. But perhaps," he suggested, grimly, "we sha'n't find either of them."

He retired from the subject obviously, if gracefully, and began to play with the poodle that had the Pullman permit. I happen to know that if there is any species of dog the doctor does not love it is a poodle, with or without a permit. The lady with three chins asked me if my husband were fond of dogs—I think she said, so fond as *that*. She glanced at the girl whom the poodle owned.

I don't know why it should be a surprise to me, but it was; that the chin lady and the poodle girl have both registered at "The Sphinx."

Directly after luncheon, for I could not afford to lose a minute, I went to Mrs. Chataway's; the agreement being that the doctor should follow me in an absent-minded way a little later. But there was a blockade on the way, and I wasn't on time. What I took to be Mrs. Chataway herself admitted me with undisguised hesitation.

Miss Talbert, she said, was not at home; that is— no, she was not home. She explained that a great many people had been asking for Miss Talbert; there were two in the parlor now.

When I demanded, "Two what?" she replied, in a breathless tone, "Two gentlemen," and ushered me into that old-fashioned architectural effort known to early New York as a front and back parlor.

One of the gentlemen, as I expected, proved to be Dr. Denbigh. The other was flatly and unmistakably Charles Edward. The doctor offered to excuse himself, but I took Charles Edward into the back parlor, and I made so bold as to draw the folding-doors. I felt that the occasion justified worse than this.

The colloquy between myself and Charles Edward was brief and pointed. He began by saying, "*You* here! What a mess!—"

My conviction is that he saved himself just in time from Messymaria.

"Have you found him ?" I propounded.

"No."

"Haven't seen him ?"

"I didn't say I hadn't seen him."

"What did he say ?" I insisted.

"Not very much. It was in the Park."

"In the *Park?* Not very *much?* How could you let him go ?"

"I didn't let him go," drawled Charles Edward. "He invited me to dinner. A man can't ask a fellow what his intentions are to a man's sister in a park. I hadn't said very much up to that point; he did most of the talking. I thought I would put it off till we got round to the cigars."

"Then ?" I cried, impatiently, "and then ?"

"You see," reluctantly admitted Charles Edward, "there wasn't any then. I didn't dine with him, after all. I couldn't find it—"

"Couldn't find what?"

"Couldn't find the hotel," said Charles Edward, defiantly. "I lost the address. Couldn't even say that it was a hotel. I believe it was a club. He seems to be a sort of a swell—for a coeducational professor—anyhow, I lost the address; and that is the long and short of it."

"If it had been a studio or a Bohemian café—" I began.

"I should undoubtedly have remembered it," admitted Charles Edward, in his languid way.

"You have lost him," I replied, frostily. "You have lost Harry Goward, and you come here—"

"On the same errand, I presume, my distressed and distressing sister, that has brought you. Have you seen her?" he demanded, with sudden, uncharacteristic shrewdness.

At this moment a *portière* opened at the side of my back parlor, and Mrs. Chataway, voluminously appearing, mysteriously beckoned me. I followed her into the dreariest hall I think I ever saw even in a New York boarding-house. There the landlady frankly told me that Miss Talbert wasn't out. She was in her room packing to make one of her visits. Miss Talbert had given orders that she was to be denied to gentlemen friends.

No, she never said anything about ladies. (This I thought highly probable.) But if I were anything to her and chose to take the responsibility—

I chose and I did. In five minutes I was in Aunt Elizabeth's room, and had turned the key upon an interview which was briefer but more startling than I could possibly have anticipated.

Elizabeth Talbert is one of those women whose attraction increases with the *negligée* or the *déshabillé*. She was so pretty in her pink kimono that she half disarmed me. She had been crying, and had a gentle look.

When I said, "Where is he?" and when she said, "If you mean Harry Goward—I don't know," I was prepared to believe her without evidence. She looked too pretty to doubt. Besides, I cannot say that I have ever caught Aunt Elizabeth in a real fib. She may be a "charmian," but I don't think she is a liar. Yet I pushed my case severely.

"If you and he hadn't taken that 5.40 train to New York—"

"We didn't take the 5.40 train," retorted Elizabeth Talbert, hotly. "It took us. You don't suppose—but I suppose you do, and I suppose I know what the whole family supposes— As if I would do such a dastardly!—As if I didn't clear out on purpose to get away from him—to get out of the whole mix— As if I knew that young one would be aboard that train!"

"But he was aboard. You admit that."

"Oh yes, he got aboard."

"Made a pleasant travelling companion, Auntie?"

"I don't know," said Aunt Elizabeth, shortly. "I didn't have ten words with him. I told him he had put me in a position I should never forgive. Then he told me I had put him in a worse. We quarrelled, and he went into the smoker. At the Grand Central he checked my suit-case and lifted his hat. He did ask if I were going to Mrs. Chataway's. I have never seen him since."

"Aunt Elizabeth," I said, sadly, "I am younger than you—"

"Not so very much!" retorted Aunt Elizabeth.

"—and I must speak to you with the respect due my father's sister when I say that the nobility of your conduct on this occasion—a nobility which you will pardon me for suggesting that I didn't altogether count on—is likely to prove the catastrophe of the situation."

Aunt Elizabeth stared at me with her wet, coquettish eyes. "You're pretty hard on me, Maria," she said; "you always were."

"Hurry and dress," I suggested, soothingly; "there are two gentlemen to see you down-stairs."

Aunt Elizabeth shook her head. She asserted with evident sincerity that she didn't wish to see any gentlemen; she didn't care to see any gentlemen under any circumstances; she never meant to have anything to do with gentlemen again. She said something about becoming a deaconess in the Episcopal Church; she spoke of the attractions in the life of a trained nurse; mentioned settlement work; and asked me what I thought of Elizabeth Frye, Dorothea Dix, and Clara Barton.

"This is one advantage that Catholics have over us," she observed, dreamily: "one could go into a nunnery; then one would be quite sure there would be no men to let loose the consequences of their natures and conduct upon a woman's whole existence."

"These two down-stairs have waited a good while," I returned, carelessly. "One of them is a married man and is used to it. But the other is not."

"Very well," said Aunt Elizabeth, with what (it occurred to me) was a smile of forced dejection. "To please you, Maria, I will go down."

If Aunt Elizabeth's dejection were assumed, mine was not. I have been in the lowest possible spirits since my unlucky discovery. Anything and everything had occurred to me except that she and that boy could quarrel. I had fancied him shadowing Mrs. Chataway for the slightest sign of his charmer. I don't know that I should have been surprised to see him curled up, like a dog, asleep on the door-steps. At the present moment I have no more means of finding the wetched lad than I had in Eastridge; not so much, for doubtless Peggy has his prehistoric addresses. I am very unhappy. I have not had the heart left in me to admire Dr. Denbigh, who has filled his rôle brilliantly all the afternoon. In half an hour he and Aunt Elizabeth had philandered as deep as a six months' flirtation; and I must say that they have kept at it with an art amounting almost to sincerity. Aunt Elizabeth did not once mention settlement work, and put no inquiries to Dr. Denbigh about Elizabeth Frye, Dorothea Dix, or Clara Barton.

I think he took her to the Metropolitan Museum; I know he invited her to the theatre; and there is some sort of an appointment for to-morrow morning, I forget what. But my marked success at this end of the stage only adds poignancy to my sense of defeat at the other.

I am very homesick. I wish I could see Tom. I do hope Tom found my message about Dr. Denbigh.

Twenty-four hours later.—The breeze of yesterday has spun into a whirlwind to-day. I am half stunned by the possibilities of human existence. One lives the simple life at Eastridge; and New York strikes me on the head like some heavy thing blown down. If these are the results of the very little love-affair of one very little girl—what must the great emotion, the real experience, the vigorous crisis, bring?

At "The Sphinx," as is well known, no male

being is admitted on any pretence. I believe the porter (for heavy trunks) is the only exception. The bell-boys are bell-girls. The clerk is a matron, and the proprietress a widow in half-mourning.

At nine o'clock this morning I was peremptorily summoned out of the breakfast-room and ordered to the desk. Two frowning faces received me. With cold politeness I was reminded of the leading clause in the constitution of that house.

"Positively," observed the clerk, "no gentlemen callers are permitted at this hotel, and, madam, there are two on the door-steps who insist upon an interview with you; they have been there half an hour. One of them refuses to recognize the rule of the house. He insists upon an immediate suspension of it. I regret to tell you that he went so far as to mention that he would have a conversation with you if it took a search-warrant to get it."

"He *says*," interrupted the proprietress in half-mourning, "that he is your husband."

She spoke quite distinctly, and as these dreadful words re-echoed through the lobby, I saw that two ladies had come out from the reception-room and were drinking the scene down. One of these was the fat lady with the three chins; the other was the poodle girl. She held him, at that unpleasant moment, by a lavender ribbon leash. It seems she gets a permit for him everywhere.

And he is the wrong sex, I am sure, to obtain any privileges at "The Sphinx."

The mosaic of that beautiful lobby did not open and swallow me down as I tottered across it to the vestibule. A strapping door-girl guarded the entrance. Grouped upon the long flight of marble steps two men impatiently awaited me. The one with the twitching mustache was Dr. Denbigh. But he, oh, he with the lightning in his eyes, he was my husband, Thomas Price.

"Maria," he began, with ominous composure, "if you have any explanations to offer of these extraordinary circumstances—" Then the torrent burst forth. Every expletive familiar to the wives of good North-American husbands broke from Tom's unleashed lips. "I didn't hear of it till afternoon. I took the midnight express. Billy told Matilda he saw you get aboard the 7.20 train It's all over Eastridge. We have been married thirteen years, Maria, and I have always had occasion to trust your judgment and good sense till now."

"That is precisely what I told her," ventured Dr. Denbigh.

"As for you, sir!" Tom Price turned, towering. "It is fortunate for *you* that I find my wife in this darned shebang.—Any female policeman behind that door-girl? Doctor? Why, Doctor! Say, *Doctor!* Dr. Denbigh! What in thunder are you laughing at?"

The doctor's sense of humor (a quality for which I must admit my dear husband is not so distinguished as he is for some more important traits) had got the better of him. He put his hands in his pockets, threw back his handsome head, and then and there, in that sacred feminine vestibule, he laughed as no woman could laugh if she tried.

In the teeth of the door-girl, the clerk, and the proprietress, in the face of the chin lady and the poodle girl, I ran straight to Tom and put my arms around his neck. At first I was afraid he was going to push me off, but he thought better of it. Then I cried out upon him as a woman will when she has had a good scare. "Oh, Tom! Tom! Tom! You dear old precious Tom! I told you all about it. I wrote you a note about Dr. Denbigh and—and everything. You don't mean to say you never found it?"

"Where the deuce did you leave it?" demanded Thomas Price.

"Why, I stuck it on your pin-cushion! I pinned it there. I pinned it down with two safety-pins. I was very particular to."

"*Pin-cushion!*" exploded Tom. "A message— an important message — to a *man* — on a *pin-cushion!*"

Then, with that admirable self-possession which has been the secret of Tom Price's success in life, he immediately recovered himself. "Next time,

Maria," he observed, with pitying gentleness, "pin it on the hen-coop. Or, paste it on the haymow with the mucilage-brush. Or, fasten it to the watering-trough in the square—anywhere I might run across it.—Doctor! I beg your pardon, old fellow.—Now madam, if you are allowed by law to get out of this blasted house I can't get into, I will pay your bill, Maria, and take you to a respectable hotel. What's that one we used to go to when we ran down to see Irving? I can't think— Oh yes —'The Holy Family.'"

"Don't be blasphemous, Price, whatever else you are!" admonished the doctor. He was choking with laughter.

"Perhaps it was 'The Whole Family,' Tom?" I suggested, meekly.

"Come to think of it," admitted Tom, "it must have been 'The Happy Family.' Get your things on, Mysie, and we'll get out of this inhuman place."

I held my head as high as I could when I came back through the lobby, with a stout chambermaid carrying my suit-case. The clerk sniffed audibly; the proprietress met me with a granite eye; the lady with the three chins muttered something which I am convinced it would not have added to my personal happiness to hear; but I thought the girl with the lavender poodle watched me a little wistfully as I whirled away upon my husband's big forgiving arm.

208

The doctor, who had really laughed until he cried, followed, wiping his merry eyes. These glistened when on the sidewalk directly opposite the hotel entrance we met Elizabeth Talbert, who had arranged, but in the agitation of the morning I had entirely forgotten it, to come to see me at that very hour.

So we fell into line, the doctor and Aunt Elizabeth, my husband and I, on our way to take the cars for "The Happy Family," when suddenly Tom clapped his hands to his pockets and announced that he had forgotten—he must send a telegram. Coming away in such a hurry, he must telegraph to the Works. Tom is an incurable telegrapher (I have long cherished the conviction that he is the main support of the Western Union Telegraph Company), and we all followed him to the nearest office where he could get a wire.

Some one was before him at the window, a person holding a hesitant pencil above a yellow blank. I believe I am not without self-possession myself, partly natural, and partly acquired by living so long with Tom; but it took all I ever had not to utter a womanish cry when the young man turned his face and I saw that it was Harry Goward.

The boy's glance swept us all in. When it reached Aunt Elizabeth and Dr. Denbigh he paled, whether with relief or regret I had my doubts at that moment, and I have them still. An emotion of some species possessed him so that he could not for the moment speak. Aunt Elizabeth was the first to recover herself.

"Ah?" she cooed. "What a happy accident! Mr. Goward, allow me to present you to my friend Dr. Denbigh."

The doctor bowed with a portentous gravity. It was almost the equal of Harry's own.

After this satisfactory incident everybody fell back instinctively and gave the command of the expedition to me. The boy anxiously yielded his place at the telegraph window to Tom; in fact, I took the pains to notice that Harry's telegram was not sent, or was deferred to a more convenient season. I invited him to run over to "The Happy Family" with us, and we all fell into rank again on the sidewalk, the boy not without embarrassment. Of this I made it my first duty to relieve him. We chatted of the weather and the theatre and hotels. When we had walked a short distance, we met Charles Edward dawdling along over to "The Sphinx" (however reluctantly) to call upon his precious elder sister. So we paired off naturally: Aunt Elizabeth and the doctor in front, Goward and I behind them, and Tom and Charles Edward bringing up the rear.

My heart dropped when I saw what a family party air we had. I felt it to my finger-tips, and I could see that the lad writhed under it. His expression changed from misery to mutiny. I should not have been surprised if he had made one plunge into the roaring current of Broadway and sunk from sight forever. The thing that troubled me most was the poor taste of it: as if the whole family had congregated in the metropolis to capture that unhappy boy. For the first time I began to feel some sympathy for him.

"Mr. Goward," I said, abruptly, in a voice too low even for Aunt Elizabeth to hear, "nobody wishes to make you uncomfortable. We are not here for any such purpose. I have something in my pocket to show you; that is all. It will interest you, I am sure. As soon as we get to the hotel, if you don't mind, I will tell you about it—or, in fact, will give it to you. Count the rest out. They are not in the secret."

"I feel like a convict arrested by plainclothes men," complained Harry, glancing before and behind.

"You won't," I said, "when you have talked to me five minutes."

"Sha'n't I?" he asked, dully. He said nothing more, and we pursued our way to the hotel in silence. Elizabeth Talbert and Dr. Denbigh talked enough to make up for us.

Aunt Elizabeth made herself so charming, so acutely charming, that I heard the boy draw one quick, sharp breath. But his eyes followed her more sullenly than tenderly, and when she clung to the doctor's arm upon a muddy crossing the young man turned to me with a sad, whimsical smile.

"It doesn't seem to make much difference—does it, Mrs. Price? She treats us all alike."

There is the prettiest little writing-room in "The Happy Family," all blue and mahogany and quiet. This place was deserted, and thither I betook myself with Harry Goward, and there he began as soon as we were alone:

"Well, what is it, Mrs. Price?"

"Nothing but this," I said, gently enough. "I have taken it upon myself to solve a mystery that has caused a good deal of confusion in our family." Without warning I took the muddy letter from my pocket, and slid it under his eyes upon the big blue blotter.

"I don't wish to be intrusive or strenuous," I pleaded, "none of us wishes to be that. Nobody is here to call you to account, Mr. Goward, but you see this letter. It was received at our house in the condition in which you find it. Would you be so kind as to supply the missing address? That is all I want of you."

The boy's complexion ran through the palette, and subsided from a dull Indian-red to a sickly Nile-green. "Hasn't she ever read it?" he demanded.

"Nobody has ever read it," I said. "Naturally —since it is not addressed. This letter went fishing with Billy."

The young man took the letter and examined it in trembling silence.

Perhaps if Fate ever broke him on her wheel it was at that moment. His destiny was still in his own hands, and so was the letter. Unaddressed, it was his personal property. He could retain it if he chose, and the family mystery would darken into deeper gloom than ever. I felt my comfortable, commonplace heart beat rapidly.

Our silence had passed the point of discomfort, and was fast reaching that of anguish, when the boy lifted his head manfully, dipped one of "The Happy Family's" new pens into a stately ink-bottle, and rapidly filled in the missing address upon the unfortunate letter. He handed it to me without a word. My eyes blurred when I read:

"*Personal.* Miss Peggy Talbert, Eastridge. (Kindness of Miss Alice Talbert.)"

"What shall I do with it ?" I asked, controlling my agitation.

"Deliver it to her, if you please, as quickly as possible. I thought of everything else. I never thought of this."

"Never thought of—"

"That she might not have got it."

"Now then, Mr. Goward," I ventured, still speaking very gently, "do you mind telling me what you took that 5.40 train for?"

"Why, because I didn't get an answer from the letter!" exclaimed Harry, raising his voice for the first time. "A man doesn't write a letter such as that more than once in a lifetime. It was a very important letter. I told her everything. I explained everything. I felt I ought to have a hearing. If she wanted to throw me over (I don't deny she had the right to) I would rather she had taken some other way than—than to ignore such a letter. I waited for an answer to that letter until quarter-past five. I just caught the 5.40 train and went to my aunt's house, the one—you know my uncle died the other day—I have been there ever since. By-the-way, Mrs. Price, if anything else comes up, and if you have any messages for me, I shall be greatly obliged if you will take my address."

He handed me his card with an up-town street and number, and I snapped it into the inner pocket of my wallet.

"Do you think," demanded Harry Goward, outright, "that she will ever forgive me, *really* forgive me?"

"That is for you to find out," I answered, smiling comfortably; for I could not possibly have Harry think that any of us—even an unpopular elder sister—could be there to fling Peggy at the young man's head. "That is between you and Peggy."

"When shall you get home with that letter?" demanded Harry.

"Ask my husband. At a guess, I should say to-morrow."

"Perhaps I had better wait until she has read the letter," mused the boy. "Don't you think so, Mrs. Price?"

"I don't think anything about it. I will not take any responsibility about it. I have got the letter officially addressed, and there my errand ends."

"You see, I want to do the best thing," urged Harry Goward. "And so much has happened since I wrote that letter—and when you come to think that she has never read it—"

"I will mail it to her," I said, suddenly. "I will enclose it with a line and get it off by special delivery this noon."

"It might not reach her," suggested Harry, pessimistically. "Everything seems to go wrong in this affair."

"Would you prefer to send it yourself?" I asked. Harry Goward shook his head.

"I would rather wait till she has read it. I feel, under the circumstances, that I owe that to her."

Now, at that critical moment, a wide figure dark-ened the entrance of the writing-room, and, plump-ing down solidly at another table, spread out a fat, ring-laden hand and began to write a laborious letter. It was the lady with the three chins. But the girl with the poodle did not put in an appearance. I learned afterward that the dog rule of "The Happy Family" admitted of no permits.

Harry Goward and I parted abruptly but pleasantly, and he earnestly requested the privilege of being permitted to call upon me to-morrow morning. I mailed the letter to Peggy by special delivery, and just now I asked Tom if he didn't think it was wise.

"I can tell you better, my dear, day after to-morrow," he replied. And that was all I could get out of him.

"The Happy Family."—It is day after to-morrow, and Tom and I are going to take the noon train home. Our purpose, or at least my purpose, to this effect has been confirmed, if not created, by the following circumstances:

Yesterday, a few hours after I had parted from Harry Goward in the blue writing-room of "The Happy Family," Tom received from father a telegram which ran like this:

"Off for Washington — that Gooch business. Shall take Peggy. Child needs change. Will stop over from Colonial Express and lunch Happy Family. Explicitly request no outsider present. Can't have appearance of false position. Shall take her directly out of New York, after luncheon.   CYRUS TALBERT."

216

Torn between filial duty and sisterly affection, I sat twirling this telegram between my troubled fingers. Tom had dashed it there and blown off somewhere, leaving me, as he usually does, to make my own decisions. Should I tell Harry? Should I *not* tell Harry? Was it my right? Was it not his due? I vibrated between these inexorable questions, but, like the pendulum I was, I struck no answer anywhere. I had half made up my mind to let matters take their own course. If Goward should happen to call on me when Peggy, flying through New York beneath her father's stalwart wing, alighted for the instant at "The Happy Family"—was I to blame? Could *I* be held responsible? It struck me that I could not. On the other hand, father could not be more determined than I that Peggy should not be put into the apparent position of pursuing an irresolute, however repentant, lover. . . . I was still debating the question as conscientiously and philosophically as I knew how, when the bell-boy brought me a note despatched by a district messenger, and therefore constitutionally delayed upon the way.

The letter was from my little sister's *fiancé*, and briefly said:

"My dear Mrs. Price,—I cannot tell you how I thank you for your sisterly sympathy and womanly good sense. You have cleared away a lot of fog out of my mind. I don't feel that I can wait an unnecessary hour before I see Peggy. I should like to be with her as soon as the letter is. If you will allow me to postpone my appointment with yourself, I shall start for Eastridge by the first train I can catch to-day.

"Gratefully yours,

" Henry T. Goward."

IX

THE MOTHER

By Edith Wyatt

I AM sure that I shall surprise no mother of a large family when I say that this hour is the first one I have spent alone for thirty years. I count it, alone. For while I am driving back in the run-about along the six miles of leafy road between the hospital and Eastridge with mother beside me, she is sound asleep under the protection of her little hinged black sunshade, still held upright. She will sleep until we are at home; and, after our anxious morning at the hospital, I am most grateful to the fortune sending me this lucid interval, not only for thinking over what has occurred in the last three days, but also for trying to focus clearly for myself what has happened in the last week, since Elizabeth went on the 5.40 to New York; since Charles followed Elizabeth; since Maria, under Dr. Denbigh's mysteriously required escort, followed Charles; since Tom followed Maria; and since Cyrus, with my dear girl, followed Tom.

On the warm afternoon before Elizabeth left, as

I walked past her open door, with Lena, and carrying an egg-nog to Peggy, I could not avoid hearing down the whole length of the hall a conversation carried on in clear, absorbed tones, between my sister and Alice.

"Did I understand you to say," said Elizabeth, in an assumption of indifference too elaborate, I think, to deceive even her niece, "that this Mr. Wilde you mention is now living in New York?"

"Oh yes. He conducts all the art-classes at the Crafts Settlement. He encouraged Lorraine's sisters in their wonderful work. I would love to go into it myself."

Lorraine's sisters and her circle once entertained me at tea in their establishment when I visited Charles before his marriage, in New York. They are extremely kind young women, ladies in every respect, who have a workshop called "At the Sign of the Three-legged Stool." They seem to be carpenters, as nearly as I can tell. They wear fillets and bright, loose clothes; and they make very rough-hewn burnt-wood footstools and odd settees with pieces of glass set about in them. It is all very puzzling. When Charles showed me a candlestick one of the young ladies had made, and talked to me about the decoration and the line, I could see that it was very gracefully designed and nicely put together. But when he noticed that in the wish to be perfectly open-minded to his point of view I was looking very attentively at a queer, uneven wrought-iron brooch with two little pendant polished granite rocks, he only laughed and put his hand on my shawl a minute and brought me more tea.

So that I could understand something of what Alice was mentioning as she went on: "You know Lorraine says that, though not the most *prominent*, Lyman Wilde is the most *radical* and *temperamental* leader in the great handicraft development in this country. Even most of the persons in favor of it consider that he goes too far. She says, for instance, he is so opposed to machines of all sorts that he thinks it would be better to abolish printing and return to script. He has started what they call a little movement of the kind now, and is training two young scriveners."

Elizabeth was shaking her head reflectively as I passed the door, and saying: "Ah—no compromise. And always, *always* the love of beauty." And I heard her advising Alice never, never to be one of the foolish women and men who hurt themselves by dreaming of beauty or happiness in their narrow little lives; repeating sagely that this dream was even worse for the women than for the men; and asked whether Alice supposed the Crafts Settlement address wouldn't probably be in the New York telephone-book. Alice seemed to be spending a very gratifying afternoon.

My sister Elizabeth's strongest instinct from her

early youth has been the passion inspiring the famous Captain Parklebury Todd, so often quoted by Alice and Billy: "I do not think I ever knew a character so given to creating a sensation. Or p'r'aps I should in justice say, to what, in an Adelphi play, is known as situation." Never has she gratified her taste in this respect more fully than she did —as I believe quite accidentally and on the inspiration of these words with Alice—in taking the evening train to New York with Mr. Goward.

Twenty or thirty people at the station saw them starting away together, each attempting to avoid recognition, each in the pretence of avoiding the other, each with excited manners. So that, as both Peggy and Elizabeth have been born and brought up here; as, during Mr. Goward's conspicuous absence and silence, during Peggy's illness, and all our trying uncertainties and hers, in the last weeks, my sister had widely flung to town talk many tacit insinuations concerning the character of Mr. Goward's interest in herself; as none of the twenty or thirty people were mute beyond their kind; and as Elizabeth's nature has never inspired high neighborly confidence—before night a rumor had spread like the wind that Margaret Talbert's lover had eloped with her aunt.

Billy heard the other children talking of this news and hushing themselves when he came up. Tom learned of the occurrence by a telephone, and, after supper, told Cyrus and myself; Maria was informed of it by telephone through an old friend who thought Maria should know of what every one was saying. Lorraine, walking to the office to meet Charles, was overtaken on the street by Mrs. Temple, greatly concerned for us and for Peggy, and learned the strange story from our sympathetic neighbor, to repeat it to Charles. At ten o'clock there was only one person in the house, perhaps in Eastridge, who was ignorant of our daughter's singular fortune. That person was our dear girl herself.

Since my own intelligence of the report I had not left her alone with anybody else for a moment; and now I was standing in the hall watching her start safely up-stairs, when to our surprise the front-door latch clicked suddenly; she turned on the stairs; the door opened, and we both faced Charles. From the first still glances he and I gave each other he knew she hadn't heard. Then he said quietly that he had wished to see Peggy for a moment before she went to sleep. He bade me a very confiding and responsible good-night, and went out with her to the garden where they used to play constantly together when they were children.

Up-stairs, unable to lie down till she came back, I put on a little cambric sack and sat by the window waiting till I should hear her foot on the stairs again. "Charles is telling her," I said to Cyrus. He was walking up and down the room,

dumb with impatience and disgust, too pained for
Peggy, too tried by his own helplessness to rest
or even to sit still.   In a way it has all been harder
for him than for any one else.   His impulses are
stronger and deeper than my dear girl's, and far less
cool.   She is very especially precious to him; and,
whether because she looks so like him, or because
he thinks her ways like my own, her youth and her
fortune have always been at once a more anxious
and a more lovely concern with him than any one
else's on earth.   She is, somehow, our future to him.

While we waited here in this anxiety up-stairs,
down in the garden I could hear not the words,
but the tones of our children as they spoke together.
Charles's voice sounded first for a long time, with
an air of calmness and directness; and Peggy answered him at intervals of listening, answered apparently less with surprise at what he told her than
in a quiet acceptance, with a little throb of control,
and then in accord with him.   Then it was as
though they were planning together.

In the still village night their voices sounded
very tranquil; after a little while, even buoyant.
Peggy laughed once or twice.   Little by little a
breath of relief blew over both her father's solicitude
and mine.   It was partly from the coolness and
freshness of the out-door air, and the half-uncon-
scious sense it often brings, that beyond whatever
care is close beside you at the instant there is—

and especially for the young—so much else in all creation. Then, for me, there was a deep comfort in the knowledge that in this time of need my children had each other; that they could speak so together, in an intimate sympathy, and were, not only superficially in name, but really and beautifully, a brother and sister.

At last, as they parted at the gate, Charles said, in a spirited, downright tone: "Stick to that, cling to it, make it your answer to everything. It's all you now know and all you need to know, and you'll be as firm on it as on a rock."

The lamplight from the street filtering through the elm leaves glimmered on Peggy's bright hair as she looked up at him. Her eyelashes were wet, but she was laughing as she said: "But, of course, I *have* to cling to it. It's the truth. Good-night! Good-night!" And her step on the stairs was light and even skipping.

On the next morning, when I knocked at her door to find whether she would rather breakfast up-stairs, I saw at once she had slept. She stood before the mirror fastening her belt ribbon, and looking so lovely it seemed impossible misfortune should ever touch her.

"Why, mother dear, you aren't dressed for the library-board meeting! Isn't that this morning?"

"Yes."

She looked at me with her little, sweet, quick

smile, and we sat down for a moment on her couch together, each with a sense that neither would say one word too sharply pressing.

"Dear mother, why *not* go to the board meeting? You don't need to protect me so. You *can't* protect me every minute. You see, of course, last night Charles—told me of what everybody thinks." Her voice throbbed again. She stopped for a minute. "But for weeks and weeks I had felt something like this coming toward me. And now that it's come," she went on, bravely, "we can only just do as we always have done—and not make any difference—can we?"

"Except that I feel I must be here, because we can't know from minute to minute what may come up."

"You feel you can't leave me, mother. But you can. I want to see whoever comes, just as usual. I'd have to at some time, you know, at any rate. And I mean to do it now—until I go away out of Eastridge. Charles is going to arrange that so very wonderfully. He has gone to New York now to see about it."

"He has, my dear?" I said, in some surprise.

"Yes. And, mother, about—about what's over," she whispered.

"Yes."

"Oh, just—just it couldn't all have happened in this way if"—she spoke in quite a clear, soft voice, looking straight into my eyes, with one of her quick turns—"he were a real *man*—anybody I could think of as being my husband. It was just that I didn't truly know him. That was all."

We held each other's hands fast for one moment of perfect understanding before we rose.

"Then I'll go, dear, this morning, just as you like," I said. She came into my room and fastened my cuff-pins for me. "Why, mother, I don't believe you and your little duchesse cuffs and your little, fine, gold watch-chain have ever been away from the chair of the library committee at a board meeting for twenty years! Just think what a sensation you were going to make if I hadn't interfered! There, how nice you look!"

The weather was so inclement during my absence that I felt quite secure concerning all intrusion for her. At noon the storm rose high, with a close-timed thunder and lightning; the Episcopal church spire was struck; two trees were blown over in the square; and, instead of ordering Dan and the horses out in this tumult, I dined with a board member living next the library, and drove home at three o'clock when the violence of the gale had abated.

The house was perfectly still when I reached it. The children were at school; Cyrus, at the factory; mother, napping, with her door closed. In her own room up-stairs, in the middle of the house, Peggy sat alone, in a loose wrapper, with her hair flying over her shoulders. An open book lay unnoticed in her lap. Her face was white and tearstained, and her eyes looked wild and ill.

As her glance fell on me I saw her need of me, and hurried in to close the door. "Oh, mother, mother!" she moaned. "Such a morning! It's all come back—all I fought against—all I was conquering. What does it mean? What does it mean?"

"What has happened? Who has been here?"

"Maria—sneering at Charles's ideas, asking me questions, petting me and pitying me and making a baby of me, until I broke down at last and wanted all the things she wanted to have done, and let her kiss me good-bye for her kindness in doing them—"

In a passion of tears she walked up and down, up and down the room, as her father does, except with that quick, nervous grace she always has, and in a painful, sobbing excitement.

Every sense I had was for an instant's passage fused in one clear, concentrated anger against a sister who could play so ruthlessly upon my poor child's woman pulses and emotions, so disarm her of her self-control and right free spirit.

"Why did she come?" I said, at last, with the best calmness I could muster. Peggy stood still for a moment, startled by a coldness in my voice I couldn't alter.

"She came to find out about things for herself. Then when she did find out about Charles's way

"OH, MOTHER, MOTHER," SHE MOANED, "IT'S ALL COME
BACK—ALL I FOUGHT AGAINST!"

of helping us she simply hated it—and she sent me after—after the letter you had. I got it from your desk, and Maria took it to find out its real address."

At that she sank again in a chair, and buried her face in her hands, hardly knowing what she was saying. "Oh, what shall I do? What shall I do?" she repeated, softly and wildly. "Yesterday I could behave so well by what I knew was true about him. Then, when Maria came and spoke as though I was three years old, and hadn't any understanding nor any dignity of my own, and the best thing for any girl, at any rate, were to cling to the man she loved as though she were his mother and he were her dear, erring child" (she began to laugh a little), "the feebler he were the more credit to her for her devotion—then I couldn't go on by what I knew was true about him—only back, back again to all my—old mistake." She was laughing and crying now with little, quick gasps, in a sheer hysteria which no doubt would have given her sister entire satisfaction as a manifesto of her normal womanliness.

I brought her a glass of water, and, trying to conceal my own distress for her as well as I could, sat down, silently, near her. Gradually she grew quieter, until the room was so still that we could hear the raindrops from the eaves plash down outside. Peggy pushed back her cloud of bright hair and fastened it in the nape of her neck. At last she said, with conviction: "Mother, Maria didn't *say* these things, but I know she thinks them for me, thinks that a woman's love is just all forgiveness and indulgence. By that she could—she did work on my nerves. But"—and her gray eyes glanced so beautifully and so darkly with a girl's fine, straight, native, healthy spirit as she said it—"I *couldn't* marry any man but one that I admired."

"I'm sure you couldn't," I said, firmly. "And, my dear child, I must confess I fail to understand why your sister should wish so patronizingly for you a fortune she would never have accepted for herself. How can she possibly like for you such a mawkish and a morbid thing as the prospect of a marriage with a man in whom neither you nor any other person feels the presence of one single absolute and manly quality?"

"Why, mother, I have never heard you speak so strongly before—"

At that moment Lena came searching through the hall, and knocking at the door of my room, next Peggy's, to announce Lorraine. The kind-hearted girl was with us constantly, and of the greatest unobtrusive solace to Peggy in those three days after our travellers had all gone, one after the other, like the fairy-tale family, at the chance word of Clever Alice.

It was on the fifth morning afterward, as I was sitting on the piazza hemming an organdie ruffle

for my big little girl—she does shoot up so fast—
that I heard on the gravel Charles's footstep.

For some time after his arrival, as he sat, with
his hat thrown off, talking lightly of his New York
sojourn, I was so completely glad to see him, and
to see him looking so well and in such buoyant
spirits, that I could think of nothing else until he
mentioned taking tea "At the Sign of the Three-
legged Stool" with Lorraine's sisters, with Lyman
Wilde—and with Aunt Elizabeth.

My work dropped out of my hands.

He laughed. "Yes. Dear mother, since you
never have seen him, I don't know that I can hope
to convey any right conception of Wilde's truly remarkable character. He is, to begin with, the best
of men. Picture, if you can, a nature with a soul
completely beautiful and selfless, and a nervous surface quite as pachydermatous and indiscriminating
as that of an ox. Wilde accepts everybody's es-
timate of himself. Not only the quality of his
mercy, but also of his admiration, is quite unstrained.
So that he sees the friend of his youth not at all as I
or any humanized perception at the Crafts Settlement would see her, but quite as she sees herself,
as a fascinating, gifted, capricious woman of the
world, beating the wings of her thwarted love of
beauty against cruel circumstance. I noticed his
attitude as soon as I mentioned to him that Lorraine
had by chance discovered that he and my aunt were

old acquaintances. He said that he would be very much interested in seeing her again. As he happened at the moment to be looking over a packet of postals announcing his series of talks on 'Script,' he asked me her address, called his stenographer, and had it added to his mailing-list. But before the postal reached her she had called him up to tell him she had lately heard of his work and of him for the first time after all these years, through Lorraine, and to ask him to come to see her. His call, I am sure, they spent in a rich mutual misunderstanding as thoroughly satisfactory to both as any one could wish. For, as I say, on my last visit in the Crafts neighborhood she was taking tea with all of them and Dr. Denbigh."

"Dr. Denbigh!" I repeated, in surprise. "Oh, Charles, are any of them not well?"

"No, no. I think he's been in New York"— he gave a groan—"on account of some delicate finesse on Maria's part, some incomprehensible plan of hers for bringing Goward back here. The worst of it is that, like all her plans, I believe it's going to be perfectly successful."

"What do you mean?" I asked, in consternation.

"From every natural portent, I think that horrid infant in arms was, when I left New York, about to cast his handkerchief or rattle toward Peggy again. I'm morally certain that he and all his odious emotional disturbances will be presenting themselves for her consideration in Eastridge before long; and, since they strike me as quite too odious for the nicest girl in the world, I hope, before they reach here, she'll be far away—absolutely out of reach."

"I hope so, too." But as I said it, for the first time there came around me, like a blank, rising mist, the prospect of a journey farther and a longer separation than any I had before imagined between us.

"I knew you'd think so. That was, partly, why I acted as I did, for her, dear mother"—he leaned forward a little toward me and took up one end of the ruffle I was stitching again to cover my excitement—"and for Lorraine and for me, in engaging our passage abroad."

He seemed not to expect me to speak at once, but after a little quiet pause, while we both sat thinking, went on, with great gentleness: "You know it's about our only way of really protecting her from any annoyance here, even that of thoughts of her own she doesn't like. There will be so very wonderfully much for her to see, and I believe she'll enjoy it. One of Lorraine's younger sisters is coming to be with us, perhaps, for a while in Switzerland—and the Elliots—animal sculptors. You remember them, don't you, and Arlington—studying decorative design that winter when you were in New York? They'll be abroad this summer. I believe we'll all have a very charming, care-free time walking and sketching and working—a time really so much more charming for a lovely and sensible young woman than sitting in a talking town subject to the incursions of a lover she doesn't truly like." He stopped a moment before he added, sincerely: "Then—it isn't simply for her that this way would be better, mother, but for me, for every one."

"For you and for every one?" I managed to make myself ask with tranquillity.

"Yes. Why wouldn't this relieve immensely all the sufferers from my commercial career at the factory? Don't you think that's somewhat unjust, not simply to Maria's and Tom's requirements for the family standing and fortunes"—he laughed a moment—"but to father's need there of a right-hand business man?" That was his way of putting it. "For a long time," he pursued, more earnestly than I've ever heard him speak before in his life, "I've been planning, mother, to go away to study and to sketch. I'm doing nothing here. Maybe what I would do away from here might not seem to you so wonderful. But it would have one dignity— whatever else it were or were not, it would be my own."

Perhaps it may seem strange, but in those few words and instants, when my son spoke so simply and sincerely of his own work, I felt, more than in his actual wedding with his wife, the cleaving pang of a marriage for him. At the same time I was

stricken beyond all possible speech by my rising consciousness of the injustice of his sense of failure here
in his own father's house, in *my* house. How weakly
I had been lost in the thousand little anxieties and
preoccupations of my every-day, to let myself be
unwittingly engulfed in his older sister's strange,
blank prejudice, to lose my own true understanding
of the rights and the happiness of one of the children—I can think it, all unspoken and in silence
—somehow most my own.

It seemed as though my heartstrings tightened.
Everything blurred before me. I never in my life
have tried so hard before to hold my soul absolutely
still to see quite clearly, as though none of this were
happening to myself, what would be best for my
boy's future, for Peggy's, for their whole lives. It
was in the midst of these close-pressing thoughts
that I heard him saying: "So that perhaps this
would truly be the right way for every one." Only
too inevitably I knew his words were true; and now
I could force myself at last to say, quietly: "Why
—yes—if that would make you happier, Charles."

He rose and came up to my chair then so beautifully, and moved it to a shadier place, as Peggy,
catching sight of him from the garden, ran up
with a cry of surprise to meet him, to talk about
it all.

I scarcely know whether her father's consciousness of the coming separation for me, or my conscious-

ness of the coming separation for him, made things harder or easier for both of us. Cyrus was obliged to make a business trip to Washington on the next day, and it was decided that as Peggy especially wished to be with him now before her long absence, she should accompany him in the morning.

On the midnight before we were all startled from sleep by the clang of the door-bell. Good little Billy, always hoping for excitement, and besides extremely sweet in doing errands, answered it. The rest of us absurdly assembled in kimonos and bathrobes at the head of the stairs, dreading we scarcely knew what, for the members of the family not in the house. Within a few minutes Billy dashed up-stairs again, considerately holding high, so that we all could see it, a special-delivery letter, the very same illegible, bleared envelope which had before annoyed us so extremely. It was addressed in washed-out characters to Miss —— Talbert. The word Peggy, very clear and black, had been lately inserted in the same handwriting; and below, the street and number had been recently refreshed, apparently by the hand of Maria.

As this familiar, wearisome object reappeared before us all, Peggy, with a little quiver of mirth, looking out between her long braids, cried: "Call back the boy!" By the time the messenger had returned she had readdressed the envelope, unopened, to Mr. Goward. Billy took it back down-stairs again; and every one trooped off to bed, Alice and mother with positive snorts and flounces of impatience.

Needless to say, Tom and Maria returned in perfect safety on Saturday. Before then, at twelve o'clock on the same morning, when Cyrus and Peggy had gone, I was sitting on the piazza making a little money-bag for her, with mother sitting rocking beside me, and complaining of every one in peace, when Dr. Denbigh drove up to the horse-block, flung his weight out of the buggy, and hurried up the steps. He shook hands with us hastily and abstractedly, and asked if he might speak to me inside the house.

"Mrs. Talbert," he said, closing the door of the library as soon as we were inside it, "I am sure you will try not to feel alarmed at something I must tell you of at once. The early morning train I came on from New York, the one that ought to get in at Eastridge at eleven, was derailed two hours ago on a misplaced switch between here and Whitman. No one was killed, but many of the passengers were injured. Among the injured I took care of was Mr. Goward. His arm has been broken. He's been badly shaken up—and he's now in a state of shock at the Whitman Hospital. The boy has been asking for Peggy, and then for you. I promised him that after my work was done—all the injured were taken there by a special as soon as possible after the wreck—I'd ask you to drive back to see him. Will you come ?"

Of course I went, then. And at Harry Goward's request I have gone twice since. He is very ill, too ill to talk, and though Dr. Denbigh says he will outlive a thousand stronger men, he has been rather worse this morning. When I first saw him he asked for Peggy in one gasping word, and when he learned she had gone to Washington turned even whiter than he had been before. He is nervously quite wrecked and wretched; has no confidence in Dr. Denbigh; and either Maria or I will go to the hospital every day till the boy's mother comes from California. It is a very trying situation. For his misfortune has, of course, not changed my knowledge of his nature. I dread telling Cyrus and Peggy, when I meet their returning noon train, after I have left mother at home, of everything that has happened here.

As though these difficulties were not enough, this morning, just before we started to Whitman, we were involved in another perplexity through the unwilling agency of Mr. Temple. He called me up to read me a bewildering telegram he had received an hour before from Elizabeth. It said:

" Please end Eastridge scandal by announcing my engagement in *Banner*.—LILY."

" Engagement to whom ?" Mr. Temple had asked

by telephone of Charles, who said none of us could be responsible for any definite information in the matter unless, perhaps, Maria. On consultation, Maria had said to Mr. Temple that in New York Mr. Goward had imparted to her that Elizabeth had told him many weeks ago that she was irrevocably betrothed to Dr. Denbigh. Mr. Temple had finally referred unsuccessfully to me for Elizabeth's address in order to ask her to send a complete announcement in the full form she wished printed.

("Whoa, Douglas. Well—mother, you had a nice little nap, didn't you. No, no; I won't be late. It's not more than five minutes to the station. Thanks, Lena. Yes, Billy dear, you can get in. Why, I don't know why you shouldn't drive.")

The train is just pulling in. Charles is there and Maria, each standing on one side of the car-steps. Now I see them. That looks like Peggy's suit-case the porter's carrying down. Yes, it is. There—there they are, coming down the steps behind him, Cyrus and my dear girl—how well they look! Oh, how I hope everything will come right for them!

X

THE SCHOOL-BOY

By Mary Raymond Shipman Andrews

Rabbits.
Automobile.   (Painted red, with yellow lines.)
Automatic reel.   (The 3-dollar kind.)
New stamp - book.   (The puppy chewed my other.)

Golly, I forgot. I suppose I mustn't use this, but it's my birthday next month, and I want 'steen things, and I thought I'd better make a list to pin on the dining-room door, where the family could take their pick what to give me.   Lorraine gave me this blank-book, and told me that if I'd write down everything that I knew about Peggy and Harry Goward and all that stuff, she'd have Sally make me three pounds of crumbly cookies with currants on top, in a box, to keep in my room just to eat myself, and she wouldn't tell Alice, so I won't be selfish not to offer her any as she won't know about it and so won't suffer.   I'm going to keep them in the extra bureau drawer where Peg puts her best party dress, so I guess they'll be et up before anybody goes there.

Peggy's feeling pretty sick now to dress up for parties, but I know a thing or two that the rest don't know. Wouldn't Alice be hopping! She always thinks she's wise to everything, and to have a thick-headed boy-person know a whacking secret that they'd all be excited about would make her mad enough to burst. She thinks she can read my in-grown soul too—but I rather think I have my own interior thoughts that Miss Alice doesn't tumble to. For instance, Dr. Denbigh.

Golly, I forgot. Lorraine said she'd cut down the cookies if things weren't told orderly the way they happened. So I've got to begin back. First then, I've had the best time since Peggy got en-gaged that I've ever had in my own home. Not quite as unbossed as when they sent me on the Harris farm last summer, and I slept in the stable if I wanted to, and nobody asked if I'd taken a bath. That was a sensible way to live, but yet it's been un-pecked at and pleasant even at home lately. You see, with such a lot of fussing about Peggy and Harry Goward, nobody has noticed what I did, and that, to a person with a taste for animals, is one of the best states of living. I've gone to the table without brushing my hair, and the puppy has slept in my bed, and I've kept a toad behind the wash-basin for two weeks, and though Lena, the maid, knew about it, she shut up and was decent because she didn't want to worry mother. A toad is such an unusual creature to live with. I've got a string to his hind leg, but yet he gets into places where you don't expect him, and it's very interesting. Lena seemed to think it wasn't nice to have him in the towels in the wash-stand drawer, but I didn't care. It doesn't hurt the towels and it's cosey for the toad.

I had a little snake—a stunner—but Lena squealed when she found him in my collars, so I had to take him away. He looked awfully cunning inside the collars, but Lena wouldn't stand for him, so I let well enough alone and tried to be contented with the toad and the puppy and some June-bugs I've got in boxes in the closet, and my lizard—next to mother, he's my best friend—I've had him six months. I'm not sure I wouldn't rather lose mother than him, because you can get a step-mother, but it's awfully difficult to replace a lizard like Diogenes.

I wonder if Lorraine will think I've written too much about my animals? They're more fun than Peggy anyway, and as for Harry Goward—golly! The toad or lizard that couldn't be livelier than he is would be a pretty sad animal.

A year ago I was fishing one day away up the river, squatting under a bush on a bank, when Peggy and Dr. Denbigh came and plumped right over my head. They didn't see me—but it wasn't up to me. They were looking the other way, so they didn't notice my fish-line either. They weren't noticing much of life as it appeared to me except their personal selves. I thought if they wouldn't disturb me I wouldn't disturb them. At first I didn't pay attention to what they were saying, because there was a chub and a trout together after my bait, and I naturally was excited to see if the trout would take it. But when I'd lost both of them I had time to listen.

I wouldn't have believed it of Dr. Denbigh, to bother about a girl like Peg, who can't do anything. And he's a whale, just a whale. He's six feet-two, and strong as an ox. He went through West Point before he degraded himself into a doctor, and he held the record there for shot-putting, and was on the foot-ball team, and even now, when he's very old and of course can't last long, he plays the best tennis in Eastridge. He went to the Spanish War —quite awhile ago that was, but yet in modern times—and he was at San Juan. You can see he's a jim dandy—and him to be wasting time on Peggy —it's sickening! Even for a girl she's poor stuff. I don't mean, of course, that she's not all right in a moral direction, and I wouldn't let anybody else abuse her. Everybody says she's pretty, and I suppose she is, in a red-headed way, and she's awfully kind, you know, but athletically—that's what I'm talking about—she doesn't amount to a row of pins. She can't fish or play tennis or ride or anything.

Yet all the same it's true, I distinctly heard him say he loved her better than anything on earth. I don't think he could have meant better than Rapscallion; he's awfully fond of that horse. Probably he forgot Rapscallion for the moment. Anyhow, Peg was sniffling and saying how she was going back to college—it was the Easter vacation—and how she was only a stupid girl and he would forget her. And he said he'd never forget her one minute all his life—which was silly, for I've often forgotten really important things. Once I forgot to stop at Lorraine's for a tin of hot gingerbread she'd had Sally make for me to entirely eat by myself, and Alice got it and devoured it all up, the pig! Anyway, Dr. Denbigh said that, and then Peggy sniffled some more, and I heard him ask her:

"What is it, dear?"

"Dear," your grandmother. She said, then, why wouldn't he let her be engaged to him like anybody else, and it was hard on a girl to have to beg a man to be engaged, and then he laughed a little and they didn't either of them say anything for a while, but there were soft, rustling sounds—a trout was after my bait, so I didn't listen carefully. When I noticed again, Dr. Denbigh was saying how he was years and years older, and it was his duty to take care of her and not allow her to make a mistake that might ruin her life, and he wouldn't let her hurry into a thing she couldn't get out of, and a lot more. Peg said that forty wasn't old, and he was young enough for her, and she was certain, *certain*

—I don't know what she was certain of, but she was horribly obstinate about it.

And then Dr. Denbigh said: "If I only dared let you, dear—if I only dared."

And something about if she felt the same in two years, or a year, or something—I can't remember all that truck—and they said the same thing over a lot. I heard him murmur:

"Call me Jack, just once."

And she murmured back, as if it was a stunt, "Jack"—and then rustlings. I'd call him Jack all the afternoon if he liked.

Then, after another of those still games, Peggy said, "Ow!" as if somebody'd pinched her, and that seemed such a queer remark that I stood up to see what they were up to. Getting to my feet I swung the line around and the bait flopped up the bank and hit Peg square in the mouth—I give you my word I didn't mean to, but it was awfully funny! My! didn't she squeal bloody murder? That's what makes a person despise Peggy. She's no sort of sport. Another time I remember I had some worms in an envelope, and I happened to feel them in my pocket, so I pulled out one and slid it down the back of her neck, and you'd have thought I'd done something awful. She yelped and wriggled and cried—she did—she actually cried. And you wouldn't believe what she finished up by doing— she went and took a bath! A whole bath—when she didn't have to! She can't see a joke at all. Now Alice is a horrid meddler—she and Maria. Yet Alice is a sport, and takes her medicine. I've seen that girl with a beetle in her hair, which I put there, keep her teeth shut and not make a sound— only a low gurgle—until she'd got him and slung him out of the window. Then she lammed me, I tell you—I respected her for it too—but she couldn't now, I'm stronger.

Oh, golly! Lorraine will cut down the cookies if I don't tell what happened. I don't exactly know what was next, but Dr. Denbigh somehow had me by the collar and gave me a yank, like a big dog does a little one.

"See here, you young limb," he said, "I'm—I'm going to—" and then he suddenly stopped and looked at Peggy and began to chuckle, and Peggy laughed and turned lobster color, and put her face in her hands and just howled.

Of course I grinned too, and then I glanced up at him lovingly and murmured "Jack," just like Peggy did.

That seemed to sober him, and he considered a minute. "Listen, Billy," he began, slowly; "we're in your power, but I'm going to trust you."

I just hooted, because there wasn't much else he could do. But he didn't smile, only his eyes sort of twinkled.

"Be calm, my son," he said. "You're a gentleman, I believe, and all I need do is to point out that what you've seen and heard is not your secret. I'm sure you realize that it's unnecessary to ask you not to tell. Of course, you'll never tell one word—*not one word*—" and he glared. "That's understood, isn't it?"

I said, "Yep," sort of scared. He's splendidly big and arrogant, and has that man-eating look, but he's a peach all the same.

"Are we friends—and brothers?" he asked, and slid a look at Peg.

"Yep," I said again, and I meant it.

"Shake," said Dr. Denbigh, and we shook like two men.

That was about all that happened that day except about my fishing. There was a very interesting—but I suppose Lorraine wouldn't care for that. It was a good deal of a strain on my feelings not to tell Alice, but of course I didn't. But once in awhile I would glance up at Dr. Denbigh trustingly and murmur "Jack," and he would be in a fit because I'd always do it when the family just barely couldn't hear. As soon as Peg came home from college we skipped to the mountains, and she went back from there to college again, and I didn't have a fair show to get rises out of them together, and in the urgency of 'steen things like pigeons and the new puppy, I pretty nearly forgot their love's young dream. I didn't have a surmise that I was going to be interwoven among it like I was. I saw Aunt Elizabeth going out with Dr. Denbigh in his machine two or three times, but she's a regular fusser with men, and he's got a kind heart, so I wasn't wise to anything in that. The day Peg came home for Christmas she was singing like the blue canaries down in the parlor, and I happened to pass Aunt Elizabeth's door and she was lacing up her shoes.

"Oh, Billy, ask Peggy if she doesn't want to go for a walk, will you? There's a lamb," she called to me.

So I happened to have intelligence from pristine sources that they went walking. And after that Peg had a grouch on and was off her feed the rest of the vacation—nobody knew why—I didn't myself, even, and it didn't occur to me that Aunt Elizabeth had probably been rubbing it in how well she knew Dr. Denbigh. The last day Peggy was home, at the table, they were chaffing Aunt Elizabeth about him, the way grown-ups do, instead of talking about the facts of life and different kinds of horse-feed, which is important in the winter. And I heard mother say in a " sort-of-vochy " tone to Peggy:

"They really seem to be fond of each other. Perhaps there may be an engagement to write you about, Peggy."

I thought to myself that mother didn't know

that Dr. Denbigh was prejudiced to being engaged, but I didn't say anything—it's wise not to say anything to your family beyond the necessary jargon of living. Peggy seemed to think the same, for she didn't answer a syllabus, but after dropping her glass of water into the fried potatoes which Lena was kindly handing to her, she jumped and scooted. A few minutes later I wanted her to sew a sail on a boat, so I tried her door and it was locked, and then I knocked and she took an awfully long time simply to open that door, and when she did her eyes were red and she was shivering as if she was cold.

"Oh, Billy, Billy!" she said, and then, of all things, she grabbed me and kissed me.

I wriggled loose, and I said: "Sew up this sail for me, will you? Hustle!"

But she didn't pay attention. "Oh, Billy, be a little good to me!" she said. "I'm so wretched, and nobody knows but you. Oh, Billy—he likes somebody better than me!"

"Who does?" I asked. "Father?"

She half laughed, a sort of sickly laugh. "No, Billy. Not father—he—Jack—Dr. Denbigh. Oh, you know, Billy! You heard what mother said."

"O—o—oh!" I answered her, in a contemplating slowness. "Oh—that's so! Do you mind if he gets engaged to Aunt Elizabeth?"

"Do—I—*mind?*" said Peggy, as if she was astonished. "Mind? Billy, I'll love him till I die. It would break my heart."

"Oh no, it wouldn't," I told her, because I thought I'd sort of comfort her. "That's truck. You can't break muscles just by loving. But I know how you feel, because that's the way I felt when father gave that Irish setter to the Tracys."

She went on chattering her teeth as if she was cold, so I put the table-cover around her. "You dear Billy," she said. But that was stuff.

"I wouldn't bother," I said. "Likely he's forgotten about you. I often forget things myself." That didn't seem to comfort her, for she began to sob out loud. "Oh, now, Peg, don't cry," I observed to her. "He probably likes Aunt Elizabeth better than you, don't you see? I think she's prettier, myself. And, of course, she's a lot cleverer. She tells funny stories and makes people laugh; you never do that— You're a good sort, but quiet and not much fun, don't you see? Maybe he got plain tired of you."

But instead of being cheered up by my explaining things, she put her head on the table and just yowled. Girls are a queer species.

"You're cruel, cruel!" she sobbed out, and you bet that surprised me—me that was comforting her for all I was worth! I patted her on the back of the neck, and thought hard what other soothings I could squeeze out. Then I had an idea. "Tell

"OH, BILLY, BILLY," SHE SAID, AND THEN—KISSED ME

you what, Peg," I said, "it's too darned bad of Dr. Denbigh, if he just did it for meanness, when you haven't done anything to him. But maybe he got riled because you begged him so to let you be engaged to him. Of course a man doesn't want to be bothered—if he wants to get engaged he wants to, and if he doesn't want to he doesn't, and that's all. I think probably Dr. Denbigh was afraid you'd be at him again when you came home, so he hurried up and snatched Aunt Elizabeth."

Peggy lifted her face and stared at me. She was a sight, with her eyes all bunged up and her cheeks sloppy. "You think he *is* engaged to her, do you, Billy?" she asked me.

Her voice sort of shook, and I thought I'd better settle it for her one way or the other, so I nodded and said, "Wouldn't be surprised," and then, if you'll believe it, that girl got angry—at *me*. "Billy, you're brutal—you're like any other man-thing—cold-blooded and faithless—and—" And she began choking—choking again, and I was disgusted and cleared out.

I was glad when she went off to college, because, though she's a kind-hearted girl, she was so peevish and untalkative it made me tired. I think people ought to be cheerful around their own homes. But the family didn't seem to see it; there are such a lot of us that you have to blow a trumpet before you get any special notice—except me, when I don't wash my hands. Yet, what's the use of washing your hands when you're certain to get them dirty again in five minutes?

Well, then, awhile ago Peggy wrote she was engaged to Harry Goward, and there was great excitement in the happy home. My people are mobile in their temperatures, anyway — a little thing stirs them up. I thought it was queerish, but I didn't know but Peggy had changed her mind about loving Dr. Denbigh till she died. I should think that was too long myself. I was busy getting my saddle mended and a new bridle, so I didn't have time for gossip.

Harry came to visit the family, and the minute I inspected him over I knew he was a sissy. If you'll believe me, that grown-up man can't chin himself. He sings and paints apple blossoms, but he fell three-cornered over a fence that I vaulted. He may be fascinating, as Lorraine says, but he isn't worth saving, in my judgments. I said so to Dr. Denbigh one day when he picked me up in his machine and brought me home from school, and he was sympathetic and asked intelligent questions—at least, some of them were; some of them were just slow remarks about if Peggy seemed to be very happy, and that sort of stuff that doesn't have any foundations. I told him particularly that I like automobiles, and he thought a minute, and then said:

"If you were going to be playing near the Whitman station to-morrow I'd pick you up and take you on a twenty-mile spin. I'm lunching with some people near Whitman, and going on to Elmville."

"Oh, pickles!" said I. "Will you, really? Of course, I'll be there. I'll drive over with the ex-pressman—he's a friend of mine—right after lunch," I said, "and I'll wait around the station for you."

So I did that, and while I was waiting I saw Aunt Elizabeth coming—I saw her first, so I hid—I was afraid if she saw me she'd find out I was going with Dr. Denbigh and snatch him herself. I heard her sending a crazy telegram to Harry Goward, and then I forgot all about it until I wanted to distract Alice's mind off some cookies that I'd accumulated at Lorraine's house. Alice is a pig. She never lets me stuff in peace. So I told her about the telegram—I knew Alice would be perturbed with that. She just loves to tell things, but she made me tell Peggy, and there was a hullabaloo promptly. Nobody confided a word to me, and I didn't care much, but I saw them all whispering in low tones and being very busy about it, and Peg looking madder than a goat, and I guessed that Alice had made me raise Cain.

Now, I've got to back up and start over. Golly! it's harder than you'd think just to write down things the way they happened, like I promised Lorraine. Let's see— Oh yes, of course—about Dr. Denbigh and the bubble. I was in a fit for fear dear Aunt Elizabeth would linger around till the doctor came, and then somehow I'd be minus one drive in a machine. She didn't; she cleared out with solidity and despatch, and my Aurora, as the school-teacher would say, came in his whirling car, and in I popped, and we had a corking time. He let me drive a little. You see, the machine is a— Oh, well, Lorraine said, specially, I was not to describe automobiles. That seems such a stupid restrictiveness, but it's a case of cookies, so I'll cut that out.

There really wasn't much else to tell, only that Dr. Denbigh started right in and raked out the inmost linings of my soul about Peggy and Harry Goward. It wasn't exactly cross-examination, because he wasn't cross, yet he fired the questions at me like a cannon, and I answered quick, you bet. Dr. Denbigh knows what he wants, and he means to get it. Just by accident toward the last I let out about that day in the winter when they were chaffing Aunt Elizabeth at the table about him, and how he'd taken her out in the machine, and how mother had said there might be an engagement to write Peggy about.

"Oh!" said Dr. Denbigh. "Oh!—oh!"

Funny, the way he went on saying, "Oh! Oh!"

I thought if that interested him he might like to hear about Peg throwing a fit in her room after, so I told him that, and how I tried to comfort her, and

254

how unreasonable she was. And what do you suppose he said? He looked at me a minute with his eyebrows away down, and his mouth jammed together, and then he brought out:

"You little devil!"

That's not the worst he said, either. I guess mother wouldn't let me go out with him if she knew he used profanity — Maria wouldn't, anyway. I have decided I won't tell them. It's the only time I ever caught him. The other thing is this. He said to himself—but out loud—I think he had forgotten me: "So they made her believe I liked her aunt better." And then, in a minute: "She said it would break her heart—bless her!" And two or three other interlocutory remarks like that, meaning nothing in particular. And then all of a sudden he brought his fist down on his knee with a bang and said, "Damn Aunt Elizabeth!"—not loud, but compressed and explodingly, you know. I looked at him, and he said: "Beg pardon, Billy. Your aunt's a very charming woman, but I mean it. I only asked her to go out with me because she talked more about Peggy than anybody else would," he went on.

I thought a minute, and put two and two together pretty quick. "You mind about Peggy's being engaged to Harry Goward, don't you?" I asked him; for I saw right through him then.

He looked queer. "Yes, I mind," he said.

"But you wouldn't be engaged to her yourself," I propounded to him; and he grinned, and said something about more things in heaven and earth, and called me Horatio. I reckon he got struck crazy a minute. And then he made me tell him further what Peggy said and what I said, and he laughed that time about my comforting her, though I don't see why. It doesn't pay to give up important things, to be kind and thoughtful in this world —nobody appreciates it, and you are sure to be sorry you took the time. When I got up-stairs, after comforting Peggy, my toad had jumped in the water-pitcher and got about drowned—he never was the same toad after—and if I hadn't stopped in Peg's room to do good it wouldn't have happened. And Dr. Denbigh laughed at me besides. However, for an old chap of forty, he's a peach. I'm not kicking at Dr. Denbigh.

Then let's see— (It makes me tired to go on writing this stuff—I wish I was through. But the cookies! I see a vision of a mountain range of cookies with currants on them—crumbly cookies. Up and at it again for me!)

The next stunt I had a shy at was a letter that Harry Goward asked Alice to give Peggy, and Alice gave it to me because she was up to something else just that minute. She didn't look at the address, but you bet your sweet life I did, when I heard it was from Harry Goward. I saw it was addressed

256

to Peg. Then I stuffed it in my pocket and plain forgot, because I was in a hurry to go fishing with Sid Tracy. I put a chub on top of it that I wanted to keep for bait, and when I pulled it out—the letter—the chub hadn't helped much. The envelope was a little slimy. I said: "Gee!"

Sid said: "What's that?"

"A letter to my sister from that chump, Harry Goward," said I. "I've got to take it to her. Looks pretty sad now."

Sid didn't like Harry Goward any more than I did, because he'd borrowed Sid's best racket and left it out in the rain, and then just laughed. So he said: "Not sad enough. Give it to me. I'll fix it."

He had some molasses candy that he'd bit, and he rubbed that over it a little, and then suddenly we heard Alice calling, and he crammed the letter in his pocket, candy and all, and there were some other things in there that stuck to it. We were so rattled when Alice appeared and demanded that very letter in her lordly way that I forgot if I had it or Sid, and I went all through my clothes looking for it, and then Sid found it in his, and, oh, my! Miss Alice turned up her nose when she saw it. It did look smudgy.

Sid hurriedly scrubbed it with his handkerchief, but even that didn't really make it clean, and by that time you couldn't read the address. Alice didn't ask me if I'd read it, or I'd have told her.

There was a fuss afterward in the family, but I kept clear of it. I wouldn't have time to get through what I have to do if I attended to their fusses, so all I knew was that it had something to do with that letter. All the family were taking trains, like a procession, for two or three days. I don't know why, so Lorraine can't expect me to write that down.

There's only one other event of great signification that I know about, and nobody knows that except me and Dr. Denbigh and Peggy. It was this way. The doctor saw me on the street one afternoon—I can't remember what day it was— and stopped his machine and motioned to me to get in. You bet I got. He shook hands with me just the way he would with father, and not as if I were a contemptible puppy.

"Billy, my son, I want you to do something for me," he said.

"All right," said I.

"I've got to see Peggy," he went on. "I've *got* to!" And he looked as fierce as a circus tiger. "I can't sit still and not lift a finger and let this wretched business go on. I won't lose her for any silly scruples."

I didn't know what he was driving at, but I said, "I wouldn't, either," in a sympathetic manner.

"I've got to see her!" he fired at me again.

"Yep," I said. "She's up at the house now.

Come on." But that didn't suit him. He explained that she wouldn't look at him when the others were around, and that she slid off and wormed out of his way, so he couldn't get at her, anyhow. Just like a girl, wasn't it—not to face the music? Well, anyway, he'd cooked up a plan that he wanted me to do, and I promised I would. He wanted me to get Peggy to go up the river to their former spooning-resort (only he put it differently), and he would be there waiting and make Peggy talk to him, which he seemed to desire more than honey in the honeycomb.

Lovers are a strange animal. I may be foolish, but I prefer toads. With them you can tie a string around the hind leg, and you have got them. But with lovers it's all this way one day and upside down the next, and wondering what's hurt the feelings of her, and if he's got tired of you, and polyandering around to get interviews up rivers when you could easier sit on the piazza and talk—and all such. It seems to me that things would go a lot simpler if everybody would cut out most of the feelings department, and just eat their meals and look after their animals and play all they get time for, and then go to sleep quietly. Fussing is such a depravity. But they wouldn't do what I said, not if I told them, so I lie low and think.

Next morning I harnessed the pony in the cart and said, "Peg—take a drive with me—come on," and Peg looked grattyfied, and mother said I was a dear, thoughtful child, and grandma said it would do the girl good, and I was a noble lad. So I got encombiums all round for once. Only Aunt Elizabeth—she looked thoughtful.

I rattled Hotspur—that's the pony—out to the happy hunting-ground by the river, till I saw Dr. Denbigh's gray cap behind a bush, and I rightly argued that his manly form was hitched onto it, for he arose up in his might as I stopped the cart. Peggy gasped and said, "Oh—oh! We must go home. Oh, Billy, drive on!" Which Billy didn't do, not so you'd notice it. Then the doctor said, in his I-am-the-Ten-Commandments manner, "Get out, Peggy," and held his hand.

And Peggy said, "I won't—I can't," and immediately did, the goose.

Then he looked at me in a funny, fierce way he has, with his eyebrows away down, only you know he's pleasant because his eyes jiggle.

"Billy, my son," he said, "will you kindly deprive us of the light of your presence for one hour by the clock? Here's my timepiece—one hour. Go!" And he gave Hotspur a slap so he leaped.

Dr. Denbigh is the most different person from Harry Goward I know.

Well, I drove round by the Red Bridge, and was gone an hour and twelve minutes, and I thought they'd be missing me and in a fit to get home, so I just raced Hotspur the last mile.

"I'm awfully sorry I'm so late," said I. "I got looking at some pigs, so I forgot. I'm sorry," said I.

Peg looked up at me as if she couldn't remember who I was, and inquired, wonderingly: "Is it an hour yet?"

And Dr. Denbigh said, "Great Scott! boy, you needn't have hurried!"

That's lovers all over.

And they hadn't finished yet, if you'll believe me. Dr. Denbigh went on talking as they stood up, just as if I wasn't living. "You won't promise me?" he asked her.

And she said: "Oh, Jack, how can I? I don't know what to do—but I'm engaged to him—that's a solemn thing."

"Solemn nonsense," said the doctor. "You don't love him—you never did—you never could. Be a woman, dearest, and end this wretched mess."

"I never would have thought I loved him if I hadn't believed I'd lost you," Peggy ruminated to herself. "But I must think—" As if she hadn't thunk for an hour!

"How long must you think?" the doctor fired at her.

"Don't be cross at me," said she, like a baby,

and that big capable man picked up her hand and kissed it—shame on him!

"No, no, dear," he said, as meek as pie. "I'll wait—only you *must* decide the right way, and remember that I'm waiting, and that it's hard."

Then he put her into the cart clingingly—I'd have chucked her—and I leaned over toward him the last thing and threw my head lovingly on one side and rolled my eyes up and murmured at him, "Good-bye, Jack," and started Hotspur before he could hit me.

Now, thank the stars, there's just one or two little items more that I've got to write. One is what I heard mother tell father when they were on the front piazza alone, and I was teaching the puppy to beg, right in sight of them on the grass. They think I'm an earless freak, maybe. She told him that dear Peggy was growing into such a strong, splendid woman; that she'd been talking to her, and she thought the child would be able to give up her weak, vacillating lover with hardly a pang, because she realized that he was unworthy of her; that Peg had said she couldn't marry a man she didn't admire—and wasn't that noble of her? Noble, your grandmother—to give up a perfect lady like Harry Goward, when she's got a real man up her sleeve! I'd have made them sit up and take notice if I hadn't promised not to tell. Which reminds me that I ought to explain how I got Dr.

Denbigh to let me write this for Lorraine. I put it to him strongly, you see, about the cookies, and at first he said.

"Not on your life! Not in a thousand years!" And then—

But what's the use of writing that? Lorraine is on to all that. But, my pickles! won't there be a circus when Alice finds out that I've known things she didn't! Won't Alice be hopping—gee

XI

PEGGY

By Alice Brown

"REMEMBER," said Charles Edward—he had run in for a minute on his way home from the office where he has been clearing out his desk, "for good and all," he tells us—"remember, next week will see us out of this land of the free and home of the talkative." He meant our sailing. I shall be glad to be with him and Lorraine. "And whatever you do, Peg, don't talk, except to mother. Talk to her all you want to. Mother has the making of a woman in her. If mother'd been a celibate, she'd have been, also, a peach."

"But I don't want to talk," said I. "I don't want to talk to anybody."

"Good for you," said Charles Edward. "Now I'll run along."

I sat there on the piazza watching him, thinking he'd been awfully good to me, and feeling less bruised, somehow, than I do when the rest of the family advise me—except mother! And I saw him stop, turn round as if he were coming back, and then settle himself and plant his feet wide apart, as he does when the family question him about business. Then I saw somebody in light blue through the trees, and I knew it was Aunt Elizabeth. Alice was down in the hammock reading and eating cookies, and she saw her, too. Alice threw the book away and got her long legs out of the hammock and ran. I thought she was coming into the house to hide from Aunt Elizabeth. That's what we all do the first minute, and then we recover ourselves and go down and meet her. But Alice dropped on her knees by my chair and threw her arms round me.

"Forgive, Peggy," she moaned. "Oh, forgive!"

I saw she had on my fraternity pin, and I thought she meant that. So I said, "You can wear it to-day"; but she only hugged me the tighter and ran on in a rigmarole I didn't understand.

"She's coming, and she'll get it out of Lorraine, and they'll all be down on us."

Charles Edward and Aunt Elizabeth stood talking together, and just then I saw her put her hand on his shoulder.

"She's trying to come round him," said Alice. I began to see she was really in earnest now. "He's squirming. Oh, Peggy, maybe she's found it out some way, and she's telling him, and they'll tell you, and you'll think I am false as hell!"

I knew she didn't mean anything by that word,

because whenever she says such things they're always quotations. She began to cry real tears.

"It was Billy put it into my head," said she, "and Lorraine put it into his. Lorraine wanted him to write out exactly what he knew, and he didn't know anything except about the telegram and how the letter got wuzzled, and I told him I'd help him write it as it ought to be 'if life were a banquet and beauty were wine'; but I told him we must make him say in it how he'd got to conceal it from me, or they'd think we got it up together. So I wrote it," said Alice, "and Billy copied it."

Perhaps I wasn't nice to the child, for I couldn't listen to her. I was watching Charles Edward and Aunt Elizabeth, and saying to myself that mother'd want me to sit still and meet Aunt Elizabeth when she came—"like a good girl," as she used to say to me when I was little and begged to get out of hard things. Alice went on talking and gasping.

"Peg," she said, "he's perfectly splendid—Dr. Denbigh is."

"Yes, dear," said I, "he's very nice."

"I've adored him for years," said Alice. "I could trust him with my whole future. I could trust him with yours."

Then I laughed. I couldn't help it. And Alice was hurt, for some reason, and got up and held her head high and went into the house. And Aunt Elizabeth came up the drive, and that is how she found me laughing. She had on a lovely light-blue linen. Nobody wears such delicate shades as Aunt Elizabeth. I remember, one day, when she came in an embroidered pongee over Nile-green, father groaned, and grandmother said: "What is it, Cyrus? Have you got a pain?" "Yes," said father, "the pain I always have when I see sheep dressed lamb fashion." Grandmother laughed, but mother said: "'Sh!" Mother's dear.

This time Aunt Elizabeth had on a great picture-hat with light-blue ostrich plumes; it was almost the shape of her lavender one that Charles Edward said made her look like a coster's bride. When she bent over me and put both arms around me the plumes tickled my ear. I think that was why I was so cross. I wriggled away from her and said: "Don't!"

Aunt Elizabeth spoke quite solemnly. "Dear child!" she said, "you are broken, indeed."

And I began to feel again just as I had been feeling, as if I were in a show for everybody to look at, and I found I was shaking all over, and was angry with myself because of it. She had drawn up a chair, and she held both my hands.

"Peggy," said she, "haven't you been to the hospital to see that poor dear boy?"

I didn't have to answer, for there was a whirl on the gravel, and Billy, on his bicycle, came riding up with the mail. He threw himself off his wheel

and plunged up the steps as he always does, pretended to tickle his nose with Aunt Elizabeth's
feathers as he passed behind her, and whispered to
me: "Shoot the hat!" But he had heard Aunt
Elizabeth asking if I were not going to see that
poor dear boy, and he said, as if he couldn't help it:
"Huh! I guess if she did she wouldn't get in.
His mother's walking up and down front of the
hospital when she ain't with him, and she's got a
hook nose and white hair done up over a roll and an
eye-glass on a stick, and I guess there won't be no
nimps and shepherdesses get by *her.*"

Aunt Elizabeth stood and thought for a minute,
and her eyes looked as they do when she stares
through you and doesn't see you at all. Alice asked
Charles Edward once if he thought she was sorrow-
ing o'er the past when she had that look, and he
said: "Bless you, chile, no more than a gentle in-
dustrious spider. She's spinning a web." But in
a minute mother had stepped out on the piazza, and
I felt as if she had come to my rescue. It was the
way she used to come when I broke my doll or tore
my skirt. But we didn't look at each other, mother
and I. We didn't mean Aunt Elizabeth should see
there was anything to rescue me from. Aunt Elizabeth turned to mother, and seemed to pounce upon
her.

"Ada," said she, "has my engagement been
announced?"

"Not to my knowledge," said mother. She spoke with a great deal of dignity. "I understood that the name of the gentleman had been withheld."

"Withheld!" repeated Aunt Elizabeth. "What do you mean by 'withheld'? Billy, whom are those letters for?"

In spite of ourselves mother and I started. Letters have begun to seem rather tragic to us.

"One's the gas-bill," said Billy, "and one's for you." Aunt Elizabeth took the large, square envelope and tore it open. Then she looked at mother and smiled a little and tossed her head.

"This is from Lyman Wilde," said she.

I thought I had never seen Aunt Elizabeth look so young. It must have meant something more to mother than it did to me, for she stared at her a minute very seriously.

"I am truly glad for you, Elizabeth," she said. Then she turned to me. "Daughter," said she, "I shall need you about the salad."

She smiled at me and went in. I knew what that meant. She was giving me a chance to follow her, if I needed to escape. But there was hardly time. I was at the door when Aunt Elizabeth rustled after so quickly that it sounded like a flight. There on the piazza she put her arms about me.

"Child!" she whispered. "Child! *Verlassen! Verlassen!*"

I drew away a little and looked at her. Then I thought: "Why, she is old!" But I hadn't understood. I knew the word was German, and I hadn't taken that in the elective course.

"What is it, Aunt Elizabeth?" I asked. I had a feeling I mustn't leave her. She smiled a little—a queer, sad smile.

"Peggy," said she, "I want you to read this letter." She gave it to me. It was written on very thick gray paper with rough edges, and there was a margin of two inches at the left. The handwriting was beautiful, only not very clear, and when I had puzzled over it for a minute she snatched it back again.

"I'll read it to you," said she.

Well, I thought it was a most beautiful letter. The gentleman said she had always been the ideal of his life. He owed everything—and by everything he meant chiefly his worship of beauty—to her. He asked her to accept his undying devotion, and to believe that, however far distance and time should part them, he was hers and hers only. He said he looked back with ineffable contempt upon the days when he had hoped to build a nest and see her beside him there. Now he had reached the true empyrean, and he could only ask to know that she, too, was winging her bright way into regions where he, in another life, might follow and sing beside her in liquid, throbbing notes to pierce the stars. He ended by saying that he was not very fit—the opera season had been a monumental experience this year—and he was taking refuge with an English brotherhood to lead, for a time, a cloistered life instinct with beauty and its worship, but that there as everywhere he was hers eternally. How glad I was of the verbal memory I have been so often praised for! I knew almost every word of that lovely letter by heart after the one reading. I shall never forget it.

"Well?" said Aunt Elizabeth. She was looking at me, and again I saw how long it must have been since she was young. "Well, what do you think of it?"

I told the truth. "Oh," said I, "I think it's a beautiful letter!"

"You do!" said Aunt Elizabeth. "Does it strike you as being a love-letter!"

I couldn't answer fast enough. "Why, Aunt Elizabeth," I said, "he tells you so. He says he loves you eternally. It's beautiful!"

"You fool!" said Aunt Elizabeth. "You pink-cheeked little fool! You haven't opened the door yet—not any door, not one of them—oh, you happy, happy fool!" She called through the window (mother was arranging flowers there for tea): "Ada, you must telephone the *Banner*. My engagement is not to be announced." Then she turned to me. "Peggy," said she, in a low voice, as if mother was not to hear, "to-morrow you must drive with me to Whitman."

Something choked me in my throat: either fear of her or dread of what she meant to make me do. But I looked into her face and answered with all the strength I had: "Aunt Elizabeth, I sha'n't go near the hospital."

"Don't you think it's decent for you to call on Mrs. Goward?" she asked.

She gave me a little shake. It made me angry. "It may be decent," I said, "but I sha'n't do it."

"Very well," said Aunt Elizabeth. Her voice was sweet again. "Then I must do it for you. Nobody asks you to see Harry himself. I'll run in and have a word with him—but, Peggy, you simply must pay your respects to Mrs. Goward."

"No! no! no!" I heard myself answering, as if I were in some strange dream. Then I said: "Why, it would be dreadful! Mother wouldn't let me!"

Aunt Elizabeth came closer and put her hands on my shoulders. She has a little fragrance about her, not like flowers, but old laces, perhaps, that have been a long time in a drawer with orris and face-powder and things. "Peggy," said she, "never tell your mother I asked you."

I felt myself stiffen. She was whispering, and I saw she meant it.

"Oh, Peggy! don't tell your mother. She is not

—not *simpatica*. I might lose my home here, my only home. Peggy, promise me."

"Daughter!" mother was calling from the dining-room.

I slipped away from Aunt Elizabeth's hands. "I promise," said I. "You sha'n't lose your home."

"Daughter!" mother called again, and I went in.

That night at supper nobody talked except father and mother, and they did every minute, as if they wanted to keep the rest of us from speaking a word. It was all about the Works. Father was describing some new designs he had accepted, and telling how Charles Edward said they would do very well for the trimmings of a hearse, and mother coughed and said Charles Edward's ideas were always good, and father said not where the market was concerned. Aunt Elizabeth had put on a white dress, and I thought she looked sweet, because she was sad and had made her face quite pale; but I was chiefly busy in thinking how to escape before anybody could talk to me. It doesn't seem safe nowadays to speak a word, because we don't know where it will lead us. Alice, too, looked pale, poor child! and kept glancing at me in a way that made me so sorry. I wanted to tell her I didn't care about her pranks and Billy's, whatever they were. And whatever she had written, it was sure to be clever. The teacher says Alice has a positive genius for writing, and be-fore many years she'll be in all the magazines.

When supper was over I ran up-stairs to my room. I sat down by the window in the dark and wondered when the moon would rise. I felt excited—as if something were going to happen. And in spite of all the dreadful things that had happened to us, and might keep on happening, I felt as if I could die with joy. There were steps on the porch below my window. I heard father's voice.

"That's ridiculous, Elizabeth," he said—"ridiculous! If it's a good thing for other girls to go to college, it's been a good thing for her."

"Ah," said Aunt Elizabeth, "but is it a good thing?"

Then I knew they were talking about me, and I put my fingers in my ears and said the Latin prepositions. I have been talked about enough. They may talk, but I won't hear. By-and-by I took my fingers out and listened. They had gone in, and everything was still. Then I began to think it over. Was it a bad thing for me to go to college? I'm different from what I was three years ago, but I should have been different if I'd stayed at home. For one thing, I'm not so shy. I remember the first day I came out of a class-room and Stillman Dane walked up to me and said: "So you're Charlie Ned's sister!" I couldn't look at him. I stood staring down at my note-book, and now I should say, quite calmly: "Oh, you must be Mr. Dane? I believe you teach psychology." But I stood and stared. I believe

I looked at my hands for a while and wished I hadn't got ink on my forefinger—and he had to say: "I'm the psychology man. Charlie Ned and I were college friends. He wrote me about you." But though I didn't look at him that first time, I thought he had the kindest voice that ever was—except mother's—and perhaps that was why I selected psychology for my specialty. I was afraid I might be stupid, and I knew he was kind. And then came that happy time when I was getting acquainted with everybody, and Mr. Dane was always doing things for me. "I'm awfully fond of Charlie Ned, you know," he told me. "You must let me take his place." Then Mr. Goward told me all those things at the dance, how he had found life a bitter waste, how he had been betrayed over and over by the vain and worldly, and how his heart was dead and nobody could bring it to life but me. He said I was his fate and his guiding-star, and since love was a mutual flame that meant he was my fate, too. But it seemed as if that were the beginning of all my bad luck, for about that time Stillman Dane was different, and one day he stopped me in the yard when I was going to chapel.

"Miss Peggy," said he, "don't let's quarrel." He held out his hand, and I gave him mine quickly.

"No," said I, "I'm not quarrelling."

"I want to ask you something," said he. "You must answer, truly. If I have a friend and she's

275

doing something foolish, should I tell her? Should I write to her brother and tell him?"

"Why," said I, "do you mean me?" Then I understood. "You think I'm not doing very well in my psychology," I said. "You think I've made a wrong choice." I looked at him then. I never saw him look just so. He had my hand, and now I took it away. But he wouldn't talk about the psychology.

"Peggy," said he, "do your people know Goward?"

"They will in vacation," I said. "He's going home with me. We're engaged, you know."

"Oh!" said he. "Oh! Then it is true. Let him meet Charles Edward at once, will you? Tell Charles Edward I particularly want him to know Goward." His voice sounded sharp and quick, and he turned away and left me. But I didn't give his message to Charles Edward, and somehow, I don't know why, I didn't talk about him after I came home. "Dane never wrote me whether he looked you up," said Charles Edward one day. "Not very civil of him." But even then I couldn't tell him. Mr. Dane is one of the people I never can talk about as if they were like everybody else. Perhaps that is because he is so kind in a sort of intimate, beautiful way. And when I went back after vacation he had resigned, and they said he had inherited some money and gone away, and after he went I never understood the psychology at all. Mr. Goward used to laugh at me for taking it, only he said I could get honors in anything, my verbal memory is so good. But I told him, and it is true, that the last part of the book is very dull. While I was going over all this, still with that strange excited feeling of happiness, I heard Aunt Elizabeth's voice from below. She was calling, softly: "Peggy! Peggy! Are you up there?"

I got on my feet just as quietly as I could, and slipped through mother's room and down the back stairs. Mother was in the vegetable garden watering the transplanted lettuce. I ran out to her. "Mother," I said, "may I go over to Lorraine's and spend the night?"

"Yes, lamb," said mother. That's a good deal for mother to say.

"I'll run over now," I told her. "I won't stop to take anything. Lorraine will give me a nightie." I went through the vegetable garden to the back gate and out into the street. There I drew a long breath. I don't know what I thought Aunt Elizabeth could do to me, but I felt safe. Then—I could laugh at it all, because it seems as if I must have been sort of crazy that night—I began to run as if I couldn't get there fast enough. But when I got to the steps I heard Lorraine laughing, and I stopped to listen to see whether any one was there.

"I tell Peter," said she, "that it's his opportunity.

Don't you remember the Great Magician's story of the man who was always afraid he should miss his opportunity? And the opportunity came, and, sure enough, the man didn't know it, and it slipped by. Well, that mustn't be Peter."

"It musn't be any of us," said a voice. "Things are mighty critical, though. It's as if everybody, the world and the flesh and the Whole Family, had been blundering round and setting their feet down as near as they could to a flower. But the flower isn't trampled yet. We'll build a fence round it." My heart beat so fast that I had to put my hand over it. I wondered if I were going to have heart-failure, and I knew grandmother would say, "Digitalis!" When I thought of that I laughed, and Lorraine called out, "Who's there?" She came to the long window. "Why, Peggy, child," said she, "come in." She had me by the hand and led me forward. They got up as I stepped in, Charles Edward and Stillman Dane. Then I knew why I was glad. If Stillman Dane had been here all these dreadful things would not have happened, because he is a psychologist, and he would have understood everybody at once and influenced them before they had time to do wrong.

"Jove!" said Charles Edward. "Don't you look handsome, Peg!"

"Goose!" said Lorraine, as if she wanted him to be still. "A good neat girl is always handsome.

There's an epigram for you. And Peggy's hair is loose in three places. Let me fix it for you, child."

So we all laughed, and Lorraine pinned me up in a queer, tender way, as if she were mother dress-me for something important, and we sat down, and began to talk about college. I am afraid Stillman Dane and I did most of the talking, for Lorraine and Charles Edward looked at each other and smiled a little, in a fashion they have, as if they understood each other, and Lorraine got up to show him the bag she had bought that day for the steamer; and while she was holding it out to him and asking him if it cost too much, she stopped short and called out, sharply, "Who's there?" I laughed. "Lorraine has the sharpest ears," I said. "Ears!" said Lorraine. "It isn't ears. I smell orris. She's coming. Mr. Dane, will you take Peggy out of that window into the garden? Don't yip, either of you, while you're within gunshot, and don't appear till I tell you."

"Lorraine!" came a voice, softly, from the front walk. It was Aunt Elizabeth. She has a way of calling to announce herself in a sweet, cooing tone. I said to Charles Edward once it was like a dove, and he said: "No, my child, not doves, but woodcock." Alice giggled and called out, quite loudly, "'Springes to catch woodcock!'" And he shook his head at her and said, "You all-knowing imp! isn't even Shakespeare hidden from you?" But

279

now the voice didn't sound sweet to me at all, because I wanted to get away. We rose at the same minute, Mr. Dane and I, and Lorraine seemed to waft us from the house on a kind little wind. At the foot of the steps we stopped for fear the gravel should crunch, and while we waited for Aunt Elizabeth to go in the other way I looked at Mr. Dane to see if he wanted to laugh as much as I. He did. His eyes were full of fun and pleasure, and he gave me a little nod, as if we were two children going to play a game we knew all about. Then I heard Aunt Elizabeth's voice inside. It was low and broken—what Charles Edward called once her "come-and-comfort-me" voice.

"Dears," said she, "you are going abroad?"

"Yes," Charles Edward answered. "Yes, it looks that way now."

"Yes," said Lorraine, rather sharply, I thought, as if she meant to show him he ought to be more decisive, "we are."

"Dears," Aunt Elizabeth went on, "will you take me with you?"

Mr. Dane started as if he meant to go back into the house. I must have started, too, and my heart beat hard. There was a silence of a minute, two minutes, three perhaps. Then I heard Charles Edward speak, in a voice I didn't know he had.

"No, Aunt Elizabeth, no. Not so you'd notice it."

Mr. Dane gave a nod as if he were relieved, and we both began tiptoeing down the path in the dark. But it wasn't dark any more. The moon was coming through the locust-trees, and I smelled the lindens by the wall. "Oh," I said, "it's summer, isn't it? I don't believe I've thought of summer once this year."

"Yes," said he, "and there never was a summer such as this is going to be."

I knew he was very athletic, but I don't believe I'd thought how much he cared for out-of-doors. "Come down here," I said. "This is Lorraine's jungle. There's a seat in it, and we can smell the ferns."

Charles Edward had been watering the garden, and everything was sweet. Thousands of odors came out such as I never smelled before. And all the time the moon was rising. After we had sat there awhile, talking a little about college, about my trip abroad, I suddenly found I could not go on. There were tears in my eyes. I felt as if so good a friend ought to know how I had behaved—for I must have been very weak and silly to make such a mistake. He ought to hear the worst about me. "Oh," I said, "do you know what happened to me?"

He made a little movement toward me with both hands. Then he took them back and sat quite still and said, in that kind voice: "I know you are going abroad, and when you come back you will laugh at the dolls you played with when you were a child." But I cried, softly, though, because it was just as if I were alone, thinking things out and being sorry, sorry for myself—and ashamed. Until now I'd never known how ashamed I was. "Don't cry, child," he was saying. "For God's sake, don't cry!" I think it came over me then, as it hadn't before, that all that part of my life was spoiled. I'd been engaged and thought I liked somebody, and now it was all over and done. "I don't know what I'm crying for," I said, at last, when I could stop. "I suppose it's because I'm different now, different from the other girls, different from myself. I can't ever be happy any more."

He spoke, very quickly. "Is it because you liked Goward so much?"

"Like him!" I said. "Like Harry Goward? Why, I—" There I stopped, because I couldn't think of any word small enough, and I think he understood, for he laughed out quickly.

"Now," said he, "I'm a psychologist. You remember that, don't you? It used to impress you a good deal."

"Oh," said I, "it does impress me. Nobody has ever seemed so wise as you. Nobody!"

"Then it's understood that I'm a sage from the Orient. I know the workings of the human mind. And I tell you a profound truth: that the only way to stop thinking of a thing is to stop thinking of it. Now, you're not to think of Goward and all this puppet-show again. Not a minute. Not an instant. Do you hear?" He sounded quite stern, and I answered as if I had been in class.

"Yes, sir."

"You are to think of Italy, and how blue the sea is—and Germany, and how good the beer is—and Charlie Ned and Lorraine, and what trumps they are. Do you hear?"

"Yes, sir," said I, and because I knew we were going to part and there would be nobody else to advise me in the same way, I went on in a great hurry for fear there should not be time. "I can't live at home even after we come back. I could never be pointed at, like Aunt Elizabeth, and have people whisper and say I've had a disappointment. I must make my own life. I must have a profession. Do you think I could teach? Do you think I could learn to teach—psychology?"

He didn't answer for a long time, and I didn't dare look at him, though the moon was so bright now that I could see how white his hand was, lying on his knee, and the chasing of the ring on his little finger. It had been his mother's engagement ring, he told me once. But he spoke, and very gently and seriously. "I am sure you could teach some things. Whether psychology—but we can talk of that later. There'll be lots of time. It proves I am going over on the same steamer with Charlie Ned and Lorraine and you."

"You are!" I cried. "Why, I never heard of anything so—" I couldn't find the word for it, but everything stopped being puzzling and unhappy and looked clear and plain.

"Yes," said he. "It's very convenient, isn't it? We can talk over your future, and you could even take a lesson or two in psychology. But I fancy we shall have a good deal to do looking for porpoises and asking what the run is. People are terribly busy at sea."

Then it occurred to me that he had never been here before, and why was he here now? "How did you happen to come?" I asked. I suppose I really felt as if God sent him.

"Why," said he, "why—" Then he laughed. "Well," said he, "to tell the truth, I was going abroad if—if certain things happened, and I needed to make sure. I didn't want to write, so I ran down to see Charlie Ned."

"But could he tell you?" said I. "And had they happened?"

He laughed, as if at something I needn't share. "No," he said, "the things weren't going to happen. But I decided to go abroad."

I was "curiouser and curiouser," as Lorraine says. "But," I insisted, "what had Charles Edward to do with it?"

"MR. DANE," I SAID, "YOU DON'T MEAN ME?"

There were a great many pauses that night as if, I think, he didn't know what was wise to say. I should imagine it would always be so with psychologists. They understand so well what effect every word will have.

"Well, to tell the truth," he answered, at last, in a kind, darling way, "I wanted to make sure all was well with my favorite pupil before I left the country. I couldn't quite go without it."

"Mr. Dane," I said, "you don't mean me?"

"Yes," he answered, "I mean you."

I could have danced and sung with happiness. "Oh," said I, "then I must have been a better scholar than I thought. I feel as if I could teach psychology—this minute."

"You could," said he, "this minute." And we both laughed and didn't know, after all, what we were laughing at—at least I didn't. But suddenly I was cold with fear.

"Why," I said, "if you've only really decided to go to-night, how do you know you can get a passage on our ship?"

"Because, sweet Lady Reason," said he, "I used Charlie Ned's telephone and found out." (That was a pretty name—sweet Lady Reason.)

We didn't talk any more then for a long time, because suddenly the moon seemed so bright and the garden so sweet. But all at once I heard a step on the gravel walk, and I knew who it was. "That's

285

Charles Edward," I said. "He's been home with Aunt Elizabeth. We must go in."

"No!" said he. "No, Peggy. There won't be such another night." Then he laughed quickly and got up. "Yes," he said, "there will be such nights—over and over again. Come, Peggy, little psychologist, we'll go in."

We found Lorraine and Charles Edward standing in the middle of the room, holding hands and looking at each other. "You're a hero," Lorraine was saying, "and a gentleman and a scholar and my own particular Peter."

"Don't admire me," said Charles Edward, "or you'll get me so bellicose I shall have to challenge Lyman Wilde. Poor old chap! I believe to my soul he's had the spirit to make off."

"Speak gently of Lyman Wilde," said Lorraine. "I never forget what we owe him. Sometimes I burn a candle to his photograph. I've even dropped a tear before it. Well, children?" She turned her bright eyes on us as if she liked us very much, and we two stood facing them two, and it all seemed quite solemn. Suddenly Charles Edward put out his hand and shook Mr. Dane's, and they both looked very much moved, as grandmother would say. I hadn't known they liked each other so well.

"Do you know what time it is?" said Lorraine. "Half-past eleven by Shrewsbury clock. I'll bake the cakes and draw the ale."

"Gee whiz!" said Mr. Dane. I'd never heard him say things like that. It sounded like Billy, and I liked it. "I've got to catch that midnight train."

For a minute it seemed as if we all stood shouting at one another, Lorraine asking him to stay all night, Charles Edward giving him a cigar to smoke on the way, I explaining to Lorraine that I'd sleep on the parlor sofa and leave the guest-room free, and Mr. Dane declaring he'd got a million things to do before sailing. Then he and Charles Edward dashed out into the night, as Alice would say, and I should have thought it was a dream that he'd been there at all except that I felt his touch on my hand. And Lorraine put her arms round me and kissed me and said, "Now, you sweet child, run up-stairs and look at the moonlight and dream—and dream —and dream."

I don't know whether I slept that night; but, if I did, I did not dream.

The next forenoon I waited until eleven o'clock before I went home. I wanted to be sure Aunt Elizabeth was safely away at Whitman. Yet, after all, I did not dread her now. I had been told what to do. Some one was telling me of a song the other day, "Command me, dear." I had been commanded to stop thinking of all those things I hated. I had done it. Mother met me at the steps. She seemed a little anxious, but when she had put her hand on my shoulder and really looked at me she smiled the way I love to see her smile. "That's a good girl!" said she. Then she added, quickly, as if she thought I might not like it and ought to know at once, "Aunt Elizabeth saw Dr. Denbigh going by to Whitman, and she asked him to take her over."

"Did she?" said I. "Oh, mother, the old white rose is out!"

"There they are, back again," said mother. "He's leaving her at the gate."

Well, we both waited for Aunt Elizabeth to come up the path. I picked the first white rose and made mother smell it, and when I had smelled it myself I began to sing under my breath, "Come into the garden, Maud," because I remembered last night.

"Hush, child," said mother, quickly. "Elizabeth, you are tired. Come right in."

Aunt Elizabeth's lip trembled a little. I thought she was going to cry. I had never known her to cry, though I had seen tears in her eyes, and I remember once, when she was talking to Dr. Denbigh, Charles Edward noticed them and laughed. "Those are not idle tears, Peg," he said to me. "They're getting in their work."

Now I was so sorry for her that I stopped thinking of last night and put it all away. It seemed cruel to be so happy. Aunt Elizabeth sat down on the step and mother brought her an eggnog.

It had been all ready for grandmother, and I could see mother thought Aunt Elizabeth needed it, if she was willing to make grandmother wait.

"Ada," said Aunt Elizabeth, suddenly, as she sipped it, "what was Dr. Denbigh's wife like?"

"Why," said mother, "I'd almost forgotten he had a wife, it was so long ago. She died in the first year of their marriage."

Aunt Elizabeth laughed a little, almost as if no one were there. "He began to talk about her quite suddenly this morning," she said. "It seems Peg reminds him of her. He is devoted to her memory. That's what he said—devoted to her memory."

"That's good," said mother, cheerfully, as if she didn't know quite what to say. "More letters, Lily? Any for us?" I could see mother was very tender of her for some reason, or she never would have called her Lily.

"For me," said Aunt Elizabeth, as if she were tired. "From Mrs. Chataway. A package, too. It looks like visiting-cards. That seems to be from her, too." She broke open the package. "Why!" said she, "of all things! Why!"

"That's pretty engraving," said mother, looking over her shoulder. She must have thought they were Aunt Elizabeth's cards. "Why! of all things!"

Aunt Elizabeth began to flush pink and then scarlet. She looked as pretty as a rose, but a little angry, I thought. She put up her head rather

289

haughtily. "Mrs. Chataway is very eccentric," she said. "A genius, quite a genius in her own line. Ada, I won't come down to luncheon. This has been sufficient. Let me have some tea in my own room at four, please." She got up, and her letter and one of the cards fell to the floor. I picked them up for her, and I saw on the card:

Mrs. Ronald Chataway
Magnetic Healer and Mediumistic Divulger
Lost Articles a Specialty

I don't know why, but I thought, like mother and Aunt Elizabeth, "Well, of all things!"

But the rest of that day mother and I were too busy to exchange a word about Mrs. Chataway or even Aunt Elizabeth. We plunged into my preparations to sail, and talked dresses and hats, and ran ribbons in things, and I burned letters and one photograph (I burned that without looking at it), and suddenly mother got up quickly and dropped her lapful of work. "My stars!" said she, "I've forgotten Aunt Elizabeth's tea."

"It's of no consequence, dear," said Aunt Elizabeth's voice at the door. "I asked Katie to bring it up."

"Why," said mother, "you're not going?"

I held my breath, Aunt Elizabeth looked so pretty. She was dressed, as I never saw her before, in a close-fitting black gown and a plain white collar and a little close black hat. She looked almost like some sister of charity.

"Ada," said she, "and Peggy, I am going to tell you something, and it is my particular desire that you keep it from the whole family. They would not understand. I am going to ally myself with Mrs. Chataway in a connection which will lead to the widest possible influence for her and for me. In Mrs. Chataway's letter to-day she urges me to join her. She says I have enormous magnetism and—and other qualifications."

"Don't you want me to tell Cyrus?" said mother. She spoke quite faintly.

"You can simply tell Cyrus that I have gone to Mrs. Chataway's," said Aunt Elizabeth. "You can also tell him I shall be too occupied to return. Good-bye, Ada. Good-bye, Peggy. Remember, it is the bruised herb that gives out the sweetest odor."

Before I could stop myself I had laughed, out of happiness, I think. For I remembered how the spearmint had smelled in the garden when Stillman Dane and I stepped on it in the dark and how bright the moon was, and I knew nobody could be unhappy very long.

"I telephoned for a carriage," said Aunt Elizabeth. "There it is." She and mother were going down the stairs, and suddenly I felt I couldn't have her go like that.

"Oh, Aunt—Aunt Lily!" I called. "Stop! I want to speak to you." I ran after her. "I'm going to have a profession, too," I said. "I'm going to devote my life to it, and I am just as glad as I can be." I put my arms round her and kissed her on her soft, pink cheeks, and we both cried a little. Then she went away.

XII

THE FRIEND OF THE FAMILY

By Henry van Dyke

"Eastridge, *June* 3, 1907.
"*To Gerrit Wendell, The Universe Club, New York:*
"Do you remember promise? Come now, if possible.
Much needed.   Cyrus Talbert."

THIS was the telegram that Peter handed me as
I came out of the coat-room at the Universe
and stood under the lofty gilded ceiling of the great
hall, trying to find myself at home again in the
democratic simplicity of the United States. For
two years I had been travelling in the effete, luxuri-
ous Orient as a peace correspondent for a famous
newspaper; sleeping under canvas in Syria, in mud
houses in Persia, in paper cottages in Japan; riding on camel-hump through Arabia, on horseback
through Afghanistan, in palankeen through China,
and faring on such food as it pleased Providence to
send. The necessity of putting my next book
through the press (*The Setting Splendors of the
East*) had recalled me to the land of the free and the

home of the brave. Two hours after I had landed from the steamship, thirty seconds after I had entered the club, there was Peter, in his green coat and brass buttons, standing in the vast, cool hall among the immense columns of verd-antique, with my telegram on a silver tray, which he presented to me with a discreet expression of welcome in his well-trained face, as if he hesitated to inquire where I had been, but ventured to hope that I had enjoyed my holiday and that there was no bad news in my despatch. The perfection of the whole thing brought me back with a mild surprise to my inheritance as an American, and made me dimly conscious of the point to which New York has carried republicanism and the simple life.

But the telegram—read hastily in the hall, and considered at leisure while I took a late breakfast at my favorite table in the long, stately, oak-panelled dining-room, high above the diminished roar of Fifth Avenue—the telegram carried me out to Eastridge, that self-complacent overgrown village among the New York hills, where people still lived in villas with rubber-plants in the front windows, and had dinner in the middle of the day, and attended church sociables, and listened to Fourth-of-July orations. It was there that I had gone, green from college, to take the assistant-editorship of that flapping sheet *The Eastridge Banner;* and there I had found Cyrus Talbert

beginning his work in the plated-ware factory—
the cleanest, warmest, biggest heart of a man that
I have known yet, with a good-nature that covered
the bed-rock of his conscience like an apple orchard
on a limestone ridge. In the give-and-take of every
day he was easy-going, kindly, a lover of laughter;
but when you struck down to a question of right
and wrong, or, rather, when he conceived that he
heard the divine voice of duty, he became absolutely
immovable—firm, you would call it if you agreed
with him, obstinate if you differed.

After all, a conscience like that is a good thing
to have at the bottom of a friendship. I could be
friends with a man of almost any religion, but hardly
with a man of none. Certainly the intimacy that
sprang up between Talbert and me was fruitful in
all the good things that cheer life's journey from
day to day, and deep enough to stand the strain of
life's earthquakes and tornadoes. There was a
love-affair that might have split us apart; but it
only put the rivets into our friendship. For both
of us in that affair—yes, all three of us, thank God—
played a straight game. There was a time of loss
and sorrow for me when he proved himself more
true and helpful than any brother that I ever knew.
I was best man at his wedding; and because he
married a girl that understood, his house became
more like a home to me than any other place that
my wandering life has found.

I saw its amazing architectural proportions erupt into the pride of Eastridge. I saw Cyrus himself, with all his scroll-saw tastes and mansard-roof opinions, by virtue of sheer honesty and thorough-going human decency, develop into the unassuming "first citizen" of the town, trusted even by those who laughed at him, and honored most by his opponents. I saw his aggravating family of charming children grow around him—masterful Maria, æsthetic Charles Edward, pretty Peggy, fairy-tale Alice, and boister-ous Billy—each at heart lovable and fairly good; but, taken in combination, bewildering and per-plexing to the last degree.

Cyrus had a late-Victorian theory in regard to the education of children, that individuality should not be crushed — give them what they want — follow the line of juvenile insistence—all the opportunities and no fetters. This late-Victorian theory had resulted in the production of a collection of early-Rooseveltian personalities around him, whose simul-taneous interaction sometimes made his good old head swim. As a matter of fact, the whole family, including Talbert's preposterous old-maid sister Elizabeth (the biggest child of the lot), absolutely depended on the good sense of Cyrus and his wife, and would have been helpless without them. But, as a matter of education, each child had a secret illusion of superiority to the parental standard, and not only made wild dashes at originality and independent action, but at the same time cherished a perfect mania for regulating and running all the others. Independence was a sacred tradition in the Talbert family; but interference was a fixed nervous habit, and complication was a chronic social state. The blessed mother understood them all, because she loved them all. Cyrus loved them all, but the only one he thought he understood was Peggy, and her he usually misunderstood, because she was so much like him. But he was fair to them all—dangerously fair — except when his subcutaneous conscience reproached him with not doing his duty; then he would cut the knot of family interference with some tremendous stroke of paternal decision unalterable as a law of the Medes and Persians.

All this was rolling through my memory as I breakfasted at the Universe and considered the telegram from Eastridge.

"Do you remember promise?" Of course I remembered. Was it likely that either of us would forget a thing like that? We were in the dingy little room that he called his "den"; it was just after the birth of his third child. I had told my plan of letting the staff of *The Banner* fall into other hands and going out into the world to study the nations when they were not excited by war, and write about people who were not disguised in soldier-clothes. "That's a big plan," he said, "and you'll go far, and be long away at times." I admitted that it was likely. "Well," he continued, laying down his pipe, "if you ever are in trouble and can't get back here, send word, and I'll come." I told him that there was little I could do for him or his (except to give superfluous advice), but if they ever needed me a word would bring me to them. Then I laid down my pipe, and we stood up in front of the fire and shook hands. That was all the promise there was; but it brought him down to Panama to get me, five years later, when I was knocked out with the fever; and it would take me back to Eastridge now by the first train.

But what wasteful brevity in that phrase, "much needed"! What did that mean? (Why will a man try to put a forty-word meaning into a ten-word telegram?) Sickness? Business troubles? One of those independent, interfering children in a scrape? One thing I was blessedly sure of: it did not mean any difficulty between Cyrus and his wife; they were of the tribe who marry for love and love for life. But the need must be something serious and urgent, else he never would have sent for me. With a family like his almost anything might happen. Perhaps Aunt Elizabeth—I never could feel any confidence in a red-haired female who habitually dressed in pink. Or perhaps Charles Edward—if that young man's artistic ability had been equal to his sense of it there would have been less danger in taking him into the factory. Or probably Maria, with her great head for business—oh, Maria, I grant you, is like what the French critic said of the prophet Habakkuk, "*capable de tout.*"

But why puzzle any longer over that preposterous telegram? If my friend Talbert was in any kind of trouble under the sun, there was just one thing that I wanted—to get to him as quickly as possible. Find when the first train started and arrived—send a lucid despatch—no expensive parsimony in telegraphing:

"*To Cyrus Talbert, Eastridge, Massachusetts :*

"I arrived this morning on the *Dilatoria* and found your telegram here. Expect me on the noon train due at Eastridge five forty-three this afternoon. I hope all will go well. Count on me always.   GERRIT WENDELL."

It was a relief to find him on the railway platform when the train rolled in, his broad shoulders as square as ever, his big head showing only a shade more of gray, a shade less of red, in its strawberry roan, his face shining with the welcome which he expressed, as usual, in humorous disguise.

"Here you are," he cried, "browner and thinner than ever! Give me that bag. How did you leave my friend the Shah of Persia ?"

"Better," I said, stepping into the open carriage, "since he got on the water-wagon—uses nothing but Eastridge silver-plated ice-pitchers now."

"And my dear friend the Empress of China?" he asked, as he got in beside me.

"She has recovered her digestion," I answered, "due entirely to the abandonment of chop-sticks and the adoption of Eastridge knives and forks. But now it's my turn to ask a question. How are *you?*"

"Well," said he. "And the whole family is well, and we've all grown tremendously, but we haven't changed a bit, and the best thing that has happened to us for three years is seeing you again."

"And the factory?" I asked. "How does the business of metallic humbug thrive?"

"All right," he answered. "There's a little slackening in chafing-dishes just now, but ice-cream knives are going off like hot cakes. The factory is on a solid basis; hard times won't hurt us."

"Well, then," said I, a little perplexed, "what in Heaven's name did you mean by sending that—"

"Hold on," said Talbert, gripping my knee and looking grave for a moment, "just you wait. I need you badly enough or else the telegram never would have gone to you. I'll tell you about it after supper. Till then, never mind—or, rather, no matter; for it's nothing material, after all, but there's a lot in it for the mind."

I knew then that he was in one of his fundamental moods, imperviously jolly on the surface, inflexibly Puritan underneath, and that the only thing to do was to let the subject rest until he chose to take it up in earnest. So we drove along, chaffing and laughing, until we came to the dear, old, ugly house. The whole family were waiting on the veranda to bid me welcome home. Mrs. Talbert took my hands with a look that said it all. Her face had not grown a shade older, to me, since I first knew her; and her eyes—the moment you look into them you feel that she understands. Alice seemed to think that she had become too grown-up to be kissed, even by the friend of the family; and I thought so, too. But pretty Peggy was of a different mind. There is something about the way that girl kisses an old gentleman that almost makes him wish himself young again.

At supper we had the usual tokens of festivity: broiled chickens and pop-overs and cool, sliced tomatoes and ice-cream with real strawberries in it (how good and clean it tasted after Ispahan and Bagdad!) and the usual family arguing and joking (how natural and wholesome it sounded after Vienna and Paris!). I thought Maria looked rather strenuous and severe, as if something important were on her mind, and Billy and Alice, at moments, had a conscious air. But Charles Edward and Lorraine were distinctly radiant, and Peggy was demurely jolly. She sounded like her father played on a mandolin.

After supper Talbert took me to the summer-house at the foot of the garden to smoke. Our first cigars were about half burned out when he began to unbosom himself.

"I've been a fool," he said, "an idiot, and, what is more, an unnatural and neglectful father, cruel to my children when I meant to be kind, a shirker of my duty, and a bringer of trouble on those that I love best."

"As for example?" I asked.

"Well, it is Peggy!" he broke out. "You know, I like her best of them all, next to Ada; can't help it. She is nearer to me, somehow. The finest, most unselfish little girl! But I've been just selfish enough to let her get into trouble, and be talked about, and have her heart broken, and now they've put her into a position where she's absolutely helpless, a pawn in their fool game, and the Lord only knows what's to come of it all unless he makes me man enough to do my duty."

From this, of course, I had to have the whole story, and I must say it seemed to me most extraordinary—a flagrant case of idiotic interference. Peggy had been sent away to one of those curious institutions that they call a "coeducational college," chiefly because Maria had said that she ought to understand the duties of modern womanhood; she had gone, without the slightest craving for "the higher education," but naturally with the idea of having a "good time"; and apparently she had it, for she came home engaged to a handsome, amatory boy, one of her fellow "students," named Goward. At this point Aunt Elizabeth, with her red hair and pink frock, had interfered and lured off the Goward, who behaved in a manner which appeared to me to reduce him to a negligible quantity. But the family evidently did not think so, for they all promptly began to interfere, Maria and Charles Edward and Alice and even Billy, each one with an independent plan, either to lure the Goward back or to eliminate him. Alice had the most original idea, which was to marry Peggy to Dr. Denbigh; but this clashed with Maria's idea, which was to entangle the doctor with Aunt Elizabeth in order that the Goward might be recaptured. It was all extremely complicated and unnecessary (from my point of view), and of course it transpired and circulated through the gossip of the town, and poor Peggy was much afflicted and ashamed. Now the engagement was off; Aunt Elizabeth had gone into business with a clairvoyant woman in New York; Goward was in the hospital with a broken arm, and Peggy was booked to go to Europe on Saturday with Charles Edward and Lorraine.

"Quite right," I exclaimed at this point in the story. "Everything has turned out just as it should, like a romance in an old-fashioned ladies' magazine."

"Not at all," broke out Talbert; "you don't know the whole of it. Maria has told me" (oh, my prophetic soul, Maria!) "that Charley and his wife have asked a friend of theirs, a man named Dane, ten years older than Peggy, a professor in that blank coeducational college, to go with them, and that she is sure they mean to make her marry him."

"What Dane is that?" I interrupted. "Is his first name Stillman—nephew of my old friend Harvey Dane, the publisher? Because, if that's so, I know him; about twenty-eight years old; good family, good head, good manners, good principles; just the right age and the right kind for Peggy—a very fine fellow indeed."

"That makes no difference," continued Cyrus, fiercely. "I don't care whose nephew he is, nor how old he is, nor what his manners are. My point is that Peggy positively shall not be pushed, or inveigled, or dragooned, or personally conducted into marrying anybody at all! Billy and Alice were wandering around Charley's garden last Friday night, and they report that Professor Dane was there with Peggy. Alice says that she looked pale and drooping, 'like the Bride of Lammermoor.' There has been enough of this meddling with my little Peggy, I say, and I'm to blame for it. I don't know whether her heart is broken or not. I don't know whether she still cares for that fellow Goward or not. I don't know what she wants to do—but whatever it is she shall do it, I swear. She sha'n't be cajoled off to Europe with Charles Edward and

Lorraine to be flung at the head of the first professor who turns up. I'll do my duty by my little girl. She shall stay at home and be free. There has been too much interference in this family, and I'm damned if I stand any more; I'll interfere myself now."

It was not the unusual violence of the language in the last sentence that convinced me. I had often seen religious men affected in that way after an over-indulgence in patience and mild behavior. It was that ominous word, "my duty," which made me sure that Talbert had settled down on the bed-rock of his conscience and was not to be moved. Why, then, had he sent for me, I asked, since he had made up his mind?

"Well," said he, "in the first place, I hadn't quite made it up when I sent the telegram. And in the second place, now that you have helped me to see absolutely what is right to do, I want you to speak to my wife about it. She doesn't agree with me, wants Peggy to go to Europe, thinks there cannot be any risk in it. You know how she has always adored Charles Edward. Will you talk to her?"

"I will," said I, after a moment of reflection, "on one condition. You may forbid Peggy's journey, to-morrow morning if you like. Break it off peremptorily, if you think it's your duty. But don't give up her state-room on the ship. And if you can be convinced between now and Saturday that the danger of interference with her young affections is removed, and that she really needs and wants to go, you let her go! Will you?"

"I will," said he. And with that we threw away the remainder of our second cigars, and I went up to the side porch to talk with Mrs. Talbert. What we said I leave you to imagine. I have always thought her the truest and tenderest woman in the world, but I never knew till that night just how clear-headed and brave she was. She agreed with me that Peggy's affair, up to now more or less foolish, though distressing, had now reached a dangerous stage, a breaking-point. The child was overwrought. A wrong touch now might wreck her altogether. But the right touch? Or, rather, no touch at all, but just an open door before her? Ah, that was another matter. My plan was a daring one; it made her tremble a little, but perhaps it was the best one; at all events, she could see no other. Then she stood up and gave me both hands again. "I will trust you, my friend," said she. "I know that you love us and our children. You shall do what you think best and I will be satisfied. Good-night."

The difficulty with the situation, as I looked it over carefully while indulging in a third cigar in my bedroom, was that the time was desperately short. It was now one o'clock on Tuesday morning.

About nine Cyrus would perform his sacred duty of crushing his darling Peggy by telling her that she must stay in Eastridge. At ten o'clock on Saturday the *Chromatic* would sail with Charles Edward and Lorraine and Stillman Dane. Yet there were two things that I was sure of: one was that Peggy ought to go with them, and the other was that it would be good for her to—but on second thought I prefer to keep the other thing for the end of my story. My mind was fixed, positively and finally, that the habit of interference in the Talbert family must be broken up. I never could understand what it is that makes people so crazy to interfere, especially in match-making. It is a lunacy. It is presuming, irreverent, immoral, intolerable. So I worked out my little plan and went to sleep.

Peggy took her father's decree (which was administered to her privately after breakfast on Tuesday) most loyally. Of course, he could not give her his real reasons, and so she could not answer them. But when she appeared at dinner it was clear, in spite of a slight rosy hue about her eyes, that she had decided to accept the sudden change in the situation like a well-bred angel—which, in fact, she is.

I had run down to Whitman in the morning train to make a call on young Goward, and found him rather an amiable boy, under the guard of an adoring mother, who thought him a genius and was convinced that he had been entrapped by designing young women. I agreed with her so heartily that she left me alone with him for a half-hour. His broken arm was doing well; his amatoriness was evidently much reduced by hospital diet; he was in a repentant frame of mind and assured me that he knew he had been an ass as well as a brute (synonymes, dear boy), and that he was now going West to do some honest work in the world before he thought any more about girls. I commended his manly decision. He was rather rueful over the notion that he might have hurt Miss Talbert by his bad conduct. I begged him not to distress himself, his first duty now was to get well. I asked him if he would do me the favor, with the doctor's permission, of taking the fresh air with his mother on the terrace of the hospital about half-past five that afternoon. He looked puzzled, but promised that he would do it; and so we parted.

After dinner I requested Peggy to make me happy by going for a little drive in the runabout with me. She came down looking as fresh as a wild rose, in a soft, white dress with some kind of light greenery about it, and a pale green sash around her waist, and her pretty, sunset hair uncovered. If there is any pleasanter avocation for an old fellow than driving in an open buggy with a girl like that, I don't know it. She talked charmingly: about my travels; about her college friends; about Eastridge;

and at last about her disappointment in not going to Europe. By this time we were nearing the Whitman hospital.

"I suppose you have heard," said she, looking down at her bare hands and blushing; "perhaps they have told you why I wanted especially to go away."

"Yes, my dear child," I answered, "they have told me a lot of nonsense, and I am heartily glad that it is all over. Are you?"

"More glad than I can tell you," she answered, frankly, looking into my face.

"See," said I, "there is the hospital. I believe there is a boy in there that knows you—name of Goward."

"Yes," she said, rather faintly, looking down again, but not changing color.

"Peggy," I asked, "do you still—think now, and answer truly—do you still *hate* him?"

She waited a moment, and then lifted her clear blue eyes to mine. "No, Uncle Gerrit, I don't hate him half as much as I hate myself. Really, I don't hate him at all. I'm sorry for him."

"So am I, my dear," said I, stretching my interest in the negligible youth a little. "But he is getting well, and he is going West as soon as possible. Look, is that the boy yonder, sitting on the terrace with a fat lady, probably his mother? Do you feel that you could bow to him, just to oblige me?"

She flashed a look at me. "I'll do it for that

reason, and for another, too," she said. And then she nodded her red head, in the prettiest way, and threw in an honest smile and a wave of her hand for good measure. I was proud of her. The boy stood up and took off his hat. I could see him blush a hundred feet away. Then his mother evidently asked him a question, and he turned to answer her, and so *exit* Mr. Goward.

The end of our drive was even pleasanter than the beginning. Peggy was much interested in a casual remark expressing my pleasure in hearing that she had recently met the nephew of one of my very old friends, Stillman Dane.

"Oh," she cried, "do you know *him*? Isn't that lovely?"

I admitted that he was a very good person to know, though I had only seen a little of him, about six years ago. But his uncle, the one who lately died and left a snug fortune to his favorite nephew, was one of my old bachelor cronies, in fact, a member of the firm that published my books. If the young man resembled his uncle he was all right. Did Peggy like him?

"Why, yes," she answered. "He was a professor at our college, and all the girls thought him a perfect dandy!"

"Dandy!" I exclaimed. "There was no sign of an excessive devotion to dress when I knew him. It's a great pity!"

"Oh!" she cried, laughing, "I don't mean *that*. It is only a word we girls use; it means the same as when you say, '*a very fine fellow indeed.*'"

From that point we played the Stillman Dane tune, with variations, until we reached home, very late indeed for supper. The domestic convulsion caused by the formal announcement of Talbert's sudden decision had passed, leaving visible traces. Maria was flushed, but triumphant; Alice and Billy had an air of conscience-stricken importance; Charles Edward and Lorraine were sarcastically submissive; Cyrus was resolutely jovial; the only really tranquil one was Mrs. Talbert. Everything had been arranged. The whole family were to go down to New York on Thursday to stop at a hotel, and see the travellers off on Saturday morning—all except Peggy, who was to remain at home and keep house.

"That suits me exactly," said I, "for business calls me to town to-morrow, but I would like to come back here on Thursday and keep house with Peggy, if she will let me."

She thanked me with a little smile, and so it was settled. Cyrus wanted to know, when we were sitting in the arbor that night, if I did not think he had done right. "Wonderfully," I said. He also wanted to know if he might not give up that extra state-room and save a couple of hundred dollars. I told him that he must stick to his bargain—I was still in the game—and then I narrated the afternoon incident at the hospital. "Good little Peggy!" he cried. "That clears up one of my troubles. But the great objection to this European business still holds. She shall not be driven." I agreed with him—not a single step!

The business that called me to New York was Stillman Dane. A most intelligent and quick-minded young gentleman—not at all a beauty man—not even noticeably academic. He was about the middle height, but very well set up, and evidently in good health of body and mind; a clean-cut and energetic fellow, who had been matured by doing his work and had himself well in hand. There was a look in his warm, brown eyes that spoke of a heart unsullied and capable of the strongest and purest affection; and at the same time certain lines about his chin and his mouth, mobile but not loose lipped, promised that he would be able to take care of himself and of the girl that he loved. His appearance and his manner were all that I had hoped—even more, for they were not only pleasant but thorough-ly satisfactory.

He was courteous enough to conceal his slight sur-prise at my visit, but not skilful enough to disguise his interest in hearing that I had just come from the Talberts. I told him of the agreement with Cyrus Talbert, the subsequent conversation with Mrs. Talbert, Peggy's drive with me to Whitman, and her views upon dandies and other cognate subjects. Then I explained to him quite clearly what I should conceive my duty to be if I were in his place. He assented warmly to my view. I added that if there were any difficulties in his mind I should advise him to lay the case before my dear friend the Reverend George Alexanderson, of the Irving Place Church, who was an extraordinarily sensible and human clergyman, and to whom I would give him a personal letter stating the facts. Upon this we shook hands heartily, and I went back to Peggy on Thursday morning.

The house was delightfully quiet, and she was perfection as a hostess. I never passed a pleasanter afternoon. But the evening was interrupted by the arrival of Stillman Dane, who said that he had run up to say good-bye. That seemed quite polite and proper, so I begged them to excuse me, while I went into the den to write some letters. They were long letters.

The next morning Peggy was evidently flustered, but divinely radiant. She said that Mr. Dane had asked her to go driving with him—would that be all right? I told her that I was sure it was perfectly right, but if they went far they would find me gone when they returned, for I had changed my mind and was going down to New York to see the voyagers off. At this Peggy looked at me with tears sparkling in the edge of her smile. Then she put her arms around my neck. "Good-bye," she whispered, "good-bye! *You're a dandy, too!* Give mother my love—and *that*—and *that*—and *that!*"

"Well, my dear," I answered, "I rather prefer to keep *those* for myself. But I'll give her your message. And mind this—don't you do anything unless you really want to do it with all your heart. God bless you! Promise?"

"I promise, *with all my heart,*" said she, and then her soft arms were unloosed from my neck and she ran up-stairs. That was the last word I heard from Peggy Talbert.

On Saturday morning all the rest of us were on the deck of the *Chromatic* by half-past nine. The usual farewell performance was in progress. Charles Edward was expressing some irritation and anxiety over the lateness of Stillman Dane, when that young man quietly emerged from the music-room, with Peggy beside him in the demurest little travelling suit with an immense breast-plate of white violets. Tom Price was the first to recover his voice.

"Peggy!" he cried; "Peggy, by all that's holy!"

"Excuse me," I said, "Mr. and Mrs. Stillman Dane! And I must firmly request every one except Mr. and Mrs. Talbert, senior, to come with me at once to see the second steward about the seats in the dining-saloon."

THAT BRAVE LITTLE GIRL, WAVING HER FLAG OF VICTORY
AND PEACE

We got a good place at the end of the pier to watch the big boat swing out into the river. She went very slowly at first, then with astonishing quickness. Charles Edward and Lorraine were standing on the hurricane-deck, Peggy close beside them. Dane had given her his walking-stick, and she had tied her handkerchief to the handle. She was standing up on a chair, with one of his hands to steady her. Her hat had slipped back on her head. The last thing that we could distinguish on the ship was that brave little girl, her red hair like an aureole, waving her flag of victory and peace.

"And now," said Maria, as we turned away, "I have a lovely plan. We are all going together to our hotel to have lunch, and after that to the matinée at—"

I knew it was rude to interrupt, but I could not help it.

"Pardon me, dear Maria," I said, "but you have not got it quite right. You and Tom are going to escort Alice and Billy to Eastridge, with such diversions by the way as seem to you appropriate. Your father and mother are going to lunch with me at Delmonico's—but we don't want the whole family."

THE END

APPENDIX

WILLIAM DEAN HOWELLS
1837–1920

Anyone could have thought of an idea for a book like *The Whole Family*, but only someone with the stature of William Dean Howells could have made that idea a reality. His participation in the project immediately gave it respectablity. Howells was not only a distinguished novelist but also one of the most influential critics in our literary history. He had the remarkable ability to appreciate writers as different as his two friends, Henry James and Mark Twain, and he generously encouraged literary talent whenever he found it.

During his many years as an editor and critic, Howells led the fight for literary realism. His book, *Criticism and Fiction* (1891), offers the clearest distillation of his literary values, but there is no better brief description of those values than the words of his friend, Henry James, who said of Howells:

> He is animated by a love of the common, the immediate, the familiar and vulgar elements of life, and holds that in proportion as we move into the rare and strange

we become vague and arbitrary; that the truth of representation, in a word, can be achieved only so long as it is in our power to test and measure it. He thinks scarcely anything too paltry to be interesting, that the small and vulgar have been terribly neglected, and would rather see an exact account of a sentiment or character he stumbles against every day than a brilliant evocation of a passion or a type he has never seen and does not particularly believe in. He adores the real, the natural, the colloquial, the moderate, the optimistic, the domestic, and the democratic; looking askance at exceptions and perversions and superiorities, at surprising and incongruous phenomena in general.

Although he also wrote short stories, dramas, autobiographical works, travel books, utopian romances, and poetry, Howells's most important creative works are certainly his novels. The two best known are his study of a failed marriage, *A Modern Instance* (1882), and his portrait of an American businessman, *The Rise of Silas Lapham* (1885). At least two of his other works also deserve mention: *Indian Summer* (1886), a story of middle-age love set in Italy, is one of his best novels of manners, and *The Landlord at Lion's Head* (1897) contains one of his finest character studies.

MARY E. WILKINS FREEMAN
1852–1930

Mary E. Wilkins Freeman was an obvious choice to write the old-maid aunt's chapter. Her grim tales of New England spinsters rank among the finest achievements of the local color movement. The best of these stories shun sentimentality, often focusing on the attempts of frustrated individuals to endure a difficult and unsatisfying world. Freeman's current reputation rests largely on two early collections of stories, *A Humble Romance* (1887) and *A New England Nun* (1891), but as her contribution to *The Whole Family* shows, she was a complex writer with a surprising range of interests.

Unfortunately, much of her work is still unjustly neglected. There are good stories scattered throughout almost all of her collections of short stories. *The People of Our Neighborhood* (1898) includes some first-rate work. Freeman's splendid collection of supernatural tales, *The Wind in the Rose-Bush* (1903), contains some of the finest ghost stories ever written in America. Freeman herself always thought highly of *Six Trees*

(1903), a collection revealing her fascination with mysticism and symbolism. Her novels have been generally ignored or disparaged, but both *Pembroke* (1894) and *The Shoulders of Atlas* (1908) merit attention, especially from anyone interested in her view of the New England mind.

Although most of her best work focuses on village life in New England, Freeman also attempted to write about other subjects. She produced a large number of stories about suburban life in New Jersey as well as a historical romance about Virginia, *The Heart's Highway* (1900), and a labor novel, *The Portion of Labor* (1901). She was also a successful writer of works for children.

MARY HEATON VORSE
1874–1966

Mary Heaton Vorse was still at the beginning of her literary career when Jordan asked her to write the grandmother's chapter. She had not yet published a book, but she had produced a number of sketches and stories which skillfully delineated American domestic life. These short pieces were eventually reworked into some of her novels, including her pleasant portrait of an American family, *The Prestons* (1918), and her moving account of the tribulations of an aged woman who resents the restrictions imposed on her by the younger members of her family, *The Autobiography of an Elderly Woman* (1911). Vorse's sympathetic account of the needs, feelings, and griefs of the elderly reflects a wider concern with the victims society tends to ignore. She went on to become a radical journalist committed to social justice, world peace, and the labor movement.

In her autobiography, *A Footnote to Folly* (1935), Vorse describes herself as "a woman who in early life got angry because many children lived miserably and died needlessly." The brutal treatment of the 1912 strike in Lawrence, Massaschusetts, stimulated Vorse's devotion to social reform, particularly the struggle of the working class. A prolific chronicler of the issues of her times, Vorse wrote countless pieces for newspapers and magazines, edited *The Masses*, and produced novels, short stories, and autobiographical works. Her concern with labor issues appears in the nonfiction compilations, *Men and Steel* (1920) and *Labor's New Millions* (1938), and the novels, *Passaic* (1926) and *Strike* (1930). Besides the autobiographical book, *A Footnote to Folly*, which focuses on the years 1912–1922, Vorse also left a record of her involvement with the Provincetown Players, *Of Time and the Town: A Provincetown Chronicle* (1942), and a satiric account of the radical intelligentsia of Greenwich Village in the novel, *I've Come to Stay* (1915).

MARY STEWART CUTTING
1851-1924

Mary Stewart Cutting has received less attention than any of the other authors who contributed to *The Whole Family*. Her name does not even appear in most standard reference works. Nevertheless, at the time Jordan invited her to take part in the composite novel, Cutting had established a modest literary reputation and a promising literary career.

The popular success of her pleasant and aptly titled collection, *Little Stories of Married Life* (1902), led Cutting to specialize in carefully plotted stories about married life in the suburbs. Her contrived plots generally focus on some relatively minor issue or personal idiosyncrasy which temporarily disturbs the happiness of a married couple. There is usually some kind of plot twist which leads to an obligatory happy ending and the suggestion that her happy couple will now be even happier. She focused many of her stories around life in the same New York suburban town and used many of the same characters over and over again. The formula worked well enough to make Cutting a popular success, but not well enough to give her a lasting importance.

Nevertheless, Cutting's speciality made her a logical choice to write the daughter-in-law's chapter. Her fiction may also have some interest for students of American popular taste or the mores of suburban family life in the early twentieth century. The degree to which Cutting relied on the same subject is reflected in the titles of many of her books: *Little Stories of Courtship* (1905), *More Stories of Married Life* (1906), *The Suburban Whirl and Other Stories of Married Life* (1907), *Refractory Husbands* (1913), and *Some of Us Are Married* (1920).

ELIZABETH JORDAN
1865–1947

Although her chief importance in our literary history probably stems from her work as an editor, Elizabeth Jordan was also a successful and prolific writer of short stories and novels. She began her literary career as a newspaperwoman, producing effective human-interest stories on subjects ranging from poverty in New York to the trial of Lizzie Borden. Her work was much admired and apparently influenced and inspired other women journalists. Jordan's first collection of stories, *Tales of the City Room* (1895), drew on her own knowledge of working journalists. The book achieved national attention, partly because one story, "Ruth Herrick's Assignment," was believed to reveal the truth about Lizzie Borden's guilt. Jordan left journalism for editorial work, but continued to turn out a vast number of stories and novels, which reveal her keen awareness of the popular marketplace.

It is not surprising that Howells suggested the idea of *The Whole Family* to Jordan or that she plunged into the project with boundless enthusiasm. Not only was

THE WHOLE FAMILY

Jordan a highly competent and incredibly energetic editor, but she also had a special flair for unusual and intriguing projects. Her editorship of *Harper's Bazar* (1900–1913) was marked by a number of clever schemes involving some of the finest writers in America. For instance, her magazine ran a series of articles in which noted authors discussed their views of life after death; the symposium was later published in book form as *In After Days* (1910) and the nine distinguished contributers included three members of *The Whole Family*: Henry James, William Dean Howells, and Elizabeth Stuart Phelps. Jordan also tried to launch a series in which writers described the turning points of their lives, but the series was abandoned after the contributions of Mark Twain and Howells appeared.

In spite of all the difficulties she faced while editing *The Whole Family*, Jordan later agreed to edit another composite novel, *The Sturdy Oak* (1917), a much more political book written by fourteen American authors who had agreed to donate their literary talent and all fees to the cause of woman's suffrage. The goal was to produce a work that would both raise money for the cause and serve as propaganda. Jordan obviously had learned from her previous experience with *The Whole Family*. This time she made sure that the plot was carefully laid out in advance to avoid any of the surprises that mark *The Whole Family*. The result was an entertaining work with a carefully developed plot and clearly political theme.

As the editor of the *Bazar* and later as an editor and literary adviser to Harper and Brothers (1913–1918), Jordan introduced the work of several new writers to the reading public, but her most impressive discovery was Sinclair Lewis, whose first novel she accepted and edited. Jordan also collaborated with Anna Howard Shaw, the suffrage leader, on Shaw's autobiography, *The Story of a Pioneer* (1915). Jordan's own autobiography, *Three Rousing Cheers* (1938), contains a lively account of her friendships with many famous writers. The chapter devoted to *The Whole Family* is always amusing, often informative, and sometimes factually unreliable.

JOHN KENDRICK BANGS
1862–1922

It is not surprising that both Howells and Jordan wanted John Kendrick Bangs, one of the most successful humorists in America, to be a member of *The Whole Family*. Clever, witty, and prolific, Bangs could always be relied on to provide an amusing piece. Moreover, he had published most of his books with Harper and Brothers and edited the humor department of both *Harper's Magazine* and *Harper's Bazar* for eleven years (1888–1899). Bangs also served as the editor of other magazines, including *Harper's Weekly* (1899–1903) and *Puck* (1904–1907). After 1907, he devoted much of his considerable energy to the lecture platform, where he was an astounding success. *Salubrities I Have Met* and other popular lectures made him one of the most sought-after comic speakers in the country.

Although his facetious and facile wit kept magazine readers entertained for several decades, most of what Bangs wrote is justly forgotten. A few of his books, however, still make for pleasant reading. His best-known and most interesting work is *A Houseboat on the*

Styx (1896), which features a cruise with the ghosts of Shakespeare, Nero, Lucrezia Borgia, Confucius and other notables. *The Pursuit of the Houseboat* (1897) is a clever sequel involving the spirits of Sherlock Holmes and Captain Kidd. *The Water Ghost and Others* (1894) and *Ghosts I Have Met* (1898) also reveal Bangs's flair for comic treatments of the supernatural. Bangs also turned his whimsical and farcical humor on a wide range of other subjects, including the detective story, Napoleon, suburban life, and American politics. Among his better known works are *Tiddledywink Tales* (1891), *Coffee and Repartee* (1893), and *The Idiot* (1895).

HENRY JAMES
1843–1916

H enry James's participation in *The Whole Family* obviously gives the book a special dignity and importance. James, who was too much of an artist to treat
any part of his own fiction as hackwork, clearly valued
his chapter, "The Married Son," which he saw as an
attempt to give the book greater significance and direction. Surprisingly, the chapter has received almost no
serious attention.

"The Married Son" comes at the end of a long and
distinguished career. James had finished the novels and
tales on which his reputation rests and had begun work
on the New York Edition, which involved a thorough
reexamination and revision of his major works. In
theme and technique, the chapter clearly reflects
James's "major phase." Its long, intricate sentences reflect the stylistic complexity of his mature artistry.
Moreover, the suggestive treatment of pyschological
themes is perfectly interwoven with what Howells
called "the phosphorescent play of James' humor." The
chapter's concern with the artistic sensibility and its

questioning of American society point to issues that James had focused on throughout his career, but which had recently come to the foreground of his thought.

He wrote the chapter in January 1907, shortly after finishing a series of eight articles on the speech and manners of American women for *Harper's Bazar* and shortly before *The American Scene* (1907) appeared in print. James was even contemplating another nonfiction book based on his recent impressions of his homeland. It was a time when James was deeply concerned with American life, and deeply troubled by the failure of Americans to cherish the most precious possibilities of civilized life. "The Married Son" is thus also reminiscent of a tale James had written in August 1906, "The Jolly Corner," in which James also confronted the question of what America's commercial mentality might do to an artistic spirit.

ELIZABETH STUART PHELPS
1844–1911

Elizabeth Stuart Phelps was at the end of a long career when Jordan asked her to write the married daughter's chapter. Phelps first gained fame with *The Gates Ajar* (1868), a best-selling novel that featured reassuring conversations about the heavenly afterlife. The book's incredible popularity in both America and abroad encouraged Phelps to continue to inform readers about heavenly consolations in *Beyond the Gates* (1883) and *The Gates Between* (1887). Phelps was also a dedicated feminist and social reformer who produced some work of genuine importance and power.

In spite of the sentimentality and didacticism that frequently mars her fiction, Phelps deserves much more attention and respect than she has received. Her best novels are probably *A Silent Partner* (1871), which focuses on a woman's attempt to help workers and deal with the business community, and *The Story of Avis* (1877), which describes the frustrations of a woman attempting to reconcile marriage with artistic ambition. Phelps's other novels also focus on the victims of society; they include a defense of fallen women, *Hedged In* (1870); an account of a woman doctor, *Doctor Zay* (1882); and a story of a minister devoted to temperance reform, *A Singular Life* (1895). Her concern with human suffering also resulted in two impressive novelettes focusing on life in New England fishing communities, *The Madonna of the Tubs* (1886) and *Jack, the Fisherman* (1887). Although Phelps's short fiction has been virtually ignored, her collection, *Sealed Orders* (1879), contains much of her most interesting and most able work.

In 1888 at the age of forty-four, Phelps married Herbert Dickinson Ward, a twenty-seven-year-old writer. Although the marriage was apparently unhappy, she collaborated with her husband on several Biblical romances. She continued to publish under her maiden name, but reference works often list her under her married name, Ward.

EDITH WYATT
1873–1958

Edith Wyatt was invited to contribute to *The Whole Family* on the recommendation of Howells, who wanted the literary family to include "some western people" and who greatly admired her stories of Chicago. In his famous anthology, *The Great Modern American Stories* (1920), Howells declared that Wyatt's stories "were all exquisite things, most artistic and most realistic things, delicate portraits of life worthy of equal place with the stories and studies" of Sarah Orne Jewett, Mary E. Wilkins Freeman, and Alice Brown. In spite of Howells's praise, Wyatt's work remains neglected.

Wyatt produced two novels, but her most important fiction appeared in her collection of short stories, *Every One His Own Way* (1901), which affirms the rich diversity of American life by sympathetically treating different ethnic types in Chicago. Wyatt portrayed immigrants with sympathy and treated conventional prejudices with disdain. Her social conscience was also reflected in her teaching at Jane Addams's Hull House and the magazine articles in which she supported progressive causes.

Great Companions (1917) reveals Wyatt as a perceptive critic concerned with important social and literary issues. Wyatt was also a founding Board member of *Poetry* and the author of an intriguing collection of poems dealing with both the rural and urban landscapes of America, *The Wind in the Corn* (1917). She wrote very little after the appearance of her second novel, *Invisible Gods*, in 1923.

MARY RAYMOND
SHIPMAN ANDREWS
1860–1936

When Mark Twain refused to write the school-boy's chapter, Mary Raymond Shipman Andrews was eventually chosen to take his place. It was a logical choice. Andrews's collection of stories, *Bob and the Guides* (1906), had shown that she could write effectively about young boys and their love of hunting, fishing, and camping. Furthermore, Andrews had recently produced her most famous and most successful short story, "The Perfect Tribute," a sentimental tale focusing on Abraham Lincoln's disappointment over the reception of his Gettysburg Address. In Andrews's tale, a dying Confederate soldier reveals the greatness of the speech to Lincoln. "The Perfect Tribute" won such praise when it appeared in *Scribner's Magazine* in July 1906 that it was reprinted in book form and went on to sell more than 600,000 copies.

Andrews retained her popularity for the next twenty years, producing a variety of entertaining works which provide a useful guide to popular taste in early twentieth-century America. She wrote some more stories about Lincoln as well as melodramatic tales of adventure set on the battlefield, in the courtroom, and in the woods. Her love for the outdoors resulted in some of her best work, including the stories collected in *The Eternal Masculine* (1913). Her other works include a novel of Napoleonic times, *The Marshall* (1912); a collection of stories about women, *The Eternal Feminine* (1916); a volume of World War I poems, *Crosses of War* (1918); and a biography of Florence Nightingale, *A Lost Commander* (1929).

ALICE BROWN
1857-1948

At the time she agreed to participate in *The Whole Family*, Alice Brown had already established a respectable literary reputation as a writer of New England local color stories. Her collections, *Meadow-Grass* (1895) and *Tiverton Tales* (1899), show a devotion to literary craftsmanship as well as a detailed knowledge of New Hampshire life. Howells and other contemporaries often ranked her local color stories with those of Mary E. Wilkins Freeman and Sarah Orne Jewett—a judgment that is still occasionally expressed by a few brave critics. For the most part, however, recent critics have ignored both her early stories about New England and the more ambitious works she attempted later in her career.

Although some critics complained that her increasingly abstruse style failed to give life to her characters, Brown's attempt to give her fiction more philosophical depth and psychological insight gained her respectful attention in the first decades of the twentieth century. The best of her later short stories appeared in *Vanishing*

Points (1913) and *The Flying Teuton and other Stories* (1918). She also produced several intriguing novels, including *The Prisoner* (1916), an intelligent study of a former convict's readjustment to society; *The Wind Between the Worlds* (1920), a book showing Brown's interest in the supernatural; and *Old Crow* (1922), a work skillfully depicting New England life.

Brown also worked in other genres. She gained some recognition as a dramatist, mostly of one-act plays. Her drama, *Children of Earth* won a $10,000 prize in 1914, but did not fare well on Broadway. She also wrote poetry and a variety of nonfiction works, including a biography of her friend, the New England poet Louise Imogen Guiney.

HENRY VAN DYKE
1852–1933

At the time Jordan invited him to assume the position of Friend of the Family, Henry van Dyke was a well-known and highly respected figure with an influential voice on religious, political, and literary matters. He was a versatile and popular writer, as well as a Presbyterian minister and a professor of English literature at Princeton University. A self-proclaimed adventurous conservative, van Dyke wrote volumes of poetry, short stories, romances, travel sketches, literary criticism, moralistic essays, and nature pieces. Marked by a graceful style and moral tone, his works represent the last remnants of the Victorian genteel tradition in America.

Van Dyke tried his hand at a wide range of literary forms, but his most popular works were *The Story of the Other Wise Man* (1896) and *The First Christmas Tree* (1897), both of which were first read as sermons to his congregation. Of his other works, modern readers are most likely to enjoy the essays expressing his delight in the outdoors and his love of fishing, especially those

340

collected in *Little Rivers* (1895) and *Fisherman's Luck* (1899). Van Dyke's fiction now seems quaintly artificial and overly didactic, but readers once respected and enjoyed the tales collected in *The Ruling Passion* (1901), *The Blue Flower* (1902), and *The Unknown Quantity* (1912). His pleasantly melodious and thoroughly conventional verses will almost certainly never regain their popularity. Once regarded as a distinguished critic of literature, van Dyke seems likely to go down in our literary history as a representative of the stifling gentility against which the early modern writers struggled. One of van Dyke's remarks provoked Sinclair Lewis into devoting his Nobel Prize speech to a scathing attack on the narrowly old-fashioned values of the American literary establishment.

Alfred Bendixen is Professor of English at California State
University, Los Angeles.
June Howard is Professor of English, American Culture, and
Women's Studies at the University of Michigan. She is the
author of *Publishing the Family* (Duke University Press, 2001).

Library of Congress Cataloging-in-Publication Data
The whole family: a novel by twelve authors /
William Dean Howells...[et al.];
Introduction by Alfred Bendixen ; with a foreword by June Howard.
Contents: The father / William Dean Howells—The old-maid aunt /
Mary E. Wilkins Freeman—The grandmother / Mary Heaton Vorse—
The daughter-in-law / Mary Stewart Cutting—The married son / Henry
James—The married daughter / Elizabeth Stuart Phelps—The mother /
Edith Wyatt—The school-boy / Mary Raymond Shipman Andrews—
Peggy / Alice Brown—The friend of the family / Henry Van Dyke.
ISBN 0-8223-2838-0 (pbk.: alk. Paper)
I. Howells, William Dean (1837–1920)
PS3545 .HQ6 2001   813.52—dc21   2001033623